Praise for *The Miniaturist's Assistant*

"What a lush, bold novel is *The Miniaturist's Assistant* by Katherine Scott Crawford, blending love, intrigue, and the role of portrait art in history for a story that is as suspenseful as it is wildly romantic. I'm not a fan of time travel tales in general, but the astounding journey of art restorer Gamble Vance through the Charleston of the present and the very long past transcends genre and takes the reader places that are entirely new."

—Jacquelyn Mitchard, *New York Times* bestselling author of *The Deep End of the Ocean* and *The Birdwatcher*

"To read *The Miniaturist's Assistant* is to be wooed by the intelligent and humorous voice of Gamble Vance. An art museum historian, Gamble takes you, the reader, by the hand on a journey through Charleston, South Carolina, passing in and out of the 21st and 19th centuries to reckon with a ghost, or is it a ghost? Lovers of art, of culture, of humanity, will want to follow Gamble's trail. Crawford illustrates the worlds of time and place with a pen so clearly shaped like a paintbrush that you feel you have crawled inside the book, or is it an 1804 miniature?"

—Amy Wallen, bestselling novelist, memoirist & author of *How to Write a Novel in 20 Pies: Sweet & Savory Secrets of the Writing Life*

"From the moment museum conservator Gamble Vance recognizes a familiar face in a 200-year-old miniature portrait, I was swept away in this immersive time-slip story. Katherine Scott Crawford deftly weaves this art historical mystery with intertwined love stories spanning generations. Readers will find their heartstrings pulled across centuries, turning the pages to see where Gamble's complicated choices ultimately will lead her."

—Laura Morelli, art historian and *USA Today* bestselling historical novelist of *The Last Masterpiece, The Stolen Lady,* and *The Night Portrait*

"A richly woven, beautifully researched historical evocative of Susanna Kearsley. Katherine writes about the past as though she lived there. You will want to read this one slowly, so you can linger with these characters and savor the setting."

—Terry Lynn Thomas, *USA Today* bestselling author of *The Silent Woman*

"Rich with historical details, this fabulously fun and transportive novel explores the great mystery of time, asking whether it's possible to live more than one audacious life. I fell in love with the characters—and with Crawford's delicious sense of adventure and assured storytelling. Highly recommended for fans of Susanna Kearsley and Diana Gabaldon, *The Miniaturist's Assistant* is a delight from start to finish."

—Heather Bell Adams, author of *Maranatha Road* and *The Good Luck Stone*

"Crawford's sweeping, Southern, and lushly romantic epic slips through time effortlessly, laying out a historic mystery as well as a love story with an immensely satisfying conclusion."

—Emily Carpenter, bestselling author of *Burying the Honeysuckle Girls* and *Gothictown*

"A tiny work of art offers a world of secrets in this delightful time-slip story, but only the most courageous will dare to unravel the layers of mystery to reveal the heartwarming truth."

—Genevieve Graham, *USA Today* bestselling author of *The Forgotten Home Child*

"*The Miniaturist's Assistant* is a multifaceted love story wrapped in a mystery that unfurls on the changing winds of history. A rollicking, page-turning tale, this unforgettable novel explores time travel, art, passion, the complexity of past sins, and the abundant promises embedded in the here and now. Katherine Scott Crawford has written a beautiful book steeped in humanity, truth, and wonder."

—Connie May Fowler, author of *Before Women had Wings*

"Katherine Scott Crawford is a daughter of the Carolinas and She writes as such, tackling this ambitious historical novel with an unflinching eye. Crawford doesn't shy away from the tangled and troubled history of the region or her heroine, a contemporary feminist who is unapologetically lusty and smart, fully prepared to challenge mores in her own time as well as those of the past she visits. The careening romance and sobering realities in this novel will leave readers with much to contemplate, a surprisingly poignant dose of optimism for humanity, and ultimately, the enduring legacy of love."

—Kimberly Brock, bestselling author of *The Lost Book of Eleanor Dare* and *The Fabled Earth*

"Full of mystery and intrigue, *The Miniaturist's Assistant* is a riveting exploration of the power of stories to transcend time and place. Crawford's prose is enchanting, the story rich and layered, and, as a bonus, she offers readers a crash course in the fascinating world of miniature portraits! Part art lesson, part romance, part history, part mystery, this novel is a thrilling testament to the myriad ways we are connected to one another and to the past."

—Jennifer McGaha, author of *Bushwhacking: How to Get Lost in the Woods and Write Your Way Out* and *The Joy Document: Creating a Midlife of Surprise and Delight*

Also by Katherine Scott Crawford

Keowee Valley

THE MINIATURIST'S ASSISTANT

Katherine Scott Crawford

Regal House Publishing

Published by
Regal House Publishing, LLC
Raleigh, NC 27605
All rights reserved

ISBN -13 (paperback): 9781646035922
ISBN -13 (epub): 9781646035939
Library of Congress Control Number: 2024944582

Cover images and design by © C. B. Royal

Regal House Publishing, LLC
https://regalhousepublishing.com

The following is a work of fiction created by the author. All names, individuals, characters, places, items, brands, events, etc. are either the product of the author's imagination or are used fictitiously. Any resemblance to actual events, places, institutions, persons, current or past, is entirely coincidental.

Printed in the United States of America

For Wylie and Willa ~

you are the best part of all my stories

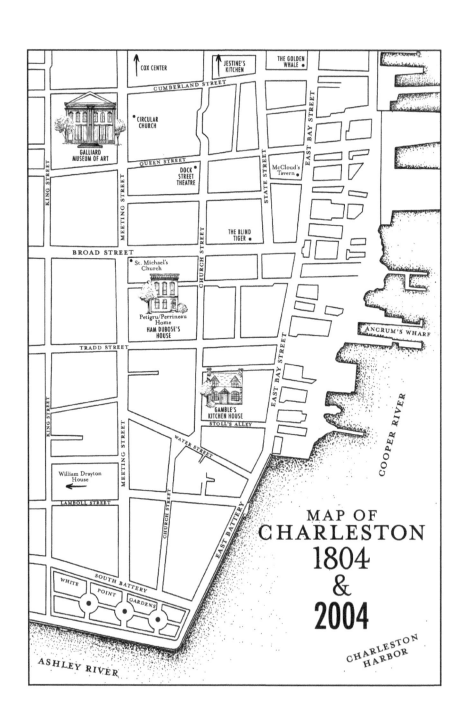

COX CENTER

JESTINE'S
KITCHEN

THE GOLDEN
WHALE ●

CUMBERLAND STREET

EAST BAY STREET

● CIRCULAR
CHURCH

GALLIARD
MUSEUM OF ART

QUEEN STREET

DOCK ●
STREET
THEATRE

McCloud's
Tavern ●

KING STREET

MEETING STREET

STATE STREET

THE BLIND
TIGER ●

CHURCH STREET

BROAD STREET

St. Michael's
Church

Petigru/Perrineau
Home
HAM DUBOSE'S
HOUSE

TRADD STREET

EAST BAY STREET

ANCRUM'S WHARF

KING STREET

MEETING STREET

GAMBLE'S
KITCHEN HOUSE

STOLL'S ALLEY

WATER STREET

COOPER RIVER

William Drayton
House
←

LAMBOLL STREET

CHURCH STREET

EAST BATTERY

MAP OF
CHARLESTON
1804
&
2004

SOUTH BATTERY

WHITE
POINT
GARDENS

CHARLESTON
HARBOR

ASHLEY RIVER

Now knowe that all Painting imitateth nature or the life in everything, it resembleth so fare forth as the Painters memory or skill can serve him to express… Of all things the perfection is to imitate the face of mankind, or the hardest part of it…

~ Nicholas Hilliard, 1547–1619, limner and miniature portraitist

There is no first or last in Forever.
It is Centre there all the time.

~ Emily Dickinson

PROLOGUE

CHARLESTON, SOUTH CAROLINA

Every visitor has an opinion about Charleston. Two tourists pedal down East Bay Street on rented bikes, and the woman asks the man if the giant antebellum homes along the Battery still belong to the original Confederate families. She shouts it over her shoulder as they wheel past parked cars, the blue harbor beyond. And this is how she phrases it: *Confederate*. He tells her something he thinks is true, but it's not.

Tour guides—the ones driving the horse-drawn carriages—tout their versions of the city's story, and theirs are probably the most accurate. At least when it comes to history's big moments: the bolded hashmarks on Charleston's centuries-old timeline, the events that make the books.

The statues in the parks tell their stories: stony, unyielding, privileged, and tragic.

But the truth is, Charleston is a town like any other. Whether it's the Charleston of the way-back-when or the Charleston of now. A town where people lived, fought in wars, got sick, celebrated things, mourned others. Where people sat on park benches and stared out at the water, like I'm doing today.

It's a town that has flipped the pages of the ages, some burnt and crackling at the edges, some faded. All written on palimpsest, every margin filled, the words overlapping, the stories latticed. Every truly old town is like this: just as buildings are built upon buildings, foundations reused and material recycled, stories are built upon stories, the voices telling them sloughing off shared DNA like old, dry skin cells.

What did that wily astronomer, Carl Sagan, once say? That we are made of the same stardust? Maybe. I think it's more that we are made of the same stories.

❧

Charleston's people want you to believe their town is special. That it is lovelier, older, more history-filled, more charming and elegant than other cities. That its family names sound an important bell, and anyone walking around still carrying one of those names owns a piece of American aristocracy, a lineage to which few belong.

Take a walk around the peninsula, for example. The peninsula is Charleston. It's the town's heart, its origins, the groundwork. But take a walk, say, down Meeting Street, and leave the crowds of commoners—the NFL T-shirt-wearing visitors from other, less thirteen-original-colonies-type states—behind. Keep crossing intersections until you mark the confluence of Church and Broad Streets. Arrive at dusk, so when you enter the neighborhood South of Broad, you attain that special and absolute sense of the otherworldly. The loveliness and the history here will vie with the distinct realization that you are simply not meant for this place: you are not of it, not at all.

Ignore the feeling, and keep walking.

I used to do this each night, after I left work at the Galliard Museum of Art on Meeting Street and made my walk home. For years I inhaled the painful loveliness which is South of Broad at dusk. I found loveliness each evening, even as I rolled my eyes at parked cars in the driveways I passed.

Why the eye roll? Yes. That is a reasonable question. It's because of the cars. You'd see them yourself if you walked this part of the peninsula at night. I'd like to say this model of car sits at every one of those old houses, but I must restrain myself from exaggeration because I am a grown-up, and restraint is what grown-ups do. So I'll say instead, these cars—which are Land Rovers, by the way—are parked at "almost every," or "every other" house on Church or Tradd or Legare or Limehouse Streets—street side, or on a skinny, grass-bisected drive next to a renovated carriage or kitchen house.

A Land Rover. That supererogatory British tank of a car: a car that serves no real function in a colonial, skinny-streeted Lowcountry city. Save, of course, as a status symbol. Perhaps they are a nod to Charleston's British origins, but I think that's stretching it. I think wealthy people in Charleston simply like Land Rovers. They remind me of folks in the mountain town of Asheville, North Carolina, where I was born and raised. There, every person (ack. Fine. Every "other" person) drives some sort of Subaru. It's just a different riff on the same status tune.

Back to my point, or at least to the point I'm trying to make, though even as I make it, I know I'll be wrong. I will know what really happened. But for now, my point is this:

Charleston, South Carolina, is a town same as any other—no matter what they would have you believe.

It took me two years to decide Charleston was a "normal" town. You see, I arrived with a handicap. This is the historian's curse: to carry a city's story like a charm, some buckeye or rabbit's foot tucked grimy and well-rubbed in a back pocket. Something to bring you luck on the journey. And I had read about Charleston. Since I was nine years old I'd read about Charleston.

It started with a book. (Doesn't it always start with a book?) We were required to choose one, and only one, for a fourth-grade nonfiction book report. The librarian at Asheville Elementary School took one look at my Trapper Keeper, decorated with a collage of classic novel covers—everything from *To Kill a Mockingbird* to *Gone with the Wind*—and handed me *National Standard's Walking Guide to Charleston, South Carolina*. She was one of those grown-ups who recognized immediately that I was an old soul. (Perhaps my stick-straight, *Little House on the Prairie*-blond hair in a time of Aqua Net and perms was the giveaway.) Librarians are good like this.

National Standard's Walking Guide to Charleston, South Carolina had been published in the 1980s, and still held to those ideas of the glories of the Old South, while flagrantly ignoring the brutality of human bondage. It illuminated the cobblestoned streets, waving palmettos and moss-filled live oaks, mouthwatering southern food (yes: "mouthwatering" is a term that truly serves here), and genteel manners, while leaving out the more salacious aspects of life which come with any colonial port city, but especially this one: pirates, scandal, whoring, slavery, drugs, defeat.

I made a meal of that book, so by the time I was in eighth grade, and our class made the annual eighth-grade trip to Charleston to do things like visit plantation houses and learn about the Revolutionary and Civil Wars, I had formed a one-sided impression of Charleston tough to crack. Even years later, as a graduate student on an archeological dig within the border of the old walled city, I'd step back from my spade and brush, wipe the wet heat from my face, inhale the musk of harbor and sea life left exposed at low tide, and wonder at the city's lasting loveliness. At the charmed lives its inhabitants must have lived.

A historian brushing 300-year-old gunk away from a stone wall hefted into being by enslaved Africans really ought to know better. But a storyteller often misses the thumping pulse of the story until she tells it herself.

I suppose, after all this, you will wonder at my sanity. Because I just spent the last who knows how many minutes trying to make my case that Charleston is normal. Average. An anybody kind of town. And now, after all that, I'm going to tell you a story which proves instead, that the opposite is true. That Charleston is unique, even magic. That something happened to me here—something wild and uncommon. Something I still think about as I sit on this park bench by the harbor, years later.

It makes no sense. Really, though—stardust and shared DNA and all—does any of it ever make any sort of sense?

I thought not.

I was twenty-four years old when I secured the graduate assistantship in the College of Charleston's Master of Restoration and Historical Preservation program. For a girl from a former frontier mountain town, where the original buildings were made from wood and the majority of artifacts we were ever lucky enough to dig up were Cherokee potsherds and arrowheads, this was big. The city opened its doors to me in ways I never expected. In a place like Charleston, however, a door can be opened and a welcome made without acceptance. Acceptance is not something you earn. It's something that comes color-coded in your double helix. In your surname. In your history in the town, a history that had damn well better go back to the 1700s, or you don't stand a chance.

Let me be brief. In two years, I'd earned another master's—this one in Art Conservation—and interned in private collections and in museums like the Frick and the Met. In three, a PhD in Conservation Research & Historic Preservation from the University of Delaware (Go Blue Hens!). In four, I returned to Charleston and secured a job, a dog, and a fiancée. The fiancée held one of those venerated surnames, owned it as if it'd been brought over on the *Mayflower* instead of a cargo vessel from the Barbados. The dog I named Kipling, as in Rudyard.

And, in years four through eight: a miscarriage, a divorce, and a distinct disillusionment with the charm and welcome of the city. Somewhere along the way, a ghost.

At least, that's what I thought she was, the night we met. After all this time, I remain uncertain.

She was not the last. (Or, for that matter, the first.) But she was, of course, the most important.

PART I

MINIATURE

miniature | noun & adjective

1. An image or representation on a small scale. 2. The art or action, orig. that of a Medieval illuminator, of painting portraits on a small scale and with minute finish, usu. on ivory or vellum; a portrait of this kind.

~ *Shorter Oxford English Dictionary, vol. 1*

Time travel…is ultimately—and paradoxically—an exercise in remembering.

~ *Maria Konnikova, science writer and international poker player*

GAMBLE

CHARLESTON, SOUTH CAROLINA
2004

At the Galliard Museum of Art, the first thing you notice is how quiet and white everything is. How fresh, blown free of dust and litter and extra. Even with strategic placement, the art there is saying it needs the clean and spare to make its point.

On the second floor, for example, each piece is placed in proportion to the viewer's response. In the atrium, at a permanent exhibit called *The In-between*, a massive, indoor tree system, constructed of intertwined twigs and branches using tension to stay upright, draws open mouths. Awe. And lots of stepping back, looking up, gaping. I watched the artist and his son install the piece—Myron Gadsden, the museum night guard, and I did—over the course of three full days. Awe does a pretty good job of describing it.

In proportion to this massive display—one that stops visitors in their tracks because it seems at once both odd and out of place, and yet as if it belongs there, as if it grew in some viney legacy from beneath the sustainable bamboo flooring—the exhibit in gallery 5, the *Miniature Portraits*, seems staid. Circumspect. It does not awe, at least not unless you look for it.

It's also dark and quiet in the *Miniature Portraits* exhibit, which is why I like it. I like the insulated walls, the muffle. The way I can sit on the yellow pine bench there as I consider the tiny painted faces beneath the glass. Centuries of faces, set like precious gemstones in subtly lit, wall-hung display cases and inside wide, shallow glass-topped drawers which slide open in near silence: history making her exhale.

I started taking my break in the miniature portraits room not long after I took the job. If you asked me now, how I went from historic house preservation to art conservation, and a complete and utter fascination with seventeenth-, eighteenth-, and nineteenth-century miniature portraits, I'd be annoyed. Mostly because I find talking about a thing often destroys it—I've always felt this way—or, in truth, destroys its magic. This is why I've been so far successful at avoiding a career in academia: At a museum there are no magic-sucking, peer-reviewed journal articles to produce. Here there is excavation without ego.

Really, though, I work with miniature portraits because the faces slay me. They just slay me—there's no other way to put it. That flush of life beneath the cheeks, the curl of hair against a virgin brow, the crook of a nose still marked in the sitter's descendants.

Portrait miniatures force an artist to home in, to relinquish excess, to concentrate. And how much, in this day and age, do any of us concentrate? How much do we see of a face? Say, the face of a friend, when it talks to us. How often do we count the crinkles at the corners of the eyes, mark the random, too-long nose hair, the sparse brow, the philtrum just beneath the nose?

We don't.

It got to where I was spending every break I had in gallery 5, instead of taking my usual amble through the graveyard of the church across the street.

"Gamble, *you're* the one who's going to shrink if you stay here any longer," I was told more than once by my friend and fellow conservator, Alice Duggar.

Alice was part of a team restoring two Renoirs found in the barn loft of a farm out in Summerville. The paintings had been wrapped in the tattered remains of a World War II parachute, stored behind a stack of 200-year-old cypress boards. The Galliard had asked (and been permitted) to display the paintings before returning them to their rightful home with a benevolent Jewish family, just outside Paris.

"Will not," I said, most mature. And Alice, who does not suffer fools though she deals daily with the decisions of foolish people, left me alone.

Then there was Myron, the night guard: "Gamble, you spend more time with those tiny dead people than you did with your own husband. That why you divorced?"

Myron said it when he found me—for the third time—standing in front of the same glass case of portrait miniatures long after closing.

"Yes," I said.

You'll want to know about the girl. The one I thought at first to be a ghost. But if you'll stay with me, just sit tight, I need to tell you about the miniatures. It will make sense, I promise. It'll all come out in the wash.

The Galliard began collecting portrait miniatures long before I arrived, but they languished in museum storage for years. This was because, in the beginning, there just weren't enough of them to constitute the need for their own exhibit. They are, after all, pretty darned small.

What happened was that one of those old Charleston families, one with a street named after them, decided to donate their miniature portraits. After, word got around in the way it does—possibly over the hoods of massive, ridiculous, shiny black Land Rovers—and other families followed suit. Then it was discovered that someone's uncle Billy (okay, William) had a fetish for collecting, and here they are. I was tapped as conservator because my former mother-in-law, who it can be said may just like me better than her own son—dropped my name to the Galliard curator over an oyster bar at some white-tie function at the Charleston Yacht Club.

No, I am not making this up. This is sometimes the way things work in Charleston. Not always: that would be clichéd. But sometimes.

I got the job.

I spent well over a year with the first batch of portrait miniatures. Conserving them takes a deep knowledge of the art itself, but also a well of patience. Resolved (and stubborn) is the hand that holds the crown. Or, in my case, the brush.

Conserving something is a whole different ball game than creating anew. Conserving forces the art historian to consider an end result she cannot yet see. To trust in the process: in the wiping away of, at times, several centuries worth of grime. To watch the pendant that used to hang on your great-grandmother's chain fob be cracked open, dissected layer by gold-plated layer, and put back together again.

You don't need all the king's horses and all the king's men when you have the right set of tools, a good bit of experience, and a doctorate in art conservation.

Oh, and also hours of time in which to drown your divorce sorrows with the use of a scalpel, resin, and the early 1800s.

I'm thirty-two years old. I've been around the block. I have come close to marriage twice and actually committed the act once. I lived abroad, once for an entire year, on a job exchange with the Uffizi Museum, in Florence, Italy. I hiked most of the Appalachian Trail the year I turned twenty-two, when I was freaked out about navigating life in the "real world." Picture me making those interminable air quotes as I say it, because that's how my father did it when I told him I was going to hike the Appalachian Trail instead of finding a job.

I attended graduate school three times. Once because I thought I wanted to be a poet. Which, of course, meant I wasn't thinking at all. Next, I decided to earn an MBA. Even my father, he of the air quotes, didn't lay any money down on that one. Let's just say I did not then, nor do I now, have a business sort of brain.

I was "restless and rootless," as my mother would say. Back then I craved adrenaline, but now I know I craved more the story of it, the drama. It was the living I needed more than anything else.

Which brings me to the miniature portraits, and the ghost. Or rather, what I thought was a ghost. But she was just a girl. A girl in an alley.

It was October, a perfect month in Charleston. You may be thinking, October is a perfect month nearly anywhere in the American South. And you'd be right: it really is.

In October in Charleston, everything is crisp, more immediate. The city loses some of its hereditary languidness. The days vacillate, as if they, like the city itself, can't decide what to be. The waking hours are warm, even hot; the nights a middling perfection of just right, the autumn wind carrying a warmth so utterly lovely you want to stand in the middle of the street, strip down to your skivvies, and bathe in it.

Or maybe that's just me. But I doubt I'm alone.

I always walked to work from my rental South of Broad, even in the depths of a wind-blown peninsula winter. I like to walk. I like the sensation of the city beneath my feet, cobblestone to lowly asphalt, because it gives me a chance to lay quiet the plane of my mind before I need to use it in a way that may affect other people.

I signed the rental agreement for the kitchen house on Church Street about six months before I hit the year mark of my legal separation. I sensed its imminence, my divorce, and knew Kipling and I would need a place to stay while we regrouped. My ex-husband owned all the cars, so the house needed to be close enough to work that I could walk or bike.

Perhaps I ought to explain my rental house. It's a 237-year-old house, across a bricked courtyard from one other, smaller house, both of which are snuggled up behind a big house. Thus is the physical reality of many of the grand old homes South of Broad. Most of the little houses sitting adjacent to or behind big homes are kitchen or carriage houses, and were once used in the eighteenth and nineteenth centuries to (surprise!) house kitchens, or horses and carriages, but have since been converted to straight-up garages or garage-apartments.

Mine was one of the original kitchen houses and servants' quarters for the main house out front, which sits on Church Street itself. My landlady used my house, and its twin across the courtyard—also a kitchen house/servants' quarters for the main house—as rental properties.

Charleston is complicated, near-to 300-year-old architecture notwithstanding. You really should see it for yourself.

Luckily, my landlady, Mrs. Catherine Mayzck Memminger, owner of everything at 353 Church, was on the board of the Galliard, liked me, and while she'd known my ex-husband since he was in short pants, felt I got the raw end of that deal. She offered me the kitchen house, flat out, during a tour I was giving to her and a group of deep-pocketed, art-loving ladies-who-lunch. A tour of the newly opened miniature portraits exhibit.

"Gamble, honey," she said, sidling up to me as we wound our way through the museum to gallery 5. At the moment, her friends were sidetracked by one of the famous eighteenth-century furniture-maker Thomas Elfe's claw-footed cabinets. "I think you should move into the kitchen house."

"The kitchen house, Catherine?" She'd invited me to call her by her given name the night we met, back when I was married to Harry.

"My kitchen house," she said. "It's two stories, with two bedrooms, one and a half baths. The living room is tiny but it's nice and quiet and there's a lovely shared courtyard."

Catherine waited, eyeing me with a patience born only to women with lots of money they never had to earn. Her yellow eyelet sheath dress held nary a wrinkle. I always wondered how they did it, these women. Didn't they have to sit down at some point during the day— you know, make a lap? When one made a lap, there were wrinkles.

"Can Kipling come?" I said.

"Kipling's that big, beautiful field Lab of yours, right?"

"Yes, ma'am."

Catherine smiled, took her hand from her raffia clutch, and laid it gently on my arm. "I insist on it." She patted me once. "You know, Harry's an ass. Handsome, but an ass. He got it from his granddaddy."

I didn't answer. I did, however, lay my hand over hers and squeeze, because I'll take solidarity from any sister I can get. We went to join the other ladies, who at my lack of leadership had wandered into the Caldwell Rotunda, where they were admiring the marble bust of George Washington.

"Gamble, why is George made up like an Italian?" One of the ladies, Mrs. Emilia Smythe said. Her tinkly voice skittered across the red and green Beaux Arts-tiled floor. "For heaven's sake, he's got curly hair."

"An Italian sculptor named Giuseppe Ceracchi made it, Mrs. Smythe," I answered. "It's in the neoclassical style."

Catherine cleared her throat. "There's a working fireplace. I'll give you off-street parking and charge you five hundred a month, including utilities. Now, that's a deal, young lady: one that does not exist in this city. But you've got to do a once-over of our holdings. I want to know what my art's really worth."

The girl, the girl. I have not forgotten the girl, though you'd think I had with the way I tend to run on. It's just for my story to make sense, you must know where I live. I live in the larger of two kitchen houses at 353 Church Street: 353A, to be exact. My kitchen house is deliciously old, and you can't take a step without the house creaking, some whispered admittance of its 237-year-old story.

Kitchen houses were the law in Charleston, once upon a time. During the colonial period, widespread fires destroyed hundreds of homes on the peninsula, and so between 1740 and 1860 homeowners were required to build separate structures, away from the main house, to serve as kitchens. This being the case, many of the oldest surviving homes in Charleston, including Catherine's, have one or two kitchen houses serving many roles over time: as kitchens, servants' quarters, stables, efficiencies, offices, and more.

At 353A Church the ceilings are low, because people tended to be short. I'm short, so this suits me more than fine. I used to like a bit of air above my head, with plenty of room for my thoughts to circle and swirl. But since my divorce, I've sought comfort and coziness. Often the house felt like a hug. There's a huge working fireplace in the small living room, complete with an original brick hearth and nooks for bread baking. It appeases my personal need for an historic aesthetic to know a person's been cooking there since 1768. The eighteenth-century brick in the courtyard between my small house and the other is sloping and lovely, just as Catherine promised. Kipling and I like to sit at the wrought-iron table out back, admiring the Carolina jessamine winding its way up the side of our house, watching chimney sweeps and blue jays do battle above the clay-tiled roofs.

Our mail carrier, whose name is Joe, brings my mail all the way to the back, which makes me feel like a real local. In the warm months—of which there are plenty—Joe wears the white shorts and matching sun helmet of the United States Postal Service. He's tall and stork-like, so he straddles the green Bermuda grass growing between the brick pavers following the line of the drive. I admire his knees. I think Joe's knees reach about the same height as my hips.

I loved my life at 353A Church, despite the dissolution of my marriage being my reason for moving there. I loved it in spite of the sleepless nights, the agony of wondering what I could've done different, the worry of time wasted, the smudging of ghosts along the stairwell. I adored, more than I ever imagined I could, the emptiness of my queen-size bed. I no longer stayed on "my side," as I had when Harry and I were married, but at first opportunity made of myself a snow angel. I slept in the middle of the bed, spread wide, my limbs stretched and pointed as long as they could get. When we first moved in, I suctioned myself to that bed like a starfish, unwilling to move until Kipling put her paws up on the foot and insisted I take her outside.

More than anything else, 353A Church became my refuge, my reha-bilitation station, when I needed it most. It never bothered the kitchen house that I was a non-native divorcée, childless and hoodwinked. That I was a low-born mountain girl in the land of palmetto trees, un-wrinkled linen suits, and monogrammed seersucker.

I always felt, not only did the kitchen house not care about these things, it held me closer because of them.

But the girl. Like I said, I saw her in an alley. Many nights, when I leave the Galliard Museum, I don't have anywhere else to be—almost always, this is the case—and I like to take my time. Church is my favorite street on the whole of the peninsula, and there's this brief window right at dusk, when everything goes so quiet you think you might actually be able to remember what it was like to live here well over two centuries ago.

I say "remember," because I'm a bit of a freewheeling believer in other lives. Well, allow me to be honest: I believe some (if not all) of us have been here before, that we hold memory in our bones. I did some scholarly work on the theory of ancestral memory, back when I was in graduate school the third time (the real time). I'm hazy on the specifics—at this point in my life, I'm not certain of much of anything—but I am sure we hold our ancestors' memories inside.

More on that later. Right now: dusk.

Dusk is a magic time—the Celtic poets were right about the gloaming—and so when the portal opens, for about an hour, between one world and the next, Church Street is an entirely different place. Everyone is in for the night, and rare is the car that travels down it, at least way down south on Church, where I live.

If you squint, using your good brain and the imagination you had as a kid but have perhaps forgotten about, you can almost see the dirt and oyster-shelled, bricked and cobblestoned roads; the carriages and horses, and the people walking about in brocade or wool waistcoats, felt beaver hats, and dresses cinched and puffy with whale-boned stays and crinolines. Because Charleston is a three-hundred-thirty-year-old city built on marshland, it can smell like it. Take a whiff and you're back: the historian's trick.

Charleston was built on a grid, like most colonial cities sprung from an original fort, and was a walled city; it even remained so after the marsh was filled in and more houses and roads were built on top. It is not too terribly difficult to figure out how to get from one place to the next—you are, after all, bordered on three sides by water. But there are still more than a few streets left from the late 1600s and 1700s. Some of these streets are alleys, and they're hidden to most everyone except those of us who live here in permanence. Or those who've managed to secure a savvy and interesting tour guide.

Stoll's Alley is one of those places. It's a long, skinny spit of a walk running east to west, connecting Church and East Bay Streets like the rung of a ladder. Open now, of course, only to walkers and the occasional cyclist, who don't mind the bump and clatter of old bricks and stones. In most places, the alley itself measures but six feet across. From the Church Street side, it looks rather normal, at least normal as weighed on a Charleston gauge. But you can tell it's a storied footpath.

From the East Bay Street side, you might miss the alley if you weren't looking for it. Many tourists assume it's one of countless private gardens: they stick a head in, but after a moment consider they're too polite to venture down. I've watched them do this with my own eyes.

I have walked Stoll's Alley more times than I can count. When I take my route home from work at dusk, however, I make a habit of stopping there, just a few feet off the Church Street sidewalk and into the middle of the first few feet of this end of the alley, and try to see what I can see.

My mother used to say that. She'd tell my brothers and me, "Let's go see what we can see." And we'd be off on some hometown adventure, whether to the backyard butterfly bush to count the monarchs, or away, on a harebrained road trip to Memphis to see our aunts. With Mom, you never knew.

The night I saw the girl, I'd stopped at the entrance to Stoll's Alley as I always do. I broke the border between it and Church Street with a mere step from concrete to brick, and then I peered down it. I pondered a walk to the harbor, but I knew that by the time I made it back it would be darker than was prudent for a woman alone. There'd been rain, and it glossed the centuries-old bricks lining the alley on this side, making it seem even more haunting and mysterious than usual.

Immediately, Stoll's Alley called to me. The words were as distinct as if someone stood at my ear, whispering into the shell of it as an actor delivers an aside: enunciating each syllable.

"Won't you come back?" she said.

When this happened, I did what any reasonable, thirty-two-year-old divorcée walking alone at nightfall would do. I adjusted the strap of the cognac leather saddlebag for which I'd culled way too much of my paycheck, and started down the alley.

And there she was, halfway down. The girl.

She was, from what I could tell, around twelve or thirteen years old, and gangly with it. Dressed in period clothes: the Empire-waisted, square-necked muslin gown of the turn of the eighteenth century—the early Regency period. Her chemisette, worn by day for modesty, I knew, glowed white and frothy in the dim.

Point of note: In America, we don't refer to it as the Regency period. Instead, for us rebellious continentals, it's the Post-Revolutionary period. Because, well, we'd straight-up ousted our regent by 1783. But for context, think Jane Austen, and the very early 1800s.

The girl was lit so bright, yet with such odd shadows by the gas lamp beside her, she appeared as a shadow drawing—a silhouette a new mother has made of her young child, to mark the tiny person that child was before she was fully formed.

The girl must be in theater, I thought. Dress rehearsal for a reenactment in the park, or something with the Footlight Players. But young. And alone.

I opened my mouth to ask, but the girl spoke.

"He needs you," she said.

Still clutched within the alley's spell but confused as to whom she was actually speaking, I whirled to look behind me. Not a soul around, nor anyone coming up the street. Not even a dog walker, and this was the time of evening they emerged. We were all alone, the girl and I.

I walked toward her, drawn as if I could not help myself. The closer I got, the more the gas lamps flickered. When I neared enough to see that her eyes were hazel, the light began a mad flashing, casting wild shadows across the brick and shell-mortar wall lining the alley. The world tipped strange on its axis.

"You must come back," she said, a tinny desperation in her voice, as if she were petering out.

I reached out—to touch what, I've no idea—when someone said, "Hey, is that private? Can anyone walk back there?"

I turned. A couple stood behind me at the sidewalk on Church Street. A decidedly modern couple: each boasted numerous tattoos.

"No. Yes." I spat out the words, unbalanced.

"Thanks," the female half of the couple said, and they entered the alley and almost passed me by before I realized I'd lost the moment, lost the early 1800s girl, and in complete honesty had no idea what had just happened. I wanted to whirl on my heels, to feel at the ancient brick wall like Nancy Drew looking for a secret door.

The couple walked past, the guy whispering to the girl. I'd place any kind of bet on its having something to do with me being nuts.

Oh, why the hell not? I thought, and held out both hands, palms up in supplication. "Wait," I said. "Did either of you see her?"

They stopped, arms wrapped round each other's waists, her hand in the back pocket of his jeans, his on her ass. She wore a delicate orange sundress, I noted, the entirety of one of her calves decorated with the siren face and voluptuous upper torso of Marilyn Monroe.

"See who?" she said.

"The girl. There was a girl, yea high." I marked a spot in the air near my shoulder. "Wearing a long dress. You didn't see her?"

The woman shook her head. "No."

"All we see is you," the guy said.

They watched me, waiting, and there in that moment I decided to suck it up and be normal, to pretend I had not just spoken with a person who wasn't really there, and I wasn't going to scare the nice tattooed couple who were probably on their vacation or honeymoon or something equally romantic, and who surely did not want to bother with a woman who was losing her marbles.

"Okay. Yes. Thanks," I said, finally.

The couple headed on, and I could hear their comments about the alley and the bricks and the wall aflame with yellow jessamine, the single house on the right so close you could touch its stucco, wonder at just how many alley-walkers it had seen over the course of its long life. I found myself in immediate need of a stiff drink.

Yes, people really do say this out loud—that they need a stiff drink. There's a reason it's a saying.

I shouldered my bag and headed back from whence I'd come. My sandals on the brick made me sound quick, as if I were scared and moving fast. The truth was, my adrenaline pumped. My heart raced. But scared? No, I wasn't scared; I was excited.

At the end of the alley I cut a sharp left and continued south on Church, setting a pace that would've made my former collegiate track-star brother proud. There was lightness in me: I felt buoyant, more alive than I'd been in years. I wound my way around an oak whose roots were busy showing the sidewalk who's boss, dodged an older gentleman walking his even older Boykin spaniel, and avoided a trash can by leaping atop one of those ubiquitous limestone mounting blocks and then landing, nimble as a dancer.

No kidding. I clicked my heels on the way down. Dick Van Dyke would have been proud.

There's an excitement historians feel when we make a find. When we uncover something about a life, or from a time, that no one has seen or perhaps made a connection to before. It reassures something infinite in us; it solidifies a truism we all trust: That somehow, through era and age, across millennia, we are connected. That our stories matter. That we share them, despite the often-dissociating construct of space and time.

It's how we get a person to walk into a museum. I mean, that's a pretty big task. In Charleston especially, there are many other things to do and see. You can eat biscuits that sing in your mouth, for example. Drink cocktails from the jazz age, mixed by clever bartenders. Take in harbor views so delightful the town put up swings. But a historian must lure a person in by other means—the means of a promise. A promise of a glimpse of the past, of an insight into how we got where we are, even with the airing of someone's two-hundred-year-old dirty laundry. A historian makes the promise that stories matter. That our choices matter, and that they ripple out, creating as many reverberations as there are waves in the ocean.

I restore art not because I want to live in the past, or because I believe it was in any way, shape, or form a better place to be. I'm a woman, for heaven's sake. The past is even trickier for my people than the present, and *that* is saying something.

Indeed, I am well aware of history's fickle soul.

But saying it like this makes the past sound just delightful, even funny. The truth is, the past is marauding. It will mow you down like a Pamplonian bull if you don't give it the attention it deserves.

I recognized her face, the girl's. That's why I was excited—why I was leaping atop giant rectangular mounting blocks like one of Walt Disney's chimney sweeps. I knew her face. I'd seen it under my own brush.

There is a portrait miniature in the Galliard Museum—in the display drawers on the eastern wall of gallery 5, in the second drawer down—which has haunted me from the moment I began to restore it. It's oval, watercolor on ivory, like near to all these pieces. It's set in a copper-plated locket, with a filigree edging, and includes a casing containing a lock of plaited hair. We don't know what happened to the locket top, but it seems that because of the presence of a set of broken clasps, there must have been one. Which means someone, at some point, wore this girl in a pocket or at a cuff or bracelet, or on a chain or scarf around his or her neck. Someone kept her close.

This girl, or young woman—seeming in her late teens—haunted me because she felt immediate. She demanded my attention. It also seemed she was trying to tell me something, from that tiny oval, from those unexpected hazel eyes, from two hundred years in the past. When I looked at her, I couldn't shake the feeling that she had a secret I was supposed to keep. Sometimes it took everything in me not to remove the miniature—not to lock it up and hide it so she wouldn't be exposed.

She wears a red fox stole draped over one shoulder. Her dark hair is pinned up, her neck white and long. Her eyes are slanted in and down, her brows raised. Her nose is pointed, her mouth curved with a wily sort of good humor.

It was the girl from Stoll's Alley. They were the same person: I could feel it in my conservator's bones.

I've no evidence with which to defend my certainty. However, I'd stake my career on it. This is why you should trust me: besides Kipling, my career was just about all I had in those days.

GAMBLE

Back at 353A Church, I kicked off my sandals and dropped my bag in the wide, shallow sweetgrass basket next to the door. Kipling met me there, still young and faithful enough to rub her body against my knee, to put her head beneath my hand and flip it back, so it fell upon the bony protuberance at the top of her skull. A brilliant move, actually, because it results in me rubbing her head.

"Hey, baby," I murmured, hesitating but a moment before giving in and dropping to my knees. I threw my arms around her neck and buried my face in her thick black coat, feeling a bum-rush of emotion. Alongside my treasure-hunter high—an energy always present at the start of a conservation project—there was a stomach-hollowing uncertainty, a foreboding I couldn't place. I squeezed Kip tighter, and to her credit, she didn't move a muscle.

Kipling was my second dog. Growing up I had another black Labrador retriever, and therefore can vouch for their loyalty, dedication, and hug-ability. Labs just know.

It wasn't until later, sitting upon my stoop, hot tea in hand, when I realized I wasn't surprised to have met the girl in Stoll's Alley. It had nothing to do with my certainty that it was her miniature in the Galliard. I wasn't surprised, because I'd seen her in the alley before.

I had, hadn't I? I'd seen the same girl, a smudge of something uncertain at the corner of my eye. It's just like when you enter a room and think you catch a glimpse of someone leaving it at the same time. But when you really focus, really look, there's nothing solid there.

My aunt Callie says when this happens, you have seen a spirit. I always thought she was right. Not because I'm nuts—my aunt Callie is, admittedly, a little nuts—but because the words felt right. The notion real.

Then I remembered. In June, when the gardens South of Broad were bursting with Carolina jessamine and camellias, and the magnolia blossoms sat fat, white, and fragrant amidst glossy green leaves, I had seen the girl. I'd stopped at the Church Street end of Stoll's Alley, just long enough to take a good whiff, and there she was. That time I assumed she was just another tourist framed in sunlight, way down at the far end of the alley, near to where it emptied into Bay Street. But it wasn't. It was the girl, outlined against the light. She said something, but I figured she was talking to someone at the other end of the alley, and I can't remember what it was.

Had she been trying to get me to listen all this time? What had I missed?

Each alley in Charleston has a legend. They're quite old, after all—some of the oldest original thoroughfares in the city. Businesses were built along them: taverns, rope makers' shops, blacksmiths' forges, and more. Duels were fought in these alleys. Young girls kissed or more, willing or otherwise. Arguments had, promises made and broken, history toyed with on a regular basis. Kegs and other such items smuggled down them. Soldiers marched. Cats slinked and dogs gamboled. For three hundred and fifty some-odd years, the wind off the water in Charleston Harbor has shot down Stoll's Alley and picked up speed, sweeping leaves and other detritus hurly-burly onto Church.

For most of October the girl was on my mind. I heard her entreating, "Come back," like a faint echo, even as I went about my daily routine. It made it tough to concentrate on work. One afternoon Alice found me in the *Miniature Portraits* exhibit, where it was apparent I'd loitered for more than an hour. She was equal parts miffed and concerned, because I was uncharacteristically tardy for a meeting. Then and there I promised myself that, during working hours at least, I'd table the mystery girl—I'd save any pondering for my walks home.

One evening, my workday through and on just such a walk, I let my mind race. I smiled half-heartedly at passersby on the sidewalk, paying scant attention to the smells of sugar, coffee, and cinnamon wafting from the open doors of bakeries and cafés I passed. I glanced up only to watch for cars and cyclists before crossing streets, and I barely acknowledged the newspaper vendor on the corner of Queen Street (Fred, a grizzled but enthusiastic transplant from New York, with whom I normally bantered over the Mets versus the Braves and the sacrosanct goodness of grits) or the sweetgrass basket weavers at the intersection of Meeting and Broad (usually Sabine and Clare, and sometimes Clare's great-niece, who was apprenticing in the art and whom I often heard Clare admonishing in Gullah to put down her pager or she'd throw it in the river).

I was preoccupied, to say the least. The mystery had me in its grasp, and I wanted nothing more than to dive into the girl's life. By this, I mean into her history: to find out who she was, and perhaps to discover why she was talking to me. I just couldn't let go of the feeling that the girl in the alley and the woman in the miniature were one and the same. Somehow, I *knew* they were connected—but other than appearance (the fact that they looked alike) and provenance (both seeming to be from early-1800s Charleston), I still didn't know why, or how.

Too, I couldn't shake the feeling that, whoever she was, she wasn't meant to be on display—that there was some secret about her I was supposed to keep.

Sounds crazy, right? Proving any of it, of course, would mean research.

But I'd have to do it with subtlety. Because what reputable historian walks up to any sort of archivist and says, "Hi, I've come to research this ghost/time traveler/crazy person who's been talking to me from the past"? And, *oh, by the way*, I think she has something to do with a two-hundred-year-old miniature portrait.

On second thought: Archivists are mysterious creatures. Maybe one would believe me.

Still, witch hunts may have shifted a bit from the 1600s—no more burnings at the stake, deaths by pressing, drowning, or hanging—but they still exist. In the art world, they hang your credibility. Ghost you from the best jobs and fellowships. This is what could happen to me should I reveal that I was funneling my considerable clout and museum resources toward the unraveling of a ghost story.

I'd have to be more than subtle, I thought, my pace slowing and my mind finally beginning to settle and stop rocking, like a canoe making an eddy after exiting a white-foamed rapid. I tucked my hands into the pockets of my suit jacket (there was a chance I'd been gesticulating

wildly as I thought-walked, one of my best and most off-putting habits)
and waited for the sedan backing out of the nearest driveway to pull
into the street. The window rolled down and a white-haired gentleman
appraised me with a raised eyebrow.

"It's dark, Ms. Vance," he said.

I nodded. It was. "Hi, Mr. Simons. I'm almost home."

"How's Kipling?" he asked, his rather austere face creasing in a smile.
You had to smile when you thought about Kipling; anyone who knew
her did. "You sure she doesn't need a date with my Rolly?"

I grinned. "Sorry, sir. She's fixed."

"Damn shame," Mr. Simons said, shaking his head. He said this every
time. "A damn shame. All right, then, you be careful walking home."

"I will. Have a good evening."

He raised a hand, waited for me to skirt the back of his car and be
on my way, and pulled out onto the darkening street.

I pondered my research plan—just how I'd get it all done—as I took
a left into the driveway of 353 Church. I tightrope-walked one of the
bricked lines down the drive like a kid, because it's fun and because
being silly sometimes calms my brain. I wondered: Would it be possible
to enlist help? Research of this strange magnitude always went well with
help.

"Gamble."

Harry. He sat at the top of my lit stoop, Kipling at his side with her
front paws draped over the wooden edge. He was scratching her ears
and she was loving it, the traitor.

"Hey, Harry." I crossed my arms. A defensive move, to be sure.

Heyward Hunt Sims was a catch, according to all reliable Charleston
sources, past and present. I should know better than most: I'd caught
him. We were together—dating and married—a total of four years, one
month, and thirteen days. Then I'd let him go. It'd been like releasing
an Alaskan salmon to the wild during the salmon run. I knew he'd be
scooped up by a brown bear pretty quick.

He waited for me to speak, loving on Kipling like it was nothing, like
it came so easy to him. It was. And it did. I should know: I'd had those
hands on me before. They were wonderful liars, just like Harry.

Harry, a very special sort of Charleston attorney, wore a fawn-colored suit with a white button-down left open at the neck, an untied bow
tie hanging. It's not a crazy color for fall here, fawn-colored. It's the

perfect menswear bridge between the seersucker and linen of summer and the light wools of a Charleston winter. You'd have to be a high-born southern gentleman who could afford to dress like someone in a glossy magazine like *Town and Country* to get this. I got it because I'd lived with one.

Harry was handsome. Looks, or the lack thereof, had never been his problem. At the present moment, his blue eyes were a bit glazed—a bourbon glaze: even in the dark, I recognized it well—but he wasn't drunk. He sat up a bit, and his jacket hung open to reveal one fine-striped suspender.

"Gamble, you've—" Harry started, and I dropped my saddlebag on the courtyard bricks with a thump.

"Really, Harry? The suspenders?"

He gave me an affronted look, then his expression cleared. "Yes, I like them. What, do they not look all right?"

"You know they look all right," I said. "They're lady lures. That's why you wear them."

"Ah, Gamble, I miss the way you talk." Harry stood, a perfect six feet, and kissed my cheek. When he lingered, smelling of mixed nuts and Old Forester, I shoved him off. I grabbed my bag and swung it over my shoulder.

Kipling stood and trotted after me when I took the steps. The original heavy wood door was unbolted and open, only the modern screened door defending the house against the last of the summer mosquitoes and sly ex-husbands. Harry was letting out all the bought air. Of course.

"Use the spare again?" I said, over my shoulder.

"Yes. Do you mind?" He followed me into the house.

"Yes."

"Well, I apologize," he said. "I thought after last time, maybe you'd want me here."

"Last time" had been a dimwitted, hormonally overloaded, serious lapse in judgment of an encounter on my vintage couch about a month before. I'd been out with friends after work, at a fish and raw bar called The Golden Whale, and spotted Harry across the glossy wooden slick of the bar top. He had been surrounded by co-workers—every one an attorney—and there was a twenty-something redhead at his side. She fed him the cherry from her drink. He took it, gave her a wink he didn't mean (Harry hated being fed), and I caught him.

I'd been fending off the advances of a real estate agent named Beau, who persisted in making me try every appetizer he ordered. (I hated being fed too.) Harry and I met eyes across the wide, long bar. We rolled them at the exact same time, then grinned at each other. It had been almost a year since I'd had sex, and Harry's problem, after all, had never been that he didn't love me. He just loved himself more.

We made it back to the kitchen house, laughing, both half-lit, inside and to the couch. And that was that. Harry's problem had also never been that he was bad in bed.

"Last time was the only time," I said.

Kipling wound through my legs, then flopped down in front of the fireplace. She laid her big head on her paws and looked up at us, brown eyes flitting back and forth like an observer at a tennis match.

I slipped out of my jacket and hung it over the back of one of my (count them) two leather wingback chairs. My arms were bare—I'd chosen a sleeveless cobalt sheath and matching cardigan for the day's wardrobe, a piece I'd shed that morning after I spilled coffee on it at work…again. Goosebumps popped along my upper arms, and I used those upper arms to yank the rubber cork from the bottle of pinot noir sitting on the coffee table. (I'd opened it the night before.)

"Shut the damn door, Harry," I said. "It's cold."

I poured the wine—a glorious glug—into a fat, purple, crystal stemless glass, one of my favorites. I did not offer any to Harry. The front door shut, and I looked up. Still there, on the inside of my house, grinning like the cat. You know: the one who ate the canary. I could almost see a yellow feather hanging from Harry's smile.

"I can stay?" he said, removing his jacket and dropping it over the back of my couch as he passed, instead of hanging it on the coat tree a mere three feet away. And that was it, really—the dropping of that jacket. Because Harry would never think, in a million years, he'd have to pick it up.

I know this sounds insane. Who cares if a smart, handsome, wealthy man forgets to put away a piece of clothing? That is small potatoes in the game of life, and we should reserve our ire for the big stuff. But the thoughtlessness: that's what did it for me. That's what reminded me. Harry—for all his good qualities, and despite the lack of a moral compass, he did have some—thought only about Harry.

I gulped my wine like this was a 1990s Gatorade TV ad, and I was

Michael Jordan. I held up a finger, shushing him until I was good and done.

I set the glass down. "No," I said.

"Gamble," he said, drawing it out.

"Harry," I returned, sharp.

He moved closer, reached out and tucked a strand of hair behind my ear. It was a classic Harry move, and I'd be lying if I didn't admit that it got to me. It always had. Mostly because it felt tender and proprietary, all at the same time. And call me cavewoman, but if you don't know how that feels, you at least must admit you have yearned for it.

"A goodnight kiss, then," he said, much more than asked.

See, this is where I get into trouble. Unlike Harry, I have a moral compass. It's darned reliable, and accurate, and has generally served me well. But I'd married the guy, hadn't I? A girl deserves to make some mistakes in her life, and he was one of mine. The big one, if you will. Harry was not a master manipulator. Don't get me wrong—the guy was old Charleston born and bred, and knew how to run a table—but he had a heart. He just tended to follow the lead of a much lower organ.

Two things: one, Harry could kiss. Like I said, physical attraction had never been our problem. Sometimes, you just want a kiss. Two, I was horny.

I know it may sound untoward, proclaiming yourself horny. Especially if the self you are is not, in fact, a college frat boy. But it's the truth: before our rendezvous on my sofa last month, it'd been a year I'd been without sex. And while I was determined that this night Harry and I would not be having any, what could a little kiss hurt?

Harry watched my eyes change and knew he had a full house. He curled a hand round the nape of my neck and leaned in, moving slowly so I'd have a chance to change my mind. (See, he wasn't all bad.) But this would not do. It was my home turf: I was in charge.

I took a handful of white cotton lapel and one suspender and yanked him down the rest of the way, locking our lips. Harry, never one to let an obvious advantage go to waste, wrapped his arms around me and got a good grip on my behind. For a petite woman, I had curves to spare. It had always been his favorite part of my particular anatomy.

A kiss can be a complicated, thinking thing, or it can run on pure instinct, be nothing more than a display of hormones. I've had my share of fabulous kisses over the course of my thirty-two years. Kisses that made me want to swear off men forever, and kisses that had me convinced I would need a ride home afterward. They call it "weak in the knees" for a reason.

Usually a kiss makes a promise, even if it's only the promise of more kissing. That is not the type of kiss my ex-husband and I shared that night. Ours held the lethal combination of mutual lust, comfort, and lack of expectation.

One thing I've also learned since my divorce: You don't have to like the guy to kiss the guy. Revolutionary!

Harry pulled me close: close enough that I felt just how much he liked *me* by the change at the front of his two-hundred-dollar trousers. He moved down my neck, and before he hit my sweet spot, the one that turned me into a brainless mess, I shoved him back. Hard.

"Nighty night," I said, swiping the back of my hand over my mouth.

Harry started to speak, thought the better of it, then, without apology and with a touch of delicacy, adjusted the front of his pants. "Good evening, Gamble," he said, ever the gentleman and absolutely sincere. "It was good to see you."

"It really was," I said, smiling. And I meant it. "Drive safe, Harry. Put the key back on your way out."

"I will." He didn't even stop to put on his jacket, just slung it over one shoulder without looking back. "See ya, Kip."

Kipling, who had since rolled onto her back with all four paws in the air and white underbelly exposed, paid him no mind. She didn't even wag. I poured myself another glass of pinot.

Sometimes, a stupid kiss with the wrong person is just the ticket.

The next day in the *Miniature Portraits* room, I stood before the drawers on the eastern wall, my hand on the knob of the second drawer down. I reached into the wide pocket of my lab coat and touched the smooth skin of a Pink Lady apple, one from the box my mother had sent from her orchard in the Blue Ridge Mountains the week before. I'd want the apple later; I always did, but I resisted taking a bite now. (No food allowed in the galleries.)

Feeling hungry but ethical, I slid open the drawer. There she was: the girl from Stoll's Alley, older and wiser—perhaps a bit more worldly, with those beckoning eyes—the head of the fox on her stole smirking more than usual.

"*Lady*. Anonymous, ca. 1804," read the label. This I should've known, since I'm the one who labeled it.

I glanced at the miniature to her left, an older, fleshy gentleman with lamb chops, a thin mouth, and high-collared suit in a rather unfortunate shade of puce. I'd put them together, the entire line of portrait miniatures, in fact. On purpose. Besides a shared provenance, I'd determined (by examining their similar use of color and technique) that "Man with Lamb Chops" (as I'd taken to calling him in my head) had been painted by the same artist. Housed in a drawer with other anonymously painted miniatures, I was still working on figuring out just who that artist was.

I looked around once, then took the key from my other pocket and unlocked the case. I popped the glass top and set it aside. I took my protective gloves from my pants pocket and slipped them on. Then, after a brief hesitation in which I considered taking the entire tray, lifted "*Lady*. Anonymous, ca. 1804" from her spot. No reason visitors to the Galliard this morning should miss out on the other painted faces because I needed the one.

Everything put away neatly, I kept my gloves on, cradling my miniature like a robin's egg. I headed for the conservators' lab in the basement.

When I started down the main staircase, two visitors making their way up smiled at me, their eyes going to the nametag at my lapel. *Nothing to see here, folks*, I thought as we passed each other.

Aloud, I said, "Good morning. Welcome to the Galliard."

"Good morning," and "thank you," they answered, in a whisper. People always feel they need to whisper in a museum. I've heard patrons hold entire conversations in whisper in the ladies' room, even as automatic toilets flushed and hand dryers roared. There's just something rarefied, even holy, about being around art. Not all the time, of course, because the modernists don't give off an aura like that—and furniture, even the kind we have in the Galliard, makes only the esoteric enthusiast feel the need to genuflect.

But perhaps I think this way because I've been on the other side of the art: I've taken it apart, laid hands on the underneath, the cracked paint, the looping signatures, the scratched chair legs and contemporary pieces made out of pick-up sticks and empty milk cartons. I've dropped, silent and nimble as a ninja on all fours, into the artists' lives, and have known them to be as messy and human as the rest of us.

In the basement, careful, I transferred the miniature to one hand, tapped the key code at the pad on the wall with the other, and hefted the door to the lab with a hip. I needed to get to my work area without alarming anyone.

It's not that I was doing something illegal or untoward—none of my fellow conservators or museum employees would bat an eye at me handling a piece of art like this—but it was certain I was using work time and resources for a personal matter. Nobody likes anybody who does that.

Taking a work tray from the shelf next to my padded desk, I set the miniature atop the protective foam sheet lining the inside. I pulled off my gloves and hung them on their special peg, clicked on my lamp, then sat and restarted my computer.

First, I did a quick search through our own archives. "*Lady*. Anonymous, ca. 1804" was acquired from Mrs. Saralee Hutto of Aiken, South Carolina, one year ago this week. Mrs. Hutto had read an article about the Galliard's new miniature portraits exhibit, and called us about donating hers. The Hutto family did not believe the woman in the miniature was a relation, and they didn't know her name or the name of the artist who'd captured her. The miniature portrait had been sitting like a paperweight on a stack of old books in the family's glass-encased, turn-of-the-century lawyer's file for as long as any of them could remember.

The closed doors on the lawyer's file, I knew, had helped maintain the miniature's pristine condition; if it'd been exposed to humidity, mold would likely have formed, and the pigment—or paint—would've flaked or most certainly faded, even indoors and out of direct sunlight.

Miniature portraits like this one, like mine, were popular in the late-eighteenth and early- to mid-nineteenth centuries among well-heeled members of the American upper class. The first miniature portraitists in the American colonies lived and worked in Charleston, as a matter of fact. Because of this, those Charlestonians who could afford to engaged the most popular and talented miniature portraitists of the day, and because they did, we are left with two-hundred-year-old portraits of people fully fleshed, deeply colored, and—I'd argue—more feeling than photographs.

Painted on ivory sliced thin from animal tusk or whale bone, and sometimes enclosed with a lock of hair (for romance or remembrance), these pint-sized portraits were often worn as jewelry or presented in display cases. Often they came in sets, as of siblings or spouses, in cases built specifically for that purpose. The simple fact that "*Lady*. Anonymous, ca. 1804" was seemingly unrelated to the family and house where it'd been kept meant it was going to be a bit of a trial to find out who the woman was and where she came from.

But I had to find out. Because, for heaven's sake, I had a ghost in an alley talking to me…and somehow, here she was, in a miniature I'd restored. I knew the memories I had of seeing her in the alley, and the odd, guilty feeling I'd felt when I saw her miniature on display, were connected. Not knowing why, though, was driving me batty. It was like living inside one of those infernal find-the-word games where you have to pick random letters from other words in order to spell something, anything, that makes sense.

I wheeled away from my desk, leaning back as far as my second-hand pleather swivel chair would allow.

"Alice," I called, down the row of conservator's tables to where my friend stood bent, hard at work, over a family portrait, circa 1750, of the Walter Rhett family. Rhett, a first-generation rice planter who rarely bowed to convention, decided to include his enslaved house workers in the portrait—not a habit of the time. Alice was determined to save the face of an enslaved boy, perhaps six or seven years old, who sat cross-legged in the corner, a hand on the family's Irish wolfhound keeping guard by his side.

"Yep," Alice said, not looking up, her brush doing a delicate tap over some spot on the canvas. I waited. A minute later, satisfied, she set the brush aside and looked my way, knuckled her glasses down her nose. "What is it?"

"Do you remember anything about that large gift out of Aiken, about a year ago? Included two portraits, a Confederate cavalry uniform and one miniature portrait? Were there any other pieces I'm forgetting?"

"I don't think so. That's the horse lady's estate, right? Mrs. Hutto? I don't remember any other miniatures besides the one of the girl with the fox stole." Alice cocked her head, her thick, wavy black hair with its wide streaks of silver unmoving on her shoulders. "I do remember Mark was dying to get into her barn, but couldn't get the okay from the woman's nephew. He's the estate executor, acting as a quasi-guardian. Mark thought there may have been more. Might want to check with him. Who knows, maybe he saw something."

Mark Whitman, director of acquisitions for the museum and a notorious art hound, was currently on a site visit in Ireland. It would've been nice to have him around: he had a sixth sense about where people seemed to stick their art.

I sighed. "I will. Thanks."

When all else fails, go see your best friend. This is an attitude I adopted in graduate school (the third time), when I was finally there for the right reasons, and when I'd also begun to see Harry on a regular basis. Whenever I found myself overwhelmed by Harry's Charleston-ness, by my anxiety over fitting into his family, and by what (if I'm brutally honest) had begun to gnaw at the edges of my intellect: the notion that we weren't entirely right for each other, I'd pop over to the College of Charleston and bother my best friend, Tolliver Jackson.

Tol was, at the time, a new assistant professor in the College's Department of African-American Studies. We met at a graduate school social my first week in Charleston, at the West Ashley house of the Graduate Dean and Provost. There'd been a game of beer pong in the carport (what can I say? We were grad students) and I'd been running the table all night. What my fellow grad students did not know was, not unlike Dr. Johnny Fever from the 1980s TV show *WKRP in Cincinnati*, the more inebriated I get, the more coordinated I become.

You remember the episode, don't you? Two of the radio station's DJs, Dr. Johnny Fever and Venus Flytrap, are participating in some on-air Drunk Reflex Test administered by a highway patrolman, involving taking shots of liquor and hitting a buzzer to answer trivia questions. Johnny Fever, a burned-out ex-hippie, gets quicker and more accurate the more drinks he consumes. Venus Flytrap, the soulful night DJ, gets tanked.

Anyway, it's classic 1980s television. Worth wasting an hour on.

But back to Tolliver and me, and how we met. Tol challenged my beer pong supremacy with a bet that he could land the ping-pong ball in a full plastic Solo cup of beer perched on my head *à la* William Penn and the apple.

I took the bet and Tol hit the shot, and half an hour later we were swinging together in a Pawley's Island hammock in the dean's backyard, barefoot and counting stars through breaks in the canopy of waxy crepe myrtle and oak overhead. Tol was a startling six-foot-five inches tall and five years older than me. His skin was such a rich dark-honey brown, all that showed when he smiled in the night was his wide, white, perfect smile. "You look like the Cheshire Cat," I told him.

He gave the ground a push with one long-boned foot, which hung easy over the side of our hammock, and up we swung, the ropes creaking from the effort. "Then that makes you Alice," he said.

I could tell Tolliver about the girl in Stoll's Alley. He wouldn't think I'd lost my mind. Tol had spent his adolescence in the foster care system in and around Atlanta, Georgia. But until age twelve he'd been raised on Sapelo Island by his mother's older sister. So his formative years had been spent in the company of aunts, uncles, cousins, and other extended family, and those folks were Geechee people who were not put off or even surprised by the presence of the supernatural.

In other words, Tol's people believed in ghosts. Though a thoroughly educated, modern man—Tolliver held a PhD in African American Studies from Harvard (no slouch, that one)—he believed too.

Plus, and perhaps more relevant to my particular conundrum, Tol was a historian. Not only that, his scholarship concentrated on relationships between Black and white families in the peninsula Charleston of the eighteenth and nineteenth centuries. I needed him, his research, his burly shoulders, and his great big brain.

Just the year before, Tol had been named Director of the Cox Research Center for African American History and Culture, located in a nineteenth-century building on Bull Street. His office was in the attic, which made it the fourth floor, and which was just how he liked it. But which made no sense, considering his circus-freak height.

I'm not being mean with the circus-freak quip. I'm five foot two, myself. I'm jealous.

The attic ceiling, Tol's office ceiling, was seven and a half feet high. Whenever Tol stood up from his desk it looked like he was going to at worst decapitate himself on a structural beam or at best bump his head. I winced every time, but nothing ever came of it.

That day I hefted open the building's solid oak front door, which tended to stick, and waved at Tasha, the Cox's office administrator, as I passed her open doorway. I took the skinny Victorian staircase two steps at a time, huffing when I reached the third floor. Valiant, I made it up the last flight and knocked once on Tol's office door before bursting inside.

"I need you, friend," I said. "You won't believe—"

Empty. I glanced around, struck by the sight of Tol's impeccable desk and the room surrounding it. The light entered the eastern window full and yellow, making the renovated attic—painted top to bottom in some historically accurate shade of cream—seem as if its occupants were bathed in butter. In the corner, framing the window on the north-facing wall, hung four graphite sketches done by different Black artists: one of a cotton field at harvest; one an architectural bisect of the innards of a slave ship; one a voting booth in rural Georgia circa 1940; and one a portrait of a senator from Illinois named Barack Obama, who'd given a powerful keynote address at the recent Democratic National Convention.

I'd commissioned each piece and acquired them on loan at Tol's request when he'd been named director. The portrait of Senator Obama was the newest addition to Tol's wall: a pencil sketch done by a faculty member in the College of Charleston's School of the Arts.

When I inquired, curious, at his choices, Tol said, "So I don't forget."

There was a squeak as the door to his office bathroom—a tiny converted closet with a sloped ceiling to match the roofline—opened, and Tol ducked out.

"How are we friends?" I said, with a pointed look at his Lucite desk: an exercise in minimalism which held only a chrome apothecary lamp, his laptop, and the slim Beaufort pottery vase I'd given him for Christmas the year before. It contained one sweetgrass rose.

"You look like you're coming out of a clown car," I added.

Tol blinked, then, nonchalant, completed the zipping of his zipper. He wore tailored dove-gray trousers and a pristine white button-down sans tie, and looked exactly like an NBA point guard who'd been tapped to walk the runway at Paris Fashion Week.

"No white girls in the attic," he said.

I ignored him. I pulled a Lucite chair—one matching the ridiculous desk—up close and sat, crossed my legs, and balanced forward on my hipbones.

I said, "Tol, I saw a ghost."

Tol took a seat in his black, real-leather chair, and smooth as a 1960s advertising exec, set his elbows on the desk and triangled his forearms. He threaded his long fingers together at the top.

"Where?" he said.

"Stoll's Alley. I stopped there on the way home last night, thinking maybe I'd walk to the harbor. And there she was." I rubbed my face, hard. "She said, 'You need to come back.'"

"'You need to come back,'" Tol repeated. "What do you think it means?"

And this is what I loved about Tolliver Jackson. In addition, of course, to his deep, sexy voice, and the salt and pepper stubble he grew during the winter, which made him look just like Idris Elba. I loved that he didn't question my sanity in the least: he did not for one second doubt that the girl had been there and had spoken to me. What Tol wanted to know was what I thought about it.

"Tolliver, how do you keep losing girlfriends?" I said, only half joking. "You are some kind of wonderful."

Tol had a habit of dating a woman for a few months, only to lose her to a much less attractive—and less financially solvent—youth minister or waiter or IT support technician.

Tol rolled his eyes. It was not becoming on a man so fully grown. "I don't know, Gamble." Then he set those eyes on me, and said, "They're not you."

Well, that took me aback. I cocked my head, considering. In an instant, I thought of the easy weekends we'd spent together over the years at our mutual grad school friends' house up the coast at Debordieu Colony, of the walks we'd taken on the blessedly empty beach there, of the hundreds of cups of coffee shared and the weekend brunches at Jestine's Kitchen, arguing over the last of the buttermilk biscuits.

It was how Tol met Harry for the first time, as a matter of fact. Tol and I were having brunch at Jestine's one Saturday, after a departmental doozy of a Friday night. Right in the middle of the meal, who should show up but my new husband. The husband Tol had yet to meet, because our courtship had been quick, and Tol had missed the wedding. (That hurt, but it's a longer story.)

In fact, I met Tolliver at the dean's house about the same time I met Harry: six months before my own wedding.

But back to brunch. I'd left Harry a note at the house that morning, telling him where I'd be, but I never expected him to show up at Jestine's. In those days—heck, probably even now—Harry slept in on the weekends until at least noon.

Harry bypassed the line that ran out the door of the restaurant, down Meeting Street and around the block onto Wentworth Avenue, I'm certain leaving raised eyebrows and grumbles in his wake. Then he spotted us and weaved his way through the crowded restaurant, which buzzed with diners talking and the clank of pan lids set over sizzling sausages. The room smelled of a gorgeous combination of sweet and savory. Harry pulled out a chair and sat himself down without so much as a by-your-leave. He reached across the table, took my coffee and sipped it before acknowledging our presence.

"God," Harry muttered, setting my mug down at his own place setting. "Gamble, honey, would black coffee kill you?"

"Harry," I said, reaching out to rub his forearm—this, I now recognize, a newlywed move—"let me introduce you to Tolliver Jackson, the friend I've talked about for so long. I'm glad y'all finally have a chance to meet. Tol, this is Harry Sims, my husband."

"Right. Couldn't make the wedding, could you? Nice to meet you, man," Harry said, for the first time looking at Tol. He stuck out a hand, and Tol took it. They shook, but after, Tol watched me and not Harry when he answered. Harry, of course, didn't notice, because he'd already picked up the brunch menu.

"It's a pleasure," Tol said. But his eyes said something else. Tol's eyes—a striking, disconcerting pale hazel from some light-skinned person way down in the roots of the Jackson family tree—said, *What the hell, Gamble?*

And that was that. The two men never liked each other, not even after four-plus years of my marriage. I simply did my best to avoid putting them in a room together. For those years, if Harry couldn't be my date to some Galliard function or another, Tol was. For the most part, the plan worked. Everyone had been happy with the arrangement...or so I assumed.

"Tol—" I started, back in the present and wondering if he meant it: that the women who left him weren't me.

But Tol wouldn't let me go there. "What else did she say?" he said.

"Who?"

"The girl in the alley. Did she say anything else?"

I nodded. "She said, 'He needs you,' and 'You must come back.'" I tucked my hands beneath my thighs to keep from gnawing at my fingernails, a nasty habit left over from childhood, one to which I resorted when anxious. "Crazy, right?"

"Hm. Who is 'he'?"

"If I knew that, would I be here? It's a mystery!" I gave up, clasped my hands like a child about to get a present. "I'm stoked, because I think she's the same woman from this miniature I worked with a while back—a lady circa 1804, in a fox stole. She just has this look in her eyes." I took a breath. "Tol, every time I look at her I feel like I know her. Like I'm privy to some secret about her I can't remember. I have to find out who she is."

Tol leaned forward with a shift of his broad shoulders, his regard so intense it made my cheeks go warm.

I said, "I started in the archives. I need to establish provenance, right? Well, nothing other than she's obviously Post-Revolutionary. The miniature portrait was alone, and the owners have no idea who she is or where she came from. But I wonder, because many times these portraits come in pairs, so maybe she's one of a sibling set, or even a couple. Which would give me more info."

I paused to take another breath. "I think I'll drive to Aiken, see if I can get Mrs. Hutto to let me into her barn. Want to come?"

Tol leaned forward, flipped opened a sleek silver day planner—because though he was a modern man, Tol liked to hold things in his hands—and began scanning. I hoped he was doing so in order to ascertain whether he was free to take a road trip into horse country, and sneak into an old lady's barn with his very best friend.

Okay, maybe not so much sneak, but persuade. Tolliver was a different kind of good at persuading than I. I was good at it because from all outward appearances, I looked like a curvy Christmas angel, or—as an ex-boyfriend researching Norse oral tradition for his dissertation once claimed—a Swedish elf. The truth is, I'm a happy person with a big smile, bright blue eyes, and pale blond hair. Because I look like this, and am in general energetic and amiable, folks sometimes mistake me for a bear of very little brain. They'd be wrong.

That being said, though it's a surface issue, sometimes the looks helped, especially when it came to getting what I wanted. I know it's possible this was, on a certain level, patently unfair: After all, using other people's misconceptions about you in order to deceive is not the most upright thing to do. But I figure, we all know what happens when we assume...

Tol, on the other hand, was persuasive because he's crazy smart, he's gorgeous, and he listens really, really well. He just waited. He took time. He had an undeniable presence. Plus, there's the deep, sexy voice. Sort of like a young Black Sam Elliott. Without the handlebar mustache. Oh, lord.

"Do you have cowboys in your family?" I said. I couldn't help myself.

Tol looked up from making a note in his planner and took a deep breath. Thank goodness he was used to me by now.

"Gamble," he said. "I am not inside your brain. Start from the beginning."

Later that evening, I stood again at the Church Street end of Stoll's Alley. The sun had set, but dusk hung on. The wind was warm, and it blew the tops of the oaks and palmettos overhead, rustling and clacking their branches, sending Spanish moss billowing like a woman's long gray hair. Leaves cartwheeled lazily down the sidewalk, catching around the front wheels of parked cars. Down the street, the gas lamps at Number 7 ½ Stoll's Alley flickered and hissed. The South Carolina flag attached above Number 10's pale-blue-painted oak door waved in a slow undulation of palmetto and crescent moon, and at once the bells began to toll, announcing the seven o'clock hour.

They rang, high and low notes, a gorgeous sound—a time-ago, time-lost sort of sound—and I touched my heels together, *à la* Dorothy. If ever there was a time for the girl to appear, it was now.

Down, way down the alley a shadow moved. There was a creak of iron, the heavy squeak of rust on rust. I looked away for a heartbeat, just over my shoulder, when a man on a ten-speed wheeled past me on Church and tinked his bell. When I looked back, there she was. The alley had darkened, the arching live oaks and myrtles more than ever a blanket above. Though I could feel cool wind ruffle the back of my suit jacket, her dress did not move at all.

I waited, surprised to find myself paralyzed. I quite literally did not know what to do next.

The girl gestured, impatient. "Come back," she said, her voice as clear again as if she spoke at my earlobe. "He needs you to come back."

I shook my head, and at the movement the girl began to walk toward me, picking her way along the brick-laid alley. I took an involuntary step backward, for the first time apprehensive. Really, consider this: how many of us would stand still if a ghost walked straight for us?

"I can't," I said, no louder than if I'd spoken to someone passing me on the sidewalk. "I'm not ready."

The girl stopped, then—in a gesture so familiar I wondered if it could be possible we were related—threw up her hands in disgust. "For the love you hold of us, do not tarry," she said.

She picked up her filmy white skirts, turned on her heel, and ran—toward the harbor end of the alley where it narrowed to only five feet wide, and where the last dregs of light spilled across from the sea, making the brick glow underfoot. As quick as she'd come, she was gone.

The next morning at the Galliard, I stood over my desk, where "*Lady. Anonymous, ca. 1804*" sat in a foam-bedded tray—its mystery woman staring up at me as if demanding to know all my secrets. I took a breath and closed my eyes, imagining the world falling away, nothing but the miniature portrait in focus, like a spotlight on a circus ringmaster, his audience in shadows.

After I had this image well contained, I spun it in my mind like a film reel, changing to a waterfall I'd once sheltered under when I was a backpacking guide. Soon the flap of papers being shuffled, the beep of the alarm code on the lab door, and Alice clearing her throat were muted by a curtain of water, a fall so thick and wild nothing could be seen through it. This was my practice, what I always did in order to give over all focus to the art at hand. So far, it had served me well.

I opened my eyes and reached for my magnifying head loop, adjusting it around the crown of my head. Then I picked up my probe and tapped at a piece of dirt caught in the tiny hinge still attached to the side of the miniature, despite the absence of a cover. No need for the microscope, at least not today. Satisfied, the corrosive dirt banished, I wiped the tiny tool on a piece of linen cloth and set it aside.

Who was she? The question was a constant, the mystery not a thorn in my side but a line on repeat, as if a pilot had been paid to string a strand of words across the sky of my memory. To fly back and forth with it all the damn day long like a banner tied behind a prop plane at the beach, with an advertisement for all-you-can-eat crab claws.

I didn't don gloves, not yet: my hands were clean, and gloves would make it difficult to safely manage the miniature as I took it apart. The miniature was already in good shape, as I'd restored it the year before. But what if I'd missed something?

I glanced again at the notes pulled up on my computer screen. There she was, number 89 in the collection. My cursor blinked next to the museum label (this was information we shared with the public, usually printed on a plaque mounted to the wall or on a stand near art on display):

89. *Lady*. Anonymous. ca 1804.
Watercolor on ivory. 2 ¼ x 1 ⅞ in. (5.8 x 4.7 cm)
Casework: Gilded copper with cast bezel and hanger;
on the reverse, beaded bezel framing compartment containing
    plaited hair
Colorplate 18b

Then, my treatment report, which I always included in my files. There, I'd noted a slight bit of mold—removed a year ago during the conservation process—but no damage to the glass, and no flaking of paint or major pigment fading. The plait of hair inside the back of the case was arranged in a simple decorative loop, tied with a fine bow using a piece of itself. I remembered the deep brown color, its richness having survived the ages.

I hadn't noted an inscription in my report, but this wasn't unusual, as miniature portraitists didn't typically sign their work: miniatures were often just too delicate and small for it. However, on occasion an artist might leave his or her mark on the paper backing, or even by manipulating a piece of the sitter's hair to form their own initials. Sometimes an artist hid their initials in the hair itself, or spelled them out using tiny pearls or beads.

I kept reading, noting the details I'd listed about the treatments I'd rendered, and my recommendations for the display and/or storage of the piece. But that was it.

I shifted in my chair, scooting closer, and chewed at my bottom lip. It didn't matter that, as a point of pride, I was unfailingly thorough with my work. That likely there'd be nothing more to find. I had to be certain.

I worked slowly to separate the locket case and the paper backing from the ivory, then set the pieces—layers of paper playing cards the artist had trimmed to fit, along with the tiny convex glass—on the padded tray. I held the miniature lightly with the tips of my fingers, careful to keep to the edge of the ivory and to place my fingers in line with the grain of it, and then finally set it down too.

Deciding to forgo use of the microscope, at least for now, I studied the compartment with the braided hair, looking for anything that might offer a clue about the sitter or the artist. But as my notes indicated: nothing. I wheeled back in my chair, waiting until I was far enough from the exposed ivory to let out a giant sigh (water droplets in breath could damage it).

Something niggled at me, an idea like a bird pecking at the wood siding outside a bedroom window. *Tap, tap, tap*, it said: *Pay attention.*

"Why is this one so important?" Alice said, having walked up without my noticing. This meant I'd really been lost in my manifested quiet place, as Alice stood a solid five-feet-ten inches tall, and in all probability weighed in at a solid two hundred pounds. Alice never announced herself; she didn't have to. She stood with both hands in the pockets of her white lab coat, waiting.

It was entirely possible I could've been examining the miniature for either twenty minutes or two hours; this was how it always happened for me. Time became flimsy, its parameters unimportant.

"I don't know," I said, rolling back, looking down again at the miniature. There was *something* there, in the knowing look in her hazel eyes, the humor in the upturned corner of her mouth. "But she is."

DANIEL

CHARLESTON, SOUTH CAROLINA
SPRING, 1805

Gamble was gone: Daniel Petigru knew this to be true. Had known it for months. Yet the knowledge did nothing to assay the emptiness in his gut. It was a hole he expected—or, if honest with himself, hoped— would have at least begun to fill by now.

Damn it all to hell. He never wanted this to happen. Had sworn he'd not allow it. But here he was, a man of forty years, with a broken heart. Again.

Daniel stood on the first-floor piazza, watching Honor in the garden. She had taken to over-pruning the roses since Gamble had left them. Her cat, a smoky gray called Jinx, wound about her heels. Honor did not even acknowledge the creature, which meant she was bothered indeed.

In a week's time Daniel was to be married in that garden. But it was not to the woman he had imagined, and there was simply nothing he could do about it.

Gamble appeared in Stoll's Alley the year before, on the first Sunday of October, 1804. She had been confused, disoriented, and clad in the most appalling fashion—like a lady actor from the Dock Street Theatre, playing a young boy in pantaloons and a man's shirt. Later, of course, Daniel would learn such was the mode of dress where she came from… from her place and time. Still, he would never forget the sight of her in those form-fitting black pants. He had been thirty-nine years old, and it was as if he'd only just realized women had legs.

Honor was the one to find her in the alley. She delivered Gamble to their home on Tradd Street at once. The three of them sat in the drawing room, perched on the edges of their cane-backed chairs, silent and trying not to stare at one another.

Finally, Honor turned to him and announced: "Daniel, it's her. I've seen her in the alley since I was twelve years old."

☙

72 Tradd Street, Charleston
October 1804

"Madam, what is your name?" Daniel asked, slowly, as though she might spook like an unbroken colt.

Startled, the woman looked at him. She absently fingered a rip in her pants, through which Daniel could see the gleam of skin. With a sudden, piercing clarity, Daniel wanted nothing more than to run his own finger along that line of white skin. He cleared his throat.

"It's Gamble," she said. "Gamble Vance. And you are?"

"I'm Daniel Petigru," he said. "It's our pleasure, my sister Honor's and mine, to offer you respite and aid you on your way."

How stilted he sounded, but then, he was nervous. And how strange a name, especially for a woman. Was it her husband's? Clearly the lady was married, or had been: there was a white line on her finger, indicating that a ring had sat there once. And she was of an age...or perhaps she was a widow.

Effie entered then, cups of chocolate and rolls from yesterday's dinner on a tray. She'd been listening from the hall, Daniel knew. Effie studied Gamble with those wide almond-colored eyes of hers—eyes that missed nothing. Daniel watched Gamble stare back, with a look far too concentrated to be considered polite. She clutched her fingers together in her lap.

"Madam Vance," he said. "Allow me to introduce Mistress Perrineau."

Gamble swallowed—he saw the movement at her throat—as she took a cup from Effie. "It's a pleasure," Gamble said.

Effie nodded at the stranger. "And mine," she said. She took one long look round the room, her frank gaze resting on his. Daniel knew what Effie was asking, but he had no answer for her or anyone else, at least not yet.

"Y'all need anything else, you let me know," Effie said.

At the doorway Effie met with Ben, who leaned against the frame, holding a cup of steaming chocolate. He blew, then took a slow sip. In his other hand he held a bench plane by the tote; he tapped it absently against his thigh. Ben wore work breeches, Daniel saw. He wondered if Ben had been able to patch the box seat of the four-in-hand, or if they'd have to order new lumber and rebuild the damn thing after all.

One of Ben's thick brows crooked up as he met Daniel's eyes across the room. Daniel knew the look—he'd been the recipient of Ben's quiet looks since their boyhood—but Daniel shook his head, the movement infinitesimal, sure to be overlooked by anyone else. *Not now*, it said.

Ben offered a nod of acknowledgment to Gamble, and, remaining silent, followed Effie down the hall. The drawing room settled into an awkward silence. Gamble cupped the chocolate in her hands but did not drink.

"Who are they?" she asked, so quiet Daniel almost didn't hear.

Daniel shifted forward and gripped his knees, the soft deerskin of his painting breeches comforting beneath the rough pads of his fingers. He picked at a dried paint splotch, giving himself an internal shake.

"Who? Effie and Ben?" he said, chafing a bit at the blunt inquiry. She was the stranger; he should pose the questions. Still, the woman was a guest and in need of aid, and Honor so obviously wanted to help her. Daniel forced a polite answer. "She's our housekeeper. More like a chatelaine, truth be told. Ben is our groom and stablemaster."

Daniel wanted to ask more, but again they all shifted to silence, for what seemed an eternity. Before Daniel could demand the woman explain herself, Honor broke it.

"From wherever did you come?" Honor asked, abandoning all pretense of propriety.

When Gamble didn't answer, Daniel shifted in his seat. For heaven's sake, *now* the cat had got her tongue?

"Madam Vance," Daniel said, impatient. But at the woman's blue-eyed glance, containing—it seemed to him—both fear and challenge, he hesitated. "Or is it miss?"

Good God, man, he thought. *Why not come out with it and ask if she has a husband?*

"It's madam…or was," she said. "But I prefer Gamble." She straightened and gripped at her knees, her knuckles paling. "Please tell me, what year is it?"

"Year?" Honor said, stunned. "Why, it's 1804. Do you not know?"

"That's what I figured, but I needed to hear it." The woman cleared her throat, and Daniel watched the movement at her slender neck, wondering what she would say next. He could not hazard a guess.

"I was born in Asheville, which is a town in the mountains of western North Carolina. A town," she said, "which doesn't exist yet. But I've come from Charleston. From the year 2004."

Daniel Matthew Petigru considered himself a bit of a revolutionary. He was born in 1765, in a revolutionary decade, but eleven years old at the start of the War of Independence. He was an artist, after all—had toured and painted all over Europe, apprenticed under the masters, lived in Rome and Paris until the revolution there became too bloody even for the artists. He returned home to Charleston to stand as guardian for Honor only after the sudden deaths of their parents.

In Charleston, they were able to keep a home through money left from his father's rice-brokering business, and his own art. Daniel knew himself to be a driven man, often losing sight of everything and anyone around him when in the grip of his art. Before he left Europe Daniel was entirely concerned with portraiture in miniature. Thankfully, miniature portraits were all the rage in Charleston. He painted them for whoever commissioned him, and he had completed over fifty in 1804 alone. Honor said he was obsessed.

Still, despite his unusual trade and knowledge of the world, Daniel could not conceive of Gamble's origins. However, it wasn't, he realized, that he thought her mad. He studied Gamble across the room, watching as she drew a deep breath, visibly lifting her shoulders. As if gathering her courage. Certainly, anyone who met the lady was sure to be convinced by her strength of character, her obvious intelligence. But to travel through time? From two hundred years in the future? It was a most incredible proposition. Impossible to believe.

"I believe her," Honor announced, and Gamble smiled, tension leaving her elvish face. For Daniel was certain he'd seen, somewhere in a faery book in Copenhagen, the face of a yellow-haired creature who looked exactly like her.

"Thank you," Gamble said.

The room sank into quiet. Then, before anyone could break it, the expression on Gamble's face shifted before their eyes, changing from relief to revelation. It was as if she'd discovered something hitherto unknown, or solved a mystery in the moment, right before their eyes.

Gamble stood, and Daniel shot to his feet. She crossed to Honor but stopped at the edge of the rug; she clutched at the hem of her untucked shirt. Honor stood too, but didn't move any closer. It was as if Gamble was an animal in need of rescue, and they afraid to approach for fear she'd make some sudden movement and injure herself further.

"It's you," Gamble said, to Honor. "You're the woman in the alley."

Honor looked to Daniel for help, but he was at a loss. Then she nodded, slowly, at Gamble, her voice purposeful and calm. "Yes, I found you there," Honor said. "I brought you here."

"No," Gamble said, working the hem in her hands, "you don't understand. I've been seeing you in the alley—in Stoll's Alley—for weeks, maybe even years. You've been appearing there, like a ghost."

Daniel took a step closer. "Madam, you must sit. Let us get you something to drink."

"I'm not delusional," Gamble snapped, her gaze suddenly fierce. The announcement seemed to fortify something within her. She faced Honor again, certain.

"You appeared to me in the alley, in 2004. You wore a white dress. You said, 'He needs you,' and 'You must come back.'" With this, Gamble turned to Daniel, determination and pleading in those startling eyes of hers. It nearly forced him to take a step back, the combination so powerful. "I studied her miniature portrait. One you painted. I knew it—I *knew* I recognized her."

"I've not made a miniature of Honor since she was a girl," Daniel said. But before he could say anything—think anything—else, Honor took Gamble's hands in hers.

"You are so very familiar to me," his sister said. She looked at him over Gamble's shoulder. "Daniel, we must help her."

There was a note in Honor's voice, something so full of hope, it rooted Daniel where he stood. He looked at the pair of them, youthful excitement emanating from his sister in waves. It was as if Gamble's presence illuminated Honor.

Daniel's mind was a whirl, but he vowed to quell his disbelief, at least for the moment. Honor wanted to help the woman, and Daniel would do just about anything for Honor.

First, they must find Gamble something appropriate to wear—for the love of Zeus, they couldn't have her parading about in pants. Society already considered the way his family lived to be out the norm; he could only imagine what they'd make of Madam Vance.

"There's much to discuss," Daniel said. "But I believe Gamble"—he hesitated briefly over the use of her given name, yet charged on—"is in need of a rest in a room of her own, and perhaps the loan of a gown?"

"Yes, quite," Gamble said. The woman stood and rolled her head on her neck, just as a pugilist does before entering the ring. It shook off Daniel's irritation, made him smile in spite of himself.

She was captivating.

Their eyes met, and it was as if he'd passed his expression to her. They smiled at each other until Honor said, "Yes, well, do come with me, madam. We're not of a height, but our mother was about your size. One of her frocks should do."

GAMBLE

It didn't occur to me until halfway to the podium, my remarks jotted on five notecards tucked inside the beaded clutch hanging from my wrist, that I'd not returned "*Lady*, ca. 1804" to her glass drawer in gallery 5. Thank goodness tonight's was a garden event, and not being held inside the gallery; otherwise, someone might open the drawer to find a conspicuous blank spot next to portrait miniature number eighty-nine.

I stepped carefully along the gravel path, lifting the floor-length hem of my navy-blue velvet gown. I never could seem to find evening wear for myself, much less everyday clothes, which didn't drag on the ground. If I'd been the sort of proactive woman who managed to have her clothes altered in time for events like this, life would be easier. Instead, I'd worn the highest heels I could find, which was a nincompoop move, to be sure. My hem caught under the pointed toe of my stiletto, and I had an instant, terrifying vision of my strapless dress coming down and exposing myself to the well-heeled, mostly gray-haired members of the Historical Society.

A large, warm hand took my elbow firmly in its grip, and an unmistakably deep voice said, near my ear, "You do this every time."

Rescued, I let Tolliver guide me the rest of the way to the podium. He bent, and for a split second I had the irrational idea he might kiss me. I turned toward him like a moth to a lamp. His breath warmed my cheekbone.

"For a smart woman, you're dumb about shoes," he said. "Break a leg."

Oddly bereft at the lack of a kiss, and wondering just what the heck *that* meant, I took out my notecards. The museum's garden was at its most spectacular on nights like this: White lights were strung in the one-hundred-twenty-foot live oak allée; crystal candle chandeliers hung over tables draped in antique cloths and anchored by wildly elaborate flower arrangements, and discreet patio heaters hummed nearby. Soft spotlights trained on the planted English urns lining the courtyard and on the delicate Demeter fountain at center with its single plume of water. Gentle waves formed on the reflection pond, catching and unfurling bits of light.

"Good evening," I said into the microphone, and seventy-eight well-coiffed heads turned in my direction. "I'm Gamble Vance, senior conservator here at the Galliard. Thank you to the Historical Society for making the *Miniature Portraits* exhibit the beneficiary of your generosity, especially so we could all be here together on this beautiful night. I, for one, am happy to welcome all of you to the Archdale Garden, which recently underwent only its second renovation since the garden was planted in 1903. Isn't it gorgeous?"

There was a smattering of applause, and I took the opportunity to look for Tol among the tables. Usually he was easy to find, being more than a head taller than anyone else. Finally, I spotted him making his way to the back of the garden, where he was stopped beneath one of the pleached oaks by a woman in a svelte red dress. He looked lean and dark, dangerous in his bespoke tuxedo (I could tell even from far away). He held a squat crystal tumbler of something; the woman in red put her hand on his arm, and he bent to listen. Had he brought a *date?*

I gathered my wits and flashed a megawatt smile at the crowd. "Tonight is a party, and so I promise not to keep us from it for long. We have the Holy City Quartet here, after all, and we want them to do their thing."

Behind the podium was a dais, where instrumentalists waited. The violinist gave a quick, friendly zip with her bow, and the crowd laughed. "But I did want to tell you a little bit about our *Miniature Portraits* exhibit, and why it's so very special to Charleston.

"Artists have created miniatures for centuries, but the one hundred years from 1750 to 1850 marked the heyday of portrait miniatures in British America and then the young United States, and Charleston claimed some of the country's most prolific and talented miniaturists. These artists painted the people of our city; what they've left us are glimpses into the soul of a century.

"Miniatures are tiny. Because of this, the artist must concentrate on a face if he or she wants to illuminate the truth of their sitter. This makes miniatures deeply personal," I said. "If you visit gallery 5, you'll note the tools used by one portraitist in particular, an artist named Daniel Petigru. Several of Petigru's pigments are on display in paint pots, along with a squirrel-hair brush, a piece of his pumice, and most miraculously, his accounts book. Because of this, and because of the sketches he left behind, we're able to name and date the people in many of his portraits: folks with family names we'd all recognize, like Pinckney, Middleton, Ravenel, Grimke, Prioleau, Rutledge, Laurens, Poinsett, and more."

I shuffled my cards, then set them on the podium, realizing I didn't need them. I took a beat, knowing I tended to speed up when talking about topics I loved.

"Most miniature portraits aren't signed by the artist: there's just not enough room. So it's through an artist's distinct style and technique that we're able—even two hundred years later—to determine which portraits are theirs, even if they're unmarked.

"While European miniaturists employed a more romantic style, sort of an idealized version of the people they were painting," I said, with a wink which had the front row smiling back at me, "American minia-turists—for the most part—strove to create portraits based in reality, using definitive brushstrokes and bolder colors. They manipulated the ivory surface in order to bring a flush of a glow to the skin, and indeed, some of these centuries' old people look as if they could step out and greet us. Spend any dedicated time with these miraculous pieces of art, as I'm lucky to get to do, and you'll begin to feel such kinship with the people in them it wouldn't surprise you to meet them in the produce aisle at the grocery store."

This earned another round of laughter from the audience, and I felt myself grow warm with their attention.

"With your generosity," I said, "we are able to conserve these pieces so they'll last at least another two hundred years, offering a glimpse into the real people of our city in an entirely new way. Though I've spent hundreds of hours with these miniatures, it never fails to move me to know they were once worn around necks, on bracelets, at cuffs, or kept as the most cherished possessions; to think people looked upon them and remembered those they loved most in the world—people they didn't want to forget."

Here I paused, because a lump had risen in my throat. I found myself with the inexplicable urge to cry, and I blinked back tears threatening the corners of my eyes. The scene before me wavered in my vision for no more than a heartbeat, but I swallowed and said, "The next time you're in gallery 5, take note of these faces. I think you'll find they're as real now as they were when they were alive. You might even see someone you know in the shape of a nose, the arch of a brow, or the twinkle in an eye."

Recovered, I folded my hands in a gesture of thanks, and offered the audience a short bow. "If you'd like to learn more about the history of miniature portraits in Charleston, please visit our website; we've updated our blog with links to articles and essays on the topic, interviews with conservators, and much of our research. I speak for all of us at the Galliard when I say we're forever grateful to the Historical Society for helping us honor the stories of Charleston's people."

I leaned closer to the microphone: "Thank you. And, y'all, don't forget to dance."

I scanned the crowd as they applauded. Tol approached on the gravel path, clapping loud and long, his grin bright in the dark. I scooped up my cards and took his proffered arm.

"You were wonderful," he said.

"Where's your date?" I said.

"What date?" He looked at me, quizzical, and stopped us in our tracks. The quartet played; voices rose and fell around us as silverware and glasses clinked.

My heels slid in the gravel and I gripped his arm with both hands to stay upright. Doggone it: I'd meant to stay light, not get myself in trouble.

"Red dress," I said, as if this explained it. I glanced around before releasing his arm and adjusting the neckline of my gown. "Jessica Rabbit?"

"Gamble—" he started, but the president of the Historical Society and his husband had found us. I put on my public smile.

"Gamble, you've outdone yourself." Brennan Lyle kissed me on the cheek. In his mid-sixties, big and brash, Brennan had worked wonders for the Society over his tenure, and I really liked him. "Wasn't she fabulous, Tolliver?"

"Always," Tol said, a note of something in his voice I would've insisted he share if we'd been alone.

Brennan's adorable red-headed husband, Christopher, gave me a wink. "Your passion is contagious, Gamble," he said. "Tol, who did your tux? It's a sin to walk around here like that. It's just not fair to the rest of us."

Minutes later, after others had joined us to congratulate me on the night and to enjoy the flit and flutter of Charleston art-world gossip,

Tol procured drinks. I accepted the bubbling champagne with thanks, sipping while I listened as a septuagenarian in a blush sequined gown insisted she was related to one of our miniatures (umpteen generations back, through a cousin). I'd not had a bite to eat, and the alcohol fizzed in my throat, warming me all the way to my toes. It was delectable to feel this way, under the trees and the sparkly white lights, and I barely noticed how chilly it was until the quartet began playing some slow song.

Tol moved behind me. He ran his palm, light, across the top of my exposed shoulder and down my arm, and took my almost-empty champagne flute.

"Let's dance," he said. Goosebumps lit along my nape. "Excuse us, everyone."

Instead of joining the dancers in the middle of the courtyard, in front of the band, Tol led me to the grass nearby, where a few outlier couples swayed, some having kicked off their shoes. I grinned and did exactly that, which made our height difference even more pronounced. Neither of us cared.

Tol took me in his arms as if he'd done so for a lifetime. He gently spun me out and then back, so close our torsos touched. I swallowed, because…this felt very different from the last time we'd danced together. (Last time, we'd been packed into the raucous, sweaty Music Farm, dancing as a group with a bunch of grad school friends.) Before I could make some (probably lame) joke about how tightly he held me, Tol said my name. The shadows made by the oak allée gave his light-colored eyes the look of dark whiskey.

"I like the way you talk about time," Tol said. "You make it seem like two hundred years is nothing. It connects folks to these pieces in a real way, as if it's something they can touch. That's a rare talent, Gamble— one not every historian can claim."

I shrugged, having to crane my head back to meet his eyes. "It's not me," I said. "It's the art. Really, these portraitists in particular, like Petigru and his contemporaries. I'm in awe of how they brought people to life. It affects me."

"I can see that," Tol said. "Your energy is infectious. You know, you really should be teaching."

"No." I shook my head. "I'm no good in a traditional classroom—I need to be with the art. Multitasking is not my strong suit. You know me: all or nothing."

"I do know you," Tol said. "I know you're having trouble keeping your mind off that miniature. Any more visits from the ghost woman? Has she told you her name yet?" He spun us in a tight circle and I laughed, wrapping my arms around his waist to keep my balance.

"Not yet. But I know I need more time with the miniature. I'd like to get her under the microscope again, take photos. Then maybe I'll be able to see if the techniques used match up with a particular artist."

Saying it aloud gave me pause. The feeling that I already knew something about the woman—the same feeling that had me standing over and over again in gallery 5, staring down at an open drawer like a person obsessed—formed a giant question mark in my mind. It was guilt, that's what it was: I felt guilty I'd put her on display, as if I was supposed to be keeping some secret about her instead.

I sighed. "I don't know how I didn't discover her identity a year ago. I would have, you know. It may be crazy to think I'll find anything new."

"Hey." Tol tucked me into his chest, and I went willingly (my neck hurt from looking up at him). "You'll find her. I'll help you."

I pressed my cheek against his smooth lapel. God, I never felt so safe as when I was with Tolliver. As we danced, the exhaustion of the build-up to the benefit, the extra hours I'd been clocking at the Galliard, and the mental work I'd been doing over the mystery woman dropped over me like a weighted blanket. I closed my eyes, relying on Tol to lead us both, to keep me upright. In this lovely fog of not thinking, I slid my hands beneath the tails of his tuxedo jacket and tucked my thumbs into his waistband. I didn't want to lose my grip.

"You're so big," I murmured. "It's hard to hold on."

Tol made a sound in his throat. "Let's get you home," he said, his voice doing that octaves-lower drop that made my toes curl.

I know. Not the most appropriate thoughts to be having about your best friend. I don't know what to tell you.

"I have to talk to people," I said, protesting. I pressed my nose into his jacket and groaned.

Tol held me away from him, to search my face. "You're falling asleep in my arms, Gamble. You can say goodbye on the way out." Taking my hand, he swiped my stilettos from the grass. I slid them on, grimacing as I used his arm for balance.

After several drawn-out goodbyes with patrons, we made it through the back gate and to his car on the street. He opened the passenger door and helped me inside. When I leaned against the headrest and shut my eyes, I felt the tug of the seatbelt across my chest and heard a click.

"Tol," I said, the need to sleep so strong my eyes refused to open. "You're a real gentleman. Don't ever change."

Dreams are funny things. Once, when I was an undergraduate, a psychology professor told me—after friends and I cornered him, tipsy, in a college bar and demanded he analyze our recent dreams—that the neuroscientist Rosalind Cartwright believed dreams are our brains' way of attempting to resolve any complicated emotions we'd experienced during the day. That they're a melding of new and old memory, and that the process changes "the organizational picture" of who we are, helping us figure things out.

One of my friends had set her beer on the bar top, where it sloshed over the side, and said, morosely: "Huh. But I don't feel organized *at all* today. I'm more confused than ever."

Our psych prof removed his elbow from the path of the oncoming spill, stood up (probably to escape), and said, "It's a big job for dreams, reorganizing like that. Cartwright thought we should look at the changes in dreams over time—that it takes more than just one night to figure it out."

In Tol's car, in the fog-heavy stage between sleep and awake, my brain underwent some sort of reorganization. Maybe it was the combination of night upon night of dreams, as Cartwright had asserted—or the combination of dream and memory—but when Tol turned off Church and down the skinny drive of my kitchen house, I stirred. When he parked I jolted upright.

The answer was right in front of me. So apparent, in fact, it seemed astonishing I'd missed it. Almost as if—like the feelings of guilt and secrecy I experienced when I looked at "*Lady*, ca. 1804"—my subconscious had tamped down on the knowledge on purpose, so I wouldn't yet wake to it.

"It's Petigru," I said. I planted both hands on the dashboard, and Tol's warm tuxedo jacket—which he must've laid across me—slid to the floorboard. "Daniel Petigru is the miniature portraitist. He painted her. The style is unmistakable; I don't know how I missed it."

I looked at Tol, who'd gone still and quiet in the dark car, waiting. "She's got to be connected to Petigru," I said. "And if she is, I can find her."

DANIEL

CHARLESTON
OCTOBER, 1804

Gamble descended the stairs wearing Daniel's mother's indigo dress, the one his mother had worn time and again, because his father had loved how she looked in it.

Daniel had been married once. He'd known women in his life—exotic women, women who spoke French and Italian, who read scandalous poetry by candlelight. But this slip of a woman standing on his mother's Persian rug, in his mother's blue dress, with her strange boots peeking out from the hem, was a mystery. He didn't know her at all. He was at a loss as to how to begin.

"You're an artist?" she said, and it jolted him.

"Yes," he said.

"What are you working on now?"

"Daniel has more commissions for miniature paintings than he can fill at the moment," Honor said. She entered with a steaming teapot in hand, then used it to fill the silver hot water cask on their father's favorite mahogany side table. "You must have him show you. They're in the carriage house."

"The carriage house?" Gamble said, surprise in her voice.

Daniel blinked. "Yes, well. Horses do not talk to you when you're trying to work."

"I can hear you," his sister said over her shoulder as she exited with the empty kettle.

Gamble wandered to the silver cask and bent to admire it. "Isn't this a fabulous contraption? It's gorgeous. It looks just like a hot air balloon, only it's stationary. Look, it has legs! As if it could walk away. What's it for?"

Now he was truly shocked, and not only from her disjointed speech and odd pattern of thought. "Is there not tea or coffee where you come from?"

She straightened. "Oh, you better believe it! There's practically a coffee house on every street corner."

Daniel smiled. It seemed he could do nothing less. "How delightful."

Gamble lightly touched the cask's delicate silver spigot. "It really is."

There was a lull, and he began to speak, not to say much of anything, only to fill the empty space because he didn't know what else to do. Gamble interrupted.

"Can we take our coffee with us?" she said.

"With us, where?"

When Gamble smiled, it lit the room just as the sun did on winter afternoons, when it came blazing in through the south-facing windows of his living quarters on the third floor. It nearly blinded him.

"To the carriage house," she said. "So I can see the miniature portraits."

It was rare that Daniel allowed anyone, except Honor or Edward Malbone—who, after all, was both friend and fellow portraitist—into his studio in the carriage house. Honor was let inside because he'd no real choice about it: she'd harangue him like a gypsy woman hawking her wares on a Prague street corner if he attempted to bar her entry. Thankfully, his sister didn't disturb anything; she just liked to be with him. There were even times she brought refreshment, then perched upon a stool and faded into silence.

Honor had done this often as a girl, after their parents died. She'd been so desperately young: a late, unexpected baby, nineteen years younger than Daniel. Sometimes she would cradle Jinx, and girl and kitten would curl together in a corner amongst his canvases and wood scraps. The kitten's low purling would be the only sound, save for the scratch of his brush. He hadn't demanded that Honor go, then, because she eased the grip of grief in which he found himself after their parents' passing, and he thought perhaps he did the same for her.

Daniel was twenty-eight years old, Honor nine, when, over the course of one summer, first their mother, and then their father, were taken by yellow fever. After receiving word in Rome of his mother's illness, he booked immediate passage to Charleston. Sea voyage being what it was, his mother was gone by the time he arrived; she'd died before he received the letter calling him home. His father held on longer, succumbing three days after Daniel's ship made port in Charleston Harbor. Their last conversation had been fevered and brief.

Would mail travel any faster by the year 2004? This was something he must ask Gamble. This and so much more.

Daniel stopped at the foot of the loft ladder, giving himself an internal shake. What was the matter with him? Surely, *surely* he could not entertain the possibility that she was truly from the future. Fantasy as such was for faery tales, not real life—not his life, at any rate.

But was it possible? Daniel could feel the idea arrange itself at the edges of his intellect, like the playing cards and other handmade papers he sliced and pasted to fit inside his miniatures—work he'd crafted and recrafted until things looked just so. Like his artistic process, Daniel could sense that Gamble's story might just stretch and reshape the world as he knew it.

At one of the nearby stalls, Gamble let Honor's mare, Cleopatra, snuffle her palm. The horse's white head hung over the stall door, and the creature strained to be close to Gamble, bumping the wood with its knees. Gamble sipped her coffee and smiled at the horse over the rim of the porcelain cup.

"Are you able to climb?" Daniel asked. "I'm afraid it's the one way up."

"This is why your studio is out here with the horses, isn't it? You're Rapunzel in the tower, only you'd prefer never to let down your hair," Gamble said. She took one last, regretful sip before setting her cup on a bench nearby. "Of course I can climb."

"Yes, well, I admit it seemed a good place to hide," he said, making a slight leg as she passed. She gripped a ladder rung at eye level. When she lifted a leg, Daniel reached out to waylay her.

"You'll catch up in your skirts if you're not careful," he said. "Perhaps we should've allowed you to remain in those shocking pants."

"Oh, I'm still wearing them." Both feet on the ground now, Gamble lifted her hem to demonstrate. "There's no way I'm wearing a corset. Talk about uncomfortable."

Daniel flushed with embarrassment, and it was as if he were ten again and had walked in on his mother being dressed by her lady's maid. What was the matter with him? He cleared his throat to cover it. "Ladies do not wear corsets in your time?"

"They do not," Gamble said, gathering her skirts in one hand and reaching high with the other. She paused midway up the ladder, bare feet balanced on a rung, her legs for all the world to see.

She said, "Most women wear dresses—gowns—only on special occasions, like to church services or parties. I rarely do. Most wear pants, just like you. We wear layers only when it's cold, and hardly even then. When I was younger, women used to wear pantyhose—tights—and slips. Shifts, you might call them. But we've done away with those too. Undergarments now are tiny: pretty much just bits of fabric on your bottom half…sort of like a loincloth. Then there's something called a brassiere you wear on top, like a tiny corset for your breasts, but nothing even as large as the short stays women wear now. It's much less complicated."

"Good God," he muttered. His memory flashed to the *chahut-cancan* he'd seen performed in Paris and the open-crotched pantalettes of the dancers.

Gamble stepped up and her petticoat caught underfoot. She slipped, and Daniel lunged, but she righted herself. On a huff, she tossed the skirts of her gown up and over one shoulder, treating Daniel to a very close view of her well-rounded backside, courtesy of those inexplicable black pants.

No fool, he chose to stay silent, and to watch.

She climbed over the railing into the loft, disappearing for what must have been a minute or two. He heard her footfall on the boards above. There was an indrawn breath, then her head appeared at the top of the ladder.

"Oh, Daniel! It's marvelous!" Gamble said.

She'd somehow, in the span of moments, tied her wild hair into a thick topknot. He saw what he thought was one of his paintbrushes sticking out of it.

Daniel knew he should've found her untoward, impertinent. Instead, he said, "Rapunzel, Rapunzel, let down your hair."

GAMBLE

The microfilm reader whirred and whapped against the reel, the sound louder than it should've been, even in the empty basement of a public library. Well, almost empty—at the sound of Tol's voice, I looked up from the desk where I'd been scanning the archives for over an hour. The far wall and the doors to the main library stairwell were glass, and through them I watched as he emerged from the upper floor, a stack of three-ring binders in his arms. Tol said something I couldn't make out to someone on the stairs above, then laughed, his teeth flashing.

With a bump of his hip he opened the door, then crossed the basement and dumped the binders on a nearby table. "Any luck?" he said.

I slowed the film to a stop, and frowned. "Not yet. What's all that?"

"The private papers of the William Drayton family. Most important-ly, the journals of Elizabeth Drayton, *née* Elliott," Tol said. "Hannah says they're the best account of Charleston society from 1800 to 1817. Maybe we'll find your mystery woman here." He took a chair from the table and set it next to me. He sat in it the wrong way: straddling it like a teenaged boy, his elbows propped on the chair back and long forearms hanging.

Today Tol wore a pale blue plaid shirt, jeans, and a pair of stylishly scuffed brogues, no socks. I smirked: sometimes he was too dapper for his own good.

"Hannah, huh? That's nice." Hannah was a graduate student from Germany earning her PhD in Library Science. She was sweet and smart, and looked like Heidi Klum.

I sent the microfilm whirring again, searching newspaper records for Daniel Petigru's name. I knew it was petty, but I was irritated. Research was not my strong suit. Maybe it was a patience thing. Still, it felt like we'd never find the woman in the miniature, but—call me crazy—I knew that if we didn't, she'd keep appearing in the alley. I didn't know how much longer I could continue doing my job if I still felt that internal pull toward her miniature, so much so it crowded out everything else. Not to mention the odd sense of guilt hovering over me like a Charles Schultz cartoon cloud...as if I'd done something wrong, something I had to fix.

Tol reached out and tucked a strand of hair behind my ear. "Why don't we switch," he said. "I'll take the newspapers and you give the journals a go."

"Fine." We both stood. Tol flipped the chair back around and held it out for me like a proper gentleman. When I sat, he leaned down. I could hear the grin in his voice when he said, near my ear, "Hannah's engaged to her tennis coach."

I pretended not to hear, opening the first binder as he sat at the microfilm machine. Soon the sound of film flipping at high speed, the turning of paper pages, and the building's massive HVAC unit—groaning just outside the basement stairwell—merged into a kind of white noise. This, and Tol working steadily beside me, helped to soothe the savage beast of my brain.

I closed my eyes and placed my hands lightly on the papers before me, picturing the miniature again: the woman with the fox stole, her slanted hazel eyes and the angle of her upturned mouth. I moved a different image into the frame of my mind and placed it beside her, like a scrapbooker arranging photos in an album: this one, the girl in Stoll's Alley in her white Regency-style dress, hazel eyes demanding that I *do* something. I took a long breath in through my nose. Then I superimposed the images, one on top of the other until only one woman emerged. I just had to find her in real life.

I opened my eyes when I realized the microfilm machine had stopped. Tol stared at me, waiting.

"Hannah said be sure and check out the entries from summer 1804 through the next spring," he said. "Apparently Elizabeth got engaged, and she had a lot to write about."

Okay. I focused on the journals and flipped to the photocopied entries starting with 1804. Elizabeth Elliott was engaged in July of that year to William Drayton III, the son of another prominent local family. Her journal entries were filled with dress fittings and other wedding preparations, family members' comings and goings, and descriptions of her awful cousins—whom her mother insisted she ask to stand as bridesmaids. I chuckled at the family dynamics: some things never changed.

Because they were photocopies, I ran my finger down the page as I scanned. Then, there it was.

There *I* was.

In elaborate, rolling script, Elizabeth had written,

12 October 1804. Engagement ball a wild Success. Madam D. proud as a peacock, says it is the most coveted Invitation of the season. I told Will it was All to show off the gas chandelirs, which are divine. Met a most unusual Woman ~ Arrived w Honor Petigru & she tld me she had never danced a reel! Imagine! Gambel Vance is her name. She is Honor's cousin just Arrived from Virginia, but I heard Rose H. tell G. Horry the lady is really Mistress to the artist. Madam D. says we mustn't speak scandal, but I thought her kind. If G.V. stays I will ask her to attend my Wedding no matter the talk.

"Tol," I said. Then, when I realized I'd barely gotten the word out, I said again, louder, "Tol."

He scooted his chair across the faded 1980s carpet, right to my side. "Got something?" he said. When I just stared at the page, my brain racing but my mouth not working, I felt his warm hand engulf my shoulder. "Gamble? Did you find her?"

I put my hand over his without thinking. Immediately he flipped it to thread our fingers together.

There. An anchor.

There was both question and comfort in his eyes, and I heard the awe in my voice when I said, "Yes. Petigru had a sister, Honor. It's her. I found her. But, Tol"—I swallowed, my mouth dry—"I also found myself."

The Blind Tiger Pub had been popular for decades for a reason: housed in a two-hundred-year-old building on Broad Street, its dark, moody, and intimate interior—with generous pours from a Prohibition-era tap—made patrons feel that even though they were in the center of town, they were hidden from the outside world. That, and also as if they'd been transported to the 1890s, when Prohibition resulted in blind tigers—another name, in Charleston, for illegal speakeasys—opening in secret all over town.

After Tol and I had exhausted our research at the archives (Hannah had to come downstairs to tell us they were closing), we'd walked to the pub, talking the entire way. The wind had blown cold off the harbor, down centuries-old streets arranged specifically to funnel it, and, above our heads, streetlamps blinked on as the sky went dark.

Seated at our high-top table, in the midst of the busy pub, it finally hit me.

"I was there," I said, gripping my cold beer bottle with both hands. "This is real."

He nodded. "It really is. The research doesn't lie."

I took a gulp of my beer and swiped a shaking hand over my mouth. "Well, at least I know I'm not going crazy."

"You are many things, Gamble," Tol said with a smile. "But crazy isn't one of them." Then he held out his bottle, and we clinked.

"Thanks for that," I said. "On one level, it's so hard to believe, right?" But the truth was, I *could* believe it. I'd been feeling my connection to the past, to Honor's miniature portrait and to Daniel's work, for weeks, months…possibly even years. The trick was, now I had to do something real about it.

If a person could feel both flummoxed and right—if there was a word for this odd combination of absolute certainty and trippy fabulism I felt snap and flicker in my veins—then that was me. I gripped the bottle again to center myself. Because still, in the midst of these conflicting emotions, I knew we had to find Honor.

Though we'd traced Daniel Petigru through the mid-1800s, discovered he'd married twice, and had lived and worked in France before and after his second marriage, we'd lost the trail of Honor Petigru after 1805. It was as if she'd vanished.

"I just don't get it," I said, stealing a seasoned fry from Tol's plate. "Petigru was well known, practically famous—one of the most prolific miniature portraitists in the US at the time. The guy painted everyone from Lafayette to John C. Calhoun. But his sister disappears at nineteen years old. There's no mention of her after spring of 1805. How is that possible?"

Tol lifted his beer but was bumped from behind by a young man pulling out a stool. "Sorry, man," the guy said. A group of his friends, obviously college students, huddled around their table, laughing and talking. Tol waved an easy hand in response and set his beer down, focusing on me despite the growing noise of the pub.

"Well," he said. "What *can* you remember about Honor's movements? Did she disappear down the alley while you were there? Talk to you about any future travel?"

I tried to concentrate, but when it came to Honor, my memory buzzed in my head like a fly trapped on the inside of a window. Sometimes the fly landed on the glass and was still. But as soon as I made any move toward it, it flew off again.

"I honestly don't know," I said, with a sigh. "And I can't even tell you why I don't know—or what I don't know. I don't think Honor even remembered calling to me from the alley. But I can't say that with any certainty. It's infuriating to be able to remember some things so clearly, but not others. Why does it work like this?"

Tol reached out and gave my arm a squeeze. "Take a breath. You're not a robot. You're a human being who's experienced the extraordinary. Nothing about this, including your memory, is going to fall into any sort of governable structure, no matter how much we want it to." He smiled, and there was comfort and humor in it. "I mean, we're dealing with human memory. And time travel. Remember what Einstein said about time?"

I let out a long huff of breath. "Einstein said a lot of things about time," I said. But Tol had quoted only one in his acceptance speech for the directorship of the Cox Center. He waited, endlessly patient, and I rolled my eyes good-naturedly. I said, "He said, 'People like us, who believe in physics, know that the distinction between past, present, and future is only a stubbornly persistent illusion.'"

He winked at me, withdrew his hand, and took another sip of beer. "But something must've happened to her," he said. "Maybe that's why she's asking for help."

"Maybe," I said. "But why didn't her brother write about her? Especially if she moved, or became ill… Even if she died, there'd be a record of the funeral."

"Not necessarily." Tol shook his head. "Remember, those records could've easily been lost in the fire of 1861."

He was right. In 1861 an enormous, devastating conflagration—incredibly, thought to have started from a kitchen accident, and nothing to do with the Civil War—destroyed a swath of the peninsula, causing millions of dollars of damage. Much had been lost, including lives, and personal and public property. If this was the case, we might never know what happened to Honor Petigru.

"I know you're right," I said. Disappointment and fried food settled in my belly like concrete. I pushed back from the table. "I'm going to run to the restroom." A glass shattered somewhere back near the kitchen, and the din of the pub paused, then immediately increased. I gripped my chairback. "Are you ready to leave? Do *not* get the check. It's my turn."

"Sure," Tol said, giving me a look I knew well. The bill would definitely be paid by the time I returned.

The all-black bathroom, a closet converted well over a century ago, was tiny. There was only about a foot of space between the toilet and the sink, which was tucked into a corner and flanked by a brass Art Deco mirror, the glass silvered and crackled at the corners. I latched the door and studied my reflection. Supposedly, the Blind Tiger Pub had ghosts, the most popular being a Prohibition-era woman in a dark dress who liked to pull people's hair.

"Have at it," I said, into the mirror.

But I knew I needed to shape up, and quick—that being ornery would get me nowhere. For heaven's sake, I was an art conservator. I knew the time and attention to detail it took, what it really meant, to peel back the layers of a story, to get to the core of it in order to reveal the beauty beneath.

"Get it together, Vance," I told my reflection.

Looking down, I spread my feet just a bit wider on the black and white penny tiles of the bathroom floor. Then I straightened as if a string had been tugged from the top of my head, and let my arms fall out to my sides: mountain pose in a water closet.

"Try to remember," I said to myself in the mirror.

He needs you to come back. This was Honor's plea each time I saw her in the alley. She was young, so the most important "he" in her life could've been her brother: a man whose work I'd been studying and conserving for years.

When Elizabeth Elliott had written of me in her journal, she'd referenced someone referring to me as "mistress of the artist." If the Charleston of 1804 was anything like the Charleston of 2004, it was town fueled by gossip—by connections between people. I'd assumed gossip was the only thing Elizabeth had meant. What if there was more? What if Daniel was the "he" who needed me to return?

I'd dreamt of the past for years. Now I was beginning to believe they weren't dreams at all, but maybe—just maybe—memories of my life in the past. Piecing them together after I'd brushed them aside for so long as if they were nonsense—as if they were just a symptom of spending too many hours at my job—felt like trying to complete an internal jigsaw puzzle.

I closed my eyes and let the noise outside the bathroom door melt away.

There'd been a garden with tea trees; I could smell the sweet mint, feel the air on my exposed neck, the brush of my gown against my belly. In that garden I'd stood next to Daniel Petigru. This time he was not a figure in a sketched self-portrait, but fully dimensional. He had kind brown eyes, and he wore a haphazard cravat, a blue paint splotch on his breeches. And I knew him.

I was pregnant, but I lost the baby, I said. *And my husband behaved as if it were nothing. As if it were something to get over, like a cold.*

He hurt you? Daniel said.

Yes. I whispered it. *He'd been unfaithful.*

Daniel stepped closer, his boots crunching the sandy lawn underfoot. He reached for me, and I felt his fingers against my cheek. *So you lost twice,* he said.

There was a knock on the bathroom door, and I opened my eyes.

"Just a sec," I said. I felt shaky, hollow, as if the breath had been sucked from my lungs. I took a big gulp of air, and stared at myself in the mirror again. My eyes looked huge, a bit wild.

I pressed a hand to my cheek, where I could still feel Daniel's touch.

It was late, but Tol came inside after he walked me back to the kitchen house. He'd been quiet all the way from the pub, and I knew this meant he was thinking hard—that he was going to say or do something either insightful or frustrating. I didn't have to wait long.

"The question is," he said, smooth as you please from the corner of my ancient white sofa, his long legs stretched out and crossed at the ankles, with Kipling's big head in his lap, "have you tried to walk down the alley when you've seen the girl? All the way down?"

I took a bracing gulp from the glass of respectable pinot noir, shaking my head in earnest when it burned. (Wrong pipe.)

I said, "No, of course not! I'm not ready to"—here I paused to regroup, holding the glass against my forehead—"go. I'm not ready to go wherever it is *she* is."

"How do you know that's what'll happen? That you'll be transport-ed?" Tol said. "You've walked down Stoll's Alley likely hundreds of times, most of them without time traveling."

"No." I shook my head. "If I follow her now, I'm gone. I know it sounds insane, but I just have this feeling the second I follow—the second I walk down that alley, this time—something extraordinary will happen."

I squeezed my body in between the arm of the old sofa and Kipling's considerable hind quarters. She stirred and looked back at me, affront-ed. When I slid my feet under her haunches, wanting the warmth, she hopped off the sofa and made herself comfortable in front of the fire-place, where my vent-less logs hummed with heat. She put her head on her outstretched paws and stared up, all moony-eyed, at Tol. Kip had a thing for handsome men.

I sighed, at a loss as to how to explain. Knowledge had opened inside me, like a bud forced early to bloom. I felt like a botanist who'd stum-bled across an undiscovered, yet-to-be-named desert flower, in a shade of red no one had seen before, its leaves fat with the promise of stored water, and spikes on its stem.

The truth was, I felt like that flower: startling, full of promise, and dangerous with it. I'd always felt like that flower.

"Tol…" I began, but drifted.

His eyes narrowed. "Yes?"

Then the sensation left, the notion of an opening abandoned. I felt as if something real had been snatched from me, and I turned to him with tears in my eyes.

"I don't know," I said, bereft.

Tol touched me, lightly, on the shoulder. "You do. Say it."

And it was back, just like that. I swallowed.

"I'm not surprised by any of this," I said.

DANIEL

When Daniel alighted in the loft, he found Gamble studying his newest commission, Mr. Nicholas Izard. The initial graphite sketch of Izard was pinned to his easel, the face and shoulders of a man emerging from a small square of vellum-mixed paper at the center of a larger canvas. The final product, of course, would be tiny: no more than two inches high and less across, on a piece of ivory cut in an oval. Daniel had taken the page from his sketchbook just that morning, wanting to see it from all angles in the light.

Unlike many of his fellow miniature portraitists, Daniel chose to sketch on paper first, rather than begin immediately on the miniature itself; after all, ivory was a fragile medium which took a tedious amount of work to prepare. With Izard, he was close, but needed a bit more time.

Gamble bent closer to the drawing, her hands clasped behind her back as if to keep from touching it.

"This is wonderful," she said, but her voice was strange. "Do you plan to use a stippling technique on the ivory?"

Daniel stepped toward her. The loft was not large, but the roof of the barn here was high, and the big window facing the garden—once used to drop hay—allowed the early afternoon sun to flicker dust motes aswirl in the air between them. Nearby, atop his small desk sat glass jars of his paints and inks, cups filled with his brushes and pencils, and a stack of sketchbooks. The room was so light-filled this time of day, he'd no need for the oil lamp.

Who was this woman? She appeared from the ether, with a story no sane person could possibly believe. Yet there was a rare and unencumbered joy to her speech—a freedom about her unrecognizable in the women of his acquaintance.

Daniel pulled at his cravat, trying to loosen it. "You know about stippling technique?" he said. "Are you an artist yourself?"

Gamble straightened, then inhaled deeply before covering her face with her hands. Would she weep? No. She exhaled, rubbing her eyes, like a person waking from a deep sleep, her fingernails, he noticed, cut short and square as a man's.

"No, I'm no artist," she said. "I'm an art conservator." At the look on his face—surely a reflection of his confusion—she gestured with one hand. "I work in a museum, where I conserve and restore miniature portraits like this one." She paused and tried again. "I help save miniatures like yours after centuries of neglect. Put them back to rights, you might say. In fact, I restored this miniature in 2003. The year before I… left. It's Nicholas Izard, isn't it?"

She could have seen it in his account book. Daniel glanced at his desk, not bothering to be covert. But the book was not there; it was, he remembered, in his bedroom in the main house. A bedroom in which Gamble had not set foot. Yet.

Daniel found himself imagining her there and cleared his throat, hoping he'd not colored. "It is Mr. Izard," he admitted.

Gamble stepped back, faltered, and gripped the seat of his painter's stool. "Oh God," she said. "Oh my God."

"Madam Vance?" Daniel thought she might swoon. He reached only to take her elbow, but she retreated, caught her heel on the hem of her frock and cursed. His eyes went wide.

She gripped the neckline of the gown, pulling at the thin fabric as though it strangled her. One arm wheeling in the air, she said, "Where the hell am I? What's going on? I followed a woman wearing a costume down Stoll's Alley and now I'm here, in 1804? And somehow, we're connected. I mean, I've spent years restoring your art. Yours! Oh God. Oh my God. I'm such an idiot. Couldn't leave hell enough alone, could you, Vance?"

Gamble stepped back again, too close to the edge of the loft. Daniel held his hands up and out, as if placing his body before a runaway horse. Could the woman not stop, be still, for but a moment—could she do nothing in the bounds?

He said firmly, "Madam, stop this at once!"

At his tone she froze. Then crumpled like a rag doll.

GAMBLE

CHARLESTON
EARLY NOVEMBER, 2004

I knew I had to tell Tol what was becoming more apparent to me as the days passed: that Daniel and Honor were much more than strangers who'd taken me in when I needed shelter and safety in 1804; that not only had I traveled to the past, I'd had a real life there, no matter how brief.

One Thursday in November, weeks into our search and after yet another unsuccessful evening at the archives (Hannah let us stay after closing), we sat in my living room, nursing our disappointment. We still hadn't managed to find out what had happened to Honor after 1804: not where she'd gone, and certainly not why she was asking me to return.

Finally, wanting Tolliver to understand more than I ever wanted anyone to understand anything, I told him what I'd remembered. I said, "I think I loved them."

"You loved him. Daniel." The statement, phrased simply, and his raised eyebrow, seeming casual, betrayed what was going on inside. I knew this, because I knew Tol. The man was the very definition of still waters running deep.

He was so serious sitting there, taking up all the space on my eighty-year-old sofa. Something about his unflagging belief in me, in my unbelievable story, broke my heart. It broke it in a good way, the kind of break which occurs only when a miracle is present.

I reached out, unable to help myself, and smoothed his raised black eyebrow with my finger. Tol caught my hand in his.

"Stop," he said.

"I loved *them*, Tol. Both of them."

Tol placed my hand on my chest and gave me a gentle push backward. I took the hint and scooted to my end of the sofa. He shook his head, reminding me of my father in disappointment mode (this was irritating), then stood with a quick and fluid grace. The ancient, wide-planked floorboards creaked as he crossed from wood to rug before disappearing into my galley kitchen.

"You give your love away pretty easy, G.," Tol said, and though I couldn't see him I could hear the suction of the refrigerator door as it opened and closed. There was a metallic pop and hiss—the sound of a beer can being opened.

Tol didn't usually drink beer. This was serious. But that was for later. For now, I was pissed.

"Don't you dare call me 'G,'" I said. "You only do that when you're trying to be someone else. Don't be someone else with me."

Tol appeared in the kitchen doorway, leaning up against the cased opening so his close-cropped hair brushed the top of the arch. He studied me, silent, as he tipped back the can and took a long gulp.

It took a second, but the words registered.

"I *give my love away easy*? What the hell is that supposed to mean?" I swallowed my temper, trying to relocate my sense of humor. Because I'd a damned fine sense of humor, and he was my flipping best friend. "Are you calling me a whore, Dr. Jackson?"

Tol grinned, all shit-eating and white in the dim room. He was backlit by the kitchen light, so I couldn't make out his eyes.

"Never that," he said.

"Well then, explain yourself. Stat."

Kipling pulled herself to her feet, walked to the door, and wagged. Tol gestured with the beer can. "Your dog needs to do her business."

"Fine." I hopped up from the couch, energized with anger, and flipped on the outside light before I hauled open the heavy wood door. The skinny screen door knocked against the kitchen house in the cold wind—wind that had the same effect as a bucket of ice water. And there I was, anger sizzling like smothered coals, dripping with the slurry ash of my own half-remembered mistakes.

How would I ever explain to Tol the intricacies of my relationship with Daniel and Honor, when I didn't quite grasp it myself? In the years since my divorce from Harry, I'd been forced—with help from a therapist (friends convinced me: I dragged my feet)—to realize I'd a complicated history with partnership. Blame it, perhaps, on being raised by a rather badass and rarely bitter single mother, but partnering up always felt to me like being collared. In my experience, some relationships required a short leash, and for me at least, those didn't last.

However, I'd come to learn that even a leash utilizing a long line had to be staked in the ground.

After my miscarriage, and in the miserable, blood-soaked days that followed (no D&C procedure for me: I'd endure the flushing out of that small promise of life like a hardy pioneer. God, I was wrecked), I discovered Harry's infidelity. An infidelity which had, it turned out, occurred over the course of our four-year marriage.

Betrayed, tear-streaked and bereft, I went to Tol. I went to Tol, truth be told, as I always did. So I suppose that should've told me something in itself, not only about my marriage to Harry, but perhaps also about my rather Herculean insistence on making all the wrong choices before ever figuring out how to make the right ones. How betrayal can run both ways. How being faithful can be more than a physical act: how it can be a rather abstract act of the heart. How the choice to lay yourself open to vulnerability, like a surgical patient with entrails exposed, means nothing—and everything—depending on who holds the scalpel...or for that matter, who stands beside the hospital bed: who holds your hand.

But Daniel: Daniel was coming back, his memory as blurry edged as an anesthesia dream. Daniel had held my hand, I think. I think, maybe, like Tol, he too had held it, just when I needed it most.

"Gamble, is that you?" Catherine's voice came clean and crisp from the dark courtyard.

"Yes, ma'am," I said, the answer automatic. I patted my own cheeks, almost as hard as a slap, to snap the hell out of it.

Kipling slipped past me. Catherine wound down the umbrella at the wrought-iron table at the far end of the courtyard; it flapped wildly in the bluster. She bent and gave Kip a brief rub, her gray-streaked blond bangs blowing across her eyes.

"A storm's coming," she said, swiping them away. "Would you ask Tolliver if he'd mind latching the shutters on both kitchen houses? He's the only one tall enough."

Ha. She knew Tol was there. I'd always wondered if she spied on me.

"I'm happy to, Mrs. Memminger," Tol said from behind me.

His voice startled, even though I'd been listening to it all night. He always called her Mrs. Memminger, no matter how many times she entreated him to call her Catherine. Tol said it was because he was both a Black man and a Southern gentleman, and that was something I'd never understand, being white and a woman.

"Thank you, dear," Catherine said, yanking the umbrella up and out of the stand with a strength I hadn't thought she possessed. She tucked it under one arm and marched past us like a knight with a lance. "The storm's supposed to hit at high tide. Y'all stay tucked in tonight," she called, before opening the back door to the main house. Light spilled onto the bricks, vanishing when it closed.

"Woo wee, permission to have a slumber party from Catherine Memminger herself," I chortled, when I was dead sure she couldn't hear. Tol had already begun to latch the shutters on the bottom floor windows at 353B. Kipling danced about his feet.

"Kip, cut it out," he told my dog, but gave her quick rub after he did.

The wind blew the next shutter open (sometimes centuries-old shutter dogs get loose), and Tol went to it, careful to avoid Catherine's fat terra-cotta pots of red canna lilies and blue morning glories. Rain polka-dotted his pristine trousers. The top two buttons of his white dress shirt were undone: he always undid them the minute he walked in my door, like some minor lord in undress—and there was a dark vee of exposed skin at his chest and throat. Light from the gas lamp flanking 353B's door glimmered on the muscle there.

Tol secured the shutter, then pointed at me in the rain-thick dusk-light, like Babe Ruth promising a homer.

"Watch it, woman," he ordered, literally making a point. "Or I might take you up on that."

"It wasn't an invitation," I said, sharp but teasing.

Or was I teasing?

I couldn't think about that now; now was a time to hold on to my ire. I slapped my thighs to call Kip, and shut the big door against the splatter. Tol could open it again when he was done.

Inside, I twisted the knob on the gas logs, making the flames flicker higher and hotter. Despite the attempt at lightheartedness, I was chilled. Recalling my time in the past, being with Daniel and Honor, encapsulated in their world—a world which at first had seemed foreign, then had so quickly felt like home—was like peeling back a bandage to check on a wound taking far too long to heal.

It still hurt. Perhaps the scar was infected. Perhaps I wasn't finished with 1804.

I stretched my hands toward the flames, toasting my palms. Kip trotted up the inner stairs of the house to the second floor, without so much as a canine glance. She was headed, I knew, to the guest bedroom, where she slept (illegally, I might add) on the guest bed. She didn't even pause on the landing. I suppose she was done with us.

I didn't blame Kip. Tol and I were quite the pair. Still, I was mad. I most certainly did not *give my love away easy*. Sure, I was affectionate. I had plenty to go around, and I didn't spread it thin. But real love? That I saved for my people. Tol was one of my people.

The old door groaned, and Tol entered, wet and ornery.

"Yikes," I said in sympathy. "It really is a storm." I'd not paid attention to the weather that week, what with being buried in research.

When Tol didn't answer but joined me in front of the fire, dripping, I tried again. He'd soaked his fancy suit to help an old lady: I could afford to be kind.

"That was nice of you to be the big strong man," I said. "Catherine and I would've never gotten the shutters closed by ourselves. Too short."

Tol gave me a passing glance. Then, as if deciding something, unbuttoned his shirt.

"What are you doing?" I demanded, unreasonably shocked.

"I'm soaked, and I'm cold, and I don't feel like staying this way," he said. "Okay if I use your dryer?"

Tol let the tails of the dress shirt drop. His white undershirt was wet too. I knew this because he stood inches away. The kitchen house was built in 1768, which meant the ceilings were low. There were very few six-foot-five people in 1768. For heaven's sake, George Washington had been considered a giant at six foot two.

Which is to say, Tol took up all the space in the room.

Am I babbling? I might be babbling. You'd babble, too, if your Idris Elba look-alike of a best friend decided to strip right in front of you on a cold night in November. And before you say it: Yes, I had seen Tol without his shirt on before. I do believe I mentioned our weekends at the beach. But clearly, something had changed.

"Fine," I managed. "The detergent's in the cabinet in the laundry room, if you want to wash it."

"Thank you," he said, taking his sweet time getting there. I think the danged man knew I was uncomfortable. He disappeared into the kitchen, heading for the laundry room on the other side, which along with the modern kitchen had been attached to the house later. "Later" being somewhere along the lines of 1920. I liked to imagine it'd housed contraband booze during Prohibition.

But back to the matter at hand.

"Tol," I called after him. The dryer lid slammed.

"Yes?"

"What do you really mean?" I said, relentless.

I turned my back to the fire, waiting until I felt the burn through my cotton tank. (I'd put on my pajamas before Tol arrived. Hey, it's my house.) The sofa was no longer safe, so I pushed the two mid-century wood and leather chairs flanking the fireplace aside and folded myself criss-cross applesauce on the sisal rug. I flexed my toes in my wool socks.

I could hear the rumble of the dryer and the clack of acrylic buttons against the metal drum as the shirt flipped inside. Tol stepped from the kitchen, shirtless. Thankfully—or, who was I kidding? Maybe not-so thankfully—he still wore his slacks.

"About what?" he said.

"Have you been working out?" I asked. I like to believe my lack of a filter is part of my charm.

Tol gave me a light-eyed look, one that said, *What do you think?* He picked up his half-empty beer and joined me on the floor. There wasn't much room, but he made it work. I'd be a liar and a blind woman if I hadn't noticed the way the muscles at his belly—insanely flat for a man a few years from forty—rippled as he sat. He stretched out his legs, so long his socked feet went under the coffee table. When he leaned back, his thick shoulders bunched.

I studied him. Though, really, when had I stopped? We were close enough that I could see the stubble at his jaw, the silver there glinting in the firelight. The mark of his ancestors—his Black and white ancestors—was evident in his face, the strong lines of his bones creating a man in full. One who confounded adequate description.

I wondered, all of a sudden, just how many women Tol had slept with in the past year. In the past month.

Oh my God, I was snooping around my best friend's sex life. Back to being mad.

"What do you mean?" I repeated.

Tol didn't pretend not to understand. "You fall in love easily. Always have."

"I call bullshit on that," I said. Yes, I know I sounded like a high school boy instead of a woman with two graduate degrees. "Since you've known me, I've dated Harry, and only Harry—who I *married.*

Then, yes, there was Daniel. That's two men in the six years we've been friends. And, again, I *married* one of them."

"You married Sims six months after you met him," Tol said.

True.

"You were in 1804 for how long, do you think? Months?" he said.

"I don't know, but it feels like it had to have been a long time," I said, frustrated at the fickleness of my memory, but certain I'd developed very real relationships in 1804. "It had to have been," I repeated, more for myself than for Tol.

"Maybe it was months, at least in 1804?" Tol said. "I don't remember you ever being gone for more than a weekend over the past several years—you've been mired in work; you've stuck around." He paused. "Maybe your absence here was brief, but your stay there longer. At least long enough to fall in love." He gave an easy half-smile, but I knew better than to trust it. "You say you loved him too. Daniel. That's what I mean. You give your love away without a thought as to who might get hurt."

Tol took another swig of the beer. It was a mechanism, I knew—something to make me believe we were having a plain old conversation here on the rug in front of my fire.

"That's not true," I said. I felt as if he were accusing me of something much worse, something like betrayal.

"Worse," Tol said, "you hurt yourself."

And that's when he did it—when he touched me. Tol had touched me before, of course: when we'd danced, or when he'd hugged me, or helped me in or out of a car or a boat, or placed a hand at the small of my back before we entered a row at the movies or at a concert or play. But this was different. He took my hand and ran his long thumb back and forth across my knuckles. It was at once soothing and electrifying.

No, I cannot explain how something can be both soothing and electrifying. But that was the effect of Tol's touch.

Mesmerized, I watched our hands. Our colors were lovely together. Tol sighed. He wasn't giving up. The man held a doctorate in history: he was unafraid of a multi-era argument.

"You're trusting. Too trusting, at least when it comes to Harry," he said.

"Very true," I murmured in agreement.

"But that's because your heart's big—as big as your brain." His thumb stopped, and I looked up and into his eyes, more pale gold now than any sort of green in the firelight. The firelight waved shadows against the wood beams bracing the ceiling, thick as a galleon's mainmast, down the corners of the house where wall met wall. The shadows made the room feel alive, as if it curled itself around us like a cat.

"I wonder if your heart can be trusted," he said.

My heart thumped like mad in my chest, and I think if Tol hadn't been holding my hand, I would've skittered backward into the fire. Sort of a like a ghost crab on the beach at night, rushing terrified into a hole at the first glare of a flashlight in the eyes.

Here's the thing about historians, art historians especially—or maybe it's just the thing about me. Maybe I'm not so much a mystery. Maybe I've taken the easy way out when it comes to love. Maybe I fell for Harry so hard and so fast because I was running from something, or someone, else. Maybe I even married Harry, knowing he wasn't right for me, because I wasn't ready. Scared and unready, and looking for a way to mask it all.

What if it was Tolliver of whom I was terrified. What if what I felt for him—the love and friendship I'd cherished for years—masked a simmering of something else beneath the surface. Tol had not once, in over six years, made any sort of romantic move in my direction. Or at least that I could tell. He'd never asked me on a date, never tried to kiss me, never even flirted with me overtly, so I'd know what he was about.

Okay, God. That last one's a lie. Tol could flirt. It made me crazy when he flirted. For the love of Sam Elliott, his flirting as of late had been set on serious smolder.

But art historians. Back to us, and the thing about us. We are caught in the past. We study it, reconstruct it, try to salvage the best and worst and most beautiful things about it. We sink so deep that at times it's difficult to figure up from down. We're like divers who rise too quickly to the surface, who risk decompression sickness because the hypnotizing mystery which is the dark bottom of the sea has left us disoriented and scared. But there is no other choice for divers and historians both: we must go deep, in order to conserve what has been lost.

We're like writers in that sense: We grow distracted by other worlds, our heads in the clouds. Even when we walk through the here and now, it's often difficult for us to clear away the fog of the ephemeral worlds in which we've been living (or, in my case, conserving).

Like poets, perhaps, some people—say, friends who are in business, banking or law, or heck, work as checkout cashiers at the supermarket: people with more sensible vocations—assume we don't live in "the real world." (Can you hear my father's voice as I say this? Because I can.) They call us airheaded, fanciful, strange.

Not the artists. The artists get us. But that's because, like artists, our job is to make connections: to weave the precious metal strands of time into some sort of plait which links past and present. We work to ensure that this weaving be not only strong and beautiful, but also relentlessly authentic. Our goal is for both the elderly immigrant grandmother and the homegrown, skinned-knee third grader to look at the same piece of art, and to feel something.

That being said, it takes a lot out of us. Maybe we are distracted, fanciful.

Once, when we were married, Harry and I were walking down Broad Street at night. We'd been to see the play *To Kill a Mockingbird* at the Dock Street Theatre and were headed to where we'd parked our car. The night was warm and thick, and even with cars and people passing—couples dressed to the nines in high heels, elegant dresses, and best suits; families ushering children who itched to be free of the church clothes their parents forced them into for the occasion—I felt transported. At the corner of Broad and Meeting Streets, the white steeple of St. Michael's Church was illuminated, an ageless, storied beacon in the starless Southern sky. The themes of the play, and the actors who uttered the lines, refused to leave my consciousness. And I felt as I always did when art touched me: I felt changed, a part of something larger. A member of humanity unbound by place and time.

I tried to explain to Harry what I was feeling: That right there, in that instant, time stood still. That we could've been any couple—a hundred years in the past or a hundred in the future—standing on the same street corner. That I could see the strands of time as they whipped and freewheeled in the humid sky above. That it made complete and utter sense to me, this street corner which had seen the processions of Martin Luther King, Jr., George Washington, Robert E. Lee, Mary McLeod Bethune, James Brown, and so many more.

But Harry hooked an arm around my neck, pulled me in for a squeeze and said, "Gamble, you're a trip." Then, "Did you see Will Blakely get into that Rolls on the street? It's got to be his dad's."

All this is to say, maybe I'd missed the signs. Hadn't noticed the forest for the trees. Couldn't see the nose in front of my face.

You get the picture.

Maybe I'd been like a cliff diver in Acapulco, my toes curled over a rocky edge, terrified of leaping but knowing the sea below, waiting like an aquamarine embrace, was where I was meant to be.

But, man, was it scary to jump. I wasn't sure I could do it. I'd already jumped into the wrong water twice, even if the first time was to Harry. And he broke my heart, made me question my judgement, and was unable (or unwilling) to comfort me when I'd miscarried—unable to comprehend the loss I felt, despite the fact the baby hadn't been planned. He couldn't fathom how I could not just "get over it and get on with it." The memory of his subsequent betrayal, even now, was an annoying ache, like a faint throb in an old, injured ankle.

Once my therapist had posed this question: Could Harry's infidelity have been my ex-husband's way of coping, of grieving the loss of our baby? I hadn't wanted to allow for the possibility then, and barely did now. After all, it hadn't been the first time he'd broken our marriage vows. Perhaps, I admitted to that same therapist, my marriage to Harry existed in the shallows long before he'd cheated. Perhaps I'd been unwilling to enter the depths. Perhaps Harry was incapable of entering them at all…or was simply not meant to enter them with me.

Nothing excused Harry's sleeping with other women. But maybe it'd been unfair to Harry for me to turn to Tolliver, even if it had been for the comfort of his friendship. I was a woman who firmly believed that friendship was more than possible between members of the opposite sex. After all, I'd grown up with brothers. I'd made a life among artists, folks who rarely bowed to convention: who saw the world in abstract and possibility, no matter how concrete and fixed it appeared to others.

If I were brutally honest (always a good thing to be, at least with oneself) then it's also true that I knew, maybe from the very beginning—maybe even from the swing in that hammock—my friendship with Tolliver was different. That it was some amalgamation other than mere friendship, ephemerous and unformed as it may've been in those years. Even that pinprick of knowledge, buried deep, was unfair to keep from Harry.

Now, over a decade later, I knew life was composed of gray matter, and there was no such thing as black and white when it came to the inexplicably beautiful and brutal mysteries of the human journey. After all, sometimes a person could walk down an alley and come out the other side entirely changed.

But back to that treacherous cliff jump into the wrong water. The second time, I'd jumped to Daniel. I broke myself, leaving him, though I knew he was never mine in the first place.

But Tol? I knew, without a shadow of doubt, that if I made that leap, took that chance, and it didn't work out—if I lost him, his friendship and his trust, his very presence in my life—I might never recover. The loss of him would alter me, would damage my soul in ways brutal and profound.

Don't ask me how I knew this. I just did. There are mysteries in life and there are certainties. Yes, I know I'm contradicting myself—I know I insisted life was all about the gray matter. Here's the thing, though: Life is really about the "also" and the "and." The ability to hold opposing ideas, disparate feelings, in each hand, at the very same time.

My love for Tolliver was a certainty. But I didn't know if my battle-weary, third-hand heart could handle it.

Heavens to Betsy: my elderly landlady knew it. She'd invited the man to spend the night with me.

Tol squeezed my hand and laid it gently on my knee. He leaned in close, and when he did I froze, feeling just like a market-goer in India, paralyzed by the sound of a rattle from some snake charmer's basket.

Tol's mouth brushed my cheek, his breath warm and lingering, and smelling of hops. "I'll pick you up Saturday morning at eight," he said.

My eyes closed involuntarily. When I opened them, he was rising from the floor.

He walked into the kitchen, emerging moments later with his dry dress shirt. He slid his arms into the sleeves, but left it unbuttoned. Show-off.

"See if you can get Mrs. Hutto to let us stay the night," Tol said. "That way we could hunt around while she's asleep."

"Look at you. Pretty *and* conniving," I said, a desperate attempt to regain my wit.

Fine. To regain my senses entirely.

Tol took his car keys from the bowl on the sofa table beside the door. Outside the wind howled, rain splattering against the living room windows. It would likely be a long and watery drive back to his house on John's Island.

"Catherine was right. You should stay." I managed not to squeak when I said it.

Tol smiled, and in his smile was the story of our years of true friendship, of companionship and trust, of a strong and authentic mutual like for each other. In that smile was sex.

"One day soon, I will stay," he said. "But not tonight. I'll see you Saturday."

I sat on the floor for some time after Tol left. I'm not going to say I'd done something so sappy as to go weak in the knees. But my legs decided they were not quite ready to support me.

This thing with Tol was a new development. Well, not so new, but a definite game-changer. I'd not expected, when I followed a ghost down a centuries-old alley, that what might come of it would include a massive shift in my most important friendship. Surely time travel was enough.

Finally, I gathered my feet beneath me. I went through my nightly ritual, shutting off the fire, locking and bolting the ancient front door, turning down the heat at the thermostat. I poured a glass of water in the kitchen, using an old jelly jar which would remain more than half full on my bedside table in the morning, because it was inevitable I'd fall asleep before I could drink it all.

This was the great thing about being thirty-two and a real live adult: you knew yourself.

Upstairs, I peeked in the guest room and whispered goodnight to Kipling. She snored, the bed dipping and rising with each canine inhale-exhale. In my own room I slipped out of my bra and dropped it over one of the posts of my bed. The bed had come with the house and was gorgeous: maple, a four-poster carved in a tobacco-leaf pattern. I ran my fingers over one of the fluted posts as I passed, the historian in me sighing with happiness.

Guilt free, and at once overwhelmed with exhaustion both physical and emotional, I crawled beneath the tatted lace quilt (another item that had come with the house) without brushing my teeth. My teeth could take one night. I'd brush with extra diligence—heck, I'd even floss—in the morning.

I took my book from the bedside table. It was rare that I fell asleep without reading; in fact, Harry used to complain when I reached for a book after we made love at night. It wasn't a comment on his sexual prowess (Harry was good at sex), it was just that stories anchored me. Plus, it was habit. Something I did for myself.

Tonight, however, I let the book rest on my chest. My thoughts swirled, and even the ritual of reading didn't manage to settle me, not after the night I'd had. A dark shape moved in the corner of my vision, and I looked over at my open bedroom doorway. There was nothing there: a case of my seeing things, or one of Aunt Callie's spirits.

It belonged to the house, whatever it was. I was not scared.

Wasn't it downright interesting, that I lay in this bed—a twenty-first-century white woman—contemplating making a move on my Black best friend? If there were ghosts there (and I knew there were), they were sure to be the ghosts of both free and enslaved house servants, people who'd stoked 237 years of fires in the fireplace below. Women who gave birth in this house. Who died here. People who walked out the same door I did every day and onto the cobblestoned streets of this complicated city, dreaming—and because of my life's work with the past, I knew they dreamed—of a life free from chains.

I was terrified of what might happen should Tol and I decide to take our relationship to the next level. But I was in no way worried over race.

If we decided to move from friends to lovers—if we made that choice, together—there'd be no backpedaling, for either of us. Our relationship would never again be the same. You see, Tolliver and I were cut from the same cloth: We were history people. We dug deep, brought the truth back with us. We refused to let go.

I set the book aside and pulled the coverlet to my chin. It was all tied up together: my changing relationship with Tol, my time with Daniel in 1804, even my career, which meant everything to me. It had to have something to do with why Honor called to me in the alley—why she continued to show up, demanding I return. The only way to move forward, for any of us, was to find out why.

I turned on my side and watched the bedroom doorway, waiting to see the ghost again: the smudge of something at the top of the stairwell just beyond. Above my head, the fan I kept on in winter to circulate heat did its lazy spin. I was safe in my bed. But the wind blew loudly outside the kitchen house, and I knew from experience that the irregular slope of old bricks in the courtyard meant it was like to be filled with water come morning.

I said a fast and fervent prayer Tol was safe at home.

PART II

PROVENANCE

provenance / noun

1. The place of origin, derivation, or earliest known history, esp. of a work of art... 2. A record of the...passage of an item through its various owners.

~ *Shorter Oxford English Dictionary, vol. 2*

In Einstein's equation, time is a river. It speeds up, meanders, slows down. The new wrinkle is that it can have whirlpools and fork into two rivers.

~ *Michio Kaku, American theoretical physicist*

GAMBLE

AIKEN, SOUTH CAROLINA
EARLY DECEMBER, 2004

Tolliver stood at a long line of white wooden fence, letting a thoroughbred sniff at his open palm. Behind him, groomed and impeccable pastureland stretched long and low toward a distant line of loblolly pines. Horses—million-dollar horses—dotted the landscape. As the saying goes, we were not in Kansas anymore.

Tol looked up, watching me watch him. He wore a pair of tailored jeans (where did he find jeans that long? He must order them from a specialty store); a thin, fitted camel-colored cashmere sweater, his white shirt collar popped at the neck, and topped with a finely waled corduroy jacket. On his feet were sturdy Italian leather boots.

I'd teased Tol about the boots, of course, when he'd knocked on my door that morning. "No cowboy boots? We *are* headed to horse country," I'd said.

"I'm not ridiculous," he'd replied.

How many Black men had been inside Mrs. Saralee Hutto's house? I wondered, smiling as Tol brushed his hands on his jeans. He smiled in return, and he gave it an extra kick, a bit more shine. It sent a current humming between us across the still-dewy grass. I fluttered my eyes, pretending to drop back in a faint against the car door. He laughed, which startled the horse, who moved off for a nearby hay feeder.

As for Mrs. Hutto: It may have been the twenty-first century, but there was no telling how a ninety-seven-year-old Southern white woman would react to my bringing Dr. Tolliver Jackson into her house that day. However, she'd agreed to our visit, and even to our spending the night, without a bit of fuss. At least this was what Mark's assistant, Shelly, reported when we'd spoken on the phone earlier.

"Mark always stays at the farm when he's in Aiken," Shelly had said. "Mrs. Hutto said it'd be no trouble. They have plenty of room; I think the house may have even been an inn at some point."

"Always?" I'd mused. "How often is Mark out there?"

Shelly just chuckled, and I could picture her rolling her eyes as she moved about Mark's messy office—a fort that she held down with aplomb while Mark remained in Ireland. "Ever since his first visit he's been convinced there's more to be discovered on that property. He makes sure to stop by whenever he's in the area—it's a classic Mark Whitman charm offensive. But they also feed him well."

Speaking of a charm offensive: Tol was striding back to the car. He took a waxed canvas driver's cap from his back pocket and donned it as if he'd been doing so for a hundred years. I squinted, imagining him in the tweed vest, knickers, and suspenders of a bootlegger *à la* 1920s Harlem.

What can I say? I'm an art historian. I like pretty things from the past.

He grinned down at me from his great height, making me feel both very small and absolutely in focus. Here's the thing about Tol, especially when it came to what people thought about him: he just didn't give a damn. My heart went all aflutter.

"Let's get moving," he said.

ॐ

What do you know? Saralee Hutto was a Yankee. Or, at least, some of her ancestors were: her mother's side were horse people originally from New York, who used Aiken as a winter colony in the 1880s. Or so she informed us the minute she opened the front door.

Still, she gave Tol an up-and-down worthy of a queen examining an erstwhile courtier. Her wrinkled, watery gray eyes narrowed behind milk bottle glasses. She couldn't have examined him more closely than if she'd used the small magnifying glass hanging on a gold chain around her neck.

"Young man," Mrs. Hutto said. "Just how tall are you?"

Tol doffed his hat upon entering. He gave a subtle bow from the shoulders and smiled. "I'm six foot five, ma'am."

"Well," Mrs. Hutto said. "You look like an African king. Doesn't he look like an African king, Corrine?"

Oh, she liked him. So. It was to be more along the lines of Queen Elizabeth and Sir Walter Raleigh. (At least until Bess Throckmorton showed up. Gulp.)

The woman standing next to Mrs. Hutto was of a similar age, wrinkled and brown as a raisin left out in the sun. She had that ephemerous look and color folks tend to turn in extreme age, where you can't tell if they're Black or white or anything in between. I always supposed— hoped, at least—this was proof, in or near the human end, that the nonsense ended with it.

The woman pursed her lips and examined Tol, claw-like hands grip- ping an aluminum walker. "Yep," she said. "He sure does."

"Call me Miss Saralee," Mrs. Hutto ordered. "This is my cousin, Corrine Hampton Wilson. You may call her whatever you like."

"Miss Corrine will suit just fine," the other woman said. They shuf- fled toward a spacious sitting room off the entry, and Tol and I followed.

The sound of footsteps came down the hallway off the foyer before we even made it to the sofas (women that old move slowly). A put-upon voice said, "I told you to call me when they arrived. Y'all shouldn't be opening that heavy door by yourselves."

"We are not incompetent, dear," Miss Saralee croaked.

The woman who entered looked to be in her mid-twenties, and very pretty in an efficient, everything-in-its-proper-place sort of way. She wore a set of deep pink scrubs and a pair of shiny leather clogs. Though her focus was on the elderly women, she took definite notice of Tol and me. Mostly Tol.

"Hi," she said, coming forward and extending a hand. "I'm Tawanna Burr. I'm the home-care nurse."

We shook hands, and before I could introduce myself, Miss Cor- rine, who'd settled with great care onto one of two Bergere chairs, said, "She's my cousin."

"And mine!" Miss Saralee squawked. She landed in her chair with a little squeak, and the two old ladies looked at each other, then laughed merrily.

"A pleasure to meet you. I'm Gamble Vance," I said, when everyone settled down. "I'm not sure how much Shelly has told you about us, but I'm a conservator with the Galliard. This is my friend Tolliver Jackson, Director of the Cox Research Center. He's here for moral support."

Tawanna wasn't sure what to make of me. I knew the look well. I cleared my throat and tried again.

"He's here to help me assess the cultural value of whatever we may find."

"I'm also her driver," Tol added.

If I'd been close enough, I'd have stepped on the toe of his nearest fancy boot.

"Well." Tawanna eyed us with interest. "I'm not sure you'll find anything. Mr. Whitman has been pretty thorough. I think he went through everything when he was here last."

"We're just trying to cover all our bases," I said. "We're looking for any sort of clue into who the woman in Mrs. Hutto's miniature portrait really was. We're hoping to discover something that might help us date and document the pieces more effectively."

"Miss Saralee!" Miss Saralee demanded. It was apparent we were to be on a first-name basis, Southern-style.

"My apology. Miss Saralee," I amended, with a dip of my chin. Miss Saralee sniffed.

Tawanna did not seem interested in portrait miniatures and their historical legacy. Straight-faced, she said, "Okay." Then she turned to her charges. "I'm going to bring y'all some decaf coffee and a snack, then it's time for your meds. I'll send Baker in from the barn. He can show Ms. Vance and Mr. Jackson around."

Tawanna turned on her heel—yep, she really did. Ruthlessly efficient and practical people do that, you know—and headed for the doorway leading into the next room. I assumed it was the kitchen.

"Thank you, dear," Miss Saralee said. She drummed bony fingers on one wool trouser-covered knee.

"Oh, almost forgot." Tawanna stopped in the cased opening. "I made up two of the guest bedrooms on the second floor: the one Mark usually sleeps in and the one across from it. End of the hall closest to the bathroom. Extra towels and blankets are in the wardrobe in Ms. Vance's room." She paused. "I just assumed you'd need separate bedrooms?"

Miss Saralee and Miss Corrine met eyes across the faded yet elegant Turkish rug. I swear, they smirked. I blushed, and Tol smiled, smooth as you please.

"We do," he said.

But I knew him, and I knew what he meant was, *for now.*

DANIEL

CHARLESTON
OCTOBER, 1804

Daniel sat on the dusty planks of the loft floor, Gamble in his arms. Though small, she was solid, her legs draped over his lap weighted with a muscularity to which he was unaccustomed in the fairer sex. He held her as he would a young child, her head braced against his shoulder. His breath brushed the pale hair at her crown. Two fine lines crossed her forehead, one deeper than the other, surely got from the outlandish expressions she made when she talked. Too, she had a slight widow's peak. He wondered how old she was.

All this, and yet he scarcely knew the woman. Emotions warred inside him; he felt a softening toward her, to her person and her story— no matter how wild and uncommon. It was in spite of all he knew to be true. How could a person feel so familiar in such a short amount of time? Daniel had led an unconventional life, to say the least…but nothing like this had ever happened to him before.

"Madam Vance," Daniel said, too quietly. He shook her gently. "Gamble. Are you well?"

The woman in his arms sighed and shifted. It seemed she curled closer.

"I'm all right," Gamble said. "Physically, at least." She leaned back, so they were almost eye to eye.

"Your eyes are brown," she announced. "Thank you for catching me. I've never fainted in my life."

"You're most welcome," Daniel said.

When she made a move to stand, he instinctively held her tighter. It was for her own good, he told himself. If she rose too quickly, she might faint again upon standing.

"Steady," he said. "Why don't we give it another moment?"

"Why don't we," Gamble said.

They stared at each other, inches apart. Daniel's breathing went shallow. He could swear he saw some change in her eyes, some acknowledgment of him as a man. But then her eyes welled, and she blinked back what might've been tears, had they been given the chance to form.

"How tall are you?" Gamble said.

By God, Daniel was growing accustomed to her unencumbered tongue. He held back a laugh. "I believe I stand at three inches shy of six feet."

Gamble smiled, the corners of her eyes creasing most attractively. Her lips were full, her mouth wide and her expression open. She gave off a guilelessness—and a goodness—which took him aback, it was such a surprise. Daniel felt his annoyance melt. How, he asked himself, could she possibly be real? He wasn't sure he could trust her, or his own feelings. Perhaps the real question was whether he even wanted to.

"That's nice," she said.

There was a whinny from the barn below, and the world came together again.

"Hallo the loft!" Honor called.

Daniel rose and helped Gamble to her feet. They brushed off their clothes, their smiles shy. Or at least, his smile was shy. He didn't believe Gamble Vance had ever been shy in her life.

"We're here," he called down, stepping to the edge.

"Did she like them?" his sister said, young and eager, even at nineteen. Daniel's heart surged with love for her.

"I did," Gamble said. Daniel put out a hand to guard her from the edge, and she considered it with amusement. "They're wonderful."

And Gamble had seen the portraits before. In the future. At least this was her claim.

Again his doubt battled with his want to help Gamble and to believe her, for Honor's sake. He breathed deeply, nostrils flaring, and ran a frustrated hand through his hair. No one paid him any attention; Gamble's attention was bent on Honor.

It was then he noticed Honor wore her green silk gown: the one she donned for parties. He smacked a hand to his forehead, and Gamble laughed. "I nearly forgot. We're expected at the Draytons'," he said.

It was the last thing he wanted to do, attend a pleasure ball, but there was no way out of it. William Drayton was a patron, and tonight his oldest son was to celebrate his engagement to the daughter of another prominent family. It would be a private ball, exclusive, and there were far too many people on the guest list by whom Daniel needed to be seen.

He took one look at Gamble, flushed and disheveled, yet her stance wide legged and confident as a sailor's on the bow of a ship. Tendrils of blond hair had loosened from her topknot, and he could see that, yes, she had, in fact, used one of his paintbrushes as a hairpin. The bristles bobbed like a twig stuck in a high and windy bird's nest when she leaned further over the edge.

"You'll make yourself comfortable in our home," Daniel said to her. "We won't be away long."

"Nonsense!" Honor said from below. "Ben has already been with a note. She's to accompany us."

Daniel watched Gamble across the enclosed carriage. Beside him, Honor did the same. It was rude to stare, he knew, but he couldn't help himself, and perhaps neither could Honor. Gamble was most assuredly *not* of this time. At the Draytons' ball, she was sure to attract notice first for being new, then for being beautiful, and last for being odd. Moments earlier, when Ben helped her into the carriage, she took his gloved hand, stopped on the hitching step, and bounced on the balls of her feet—on purpose—as if the step were a joggling board, and she a child. Her earlier dark mood seemed lifted. Daniel felt as though the weather had shifted in an instant; he could not help himself: he prayed it was more than a sunblink.

"The past is a kick," Gamble declared, on a loud and joy-filled laugh.

Truly, the woman was a grenadier. Who knew what bomb she would throw next, and into a crowd?

Gamble's appearance was an illusion, for she was the picture of innocence. But from the appearance of her borrowed gown, she must've at least allowed for stays. While Honor reported that Gamble had balked at the curling tong, Effie obviously managed to coif the wild mess of Gamble's hair. It was brushed, puffed, and smoothed into a simple but elegant updo.

Daniel's mouth twitched. Effie was both genius and general.

He studied Gamble across the carriage as she grimaced, reaching up to pat gingerly at Effie's work. If she was to be believed (Daniel made himself think this), Gamble knew more about the world, their world, than they did of hers—certainly knew what would happen, years in the future. If it were left up to Daniel, he'd keep them home and ply Gamble with food, drink, and questions.

"You look wonderful in Mother's gown," Honor said. "Doesn't she, Daniel?"

At first Daniel didn't answer. His instinct was to throttle Honor. How could his sister imagine it'd be within the realm of good taste to bring Gamble along to the Drayton house? The ball had been planned for weeks, the guest list surely taken just as long to perfect. Daniel could imagine the titter sent through that house at the arrival of Ben with Honor's note—good God, the gossips would be out for blood. He'd be fielding questions all night.

Then Honor cleared her throat and said, "Daniel?" with such sweet uncertainty it took him back to her childhood. Daniel blinked. How did Gamble look? He wasn't sure he could rightly say.

Earlier, when Honor and Gamble had exited the house, Effie trailing behind with their cloaks, he was caught off his guard. The dress Gamble wore was their mother's to be sure, which meant it was more than a decade old and sure to be out of current mode. But that didn't signify, for it was stunning on Gamble.

Daniel remembered his mother coming down the stairs in it. More, he remembered his father's reaction. His mother had been petite, as was Gamble, with hair a kinship blond. Because the dress was a bright teal, bordered with decorative gold-stitched accents on the sleeves, high waist, and hem—the rich color unique to ladies' frocks as he knew them—it brought out the flush in his mother's cheeks, the gilt in her hair. He could see, even before his father told her she was beautiful, his mother felt it for herself.

When Gamble emerged from the house, framed by the painted black door and the tawny color of the stucco behind—a scene almost Italian in sumptuousness and hue—Daniel knew, suddenly, what it meant to have his heart skip a beat.

Gamble wore a velvet spencer jacket of deep blue, borrowed from Honor. It was her new one and a favorite, the loan of it evidence of Honor's swift and growing affection for the woman. A woman with them but one day. A woman certain to leave, should she have the chance to return to her own time.

Daniel met Gamble's eyes. "Yes, she does," he said.

Gamble lifted her arms, studying the fall of the full sleeves of the dress. She looked to Honor. "Will it be okay? That I don't look more like you?"

Honor's lips made a brief line as she considered. "There will be talk, but then there's always talk. An older dress isn't so unusual, and this one's not too far off the mark. Besides," she said, "you've still the high French waist. It's the color that may give pause—most ladies will wear pastels—but we can tell them some bit about your things being misplaced."

Daniel cleared his throat. "We'll need a plausible story," he said.

Gamble snorted, which irked Daniel. He wondered if she laughed at him.

"Plausible?" Gamble said. She looked at them both, her face flushed and eyebrows raised, a hint of what might've been anxiety sending her voice higher. "Is anything about my being here plausible?"

No one spoke, and the carriage settled into an awkward silence. Daniel met his sister's eyes in the dim, and he read the questions in them.

After a moment, Gamble leaned forward with a rustle of skirts and pushed back the heavy leather curtain, allowing in the cold. She poked her head outside. The lamps were already lit all the way down Tradd Street, casting half-moons of light onto the sidewalk. When the carriage took a too-sharp turn south onto Legare, she gripped the door with what looked like an acrobat's ease, seeming without fear.

"Whatever is she doing?" Honor whispered to Daniel, louder than he would've liked.

"I'm looking at the world," Gamble said, overhearing and not bothering to hide it. "It's incredible." She fell back against the bench with a broad grin.

"Do you hear it?" Gamble said.

Daniel and Honor looked to each other, perplexed. "Hear what?" Daniel said.

"The clatter of horses' hooves on the cobblestones. The hiss of the gas lamps. The rush and crackle of wind in the palmettoes." Gamble shook her head as if in disbelief, then held out her hands, palms up, like a woman begging for something in response.

"There's no background noise!" she said, awe in her voice. "No noise of the busy world, polluting everything. No music blaring. No cars. I bet tonight, if we walked to the harbor, there'd be a million stars in the sky. I bet if we climbed the steeple at St. Michael's, we'd be able to see for miles. But the quiet, oh—it's the loveliest thing I've never heard in my life."

"What is a car?" Honor said, before Daniel could.

GAMBLE

AIKEN, SOUTH CAROLINA
EARLY DECEMBER, 2004

Baker Collins was less than thrilled to be leading Tol and me into the high and dusty upper rooms of Miss Saralee's barn instead of tending to thoroughbreds, but he was too much the gentleman to say it out loud. Still, long pauses and raised eyebrows conveyed plenty when one was built like an Irish tank, thank you very much.

Earlier, on ground level, Baker's red, bushy eyebrows shot straight up when I told him what we were seeking. Really, it would've been an eye roll if we'd been anywhere other than in a famous old horse town in South Carolina, and his proprietress and her keen, albeit milky, eye not a hundred yards away in the main house.

"One of those tiny paintings?" Baker said. "We gave y'all everything we found. Heck, Mr. Whitman spent so much time here, I thought he was gonna move in. That man's a bloodhound. If it was here, he'd've found it."

"But Miss Saralee's nephew wouldn't let him in the barn," I argued. "There could be more."

"David Hutto doesn't want y'all here now," Baker said.

"No," Tol agreed. "But his aunt does. And she pays the bills."

Baker and Tol smiled at each other—two full-grown men appreciating the power of a dowager duchess over an unfortunate relation—and I pressed my advantage.

"It's not just a miniature portrait," I said. "It could be something else—a notation in a logbook, a signature on a painting, a random letter. We just want to know where the woman in the miniature portrait came from. Or at least what her name was."

Baker's expression clearly said, *Who cares?* I ignored it.

"It's a crapshoot," Tol said. "And we may find nothing. Thanks for humoring us, bro."

Baker shrugged and turned to lift the heavy wooden latch on the door leading to the barn's second floor. I looked up at Tol and smirked.

Bro? I mouthed, mocking. Tol rolled his eyes. Obviously being beyond Baker's gentlemanly restraint. Great big man with a PhD.

The boards in the stairs protested as we hiked up to the second floor. They were gray and thick-planked, and though the construction mimicked the barn's exterior, it was very different upstairs than it was down. Down, there were stalls running along each side of the barn with a long, wide, brick-sanded run down the middle. At the center of the building, two good-sized offices with a restroom, and across the run on the opposite side, a large tack room, packed with an assortment of saddles, bridles, and helmets, and smelling of oil and leather. It seemed very modern.

But upstairs felt like a different century. The second floor was massive, one main room encompassing the entire front half of the barn, with a large loft above as a third floor, accessed by a ladder nailed to the wall. Giant windows, one with a pull door to release hay, like a garage door, flanked the wall facing the drive and main pasture. They were closed now, but light flooded the room. Stacked along each wall were mysterious wooden crates of various sizes, draped with canvas drop cloths.

We'd come up first into a short hall, where there was a bathroom, and two rooms across from each other. I managed to glance in the open door of one—a bare single bed, ceiling fan, small dresser, and lamp—before the hall emptied into the large main room. Baker stepped back into the long hall and turned.

"Stay as long's you like," he said. He nodded at us, the Irish tank's version of an acknowledgment, and headed for the stairs. "Lemme know if you wanna ride later," he called. "Or even tomorrow."

"Ooh, a ride! Tol!" I squealed. Yep, like a little girl. A little girl with a thirty-two-year thing for horses.

At the same time, Tol said to Baker, "We will. Thanks for your help."

When Baker left, Tol shook his head at me. "Nope, not today, Gamble. Look at this place: it's huge. We're not here long. We need to optimize the time we have."

I frowned. "You're right." I walked to the stack near the window, flipped back the corner of a dusty drop cloth. There was a pile of crates beneath.

"Play that song again?" Tol said, a laugh in his voice.

I looked over my shoulder. He'd returned the driver's cap to his back pocket. Dust motes swirled in the air above his head, catching the light like miniature lightning bugs. Even in the giant room, with its twenty-foot ceilings and wide, open floor plan, with all that air to breathe, Tolliver seemed solid, grounded to the earth. I depended on him so much, I'd stopped noticing it. He'd become a given in my life: his steady goodness and faithfulness something I'd taken for granted for far too long. Years too long, in fact.

And here he was, giving up an entire weekend—a weekend in which he could be watching basketball or eating at nice restaurants or squiring around beautiful women (I shrugged off this notion, as it chafed)—to be with me. In a dusty barn in Aiken. With two old ladies who got way more of a kick out of each other than perhaps they should.

Steadiness—or, more appropriate: steadfastness—was a quality of note. Something to be desired. I had not desired it, as a young person living my original Charleston life, the one I'd begun when I arrived in my twenties and met Harry. Steadfastness was not a quality Harry could claim, that was for sure. It was rare that Harry did the same thing twice; he'd forget to let his own dog back in the house if not reminded, and often forwent showing up for one of my work events if he got into something else. (Something else being bourbon, or tennis, or sailing, or heaven knows what.) More telling, he didn't see the problem with doing so.

You show up for the people you love. This, my life thus far had taught me. This I knew to be true. To be an infallible code by which to live: an ancient clan motto carved in Latin in the lintel above the door of a medieval castle. The sort of castle built on bedrock. One that had, throughout centuries, been home, fortress, and sacred place.

Tolliver always showed up. In six years there was but one time he hadn't.

"Why didn't you come to my wedding?" I said.

Tol was bent, shimmying open the top drawer of the old desk. It wanted to stick, but then gave. He stood.

"What?" he said. "You know why."

Right. The conference at Florida State University. When he'd been in Tallahassee, lecturing on the African diaspora in seventeenth-century Florida, just as I was standing at the altar of Grace Episcopal Church in Charleston, promising myself to a man with a rather flexible interpretation of the word *vow*.

"You could've skipped the conference," I said. In fact, I'd wondered if Tol had pitched his paper to the conference panel after he knew the date of my wedding. As if he'd been looking for a reason to miss it.

Tol bent over the open drawer and began pulling out papers and setting them on top. "That wouldn't have been professionally kosher, would it?" he said mildly.

"It was my wedding," I said, and even I could hear the note of pleading in my voice. The hurt.

I found myself with feet spread like a gunslinger, fists clenched at my sides. My stomach churned. I'd wanted to know the answer to this question since my wedding night.

Tol stilled. "Don't, Gamble," he said softly.

"It was my *wedding*," I repeated.

"To *him*!" Tol shouted.

The shout reverberated off the barn walls, and it shocked me. I think it even shocked Tol. He braced his hands on the front edge of the desk, shoulders tight. His curved spine formed an indentation between the long muscles of his back—a shallow channel from nape to waist beneath his fine sweater. He still did not look at me.

I couldn't make a sound, even if I wanted to.

Finally, Tol said, calmly, "I couldn't watch you get married, Gamble. I just couldn't."

"To someone I'd only known for six months," I said, finding my voice.

This was it—we were doing this. I needed the truth. Tol's opinion of me meant more than I wanted to admit. His absence on what had been—at least then—the most important day of my life felt wrong. It stung, and the sting had not eased in the years since.

"To someone who wasn't me," Tol said.

DANIEL

WILLIAM DRAYTON HOUSE, GIBBES STREET
OCTOBER, 1804

Once they entered the main hall of the Drayton house, Gamble stopped short. Excited conversation, like the hum from a swarm of gossiping bees, floated down the staircase from the ballroom on the second floor. Thomas Huger escorted his wife, Mary Ellen, up the steps; Daniel recognized them even from the back, because he'd sat with them for hours, drawing their faces.

The garnet- and gold-stitched hem of Madam Huger's silk robe disappeared around the stairwell, and Daniel nearly walked into Gamble. He took her shoulders to steady himself, then promptly dropped his hands.

"What is it?" Honor said.

Gamble, stock still, stared in what looked like horror at Winnie, one of Drayton's enslaved house servants, who greeted them.

"Madam, may I take your jacket?" Winnie repeated. Winnie's brown-eyed gaze was neutral in a round face, every bit of hair tucked into a cotton bonnet. She held her small, dark hands tight against the white of her apron. Gamble stood frozen, her eyes wide.

"Gamble?" Daniel prompted.

"What?" she said, as if someone had asked her to chart a course for India.

Honor reached up and, gently, began to remove the blue spencer from Gamble. Obviously shaken, Gamble gathered herself and slipped out of it. Daniel handed over his wool cloak and the ladies' jackets, echoing their thanks. Winnie draped them over an arm as she dipped her cap, made a quick curtsy and moved on, already greeting other partygoers entering behind them.

"You don't enslave people," Gamble said.

It was not a question. Gamble gripped Daniel's forearm; he felt the heat from her palm through the wool sleeve of his tailcoat. "Effie told me she's free—Ben and Cooper too."

"You met Cooper?" Daniel said, confused. "When?"

Gamble's wide mouth pressed into a line. She seemed impatient, insistent; that Daniel knew the swing of her moods already was a wonder. "Honor introduced us in the back garden. I asked about the tea trees. Daniel," she said, giving his arm a firm shake. "You do not enslave people."

"No," Daniel said, making his voice as calm as he could. "Our parents were Quakers. Effie and her brothers are hired—Effie and Ben have been with us since I was a boy. Cooper and Honor were babes together."

"I forgot," Gamble said, as if he'd not spoken at all. She looked around, wild. "How could I forget? But it's 1804. Of course."

With the absence of the spencer jacket, Gamble's neck and a substantial portion of her chest were bare. Effie must have cinched Gamble's stays tight, and that and the combined snugness of the high waist of her gown and its low, rounded neckline put the upper curve of Gamble's breasts on display. They moved up and down in agitation, and her skin—which to Daniel's practiced artist's eye seemed honeyed from the sun—glowed in the candlelight from the French gilt chandelier above. Her skin looked impossibly smooth.

Despite Gamble's obvious distress—despite the crowd forming, the sound of musicians warming up on the floor above and Honor's repeated, "What is it? Is something the matter?"—all Daniel wanted to do was to draw her.

God's truth: he wanted to do much more than draw her.

"Daniel, Miss Honor! How good it is to see you both."

Someone took Daniel's shoulder, and he turned to find his friend and fellow miniature portraitist, Edward Malbone. Two of Malbone's current patrons, Mr. and Mrs. Heyward Pringle, followed behind.

"Hello, Ed," Honor said, her smile warm. She took in their group at a glance; they'd crowded the main hall. "Let's move upstairs, shall we? We're blocking the entry like this."

Gamble squeezed Daniel's arm tighter, and instinctively he put a gloved hand over hers and held on. He knew then that no matter what he believed, he'd be there to steady her. They ascended the staircase two by two. Introductions and pleasantries were exchanged; Daniel was cognizant of at least that much. So distracted was he by Gamble's grip on his arm and, if he was honest, her décolletage, that the fog didn't lift until Ed said, "What a pleasure it is to make your acquaintance, Madam Vance. I've known Daniel and Honor for years, yet they never mentioned cousins in Virginia. And such a lovely cousin, at that."

Virginia. Daniel sent a pointed look at Honor, who'd always been quick on her feet. In the carriage, they'd discussed a potential backstory for Gamble—a biography of sorts that wouldn't arouse suspicion. But they arrived at the Drayton house before any such story had been agreed upon. Apparently Honor had taken it upon herself to create one.

Virginia was perfect: it could explain Gamble's accent—which was southern but not Charlestonian—and why she might be lodging with their family for an indeterminate amount of time.

"I'm from the Quaker side," Gamble said, and any trace of upset vanished. What control that must take, Daniel thought. What a mystery she was. But a pleasure ball was no spot for pondering, and they rounded the blocky newel post at the landing as the din of the party increased.

"We tend to be the quieter cousins," Gamble added.

Ed laughed, and Daniel could see he was enchanted. They could form a society.

"Are you an artist, too, Mr. Malbone?" Gamble said. "Is this how you and Daniel know each other?"

Daniel could not say why, but if pressed, he'd swear Gamble already knew it to be true. But then, of course she did: if Gamble was what she said she was—a time traveler, a student of art and artifacts, especially miniature portraits—she must know of Edward Greene Malbone. Ed's reputation was such that he took commissions from prominent families up and down the Eastern coast. His work was luminous, affecting. He'd mentored Daniel more than any Paris apprenticeship: taught him to really see a face—to stretch his powers of observation further than he'd thought possible, and to capture the life there, the flicker in the eyes which color and technique could bring.

Could it be Ed was to be revered, two hundred years in the future? Daniel hoped so.

"Please, you must call me Edward," Ed said. "I am, yes. But this is how Daniel and I came to be friends. We were acquainted on my first visit to Charleston."

"It's been close to twenty years since," Daniel said, clasping hands with Ed. "How happy we were to get your note. We hope you'll call on us tomorrow? It's sure in this melee we won't have a chance to trade stories." The last time he was in South Carolina, Ed had extended his visit by two months and lodged with them on Tradd Street; they'd painted together in Daniel's studio. As always, Daniel learned more in his weeks observing Edward Malbone than he had in the finest salons abroad. But besides that, the man was a true friend.

"How long will Charleston have the pleasure of your company, this visit?" Honor said.

Ed smiled, and it gave his fine, sensitive face a merriment it tended to lack. His pale brows went up over serious brown eyes. "As long as Charleston will have me," he said.

"We'll have you as long as you care to stay," Daniel said, grasping their clasped hands with his free one. Ed did the same, and they released and shifted as partygoers moved about them like water fording a rock in a stream.

Daniel felt Gamble go still, but it was a different sort of stillness from her abrupt meeting with Winnie. Watching Ed, her eyes narrowed to blue slits and the shallow wrinkle in her forehead deepened into a line. It looked as if she studied him for clues.

Daniel could not help himself: he bent so close to her ear he could almost feel the soft skin at the seashell curve. "What is it?" he whispered.

Gamble shook her head, *No*, and was once again gregarious and amiable: at once the enchanting escort. Daniel couldn't help but wonder why she did this, and where she'd learned it. He felt certain she was lying.

Indeed, when it came to learning anything about Gamble, Daniel felt as if he pushed against some wall, on the other side of which lay some truth he couldn't access.

"Petigru, Malbone—you're causing a jam. Come, gentlemen, let's take these beautiful ladies into the room so we may do a proper job of showing them off."

It was Heyward Pringle, aged and infirm but determined as ever to attend every last ball he could. Mr. Pringle handed his top hat to Winnie without looking at her, made a swooping motion with his arms at their little crowd. "Come now, young ones. We'll miss the dance."

"Onward," Gamble murmured. She took her skirts in hand with what looked like, but could not have been, a practiced ease.

The Draytons had opened the parlor doors, so the entire street side of the second floor was fashioned as one long room, the furniture pushed aside and rugs rolled up for dancing. The musicians, fully warmed, launched into a Scotch reel. Guests, most of whom Daniel knew from either a family association or an artistic one, spread out accordingly—some to the walls and clustered about the hearths to make room for the dancers, and some into the dance. People laughed and clinked crystal glasses of Madeira. The briny and buttery smell of bowls of shrimp pilau and steamed oysters being carried through the crowd on silver trays by liveried servants made for an intoxicating atmosphere.

Daniel felt the wall inside him begin to crumble. Really, it was an impediment between what he knew to be true about the world and the events of this remarkable day. All he really wanted to do in the moment was to simply *be*. To shed his many roles. To be neither guardian nor older brother, nor even artist, but just a man at a ball—nothing more.

The music swelled; someone laughed uproariously. The room grew warm from the bodies and the fires in the Dutch-tiled fireplaces at each far wall. Daniel rolled his shoulders ever so slightly beneath his tailcoat, letting them sink away from his ears. There.

Daniel, who did not love a dance though he couldn't deny the potential for subject matter, found himself happy there. He knew it was because of the woman beside him, who was taking in the room. It was likely Gamble had never before seen anything like it, and if she had, it was sure to be a world revealed only on canvas. He couldn't imagine she ever considered she'd see it in person.

Light blazed from the newfangled gas candle chandeliers. It glittered on silver platters atop the well-lit and generously stocked sideboards, on the beveled glasses, in the jewels at women's necks and in their hair combs and diadems. He glanced at Gamble's hair, just to be sure she no longer wore his paintbrush. Still properly coiffed. Effie was a saint.

"Is that Nicholas Izard?" she said. "And there, by the bookshelves, Allistair Drayton and his son, William?"

"Yes," Daniel said, not taking his eyes from her. As Gamble spoke she turned her head to each corner of the room, sharply, like the second hand on a watch.

"Mrs. Thomas Huger. Henry Smythe. Laurens. Montagu. And, oh, is that...Sarah Gadsden? She looks different. In her miniature the face has faded to a rather unfortunate puce. Some ignorant descendant kept it hung in the sun."

Gamble's voice shook. It was subtle, but Daniel heard the shock, perhaps, of her improbable journey as it leaked into her speech. He squeezed her hand, spoke in *sotto voce*. "You know them all? Is your memory that strong?"

A quartet of dancers swung by, and even in the control of the song, in their practiced steps to the beat of the music, Daniel saw abandon on the dancers' faces—that sheen near the brow which meant exertion and fun. Honor tapped her foot and clapped with appreciation. His sister loved to dance. He hoped Ed would ask her.

But Gamble. Gamble watched it all, her gaze hawk-like. She was not searching, Daniel realized. She was imprinting.

"I've stared at these faces on ivory for more hours than I can count," she said. "Months of hours. I restored them with my own hands, cleaned the grime from their faces, repaired lockets and even touched locks of their hair. So, yes"—here her voice went up on a high note—"I know these faces."

He watched George Horry, ever the slick one, sharpen his gaze on Gamble and make his way toward them around the rim of the room. The man's black velvet cutaway jacket gleamed; his cravat was snowy, and expertly tied.

Daniel detested Horry. He stepped in front of Gamble, giving his back to Horry and any other gentleman looking for an introduction to the strange newcomer.

"They're just people," Daniel said, attempting to soothe. He wanted to smooth the line across her forehead with his fingertips. With his lips. To recover, he said lightly, "Did you study my face?"

"I studied you," Gamble said, without taking a breath. "I stood in front of your self-portrait every day for six months. I touched your jars of ochre and sanguine. I ran my fingers down the lines of your journal." She hadn't been looking at him, but she looked up then. "I couldn't tear myself away. It became so that you were more real to me than my own husband. When Honor led me out of the alley, I knew. I knew we were going to your house the moment we stepped onto Tradd Street."

She smiled, rueful. "But don't ask me how."

"Mr. Petigru, you must introduce us to your charming houseguest. What an unexpected addition to the winter season she'll be."

It was Mrs. Heyward and Mrs. Marion, matrons flanked by their unmarried daughters. The corner of Mrs. Heyward's lightly rouged mouth crooked in anticipation. Daniel recalled something his mother once said of the woman: a yellow jacket hiding among the flowers of an otherwise lovely azalea—always waiting until things got nice and warm to emerge and sting.

At Mrs. Heyward's comment, Daniel felt the eyes of other party-goers alight upon his group. Nearby people shifted their attention, bodies turning toward them with ears pricked up like petals to the sun. Horry had yet to relent, blast the man: he stepped up with a tight nod to Daniel and a small bow to the women, then presented Gamble with an unrequested flute of champagne.

"You must be parched, madam. Allow me," Horry said, his black, Beau Brummell-styled hair tipping forward and back at the movement, despite the amount of Macassar oil surely used to hold it in place. Gamble took the glass and smiled, close-lipped, but did not respond.

Daniel knew what was expected of him. "Madam Vance," he said. "May I have the pleasure of introducing Mrs. Heyward, her sister-in-law Mrs. Marion, and their daughters, Miss Rose Heyward and Miss Meg Marion. And, of course, Mr. George Horry." He forced a smile. "Madam Vance is our cousin, lately of Virginia. Honor and I are happy the Draytons included her so graciously in their party."

Finally, Gamble spoke. "Yes, I'm afraid my arrival was a bit of a surprise, though unintended. Our correspondence got lost in the post, otherwise my cousins would've had word of my arrival long before now." She gave a winning smile. "How gracious they were to receive me without notice, just as all of you are. Charleston is as beautiful as I remembered."

"So you're familiar with our city," Horry said, and by God if the man didn't put a foot inside their group, so that his shoulder made to cut Daniel out ever so slightly. Enough was enough. Daniel scanned the crowd for Honor.

"I am," Daniel heard Gamble say, as he registered his sister and Ed making their way through the throng near the parlor doors.

Honor touched Miss Rose Heyward's elbow and greeted the older women before slipping her arm through Gamble's.

"You must not wear her out, Mr. Horry," Honor said, with a gay frivolity so unlike her that Daniel turned toward the band to hide his reaction. "My cousin only just arrived from so far, and already we've insisted she enjoy our society on her first night." She dipped her head to Gamble, who gave Honor a grateful look. "Come, let's find a seat for a moment, shall we?"

Honor turned, Gamble in tow, and Ed offered an arm to each. They made a path to a set of small tables set near the piazza doors. Honor sank into a chair with a faint flutter of skirt. Gamble watched her do so, then followed suit. *Look at her*, Daniel thought, as Gamble mirrored Honor's every action: tucking her hands in her lap, crossing her ankles just so.

"Charming, your cousin," Horry said, droll, beside him. "Is she widowed?"

Daniel sipped his Madeira before answering. "Just so," he said. "Penniless, you know." Before Horry could react, Daniel bowed. "You'll excuse me."

Daniel went to stand by Ed, who seemed to keep guard by leaning against the window behind the ladies. In the reflection, colors flashed—gowns and jackets spinning across the glass, the chandeliers flickering. Daniel didn't know what he'd been thinking, only that Horry was a horrible snob. Best to get him off the scent quick.

Honor raised an eyebrow and Daniel shrugged. He stood at Gamble's shoulder, for a brief moment thinking how the four of them must look like a portrait—two couples at a society ball—before leaning down to Gamble. She stilled at the movement. It struck Daniel then: perhaps she was just as aware of him as he of her.

He had many questions, each too private to ask here. "Are you well?" he said. Gamble looked up, emotion flickering in her eyes, but she seemed hesitant to respond. Finally, she shrugged.

"How can I be?" she said.

GAMBLE

"What?" I said, shaken.

But I'd known, hadn't I? Somewhere, deep in a place I wasn't ready to access because I was afraid, I knew how Tol felt about me. Or at least I hoped for it. Because what sane person welcomes the torture of being in love all by their lonesome?

Tol drew up to his full height and folded his arms, staring across the barn at me like some disappointed deity. "You knew," he said.

I shook my head, desperate and incapable of hiding it because I never hid anything from Tolliver. Anything, except for what was apparently my serious and long-stifled love for everything about him.

Okay, almost everything. Tol was way too tall: I had to crane my neck to look up at him when we were close. He was right far more often than I found comfortable, and it was rare that he let his emotions get the better of him. Which was annoying, to say the least.

"I didn't," I said. Liar.

Tol seemed to come to some sort of decision. He loosened his arms and sat on the edge of the desk. If he crossed his ankles next, all devil-may-care, I'd hit him.

"Liar," he said, dangerously soft. His face went still as stone. I could've cut glass with the edge of that jaw of his. He crossed those Italian leather boots, looking like nothing so much as the central actor in a Ralph Lauren commercial. Ridiculous.

I leapt forward, nearly tripped over the edge of a drop cloth, then righted myself with aplomb. I marched across the cavernous room but drew short a good three yards away, because the man was a giant kettle ready to boil.

Also, because I was a chicken-shit.

"I'm not lying, Tol," I said. My heart pounded and my breath quickened: my brain may have been wild with what ifs, but my body knew how important this was. "I'm not. Or I don't mean to lie. I'm scared."

"Me too," Tol said. "But something's got to give. I'd never pressure you, Gamble. Hell, I waited six years, 'cause I can't stand to be wrong. But I can't wait anymore."

He chuckled, rueful and deep, and it made me want to crawl inside his clothes. He said, "If you don't love me, you don't love me. I can take it. I might finally accept that job with the Smithsonian. Get the hell out of South Carolina."

"You move to D.C. over my dead body," I said, trembling. I mean it: I literally trembled.

"You mean without you?" Tol said, and smiled.

It was a real smile, white in the dim, the dimple showing in his cheek. Sun streamed in from the tall window on the front wall, tracing a line of light along the floor between us, like some boundary or demarcation. Like something we had to cross.

"Damn right that's what I mean," I said, the shaking easing a bit. I wiggled my fingers, just to make sure they were still there. Shocked, I realized it was true.

If Tol was going anywhere, I was going with him.

"Come closer," Tol said.

DANIEL

WILLIAM DRAYTON HOUSE
OCTOBER, 1804

"Shall we leave?" Daniel said to Gamble.

The truth of it was, he didn't know how he could manage to stay there much longer, in the midst of a crowded ball, after what she'd said about studying his portraits. His art. In the year 2004.

None of it reasoned out. He couldn't see the end of their story—couldn't fathom how any of it would turn out—but the need to be alone with Gamble, this woman he barely knew, was ardent and consuming.

Daniel felt as he did whenever he was into the last days of a portrait, when all that remained were the subtle touches necessary for a face to come alive: the white to make the eyes focus and shine, the pink flush along a cheek, the shadowing of a jaw. All the tricky, fastidious brushstrokes that made the person in the portrait real: the touches that gave them life.

In these moments at his easel, bent close to the miniature tacked there, Daniel wanted the world to let him be. For everyone and everything in it to leave him the hell alone. He wanted the very same, right then. He wanted to consider nothing but what Gamble said to him, and what he meant to do about it.

"We should," Gamble said. "But not before I've danced at least once. I'd never forgive myself if I left here and didn't dance."

Daniel swallowed all the things he knew he shouldn't say, and inclined his head. "Then may I request the honor of a dance, Madam Vance?"

"What a question," she said, grinning up at him with cheek, displaying a set of the straightest, whitest teeth he had ever seen. If she smiled like that with any sort of frequency, all would see she was not of this world.

Gamble shrugged, adding, "I'm not interested in dancing with anyone else."

☙

The cotillion, Daniel thought, always made him feel like a boy again. He hoped it'd finally gone out of fashion, and perhaps they might have a reel instead—something where he could swing and leap and lift his feet a bit, and look fine—but it wasn't in the cards. And since this was a private ball instead of a public one, partners were scarce. It was either dance with someone else—something he did not want to do—or dance with Gamble, something he very much did want, simply because it gave him a reason to touch her.

He led Gamble to the floor, and they took their places across from each other near the center of the double row. She was shorter than the women she stood between, and again he was reminded of some mischievous mythological creature plucked from the pages of a faery tale. His mother's gown, though cut much the same as the others, had in the candlelight even more of a look of the past about it. Even with its similar high waist, low, squared neckline, and ethereal fall of skirt, the sleeves were long and queenly; the teal green, to him, the brightest color in the room. It made Gamble's eyes light up like some West Indian sea.

Daniel gave himself an inward shake. Even in his head he sounded like a fool.

He said, across the space between them and above the din of the party, "Have you danced the cotillion before?"

Gamble shook her head. "Nope. I plan to pick it up as we go along."

The young woman to her right, William Drayton III's bride-to-be, Elizabeth Elliott, reached over and touched Gamble on her gloved forearm. "Oh, it's easy," she said. "Just keep watch on the line and do the same as the couple before you. I'm Lizzie, by the way."

"Hi, Lizzie. I'm Gamble," Gamble said, as the fiddles pulled.

It may as well have been a country dance, rowdy as the party had become. Along the elegant, silk-papered walls guests clapped and laughed, heads bent in conversation. Glasses were refilled with Madeira and punch, sweetmeats and candies consumed, and cups of chocolate distributed. Candle and gaslight gleamed on new pantaloons and silk frocks, on pretty legs and curtsies made, cards exchanged. Old Washington Manigault wore his wig, as if it were the days of the revolution; John Montagu, seated beside him in a loud pink waistcoat, smoked a pipe carved from ivory. There were no children in sight. It was very much a revel.

Once, Ed had told him that balls in Charleston, public or private, were like nothing he'd seen before. In New England, Ed said, balls were ordered affairs, every flip of a lady's fan or sip from a cup filled with coded social nuance: *Yes, I will accept this dance. No, I am not interested in courting. Place a hand here, step to the left. Do not cross a room unaccompanied.*

Daniel had laughed, assuring his friend that Charleston was buried beneath social nuance. Yes, Ed agreed, but southerners were bred for revel. They seemed to wrest some of their love of excess from their colorful Barbadian ancestors—they were not tied to Puritanism, like their neighbors to the chilly north.

In addition, Ed argued, in Charleston there was wholehearted attention to libation. He'd yet, Ed added, to attend any sort of social event in the city that had been without an excess of dragoon punch.

Daniel and Gamble took hands, and when it was their turn, trotted down the path made by the rows of fellow dancers. She wore a pair of his sister's elbow-length gloves, the white silk supple from use, and thin at the fingers. She smiled at him, wide and joy-filled, showing teeth. Women didn't smile like that, not here.

Gamble's cheeks flushed, and her bosom rose and fell with each step. Her eyes flashed, the shallow wrinkles at the corners fanning out when she threw her head back and laughed.

Daniel kept a firm grip, fearing she'd slip away.

GAMBLE

"You first," I said.

"Gamble," Tol said, and there was chiding in it.

I straightened the hem of my chambray shirt, which had come untucked from my jeans. I'd tossed my down vest on a chair nearby, knowing I'd get hot when we started moving crates and art around. I wore a pair of tall Dubarry boots—boots upon which I'd spent a month's paycheck, because on top of looking damned good, they were serviceable and unafraid of muck. *I* knew how to dress in horse country.

It was a bit like checking my armor, that straightening (okay, tugging) of my shirt. I gripped the butter-soft denim—so worn it was nearly-white—because I honestly did not know what to do with my hands. If I were twelve, I'd have chewed my fingernails.

Tol must have seen something in my face, because he stood, oh-so-slowly, from his perch on the edge of the desk. As if wary he might spook me and I'd run.

"How about we meet halfway?" he said.

Oh, heavens.

It struck me then how meticulous Tol had always been, careful and calm. I was by no means flighty, but I'd never been able to contain my emotions, my natural energy. We were utterly different, yet so very right: our pull like the opposite ends of the same magnet.

"Right," I said, clearing my throat as though it'd not been used in days. "We meet halfway. I'm a modern woman. A feminist. I'm not coming all the way to you."

"Plus, you're scared," Tol said. There was no teasing in it.

"Plus that," I said.

We stepped forward at the same time. I had to lean back to get a good look at him, and when I did I noticed his chest move up and down, his breathing more rapid than it appeared at a glance. Maybe his heartbeat was as wild as mine. God, I hoped so.

"Gamble," Tol murmured. I put my hand in his. He waited about a millisecond, then tugged, and we pressed together, arms curled about each other's waists. He bent.

"Wait," I said, putting a hand on his chest. Yep, his heart beat crazy fast, just like mine. I could feel it beneath the cashmere and muscle, against my open palm. "I think you just told me you loved me."

Tol laughed, loudly, and I couldn't help but grin. But I'd be damned if I did not get a straight answer. I studied his face—the black and silver stubble at his implacable jaw, the faint, wonderful wrinkles at the corners of his eyes when he smiled. Those disconcerting hazel eyes so solemn: focused only on me.

"I almost did," Tol said. "But not quite. I believe I said, 'If you don't love me.'"

Oh, I wanted to kiss him, though my mind was a mess. The feel of his arm circling my back, holding me in such a new way, yet with such ease it was as if he'd held me for years, made me want to give up the ghost. To kiss first and ask questions later. But I needed his answer.

"Do you?" I said.

He untucked my shirt and gripped the fabric in a fist. I felt the cool air of the barn, his knuckles warm against the skin at the base of my spine.

"Yes, Gamble," Tol said. "I love you. I've loved you since the night we met. I tried to stop. Do you know how many times I walked down the street to wherever we were meeting up, praying when I saw you on the sidewalk, or waiting at a table, the feelings I had would be gone? Thousands of times. But there you'd be, waiting for me. And still I loved you. You put me through hell, woman."

"I'm sorry," I said.

And I was. But there on the second floor of Miss Saralee Hutto's barn, standing in each other's arms, I felt as if the glass of my life had been wiped clean—all the smudges rubbed away. I felt like a person with poor eyesight must feel when they walk out of the optometrist's office, into the sunlight, and slip on brand-new eyeglasses for the first time. Prescription eyeglasses, made only and individually for them. How the world you thought you knew was alive and wonderfully sharp; how the tiniest leaves on faraway trees became visible; how now you could read road signs from fifty yards away.

How everything became that much clearer.

"I don't want you to be sorry," Tol said gruffly. He gripped my shirt tighter and lifted me to my toes. He bent, his breath warm on my lips. "I want you to say it."

I exhaled happiness, slid my hands up to his shoulders. I'm proud my voice didn't shake.

"I love you," I said. "I think—no, I know—I've always loved you."

Then I grinned all over again, because I couldn't help myself. "God, but, Tol, I *am* sorry. I'm sorry it took me so damn long."

You do not kiss your best friend and walk away unscathed. This is something I should've realized before Tol and I kissed in that barn. Before we set into motion a story that would break both our hearts before we could ever put them together again.

As it was, once we declared our feelings out loud—feelings held in check for six long years—neither of us thought about anything but getting our hands on each other. And our mouths. And other things.

Tol kissed me just as you might imagine: as if he'd hungered for my mouth for a very long time. For my part, I would've been perfectly happy to swallow him whole.

I don't know how long we stood there, kissing. I was lost in the feel of his tongue in my mouth, of the press of his large, capable hands on my hips and in my hair, of his whispered, deep, "Gamble," over and over again. He moved down my neck, pressed his nose there and breathed in. When he opened his mouth against my skin, my entire body quaked.

I tried as quick as I could to crawl inside his clothes. I didn't care if the old ladies walked in on us, if the barn caught fire around us. I didn't care what day it was or what my job was or why we were there. Hell, I didn't care who I was or who he was. All I wanted was more. All I wanted was Tolliver.

He picked me up, and I wrapped my legs around his waist, locking my ankles. I don't know if our mouths separated until my backside touched the cool oak of the desktop. Immediately we were at each other's shirts, hands fumbling with buttons and tugging at hems, wanting them over our heads. Wanting them gone.

He cupped my breasts, running his thumbs across my nipples so I felt his touch through the cotton, and my legs fell open. Was this all it took? Tol touched me, and every inhibition flew right out the window? I was a (not-so virgin) sacrifice. It was Achilles and Briseis all over again. I'd been reduced to ancient, animal lust. I'd lost the ability to reason.

I worked Tol's shirt and sweater up to his arm pits and ran my hands across his stomach. I was spreading my hands over his chest (if it turned out he waxed, I'd have to give him hell for it) when I realized we were seconds away from consummating our newly declared love. Right there on Miss Saralee's antique desk. And it wasn't even dark yet.

Tol bent and pressed his lips to my collarbone, and I tucked my heels behind his thighs and pulled him in as close as was humanly possible while still wearing clothes. The hell with it. Sex had surely been had in barns for centuries.

I reached for his zipper, and he kissed me on the mouth, quick and hard. "Wait, Gamble," Tol said, his voice sinking to a register lower than I'd thought possible. I ignored it.

Okay, I didn't ignore it: it made me hotter. I've already mentioned my fondness for Sam Elliott's deep voice. I loved Tol's voice more. The fact that this was Tol, and I loved him—*I loved him!*—made everything else vanish. No kidding: we could've been anywhere in the world. All I knew was the breath of space between us, and the heat we stoked there.

"Gamble, we can't." Tol gripped my hand—the one working his zipper down—brought it to his mouth, and kissed it with a tenderness that caught me by surprise.

"Okay," I said, breathing heavy. Needing to touch him, I pressed a hand against his jaw. "Okay."

Our chests moved in a matching rhythm, and we stared at each other until Tol dropped his head, touching his forehead to mine. He took my other hand, the one he'd kissed, and wrapped it round the back of his neck. He pressed his lips, slick from my mouth, to the thin skin at the inside of my forearm, near my wrist, and I shivered.

"Wait," I said. "Why can't we?"

If I'd been able to retain coherence, I might've made more sense of this. But we were consenting adults, Tol was my best friend, and we'd established that we loved each other. We could have sex.

"We can't be together, not like this, until you're free of him," he said. "Daniel."

Tol was steady; I heard the resolve in his voice. I uncurled my arms from his neck, tugging at his shirt until I'd unrolled it to his waist. I looked down then, a stalling tactic, and smoothed his hem. "I'm free of him," I said.

How could I not be? All I could think about was Tol. About the two of us, together. It was the whole of my world in that moment. We were snow-globe people, safe and suspended in water.

Tol tugged the lapels of my shirt together, then did up my buttons with a swift and capable tenderness. He didn't answer. I felt the sudden and inexplicable urge to cry.

"Tolliver?" I said. This time, my voice shook.

Tol took my face in his hands and looked into my eyes. "We need to be sure this is real," he said.

Well. That stung. I breathed deeply through my nose, then took his face in my hands. Anyone walking in on us then would've found the scene strange, us holding each other's face, but I couldn't have cared less.

"It's real. You know it is," I said. The mad banished the urge to cry. I did my best not to yell.

Tol kissed me, then, before we were lost in each other again, hugged me tight. I rested my chin on his shoulder. When he spoke, I felt the words in my chest cavity, in the space around my heart.

"When we get home, after we're finished here, we need to be sure this is real. That you're ready for us." I felt Tol swallow. Then, he said, "Gamble, you need to go back to Daniel."

DANIEL

CHARLESTON
OCTOBER, 1804

They stood outside the Drayton house, awaiting their carriage in the dark. Daniel could feel the wind off the Ashley through the trees in the side garden; he turned his back to it, unprepared for the cold. The gas lamps flickered amber light in a dance across the brick-laid walk before disappearing into the shadows of the oaks. Only a few steps through the dark, and then there was the road, the clinking shake of a bridle and the snuffle of horses, a night full and waiting.

Daniel had left Honor in the good care of Ed, under the assurance he'd see her safely home. Inside, when Daniel had glanced about for a chaperone, knowing the talk that could come of his sister and friend alone together, despite their age difference, Honor had fixed him with a stern and determined eye.

"Daniel, I am nineteen years old," she said. "And Ed is a family friend. He came over with the Pringles, anyhow. They can all of them see me safely home when the music is through."

The hour approached ten of the clock. Drivers waited at carriages parked along the curb all the way down the street, some seated and alone, others talking quietly in the dark. Honor and Ed, he knew, would be out much later. It was typical for a private ball, especially one celebrating the engagement of the son and heir of a family like Drayton's, to last until the morning's wee hours.

But the gossipmongers would not be satisfied by Gamble's answers to their questions should they stay—answers surely impossible for her or anyone else to give.

"Shall we walk?" Gamble said.

There was a distinct chill in the air, and while Daniel knew he'd be fine walking about in his long cloak, Gamble's shorter jacket wouldn't keep her warm for long.

"Are you certain?" he said. "You don't have a cloak, though you're welcome to wear mine."

"I might," she said, slipping her arm through his as though she'd done so for years. "But you forget: I'm from the mountains. The air here isn't cold to me—it's delightful."

Daniel pulled the lapels of his cloak up toward his ears. He waved off a hackney which had seen them and slowed its horses near the curb, and switched to Gamble's other side, so he walked closest to the street. The cold had blown away the humidity which had hung about through early autumn; the night felt expanded and unencumbered.

A bright moon shone through the bare and spidering branches of a streetside set of oaks; it paled the houses along the road in a wash of watered-down silver. Most homes were quiet, the night calm and still, until they entered again a street of taverns and shops. Ahead, a man stepped from a door and doffed a top hat, and sound spilled out with him: a bark of laughter, an answering shout, the clink of plates and glasses. Then it was gone.

The breeze shifted, the rich sulfur smell of low tide sweeping in from the harbor. Daniel imagined it: the moonlight on the harbor, the muddy pilings at the wharves illuminated, the scurrying crabs and the soft thwap of the sea against the city. He closed his eyes briefly against the image. He felt very much alive.

Their strides were well matched. Despite their inexplicable situation, Daniel was selfishly glad of the ball, for the occasion had allowed Gamble's hair to remain uncovered. He couldn't help but admire the sheen of her hair in the dark, lit the color of old gold at her crown each time they passed beneath a lamp. During the dance, tendrils had escaped near her ears, and they waved down now to rest bright against the deep blue velvet of her high collar.

"Does it look much like this, in your time?" Daniel said. "Charleston?"

"It looks very much like this," she said. "Minus the horses and brick and stone streets, of course. And there's more of, well, everything. There're still a few original cobblestone streets left—most in the French Quarter, down near Adgar's Wharf."

"Adgar's Wharf?" Daniel said. "I don't know it."

She put a finger to her bottom lip. "No, wait—it would be Ancrum's now. Ancrum's Wharf."

Daniel waited, and Gamble breathed in through her nose. She seemed to consider her words. "There'll be more war, of course. But a great and awful one, over fifty years from now, will change the face of Charleston—of the entire country—forever. Charleston will burn. There'll be another occupation."

This nearly brought Daniel to a standstill. It had been little more than twenty years since the British occupation of Charleston. He'd been fifteen, then, and living abroad, apprenticed to an artist in Paris. Unable to return home for fear of being pressed into the British navy. But every Charlestonian alive in those days told stories of the Siege, and the disastrous explosion at the powder magazine. Daniel's two younger siblings, January and Philip, had died from malaria during the occupation; his mother laid the blame on Sir Henry Clinton and General Cornwallis until the day she died.

Daniel touched a hand to the brim of his top hat as two Negro men, one carrying a satchel of papers, stepped off onto the street to let them pass.

"What will bring it about?"

Carriage wheels and horses' hooves clattered on the cobbles as a coach crossed in front of them at Lowndes Street. A strong odor of brine and food scraps wafted past, and Daniel knew the tide had shifted. Other than that, even here things were almost quiet, the world seeming abed.

"Slavery—or the question of it—will be the cause of that war," Gamble said.

"I'm not surprised," Daniel said, and he wasn't.

Daniel had been taught by his Quaker parents that slavery was an evil. And though he and Honor had fallen away from the Friends and had not even been to Meeting since the deaths of their parents, their religious training—at least inside the home—had been rigorous and real. Lydia Dillwyn Petigru had seen to that, by God: to his mother the practice of slavery was more than distasteful, it was an immorality—and a stain upon their city. When in 1790 Quakers petitioned the United States Congress for slavery to be abolished, both his parents had been a part of it.

A series of images flitted through Daniel's memory: the old Quaker Meeting House on Queen Street. His parents and other Friends gathered in their parlor on Tradd, furniture pushed aside and chairs and benches set in a circle, a bend of wigs and dull bonnets, the strong voices of men and women raised in worship or sharing or dissent. Daniel had sat high on the stairs, just out of sight, to listen on those nights, sometimes with Ben beside him. At the sound of footfall—usually Effie's—they'd scatter: Daniel to his room, Ben to the kitchen house.

"Please don't tell me more," Daniel said. "I think it must be dangerous to know too much of one's future."

"I can respect that," Gamble said. "But I think you'll be fine."

"Oh, will I?" Daniel said, with humor. She might look like a faery from some lush European storybook, but she sounded like nothing so much as a gypsy.

"Yep. You're a man ahead of your time, Daniel Petigru."

At the confluence of Gibbes and Legare Streets, they paused before crossing. When Daniel made to step into the street Gamble held him back.

"What is it?" he said.

"I just want to look," she said. "You know, in 2004 there'll be a coffee shop just there—remember how I told you there's one on every corner? Where the apothecary is now there'll be a law office—a barrister's office—and that single house will become divided apartments. The bottom floor will be a little design studio, where Charleston housewives will buy trinkets and pretty pillows for their couches. It'll be different, yet in some ways, very much the same."

Could you stay? Daniel wanted to ask, but he knew he would not. Gamble didn't belong here, not in 1804, and not with him, no matter how much it felt, in this moment, she did. The way she flinched each time she encountered an enslaved Negro, how she answered a gentleman's inquiry with bold answers and unguarded speech—to say nothing of her refusal to wear proper stays and cover her hair—revealed her as unfit for this world, his world. It was obvious women, and men, and the relationships between them, were to be markedly different two hundred years hence.

In turn, Gamble knew too much about what was to come. History was never kind to the soothsayers.

They neared McCloud's Tavern, the wooden sign swinging and creaking in the wind, and Daniel looked down when Gamble shivered. Finally, she felt the cold. Inside would be a brazier and a coal fire, hot tea, brandy, and mulled wine. And other people.

"May I buy you a drink?" he said, hoping she'd refuse.

The lamps flanking the tavern's ancient wooden door flickered yellow light onto Gamble's upturned face. When she looked at him her eyes were full of worry.

"No," she said. "Can you take me to Stoll's Alley? I think I should try to go home."

Stoll's Alley was quiet and dark, the houses along it shuttered at the late hour. Only one lantern, at number 7½, remained lit. Its light was not strong enough to reach the brick path, and Daniel and Gamble stood in shadow. When she swallowed, he heard it.

"What next?" he said.

"I honestly can't tell you," Gamble said. Again she pressed hands to her face, covering her eyes. When her hands slid away her eyes were large and red-rimmed, her voice shaky. "I can't tell you how I can remember the lay of these streets and stores in my own time, or aspects of my work, but not what happens to you. None of it makes sense." She took a shaky breath. "All I know is I walked down this alley in 2004, and walked out of it—two hundred years later. I can't remember why. I don't know what I did to make it happen."

Daniel took her shoulders, the velvet of the spencer jacket soft beneath his hands. He found himself both wanting to shake Gamble—to make her admit, for God's sake, that none of this could be real—and at the same time, to comfort. It was a most infuriating combination.

Instead, he said, "Steady on. Is there truly nothing you remember?"

She looked up. "Honor was here, even if she doesn't remember it. She spoke to me, and I followed her." Gamble looked past him, searching the alley, her tone low and anxious. "What if I can't go without her? What if I can't get back?"

Enough. Daniel released her and stepped aside. "You must try. Go now." He steeled himself as he said it, but against what, he wasn't sure. His inexplicable attraction to Gamble seemed bound up in a fabulous madness.

"I can't be here," she said. "I'm not supposed to be here."

Then, without another word, she walked away from him. At the first iron gate set in the alley wall, darker and darker under the trees, she picked up her pace, then ran.

Daniel felt his heels lift, his weight shifting forward onto his toes. It took real effort not to chase Gamble down. When she disappeared with a flash of skirts into the pitch at the center of the alley, he gasped.

He jogged forward, incognizant of the awkward slant of the bricks underfoot, of the dark, of anything but Gamble.

At the center of the alley, just beyond the wall to the right, a single white house loomed, faint against the night. Looking ahead he could see, like a muted blue opening, the gateless terminus of the alley where it emptied onto Bay Street. Daniel spun and searched the wall, the wooden door set into it, a nearby gate. He felt moss and mortar under his hands. There was no way on earth Gamble could've made the end of the alley so quickly.

It was as if she'd vanished.

His stomach felt empty; suddenly he needed to brace himself against the wall. He set his back against it and ran both hands through the hair at his crown.

Then: "Daniel," someone said, just as he pushed off the wall to find his feet again. The voice sounded tinny and far away.

Impossible. Gamble stood at the alley's head, back where they'd started, Church Street behind her. The alley measured a mere six feet across: there was no way she could have passed by without his knowing, even in the dark.

He rushed to her. He managed to stop feet away, almost at a skid. She looked small in the teal dress, her outlines blurred in the weak light.

"Daniel," she said again, her voice hollow. "It didn't work."

The house was silent, Effie having retired long before to her quarters in the kitchen house. Daniel slid Gamble's jacket from her small shoulders. He could not help but watch, and wonder at the feel, as the velvet moved from her diaphanous sleeve across a short length of bared skin until it met the silk of her glove. When she turned—disheveled and glowing, her neck free of jewelry but containing, he noticed for the first time, quite a few small freckles drawn like a constellation near her collarbone—he was not at all certain what to do or say next.

For most of their walk home from Stoll's Alley, Gamble's silence seemed despondent. Finally, as they neared the house, she'd said, "Do you believe me now?"

How could Daniel deny what he'd seen with his own eyes—Gamble had been there, then gone, then back again, as if transported. And she was no magician, he knew. Just a woman out of time.

"How can I not," he'd replied.

Now Daniel felt the emptiness of his house and their aloneness in it with sudden clarity. Before he could stifle the words, he said, "You said you'd studied me. My notebooks. My portrait. Why?"

Gamble drew off one glove and then the other, fingertip by fingertip, then laid them on the walnut hall table in the small foyer. Daniel watched as she caught her reflection in the ornate French mirror, a gift for his parents on the occasion of their marriage: one of their few luxuries. Gamble squinted at her reflection, then drew out the pins Effie had placed in her hair. It fell, unencumbered, pale and straight as silk, over her shoulders. His chest tightened.

Turning, she lifted her shoulders, seeming unable to help her answer. "I can't explain why. I wish I could; it might make things easier. But I was drawn to your face," she said. "I'd spent so many painstaking hours with your miniature portraits. That's what a conservator does: in order to save your work, I had to research your life, your career—to use what I learned to determine which miniatures were yours. How could I not help but become fascinated with the man who'd created them?"

Here she paused, then shook her head as if to clear it. "I don't know. Maybe remembering is like being in a state between dreaming and waking…maybe it's just as ambiguous. Maybe it has to do with my frame of mind, whether I can be calm enough to have a sense of clarity? It certainly feels like there are times my memory floods, and times it trickles." She laughed, low. "I'm the boy with his finger in the dyke. Maybe I should just pull it out."

Daniel didn't say a word, only waited, his own thoughts as disjointed as her speech. He was considered a bit of a bohemian by his fellow Charlestonians. Perhaps he should warn Gamble it was improper for them to be alone in the house like this. But he couldn't find the will. He wanted to wrap his hands in that hair. To use it to pull her close, like a thick line of rope.

Daniel wanted, he thought with brutal honesty, to use it to possess this wild and original creature—to catch her once, if just the once, before she disappeared forever.

He couldn't keep her, Daniel knew. It was impossible to make promises to a woman like Gamble, who had no obtainable history, no lineage, no family, at least in this Charleston. It was boldly apparent that 2004 was a place of much greater freedom than she'd ever find with him.

Daniel couldn't recall whether Gamble had truly said she was unmarried, or even widowed. Despite his tendency toward freethinking, Daniel knew he shouldn't take her to his bed—a woman such as she was, of good, though unconventional breeding—without offering for her hand. Without speaking to her family.

But not once had Gamble spoken with any depth about life in her own time. Daniel didn't know if she even had a family—a father, or even brothers or sisters as fair-haired and impudent as she.

How could it be that this woman, this stranger, took up all the creative space in his mind. Usually Daniel found himself consumed by his art. If he wasn't painting or sketching, he was thinking about painting or sketching, or carving out and cleaning his ivory, or perfecting his technique. His art was his world, outside of caring for Honor. How would he return to it after Gamble left? Once she left, would the grip ease in his chest? Would the lust leave his belly?

"I'll retire to the stable," Daniel said, hoarse: an attempt at saving her reputation. "Can you see yourself to your room? Effie made up the one next to Honor's. At the end of the hall on the second floor, on the right."

"Daniel," Gamble said, her voice soft as the silk gloves she'd discarded. "I was so unhappy. And then I walked down Stoll's Alley, and I found you. Finally, here you are—a man it seems I've been looking for without even knowing it."

Daniel stepped back and felt the post of the stair rail touch his spine through his jacket. His skin felt too tight, his wool breeches and well-worn boots at once stifling. And by God, if he did not loosen this confounded cravat, he'd choke to death. He ran a distracted hand through the thick brown hair at his crown, sending it sticking up like a cock's comb.

Gamble was small, and lovely, and yet Daniel was terrified of what she might say and do next. More, he didn't know how to keep himself from touching her, were he to stay in the house.

"It has been my pleasure to attend you," he said, awkward and desperate. Feeling like nothing more than a schoolboy. "But tonight has been wearying for us both. I should bid you good night."

Gamble approached, and backed up against the railing as he was, Daniel had nowhere to go. That is, unless he decided to flee the house like a boy racing from the threat of the strap. He stilled when she put a hand on his shoulder, balanced herself, and drew first one dancing slipper off, then another. She held them by the heels, and then took his hand in hers, ungloved.

"I don't know how much time we have," Gamble said. "But I'm tired, and I'm scared, and I think being with you would make me feel less alone. I'd like you to show me to your room."

On the third floor Daniel opened his bedroom door and Gamble went in without a qualm and did not so much as blink when he closed it behind them. It was cold, and thinking to build a fire, he went to the hearth.

"Daniel," Gamble said. "Don't do that. We don't know when Honor will be home. Am I wrong? Do you want me?"

He went to her, laid his hands on her shoulders. He couldn't let her think otherwise. "Of course I want you," he said. "I've wanted you since the moment I saw you. But you needn't give yourself to me like this."

Gamble smiled, small and knowing. She slid the black evening jacket from his shoulders. He let it fall, let her drape it over a chair nearby.

"I know I don't," she said. "And I'm not giving anything away. I want you too."

Daniel untied his cravat, past arguing about the morality of bedding a woman he scarcely knew, one who was not, nor was ever likely to be, his wife. His need for her was that great.

"Is lovemaking like this in your time?" he said. "Are men and women so free?"

"Lovemaking—or sex, as we call it—is exactly what it is," she said. "Two people who are attracted to each other, doing something about that attraction. But no, the social contract is different than it is now. Sex isn't seen as a commodity, as something to be bargained over. It's certainly not something a woman gives up. It's my choice. I want you, Daniel. Just you. Not your house, not your name or your reputation. I don't need those things. I can take care of myself."

Daniel let his cravat drop and pool on the floor, then unbuttoned the top of his linen shirt and pulled it free from his deerskin trousers.

"I've never lain with a woman who didn't want something from me," he said. It was as honest as he'd ever been, yet he could be nothing else with Gamble. "I was married before, did I tell you that? I was seventeen, and she was French. The daughter of an artist to whom I'd been apprenticed. We divorced within a year and a half."

Gamble stepped close, then gave him her back and looked over her shoulder. "I need you to undo my dress and stays," she said, her voice clear. "We don't have these sorts of things where I'm from, and I have no idea how Effie did them up."

When Daniel opened her like a gift, her stays undone, her exhale was audible. "I always wondered how women did it," she said, "being trussed up like turkeys all year long." Gamble turned round, looking like nothing more than Botticelli's Venus—like Eve at the shell—before she let the dress and stays fall from her body to pool about her feet.

She stood there in nothing but pantaloons so thin Daniel could see the dark shadow of pubic hair at the juncture of her thighs. She didn't bother to cover herself, yet seemed proud and uninhibited in her nakedness.

"I've been hurt in my time," Gamble said. "So badly hurt I thought I'd never come out of it. All that kept me going was my work—the work I'd done with your art, the hours I spent studying the faces you captured on ivory. I want you, too, Daniel. Just you. I don't need anything in return except comfort and connection."

"Sweet lady," Daniel found himself saying, like a silly swain, an aging Romeo. "I believe I can give you those things."

Gamble took the hem of his shirt and lifted it. Daniel helped. When it cleared his head and fell away, she pressed herself against his body, tangled her fingers in the thick hair at his nape.

"Enough with the talking," she said.

Since the day Gamble stepped into his home, Daniel had imagined her there, in his bed. Still, the sight of her now, on her side, her waist curved like a sand dune and the bed covers trailing from her naked hip, didn't seem real. Daniel wondered if she slept.

Their lovemaking had been breathless, far too quick, and—from her unabashed cries of pleasure, he believed—their satisfaction mutual. Still, she was a mystery. He felt tethered to Gamble in some inexplicable way, and yet he'd many more questions than answers. Why had she been granted this ability to travel through time, and why to him? He didn't know how long she would stay, or if she'd stay at all. All he knew was she was there now, and she had brought with her a joy that, after his divorce and the deaths of his parents, he'd not imagined he would find again.

The world outside his window was silent and dark, and Daniel wondered at the hour. While Gamble slept, he lit a fire. It popped and hissed, still strong. The flamelight moved along her body like a caress.

He traced the line of Gamble's spine with the pad of his pointer finger. When he reached the boundary of the cover he slipped his hand inside, dipping into the warm crease of her buttocks. She sighed and rolled to face him. The blanket slid off completely.

"Hi," she whispered.

Daniel drew back his hand when she turned, but she caught it up and placed it on her breast. He'd no idea what the woman would do next. He rolled her nipple between the pads of his fingers, unable to stop himself. She arched into his hand.

"Hello," Daniel said. When Gamble took his cock in hand, already firm, he groaned. "You are wanton," he said, with appreciation.

"Not used to that, are you?" she said. She scooted closer, positioned herself against him, and looked directly at him. "We modern women embrace our sexuality. It's one of the perks of the twenty-first century." She smiled and licked her lips, and if it was possible, he grew harder. "That and birth control."

Daniel laughed. Before he could consider all the fantastical things she'd told him in the night—about birth control, and sexual freedom, and the fact that women and men of all stations, if they wanted, engaged in sexual congress without societal repercussion well before marriage, and even lived openly with one another without the bonds of the institution—she hooked a leg over him.

"Gamble," he murmured, besotted. "I'm out of French letters."

With that deft small hand, she fitted him at her slick opening and looked up, eyes narrowed and impossible to read in the firelight.

"I'll protect you," she promised.

GAMBLE

After a row of an argument, which would've sent two lesser mortals to their far corners, never to speak again, Tol and I decided to continue in relative silence our search for the identity of the woman in my miniature portrait. He'd pulled all the drop cloths from the stacks of boxes and crates, and he used the claw of a hammer to retract the nails at the tops of any crates that looked like they might house paintings. I'd climbed the ladder into the loft, wanting to get away from him for a little while but unwilling to put aside the search. Tol was right: we didn't have much time.

Still, I stewed from my spot cross-legged on the loft floor, where I read through papers I'd discovered in what looked to be a twenty-year-old accordion file. I scanned for clues, laying papers aside one by one as I worked. Most were barn accounts, listing hay and seed bought and stored, farrier's and veterinarian's bills marked with 1980s dates. Nothing yet to indicate any account of art.

But I could do two things at once. Just as I was about to yell, "I am not returning to 1804!" for the twentieth time, he gave a whoop.

"Think I found something," he said.

I uncurled myself from the floor and brushed off my behind, then walked to the edge of the loft. "Really?" I said, not wanted to get excited until I knew we had a winner. "What?"

"Come down and see," Tol said. He stood next to an art crate with its top off. He'd shed the fancy sweater and rolled up the sleeves of his shirt, the buttons undone at his neck.

"Fine," I muttered, still mad. "I'm coming."

I climbed down, then jumped from the second to last rung. Up in the loft, I'd kicked off my fancy boots, and I'd been walking around in my socks. My now very dusty socks. Tol looked at my feet and grinned.

"You're a ragamuffin, Gamble. Just a straight-up mountain girl. How'd they ever let you into Charleston?"

"I fooled everybody," I said, refusing to be charmed. "Let me see."

Tol pulled a large canvas, about two feet long by three wide, out from inside the crate and brought it to the desk, where he'd clicked on the lamp.

"This is your girl, isn't it?" Tol said.

For a moment I lost the capacity to breathe. It was Honor, but a much older Honor than when I'd known her in 1804: here, she looked to be in her middle to late forties, surrounded by what had to have been her family.

She wore a blue taffeta dress in the wide-skirted, wasp-waisted style of the 1830s, with mutton sleeves and a deep, wide neckline. A tiny oval broach was pinned at center, near the slightest impression of a décolletage. The family was posed in a room I didn't recognize: it had gracious high ceilings, sheened-green painted moldings, and an intricate chinoiserie wallpaper showcasing Asian flora and long-necked wading birds. Packed bookshelves were punctuated on each side by two individual portraits: a man in a gray wig standing at a desk, and a woman in red on horseback, both wearing what looked to be mid-to-late-eighteenth-century dress. If my memory served—and, heaven knew its reliability could be a toss-up—the portraits were of Daniel's and Honor's parents, Ramus Petigru and Lydia Dillwyn Petigru, who died fairly young and under tragic circumstances while Daniel was apprenticed in France.

These, I'd seen. Like a reel of movie film, memory went unspooling in my mind, speeding and then slowing to stop. These Petigru portraits had been in the front two rooms of the house on Tradd Street—each above a fireplace. Could it be that, much like today's fixer-upper craze, this room had simply been redone?

I remembered in 1804 standing on tiptoe before the portrait of Daniel's mother, bracing a hand on the mantel. I'd admired the insouciant red of her riding habit, the rakish white feather in her hat, and the look in her eyes: a look that held both daring and humor. Even in my distress then, at landing so unceremoniously in the early nineteenth century, there had been something grounding in her gaze. Then, as now, I wished I'd known her.

Shaking myself from reverie, I concentrated again on the painting of the family. Honor and a handsome dark-haired man in shiny black riding boots, surely her husband, were at center. Their hands were clasped at her shoulder, and to see it I drew breath: it looked, at least here, like a love match. At stage right was a girl—a young woman, really, for she looked in her teens—seated, a hand trailing in her wide butter-cup-yellow skirts. She had lovely brown hair and sharp blue eyes. There were three boys, the oldest of whom stood next to the dark-haired man, dressed in cravat and tailcoat, his younger brothers before him. The younger boys wore high-waisted honey-colored trousers and short blue jackets, their brown hair cropped but longer and mussed at the crown. They had snub, still-forming noses, and looked to be about nine and seven years old, respectively. There was a great black dog seated between the youngest boy and the girl. Some sort of hound, perhaps. Its head was draped over the boy's shoulder, its clear-eyed gaze directed at the painter.

My breath came back with a pang. Daniel was—had been—deeply talented. He could layer a painting with feeling, personality, mood—both collective and individual—where others (many others, but especially other Jacksonian-era portraitists) only scraped the surface.

"I think it is," I finally managed to say. "She's much younger in the Galliard miniature, but this is Daniel's work. Let's flip it over."

Tol flipped the painting carefully, holding it without setting the canvas all the way down on the desk. I leaned in close. My instinct told me something was going on here, something important not just to me, but to Honor. The questions I asked myself over and over again sounded in my mind: Why did she continue to plead with me in the alley? Why "he needs you"? All along, I'd assumed it was Daniel who was the *he* who needed me—that Honor was a sister trying to help her brother. But here we'd found Daniel, in 1832, still in Charleston, still painting prolifically even in his sixties.

There was a looping signature on the back of the frame, one I recognized as well as my own. A small index card was attached above the signature. The information on the card was typed, and read, "The Parker St. Denis Family: Mr. Parker Pierre St. Denis, Mrs. Parker St. Denis (née Honora Petigru (Huger)); her daughter, Catherine Eleanor Huger; their sons, Parker Percival, Henry Ely, and Daniel Montagu St. Denis. Charleston, South Carolina. By Daniel Matthew Petigru, 1832."

Before I could help myself, I touched the ink with a fingertip. "Well, this proves it," I said. "Her name was Honora Petigru. I suppose she must have married twice, becoming Huger and then St. Denis. But I knew her as Honor."

"There's something at her neck," Tol said.

"It's a miniature," I murmured. "Which tells us how important the art form was to this society. Anything showing up in a family portrait was important." My eyes strained at the tiny oval Daniel had painted at Honor's neck. "It's a locket," I said. "There're two people in it. It might…it might even be Honor on the left. I really need a magnifying glass or microscope to be certain."

"Why would she wear a locket of herself?" Tol said.

"I can't be certain it's Honor," I said. "The other side is harder to make out; there's been some damage. It could be a child, even a baby."

I rocked back on my heels and pressed a hand to my lower back. Discovery was one thing, but this was my life. And I didn't know what to do next.

"Well," Tol said. "What of big brother? What of Daniel?" He turned the painting over and gingerly set it down. "There's only one real way to find out."

"For Christ's sake, Tol, I'm not going back!" I said, irritated and loud. We had the names now: we knew who the people in the portraits were, what I meant to them and what they meant to me. There was nothing else. It was time to get on with our lives, for God's sake. Why was he so set on my digging deeper? "We got what we came for. Heck, we got more. Maybe Miss Saralee and Miss Corrine will let us take it all back to the Galliard. That way I can magnify it."

"Of course, it matters," Tol said, in his best professorial voice, ignoring most of what I'd said.

"Why?" I stalked away from the desk, hating the whine in my voice but too frustrated to do anything about it. We'd come so far. We needed nothing else.

I spun on my heel and marched back, poking him in the chest. "We love each other. You admitted it, same as me. What else is there?"

Before I could make another peep, Tol grabbed my hand, tucked it into his chest, and pulled me close. Then he laid a big, fat kiss on me. In spite of myself I opened my mouth to his. We tangled for a bit, then he groaned and pulled away.

"There's more," he said, deep and determined and so utterly Tol-like I was powerless against his certainty. "Honor said, 'He needs you.' She said, 'You must come back.' What if she keeps showing up and begging for help? Would you be able to forgive yourself if you gave up on her?"

He took a deep breath and bent low so I could look him in the eyes. "You need to fix things with Daniel too. You've got resolving to do in 1804, Gamble. I need you like I need water and air, but I won't have you unless I can have all of you."

"Well," I said, stunned.

❧

Later that evening I stood in the doorway of Tolliver's guest bedroom in Miss Saralee's house.

"Three paintings signed by Daniel Petigru, Edward Malbone's travel journal, and a seascape by 'an unknown lady,' circa 1850. I'd say that's pretty damn good," I said.

I'd taken a long, hot shower, and it'd washed away some of the intensity of the afternoon. I finally felt a sense of equilibrium. Plus, I was relaxed: I wore the fluffy plush robe I'd discovered lying across the canopied bed in my own guest room, my wet hair turbaned in a thick terrycloth towel and a dripping toothbrush in hand. My feet were bare.

Tol sat on his bed in a gray slub T-shirt and a pair of plaid pajama pants, his long legs stretched out, feet against the footboard. He wore his wire-rimmed reading glasses, a tome of a book on his lap. No wonder it was rare these days for him to teach: the coeds probably went nuts.

He tipped the glasses down with one finger, to look at my toes. After he got his fill, he pushed them back up and eyed me, wary.

"It is good. Mark, especially, should be pleased," Tol said. "Now go to bed, Gamble."

"Okay." I grinned, stepping into the room.

Tol leapt from the bed with more speed than I would have expected from a man of his size, spun me around quick as you please, and shoved me out the door.

"Goodnight, Gamble," he said, closing the door between us before I could even turn around. The lock clicked into place.

I leaned into the door and cupped my hands around my mouth like a megaphone against the solid oak. I contemplated making chicken sounds, but instead whispered, "I love you, Tolliver Jackson."

DANIEL

Daniel had not expected the French hero of Brandywine to be a bean pole of a man, but he was. Still, this did not detract from the man's obvious charm, his palpable presence. He was—despite his unblemished blue military jacket, trimmed in gold thread, epaulets on the shoulders, white deerskin trousers and high black officer's boots—a true soldier, and one not long from war.

"General Lafayette," Daniel said. "Would you turn your shoulders toward the window, into the light? Yes, that's it."

The autumn sun was at a perfect four o'clock position in the sky, and Daniel wanted to capture Lafayette's face in it. The older man did not wear a wig—hadn't even powdered his graying red hair, as many men his age did for a portrait, and he had a most open face, unusual for a soldier and diplomat.

He did not seem tired by the hour, or by Daniel's constant ministrations and adjustments to his pose, as so many of his sitters did. Much of this had to do with Gamble, who was acting as his artist's assistant and had been charming the marquis with questions.

Daniel stepped to his easel, where the miniature was tacked. He took up his pencil again, stippling the cheekbones. Lafayette had such a presence—he was alive in a manner others were not, so much so Daniel could almost see a spark in the air around the man. Daniel was determined that this was the way Lafayette would appear in miniature too. Later, he'd use different strokes and even a wash in order to allow the luminosity of the ivory to emerge on the face. The technique would be laborious, but well worth the effort.

For a moment, in the warm sun coming in through the tall drawing room windows, the major general closed his eyes. Daniel studied his expression, silently cataloging what he knew about Lafayette's life: the man had been a hero and a revolutionary in two countries; he suffered years in an Austrian prison, had seen monarchies rise and fall. He was nearing fifty years of age, Daniel knew. It was a long way from Paris.

"Favorite thing to eat in Charleston?" Gamble asked.

She perched on the edge of his mother's favorite chair, one upholstered in a damask of the most riotous red and pink fabric, but instead of sitting in a more demure fashion, with ankles crossed at the floor, her feet were tucked beneath her. Daniel felt certain she was cross-legged like a child beneath her skirts.

In addition, she was likely without stays. Daniel knew this because, well…he'd known her intimately that morning, just before she'd been dressed. An image of Gamble smiling at him over her shoulder, her gown open to the line of her backbone, made him shake his head to clear it. You couldn't tell it to look at her, but the woman was a siren. Circe herself.

"I adore everything about Southern cuisine," Lafayette said. "But I must admit, Madame Vance, I was served a rum and brandy punch at the Charleston Theatre which tasted of heaven, and so this drink may be my favorite. Alas, this is not food, no?"

"No," Gamble said. "But that's okay. I've been jonesing for the dragoon punch too. It's addictive."

Lafayette turned his head, interrupting Daniel's study of the hollowed, tricky space between cheek and ear, and looked to him. "Monsieur Petigru, do you know of this word 'jonesing'?"

"I do not," Daniel said, raising an eyebrow at Gamble. It was, by his count, the seventh unfamiliar word she'd uttered since breakfast.

"It means that you want something so much, you can't control yourself around it," she said. There was a laugh in her voice. "I feel this way about candied chocolate."

"Ah," said Lafayette. "Now I understand."

I feel this way about you, Daniel said silently to Gamble.

Mercifully, she stayed quiet. Daniel was able, then, to finish this first sitting before they lost the sun. He tried to remember if he'd enough oil in his lamps in the loft to work into the night, and whether his ivory was washed, sanded, and ready. He hoped so. His miniature portraits always turned out better if he could go from first sketches on ivory to more detailed pigmentation straightaway. Too, he found himself inspired by Lafayette: his mind awash with color and possibility, with the complicated look in the man's eyes—a look he yearned to translate. It was a familiar feeling, albeit fleeting. Inspiration, he knew, must be grasped, and grasped tight, whenever it could be caught in hand. If not, it would likely be days, even weeks, before it returned.

They'd scheduled only one other sitting, two days from now. Lafayette's social obligations were many, and it was rumored he would not be long in Charleston. The general was making a hero's return to some of the places he'd visited while serving under President Washington, and he was to be feted by families in many states. A great favorite of Washington's, Lafayette was beloved for his heroism in the Revolution. And rightly so.

Daniel smiled to himself: just the night before, Gamble had told him that in the year 2002, the United States Congress would make the Marquis de Lafayette an official citizen of the United States.

"What are your plans for the remainder of your visit, General?" Gamble said.

She straightened, set her feet on the floor with a rustle of skirts, and reached for her coffee. She seemed loose and natural, as if they were compatriots, at their ease in a private salon, instead of near strangers who'd met but days before.

Lafayette kept his head turned toward the window but cut his eyes in her direction, as if not wanting to spoil Daniel's situation. "I'm to sup with several families who hosted me when I was here before, and there is, I believe, a ball being held in my honor at the home of Benjamin Huger. Madame Lafayette and I should like to celebrate Christmas in Charleston, but alas, we're for Philadelphia before then. A reunion of my comrades."

Gamble lit up like a candle. "Will you see President Adams?" she said.

"I shall," Lafayette said. "No visit would be complete without our fellowship. And I hope, too, to see Monsieur Jefferson and his daughter."

Here the Frenchman's face went still, the lines of it deepening, aging him. "I'd have been full of joy to have seen once more *Monsieur mon tres cher frere* Alexander, Colonel Hamilton, before his unspeakable murder. I could kill Burr myself."

Lafayette sighed. Before either Daniel or Gamble could respond, the Frenchman's face cleared. "My sincere apologies, Madame Vance. I am yet unaccustomed to the loss of my friend." He gave a small smile, the diplomat reemerging. "I must admit, I long for a visit with Madame

Adams most, after Thomas that is. She is a thoroughly delightful creature."

"I couldn't agree more," Gamble said.

"Ah, so you are acquainted with Madame Adams?" Lafayette said, and Daniel set his pencil aside, brushing gray dust from his hands as he stood.

Of course the woman had not met the wife of the second president. Abigail Adams was sure to be known to history. Lafayette, of course, could not know this, and Daniel didn't want Gamble to have to lie. She had a glass face: he doubted the woman could lie even if she wanted to.

"Miss Gamble?" Effie had stepped into the room without Daniel noticing, he'd been so taken by his own work and then alarmed by Gamble's gaffe. Effie held his mother's riding cloak. "Miss Honor says it's time the two of you took that ride she promised."

"Oh yes!" Gamble unfolded herself from the chair—she was indeed wearing slippers, so at least there was that—and flew to Lafayette, who had risen when she had. He held out his hands, and she took them as if she'd known the famed hero since her girlhood.

"What a pleasure it's been to spend the afternoon with you, General," Gamble said. "Please forgive me for leaving, but I promised Honor we'd ride to Oyster Point."

"The pleasure is mine," Lafayette said. He brought her hands to his lips and bussed her knuckles. "You're delightful company, madame. I hope this will not be the last time we meet."

Gamble grinned at him—again, that free, open smile of hers could be called nothing else. She squeezed his hands, leaning in. "Oh, I hope so too," she said.

She took the cloak from Effie and shrugged into the outmoded garment like nothing so much as a young boy, the jacket's long red peplum flapping with her efforts. Effie tried in vain to assist, but Gamble was off.

"Thanks, Effie," Gamble said. "Bye!" She left the room quick as a cricket. After a moment, they heard her footfall on the stairs. It sounded as if she took them two by two.

Effie cast her eyes to the ceiling, which made Lafayette chuckle. She said, "Need anything, Mr. Daniel? You're about to lose your light."

"No," he said. "I believe I'm satisfied. But thank you. The general has a supper engagement with the Pinckneys, and with Honor and Gamble away I'll sup in glorious solitude. Don't trouble yourself tonight."

"All right, then," she said, then turned on her heel, abandoning them for the kitchen house. He waited for it: Yes, Effie's footfall on the stairs was measured and reasonable; at least one member of his household had their passions in check.

Lafayette walked to the balcony door, close to where Daniel had placed him to attract the southerly light, though Lafayette did not make to open it. He merely peered out through the mullioned glass.

"You say Madame Vance is your cousin, from Virginia? She is most unusual."

"She is," Daniel said, joining him. What else could he say? The man had Gamble pegged. On the street below, the front door of the Tradd Street house opened, and Honor and Gamble spilled out on a laugh and a flutter of skirts. He wished he knew what they were laughing about. A moment later, Effie followed with Gamble's bonnet in hand, which the woman took with a look of chagrin.

"'Zounds, will the woman ever wear a hat?" Daniel exclaimed without thinking, as her uncovered blond head disappeared into the curricle.

Lafayette said dryly, "I think not, monsieur. She is rather unconcerned with public opinion, is she not? Though it surely must concern itself with her."

Daniel turned sharply. But Lafayette's blue eyes held nothing but amusement, and he gave Daniel a decidedly Gallic shrug. "How can it not? People will talk of the unusual, and the beautiful. Your Madame Vance is both. How will you keep her?"

Keep her? How can I? Daniel wanted to say. Wanted to shout, if truth be known. But instead he said, "What makes you think I want to keep her, sir?"

The French hero put his hand on Daniel's shoulder. He did not clap it there, as a blustering soldier or puffed-up dignitary might; instead, it was a touch of gentle empathy.

Lafayette patted once. "She's an original, my friend. *Les femmes* like Madame Vance are not born each day. Besides, she is a widow, *no?* What is keeping you from pursuing her in this fashion?"

Daniel watched as Ben closed the carriage door behind the women, then slung himself up into the driver's box. Ben smiled—teeth white in his shadowed face—at something Gamble said to him, but it was apparent he was trying not to. Daniel had known Ben since they'd been in toddling strings; the man was the steadiest, most reserved sort he knew.

"Madame Vance is not of this world," Daniel said.

Daniel found with Gamble in his home and in his life, the days passed at breakneck speed. November was gone as quickly as if it were a candle flame someone had pinched with the pads of wet fingers, leaving but a trail of smoke. It wasn't that the days were not pleasurable. They were. In the mornings, often after he or Gamble had slipped from the other's bed before the house had awoken, they'd take their breakfast in his studio. Gamble would sip her coffee with relish—truly, he'd never before seen a woman take so much pleasure in the drink—and together they would work.

While Daniel sketched or painted, Gamble would clean and bleach his ivory. She was painstakingly thorough: an obvious professional. One late afternoon, after they'd been at work since dawn, Honor bringing trays so they could remain uninterrupted, he'd stilled at his easel.

He said, "Gamble, there's no need for you to work yourself so. You're not my servant."

And she'd straightened from her bent position over his desk, where she had been picking through his artist's box. Her uncontrollable hair was turbaned in a sanguine scarf, to keep it out of her eyes. She fingered several of the tools and stones there before choosing a piece of pumice, which she used to sand the ivory smooth.

"Daniel," Gamble said, sighing with what he knew was exasperation, but not halting her work. "This is what I do. Let me."

In the evenings before supper, they'd stroll through the city, often finding themselves along the sand and shelled path at Oyster Point. Gamble did not shirk from the cold air sweeping off the harbor; nor did she balk at the piles of downed palmettoes, wood, and debris still lining portions of Water and East Bay Streets on their way. Daniel had heard tell the hurricane which pounded Charleston the month before Gamble's arrival had left one million dollars' worth of destruction in its wake. She didn't seem surprised. In fact, she told him of storms in her century so relentless they lifted houses from their foundations and had Charlestonians paddling canoes down the center of Broad Street.

One evening, the sun sinking in a melting of orange and gold behind the live oaks at their backs, he pointed at the small island in the harbor.

"Look," Daniel said. "They've not repaired the palisades at Fort Pinckney. I wonder if the governor waits on logs or labor, or both?"

Gamble followed his hand, her eyes narrowed. "I wonder," she said, with a bitterness Daniel had not yet heard in her, "if the overseer simply waits on more enslaved workers. A boat full of them drowned trying to make it out to barricade the fort during the storm, you know."

"No," Daniel said. Gamble's was a voice from the future, and sometimes when she spoke like this, toneless and quiet, it made the small hairs rise at the nape of his neck. "I didn't."

"It's only the first hurricane of the century," she said, watching the water. "There'll be others."

Sea craft bobbed on gleaming blue-green water. The sunset cloaked small boats with sailors' casting nets close to the winter-yellow reeds nearby, a naval vessel at anchor, and four other ships leaving the wharves for parts unknown. The harbor was busy, even at dusk.

"One hundred enslaved workers drowned in this storm," she said. "Aaron Burr will write about it in his journal. He's somewhere in the south now, you know, trying to avoid a murder charge."

Gamble paused. She crossed her arms, rocking forward on the balls of her feet. The white shells crunched beneath her boots, and she gripped at the wide lapels of her borrowed brown greatcoat. Behind them a small white dog barked from the upper porch of a single house—they'd seen it earlier, its pink snout poking through the wood railing—and a carriage went by, slow enough to wonder; workers hammered nails and moved wood at the peninsula's southernmost point, shuttering the bathhouse there until the warmer months. Two gentlemen on horseback trotted by, tipping their tall black hats in unison. Everything as it should be, Daniel thought, with no small amount of cynicism.

He turned back to Gamble in the growing dark, observing the blowing strands of her hair as they loosened from the chignon Effie had fashioned, hidden beneath a wide hood. He sketched her profile with an invisible artist's hand: the cockleshell curve of her ear, its elfin tip red against the cold; the line of her mouth, lips pressed together hard in thought; the shallow creases at the corners of her eyes, noticeable just when close.

When Gamble did this—when she with intention made herself small, removing herself not in presence but in mind to a future and a time Daniel couldn't know—he felt helpless, useless, and, God help him, unmanned. Gamble was a creature of such mystery, so much her own yet adaptive to change, so willing to envelop herself in her surroundings, to sink deep into her particular reality. Daniel felt when she went still like this, becoming a sage once more, she took herself away even further, on some inexplicable journey whose destination was far from him.

Daniel gave himself an imperceptible shake. He raised an eyebrow, wanting nothing more than to root her in the present moment. He said, "I don't think it a coincidence your arrival was preceded by a dangerous and powerful storm."

"Ha!" she said. He noted that her eyes seemed closer to gray near the wintering sea. She shaded the sunset with a hand across her brow like a salute. Better to have worn a damned hat.

"You are funny, Mr. Petigru," she added. "And you're probably right."

"Gamble," Daniel started, knowing if he did not force the words, he might languish in silence far too long. Long enough for her to hate him. "You're not meant for this place. For this time. For me. Are you?"

"No," she said. "But I want to be."

GAMBLE

Early December, 2004

We loaded up Tol's serviceable sedan with our historic booty, the journal wrapped in the robe I'd worn the night before (donated with permission by Miss Corrine), the painting nailed up tight in its wooden crate. It pained me to watch Honor's forty-something-year-old face disappear into the slot of wood, even knowing I'd see it again in the lab at the Galliard.

It was painful, I think, because I hadn't been there. Because Honor had had a life, and children, and I'd missed it. Because Daniel, when he'd painted her thus, would be into his sixties, possibly a very different man.

It was not that I missed them in a way that made me wish for a different life. I was a woman of my time, no matter how much I appreciated the past. But Daniel and Honor had been mine, just for a little while, and for that I would always love them.

I backed away, and Tol closed the hatch with a click. The morning was quiet and wet, warm for early December. Low-slung fog hung over the pastures, blowing through the horse fence lining the long sandy drive, making everything behind it—the trees, the empty grass, the barn on one side and the big Victorian house on the other—opaque. Like the faded relief of a woman's face in an opal brooch. The fog seemed on its way to someplace else.

"You ready?" Tol said. Then, as if he'd been doing it for years, he tugged on my ponytail. He pressed two fingers against the muscle at my nape. I tried not to purr.

"Yep," I said. I rolled my head on my shoulders so my hair touched his arm, then dropped back to look up at him. This was what it was going to be like to stand beside Tol for the next fifty or more years, if I wanted to see into his eyes. "Are you?"

"Yep," Tol said, and winked. He squeezed my neck, released. "You like them, don't you?"

He meant the old ladies. "Of course I do," I said. "I wish we could pack them up and take them back with us. Don't you? They loved you! One minute more and Miss Saralee would've patted you on the fanny. We're getting away just in the nick of time."

Tol caught my hand and threaded our fingers. "Naw, they belong here. Unlike us."

That smile of his, I swear. It did something unexplainable to my insides. How had I missed it all this time? How had I missed *him*?

"Oh, I could do very well on a horse farm," I said. "I've got the boots. Plus, I can ride." Tol leaned down, and just before our lips were about to touch, I added, "You'd have seen it for yourself if you'd let me."

"Gamble," Tol said, his breath warm on my face, smelling faintly of the cheese grits and jelly toast we'd had for breakfast. "No one has ever kept you from doing anything you wanted in your life, especially not me."

Then he kissed me. He kissed me, at just before eight o'clock in the morning, standing there in the gravel drive of Miss Saralee Hutto's venerable Aiken horse farm, in full view of her house, with fog swirling about our ankles. Tol's intent was not to be chaste. Before I knew it, I'd wound my arms around his neck and he'd bent over me as if he'd scoop me up if I let him. If I just said the word.

I pulled away with a gasp. Yes, a gasp—just like in the movies. I pressed my hands against his chest, keeping him at bay. He looked at me as if I were a plate of oysters on the half-shell on a candlelit table at FIG. And I knew how Tol felt about those oysters. We ate there every time one of us had a coup: when we won a grant for the Galliard or the Cox, published a paper in an academic journal, or launched a new exhibit.

"Wait," I breathed. "Just a minute. Stop. *You* are. *You* are keeping me from what I want."

"What's that?" Tol said, doing the looming and curling thing again, and I knew soon I'd be unable to do anything but relent.

I smirked, and quick as a flash ducked under his arm. "You know what," I said, backing toward the passenger side of the car.

He stood to his full six feet five inches, tucked his chin, and said, "Fuck."

He didn't mean it the way it sounded. It was rare Tol was crude. He meant it as an expletive: a heartier version of "crap." Like, "Crap, she's right."

Still, "fuck" was especially apropos here.

"Yep," I said. I offered no quarter. This celibacy of ours was his deal. "My sentiments exactly."

When we were back on the peninsula, exiting I-26 East for Meeting Street, Tol glanced over. "Do you want to go by their house?" Tol said.

Outside the car, restored and dilapidated single houses flashed past—many the former homes of enslaved people who had "lived out" from their early masters. This area of the peninsula was experiencing a renaissance along with the rest of Charleston, the old houses being bought up by new Charlestonians with a yearning to be a part of history and a fixer-upper gleam in their eyes. But life was tricky, and, let's face it, never fair. So, at the same time as it saved these irreplaceable old houses, restoration sometimes drove out the poorer, ancient Black families whose ancestors had made lives on these streets for centuries.

I didn't know what the answer was to such a displacement, but I knew it all came back to slavery. History in every old American city—but especially in an old Southern port city like Charleston, the literal gateway of the North American slave trade—ran, always, in brutal parallel.

I turned from the flash of houses outside the window, slowing as the car did, and narrowed my eyes at Tol. "Whose house?" I said, suspicious.

Tol braked when the light turned red at the corner of Meeting and Market Streets. His look was direct and unapologetic. "Theirs: Daniel's and Honor's. You said the house was on Tradd, right? I know you know which one it is." He looked back at the intersection. "I think *I* know which one it is."

I scrutinized my translucent reflection in the window until it disappeared into the outline of the nineteenth-century buildings behind it. After several blocks, we turned onto Tradd. As we took the corner I watched a silver-haired woman, likely in her early sixties, lift the latch of a tall wrought-iron gate, with a young boy, about three years old, in her arms. The gate latch clicked back into place behind the woman, and her life was hidden; whatever she and the boy were about to do next vanished into the garden of that house. Her grandson would grow up thinking it normal to play in a centuries-old garden, on one of the most sought-after streets in the south.

I loved this street. Long before I'd moved to Charleston, Tradd had been one of my favorites. The eighteenth-century houses here, older and less grand than the nineteenth-century showcases of Bay Street, had a saltier, more complex history. During colonial times, Tradd had been home to many seafaring merchants and their counting houses. During the later Antebellum period, the upper classes of the peninsula, it was said, turned their noses up at what they considered a former "tradesmen section" of the city. It had to make any cultural historian, any lover of the hoi polloi, smile to know that the same homes were now being advertised at multi-million dollars a pop.

In my mind at least, Tradd Street represented Charleston during a time when the city was more diverse than it would become in the centuries hence. In the late 1600s and 1700s, Charleston was an incredibly multicultural town. There were more women and free people of color-owned businesses than there would be by the 1800s, and—a graduate professor of mine once said—you could stand on a street corner on the peninsula and hear at times six different languages being spoken. It was not a perfect place, and all the evils of colonial life—misogyny, racism, and more—plagued it. But slavery, especially after the turn of the nineteenth century, would make Charleston more closed-minded and insular.

This wasn't the entire story of eighteenth- and nineteenth-century Charleston, of course—we all know humanity is complicated; at least, I hope we do—but slavery is the central, horrific, and undeniable thread. Those who deny it do so in ignorance and at their own peril.

But back to my beloved Tradd Street. Tradd's loveliness was contained. When you walked it, you were enveloped in age and quiet. While Bay Street was the eighteen-year-old belle of the ball, donned in the most fashionable gowns and educated by tutors chosen by her father, Tradd was a woman older and full in her power, aware of the world, revealing an unapologetic décolletage and wearing skirts that showed her ankle because she was unafraid of muck.

At least, this was how I saw it. Tol said I was as bad as a novelist, forcing personification and character onto inanimate objects like plants, houses, cars, and streets. But I couldn't help it: I saw life in layers.

Tol pulled the sedan into an empty space across the street from Daniel and Honor Petigru's house. Effie, Ben, and Cooper Perrineau's house.

"Want to get out?" he said.

No. I did not want to get out. I knew what the house looked like, thank you very much. I knew how many steps it took from the car-riage block to the front door. How the stucco warmed to a tawny color at sunrise and sunset, a color more akin to Italy than the Barbados, where Charleston got its original Caribbean-bright colors. I knew which boards creaked in the third-floor hall (at least if they hadn't been fixed in the past two hundred years), and why there was a chip in the mantel above the drawing room fireplace; Ben had made it with the corner of a French burr walnut marquetry table he'd moved at Honor's request. But he'd tripped on the corner of the Turkish rug, and one of the brass-encased feet had banged the mantel.

I most certainly did not want to see—could not bear to see—Dan-iel's studio turned into a garage. Especially if it housed a Land Rover.

But this—me facing this house, and my past in it—might help me help Honor. It might help me finally close the book on my relationship with Daniel, which was important to Tol. And I could do hard things for Tol.

"Okay," I said.

We got out of the car and crossed to the house without touching. The crepe myrtles along the street swayed their whitened branches in an easy wind; a middle-aged man in a navy sport coat and khaki pants dragged a trash can up the short bricked drive of the house next door. Somewhere someone's terrier yipped.

I could feel Tol putting a purposeful distance between us. At the single house's skinny front door (no match for the American giants of the twenty-first century), painted a satin black, he waited. I stepped to the top of the ancient stoop. My feet settled into slight dips in the limestone, made by over two hundred years of feet. I took the antique knocker in hand—a brass Huguenot Cross—and tapped it twice to the aged metal plate beneath. We waited.

"Do you want kids?" Tol said. He may have stood on the sidewalk below, but his head was still higher than mine.

"What?" I sputtered.

Before I could manage to say anything else, the door opened. The man standing there was not much taller than I. He looked to be in his early eighties, with a shocking full head of thick, waving white hair, a steady brown-eyed gaze, and a long, straight, regal nose. A Petigru nose.

"Daniel?" I whispered.

DANIEL

CHARLESTON
DECEMBER 1804

Daniel finally looked up from his work. It was after sunset, the sky outside the barn clinging to light but not long for the dark. It held a glow about the edges of the window, like gilt in a picture frame.

Not wanting to pull the drapery and cover the barn window, both he and Gamble wore cotton and wool blankets about their shoulders. They'd lit the oil lamps at dusk: the one at his desk, where Gamble worked, and the one on the table next to his easel, where he sat now, his brush unmoving in hand. Whenever a breeze slid through an unfilled crack in the wood walls, the silver candelabra with its six half-melted candles on the table next to his simple studio bed fizzled and hissed; another candle in a rough wooden pot flickered at the top of the loft ladder. Below them the barn was dark and quiet, smelling of horses, leather, and hay.

Daniel took up his brush again and added a last line of hatching to the chin of Mrs. Silas Pringle. The delicate crosshatch, combined with transparent washes of color, were as detailed as a tiny mosaic. It was a laborious process, but Daniel was determined not to shape the face as it could be—like some sort of European portraitist's ideal, dreamy and ephemeral—but rather as the lady really was. He set the tiny squirrel-hair brush into the lip of his easel.

Gamble was entirely focused on his paint pots. She'd examined the colors for the past two hours, playing with his mixtures of Indian yellow, ivory, and blue verditer in glass jars and small bowls she'd collected from the kitchen. There was yellow paint on her knuckles and at the tip of her nose, where it was sure she'd scratched with a messy finger. She looked like a medieval apothecary—or, more apt, a sorceress intent on her potions.

Earlier that afternoon, she'd insisted he again talk her through his colors, all of which—except for his white—he ordered from a color-man on King Street. White tended to be unique and particular to every portraitist, at least the ones he knew. His, he told Gamble, must be a "French white, dry and well levigated." She'd repeated it to herself when he said it, like a catechism.

"This will help me in 2004," she'd said, earlier that afternoon. "We never repaint faces if there's too much damage or fading there—other parts of the portrait, like clothing or drapery, yes, but we don't mess with the face. However, if I know how you mix your white, I might at least be able to conserve *your* faces so they look as close to what you intended as possible."

After Gamble had said it, she stilled like a thief caught at the larder. Daniel didn't say a word—tried his best not to even look at her, to show he knew what she meant. Because what she meant, of course, was that she would keep trying to return to 2004. That she'd leave them.

"Gamble," Daniel murmured now, clasping his knees. The weathered buckskin of his father's old breeches—the ones he liked to paint in for comfort—was smooth beneath his palms, and he rubbed his hands over his thighs to bring himself back to the present. She looked up at the sound of his voice, the lamp light crowning her hair. "We've stayed quite secluded, haven't we?" he said. "Like a couple in their dotage. Have I kept you too much from society? Is there more you'd like to see?"

"I prefer to think of us as a pair of wolves," Gamble said. "You know, needing the pack, but preferring the solitude of the woods, and each other's company."

"Wolves?" Daniel said, then laughed.

Gamble grinned. The paint blotch at the tip of her elvish nose was most certainly ochre. "Yes, wolves. I saw this fabulous PBS special on Alaskan gray wolves once. They're fascinating. Most of the artists and art historians I know are like wolves: we need to be with other people, out in the sound and the light, because being part of a pack feeds our work—our art. But we also need just as much to be alone, out of the crowd. In solitary spaces. That's where the magic happens."

Daniel pushed off from the stool and went to her. There was a clean rag on the desk; he used it to wipe the paint from her nose. Sometimes, it was as if she spoke a foreign language.

He said, "Are you talking again of television?"

Gamble wrinkled her nose, but she took hold of the corner of the blanket he'd draped about his shoulders, which hung at his side. She pulled. "Yep. Good old moving pictures. It'll be another seventy or so years before someone figures out how to make them."

Daniel moved closer at her urging and fingered a lock of hair which had come loose from her turban. "I want you to answer me, Gamble. We can go anywhere—you could see more of Charleston as it is now, or we could even take a ship to Boston. I turned down a recent commission I could write and accept. If you wanted it."

Gamble looked up, her eyes full of what he might call love, if he could make it out. She covered his hand with her own and held it against the blanket at her shoulder. "You turned it down for me, didn't you? Because I was here."

"Yes," he said. "It didn't harm me to do so."

"Still." She reached up with her other hand, the paint-grubby one, and gathered the blanket together at his chest. She pulled him down until their foreheads touched. "You didn't need to do that."

"You didn't need to stay," Daniel said. "But you did."

"Need," she said, her voice low, "had nothing to do with it."

"We could go anywhere," he repeated.

"Daniel." Gamble kissed him briefly, then touched her forehead to his again. "I've met the hero Lafayette, held my tongue next to John C. Calhoun, and heard an anti-slavery speech by Ann Tuke Alexander—a bona fide Quaker feminist! I met Washington Allston, whose work I've studied for years—his name was literally the answer to test questions when I was in graduate school. I danced the cotillion and the scotch reel, and drank Charleston Light Dragoon Punch, from the original recipe. I drove a curricle and I've worn a whalebone corset. I think I've had quite the nineteenth-century experience.

"But more than any of those things," Gamble continued. "I've been with you and Honor. Here, in your studio and in your home. And it's been my saving grace." She stopped, and he said nothing. They breathed each other in. He watched her throat move.

"Plus," she said. "You did promise to take me to Christmas Eve service at St. Michael's, did you not?"

Daniel swallowed everything he wanted to say and everything he did not. "That I did."

"Well," Gamble said. "There you have it. What more could a girl ask for?"

❧

Daniel had not seized the moments of his life—even the minutes and hours of his life, his present—since he'd been a young man in Paris, before the deaths of his parents. Yet here he was, a man of thirty-nine years, acting as though there was no tomorrow. As though everything he had and had known existed solely in those moments. In that room.

He assumed, after Gamble was with them for months, that her actions, her very person and his own reactions to her, would cease to astonish. That he'd return to his daily life, moving through it in the same pattern he had moved through before. Acting as brother, head of house, friend, and artist. He assumed that the separate, working parts of his life would fall back into place, like tumblers in a lock.

Daniel had not lived as a monk before Gamble. His former wife, Simone, had been exciting and wild, yet emotionally as fragile as a hothouse flower. When they abandoned the hothouse of their courting and entered the real world beyond her father's—his patron's—house, and into Daniel's artist's garret in the attic of a Paris tenement, Simone wilted. Life as the wife of an impoverished young artist did not suit her. She'd no interest in returning with him to America, and Daniel had always known he would not stay away forever from his family in Charleston.

What's more, Simone expected Daniel to paint grand works: masterpieces on massive canvases, pieces like the art of de Steuben or Gros—men Simone had met in her father's salon, men she admired. But Daniel's interest, even as a young man, had always been in the human face. He felt pulled to paint personality. To show, from within a most circumscribed space, the entire portrait of a human soul.

Upon his return to Charleston, Daniel avoided romantic entanglements. After one failed marriage, he'd no interest in attempting another. Women of his social class sought matrimony, so Daniel sought his pleasure, when necessary, elsewhere. There'd been a widow, a decade older than he and just as uninterested in a long-term bond. She'd no intention of giving up the autonomy she had over her own estate—something that was sure to transfer to a new husband.

Then there was the brothel on West Street, which Daniel visited once or twice a year, when he thought he might go mad if he didn't.

That, of course, was carnal pleasure. Mere physical relief. With Gamble, Daniel's world seemed as if it were itself a portrait in miniature, as if when he concentrated with all his might on this small, contained space—on his life with her—what was beyond the frame fell away. As if everything else were excess, unnecessary. Surely, it was healthy for neither heart nor head to rely upon one person so much for, well...so much. Something must give.

When Gamble reached out and began with deft fingers to unbutton the fall front of his breeches, Daniel decided he'd contend with those concerns later.

Later, with the candles burned out and the oil near to smoking in the lamps, Daniel faced Gamble on the small studio bed. He propped himself on his elbow and drew the blanket up and over her nakedness. She lay on her back, studying the barn ceiling. At the movement she took the edge of the blanket from him, pulled it to her chin, and threaded her fingers atop her chest. She raised an eyebrow.

"Yes?" she said.

"I have to ask it," Daniel said. It was futile. Idiotic. But necessary.

"Daniel," Gamble said.

"Will you stay?" he said. "Here, with us, in this time? I believe we could make a good life."

Gamble sighed, regret in her voice. "There's a very good chance we could," she said. "But, no."

Daniel wanted to argue, to make his case as if he were a barrister before a jury of peers. They were astonishingly well-suited for each other, could she not see it? He'd never worked alongside anyone—not even Ed—with such ease. Honor already considered Gamble a sister. Charleston society had no idea what to think of her, but it found her fascinating. Daniel would place any sort of wager on society finding her fascinating until her hair turned white.

Then something occurred to him. When Gamble said she wasn't married, he'd assumed it meant there was no one else. The thought of her with another man was a clenched fist in his belly. It was a question he should've asked long before now.

"Is there a man you love in your time?" Daniel said. "Someone to whom you are promised?"

"Yes," Gamble said, so quick and with such force it seemed to startle her. She scooted to sit, bringing the blanket with her to her collarbone. She pushed heavy hair behind her ear, then covered her mouth with splayed fingers. It was nearly an exact replica of the movement she had made on the day they met. When she'd found herself in 1804, in their parlor, confused and afraid.

"Gamble—" Daniel began, but she looked at him with such an odd combination of surprise and certainty he stopped.

"Wait," she said. "What I meant to say is, yes, there's someone I love. I love my best friend, Tolliver. He's a wonderful person, Daniel—you'd feel it if you knew him. He's kind and smart, and he takes his time with things. With me." Here she paused. "You two are alike in that way, which is why I may have felt so comfortable with you, so soon after we met."

Daniel didn't know how to respond. It seemed as if Gamble had only just realized something which startled her. He loathed this Tolliver. But he cleared his throat and said, "He's your friend?"

"My dearest friend," Gamble said. "He's also a Black man."

Daniel sat up, hitching his breeches around his waist and fumbling with the fall front, angry. At the wet shine in her eyes he breathed through his nose, forcing himself to calm. He leaned back against the wall at the head of the bed, letting their shoulders touch. Gamble was silent.

A Black man. So much now made sense. Still, he said, "You know we're Quakers, Gamble. We don't share the views of others. Effie and Ben are paid to serve us—we'd never think of owning slaves."

Gamble shook her head. "It's still too hard. Even knowing you and Honor are on the right side of history. I couldn't live with slavery. It's everywhere. It would be everywhere I went in this city—in the entire country. It'll be 1863 before emancipation. Another year until the House of Representatives ratifies the Thirteenth Amendment to the Constitution—the amendment that will finally free them forever. That's sixty years from now, Daniel. Sixty years. By then, we could be long dead."

Daniel didn't speak. He laid a hand over hers and waited. She breathed deeply and began again.

"Even knowing of the goodness and grace in *this* home, I couldn't walk through this city, make a life, maybe even a child, with you, and breathe the same air of people who hold others in bondage. As chattel," she said. "It's pervasive. Slavery's in the soil of Charleston. It seeps into everything—the politics, the food, the tiny everyday things—and it stains like blood. And bloodstains never go away, no matter how hard you scrub."

Gamble shook her head again, her eyes wet with unshed tears. Pleading. "God, we're still dealing with its aftermath in 2004. Slavery is the great and awful curse of this country."

"Yours could be a voice of reason," Daniel said, but even as he did he knew it would never work. Gamble met the eyes of every Negro they passed upon the street. She greeted them freely. When they were at Thomas Pinckney's last week for Daniel to make his initial sketch for the bridal portrait of Pinckney's intended, Eliza Izard, Gamble took a tray of food from the hands of an enslaved house worker, spoke to him most informally, and served the plates herself. Everyone watched in shock; the only reason no one commented was that it had happened so quickly. Though Daniel knew there'd have been talk after they left.

Gamble did it without thinking. She was as likely, through her actions, to have a slave inadvertently whipped as she was to find herself run out of the city. Accused of fraternizing with Negroes. Dubbed a race-baiting abolitionist. Her association could affect his art commissions and even Honor's future marriage prospects in the most painful of ways. If this happened, Gamble would never forgive herself.

It was impossible for her to stay. He knew this, yet he couldn't help himself.

"No, Daniel," Gamble said. "I'm not meant for 1804, and 1804 is certainly not meant for me. Though I've loved being here, and I've loved you."

Daniel squeezed her hand and felt his heart break. In fact, it may have been the first time his heart had ever broken over a woman, save for the death of his mother.

"And I you," he said. He made himself ask. "When will you go?"

Gamble swallowed, a vertical crease forming between her eyes. Daniel could not imagine another man getting to trace it with his fingertip. "I don't know I'll be able to go," she said. "After all, it didn't work last time. But I'll wait until Christmas to try."

After she'd tried and failed before, they'd spoken of how it had felt to come through the alley, how she'd but followed Honor down it the first time. Gamble didn't know if the passage opened at a certain time of day, or if there was any ritual to it. All Gamble said was that Honor had called to her, and Gamble followed. She could not recall anything of her journey through time, only that when she'd arrived in the middle of Stoll's Alley she'd been shaken, unsteady, her heart beating painfully in her chest, her skin clammy.

"I've never met anyone like you," Daniel said, and he meant it. "I shan't know what to do with myself, after you go."

"I will," Gamble said, and her smile held knowledge of his future. When it faded, her expression grew solemn, and she threaded her fingers through his hair. She took his skull firmly in hand and looked into his eyes with such intent, Daniel knew the moment would be seared into his memory until old age met him.

"You are not my man, Daniel Petigru," Gamble said. "But, oh, you are such a good man."

GAMBLE

The elderly gentleman looked from me to Tol and back again.

"May I help you?" he said.

He could've been Daniel as an octogenarian. They had the same brown eyes, the same thick, unruly hair. It seemed time had made the choice not to lay a changing hand on these things—had made some cosmic decision not to age them beyond recognition.

Beside me, Tol extended a hand. "Forgive us for coming by without calling first," he said. "I'm Tolliver Jackson, the director of the Cox Research Center over on Bull Street. This is Gamble Vance, an art conservator with the Galliard Museum. We're working on a genealogy project of sorts. We have a particular interest in this house. Do you have a few moments now for some questions, or is there a better time?"

"Young man," the gentleman said—for it was obvious, he was a gentleman. "I've got nothing but time. Come on in."

"Thank you, sir," I said, finding my voice. He shuffled back from the door and held it open for us, and we entered the place where I'd lived, and loved, two hundred years in the past.

When the man closed the door behind us, my eyes adjusting to the new light, I said, "Is there any chance you're related to the Petigrus— the family who lived here from about 1765 to the late 1800s?"

The old man turned. He'd stopped in the large cased opening between the drawing room and the wide foyer.

"As a matter of fact, I am," he said. "The artist, Daniel Petigru, was my seven times great-uncle. I'm Hamilton Dubose, by the way. It's a pleasure to meet you both."

Well, that explained the resemblance. I knew, of course, that Daniel had married after I left. That he might've had a family of his own. We knew Honor had.

All at once I felt relief, and if I was honest, a sting of regret, as if I had stepped on a tack but managed to catch my foot before it went too deep.

"It's our pleasure," Tol said, placing his hand lightly on the small of my back. The way he did when we'd go to the movies, and he'd let me pick the row, or when we'd leave a restaurant, and he'd indicate for me to go first. It made me feel steady and cared for.

"Yes," I said. "Thanks so much for being willing to talk with us."

"Do you mind if we have a seat? I've got arthritis in my knees and I get shaky if I try to stand for too long. This sounds like a conversation in need of a couch." Mr. Dubose raised one bushy gray eyebrow, a hint of humor at his mouth.

"Of course!" I said.

In the living room I tried my best not to stare. The house was thoroughly modern: a TV in the corner and a low glass coffee table, spotted by water rings and flanked by a wide mid-century leather couch and two striped, comfortably faded armchairs. I heard music coming from somewhere in the back of the house. Yep, I thought, cocking my head: it was Sam Cooke. I *liked* Hamilton Dubose.

Despite the home's obvious occupation, there was a lonely quiet to it. A slight, barely detectable sadness about Mr. Dubose. I studied the room, trying to be covert. The art was well-placed, and there was one of Daniel's and Honor's parents' pieces on the far wall: a giant armoire made of oak, with Jamaican mahogany paneling. I wondered if Mr. Dubose still had the ornate mirror.

A faded lace cloth covered the marquetry table by the front windows, lit by a dusty Tiffany lamp. This house had been touched by a woman, but I didn't think she was there now.

"Has a Petigru always owned the house?" I asked.

Mr. Dubose, who'd seated himself in one of the ancient armchairs, patted the armrests with gnarled, veined hands. "Yep. It's been in my family since the beginning. Well, there was one owner before Daniel Petigru's parents. But that's it. Otherwise, it's been us."

He smiled, and there was regret in it. "It's just me now. My wife, Anna, passed in 2002. Pancreatic cancer."

"I'm sorry," Tol said. Mr. Dubose looked up and nodded.

"Thank you," he said. He clapped his hands once over the armrests and looked back and forth between Tol and me. "So. What do y'all want to know?"

❧

Hamilton Dubose—or "Ham," as he insisted we call him—knew quite a bit about the house, and about Daniel. It was disconcerting to hear him speak of a man I'd known intimately and well, and to speak of him as an ancestor: someone long dead, seemingly unconnected to the present except for a long and age-plaited line of DNA. You might think it'd be strange and uncomfortable to hear of Daniel's history, and the house's history, with Tolliver—the man for whom I'd so recently declared my love—sitting next to me. But it wasn't.

It wasn't because I was me, and Tol was Tol. Our long friendship bound us. We knew each other down to the core. That friendship prepared us for this moment in inexplicable ways. Plus, Tol was a man unintimidated by the past. He knew it, and he knew himself.

Tol met my eyes, asking a silent question. I shook my head. I wasn't ready to talk about Daniel yet.

"Well," Tol said. "We're particularly interested in the house during the post-Revolutionary period—what most people know as the Regency period. Mainly from about 1800 to 1810, when Daniel Petigru and his sister, Honora, lived here. Petigru painted prolifically then: most of his work in the Galliard comes from this period. We believe the Petigrus may have played host to a woman in the fall of 1804, a cousin, who assisted Daniel in his studio. Were there any family stories you heard that might help us?"

"I'm afraid Anna was the family historian," Ham said. "I never took too much interest in it. As a boy I was fascinated by the Revolution, though, so I loved that the Marquis de Lafayette had visited here. Least that was the rumor."

"He did," I said, without thinking. "He sat for a portrait upstairs, by the balcony windows."

Both men stared at me, and Tol's eyes went narrow. I coughed. "At least that's what we believe, based on Daniel Petigru's account book in the Galliard and his pencil sketches of Lafayette."

"Well." Ham smiled. "Glad to know it wasn't all family legend. I always liked the general, myself. Anna thought he was dashing."

He was, I wanted to say. Instead, I grinned, and said aloud, "Me too."

Leave it to Charlestonians to talk about folks dead for centuries as if they'd seen them just yesterday in the bread aisle of the Piggly Wiggly. People who spoke of the past and of time as thinly veiled and vaguely boundaried, as I knew both to be, were my kind of people.

"The Petigrus were Quakers, weren't they?" Tol said. "Pretty unusual for Charleston."

Ham nodded. "It sure was, especially later. Y'all probably know this, being historians, but there was a small but strong contingent of Quakers in Charleston at the turn of the nineteenth century. The Quaker Meeting House was over on Archdale Square, but it got burned by firemen during the Queen Street fire in the 1830s. Daniel's parents were staunch Quakers and didn't believe in owning slaves. In fact, when I say this house has stayed in the family, I should say it also belonged to the Perrineaus—there was a brother and sister, maybe more, by that name. Free people of color. They'd been with the Petigrus since Daniel and Honora's parents were first married."

Ham rocked forward a bit, resettling. "I hate that we don't know much about them. But I do know when she was in her middle age, Honora had a writ of habitation—sort of like a deed—drawn up, which she signed over to Benjamin Perrineau. The trail vanished for Anna there." He rubbed a knobby hand over his knee. "I'm pretty sure neither Daniel nor Honora ever owned a slave or used enslaved labor in their homes, and that must've been pretty tricky for Honora considering she married into two slave-holding families."

"My guess is she was a strong-willed woman," I said, careful this time.

"Yep, well, she must've been, to have both her parents die when she was just a kid, really, and then be raised by Daniel, who was so much older and, by all told, a bit of a Bohemian artist type," Ham said. Then, after hesitating, he said, "You know, we're proud of them."

"You should be," Tol said.

Ham searched the younger man's face. His brown eyes held a heavy emotion—a history—to which I couldn't put a name. He took a breath.

"I never heard anything about a strange houseguest about that time," Ham said, "but it doesn't mean there wasn't one. The Petigrus seemed to keep to themselves, though an artist named Edward Malbone stayed with them a few times, for quite a while. Houseguests stayed months at a time back then, can you imagine it?"

"I can't," Tol said, a smile in his voice. "My foster sister lives in

Detroit, and every time she and my nephews come down they stay for two weeks. She says the sunshine's good for her soul. But I'm more of a 'fish and houseguests stink after three days' kind of guy.'"

Ham guffawed, and the two men exchanged a kindred look.

I said, "Remind me not to overstay my welcome with you two."

"I wish I could help you with this mysterious houseguest," Ham said, after a moment. "But Anna and I gave everything we had to the Galliard right before she died, including Daniel's account books. My guess is, if it was anywhere it'd be there. The man kept meticulous records. Nothing interesting, though—just who commissioned him, payments rendered, that sort of thing. Up until he married and went to Paris. But, of course, Ms. Vance, you'd know that."

Paris. When I'd been with him, Daniel said he'd never go back. But he did—and with his second wife, this much at least I knew. Why couldn't I remember why? What could've changed his mind? Was it Honor? The questions spun in my head like a pair of jeans in a dryer, the metal snap clanking against the drum every time it got tossed around. I needed to be somewhere I could focus, and slow it all down.

"Please, call me Gamble," I said, rising. "We'll let you get back to your day. Thank you so much for welcoming us into your home."

Tol looked at me sharply but followed my lead. "May we have your phone number, Ham, to call if we think of anything else?"

"Certainly." Ham rose slowly, but once up, seemed spry. He held up a finger. "I'll just pop into the kitchen for a pen and paper."

Ham left through the door flanking the fireplace and disappeared into the room behind it, which in 1804 had been Honor's bedroom. His footsteps faded and it seemed as though he'd entered another room after that. An addition, perhaps. If they'd added a kitchen onto the house at some point, it was likely to be located either upstairs on the second floor or on the first floor at the back corner of the house.

"Gamble, don't you want to look around? See if anything else sparks your memory? He's a kind man; he'd probably welcome it," Tol said. He was still seated. Maybe he hoped I wouldn't run. "Or does it hurt too much?"

Tol managed to look at ease in that thirty-year-old armchair, but his voice held a note of uncertainty. As if he treaded in unfamiliar waters and was doing his damnedest to stay calm and afloat. I wanted to ease his mind—to affirm I wasn't going anywhere. I was with him, and only him. But I also wanted to be honest, because we'd always been honest with each other.

"It does hurt, but much less than I expected," I said. "It's the same house, but it's different. I don't feel them here. I thought I would."

There was a shuffling of weathered boat shoes, and Ham reappeared in the doorway. He said, "You know, I just remembered. We did find a couple of those miniatures, only this year. My granddaughters were playing out in the garage—they found the miniatures by themselves, no frame or case of any sort with them. We'd been in the process of removing a wall to make room for an apartment to use as rental property. They were wrapped in a piece of wool. Just sitting on a beam inside the wall."

I didn't breathe. Thank goodness, I had Tol to breathe for me.

Tol said, "Is one a portrait of a blond woman?"

Ham looked startled. "Yes. Actually, they both are."

Tol and I stood, and he took my hand. "May we see them?" Tol said.

DANIEL

CHARLESTON
DECEMBER, 1804

So much went on inside a house, Daniel thought. So much to which the outside world was never privy. Passersby caught glimpses of the private lives of their neighbors, even strangers, if the curtains were drawn back and the lamps lit. At night on the peninsula, especially south of Broad Street and especially if someone was hosting a dinner party, the windows on the first floor of a house served as frames onto a scene. So, too, did glances over walls and into gardens, first-floor piazzas on full view. Servants might scurry about carrying heavily laden dinner plates. Couples might argue, never knowing their anger had been illuminated.

In his loft studio, however, Daniel felt a sense of privacy, of containment, which seemed magical and rare. Being there with Gamble at night reminded him of his attic apartments in Paris. It reminded him of being twenty years old again, with a singular focus, under the complete spell of a city and of his art, in spite of the beautiful, beckoning outside world. In Paris he'd been surrounded by other artists, part of a company of portraitists serving the Parisian upper class. It had been a like-minded community, often wild, filled with music and wine.

But when he'd return to his meager apartments, Daniel felt content. He worked until any small hour he pleased, pausing only to stretch his fingers. He took his tea at the window, watching the world below, following the green curve of the Seine until it disappeared between shops, multi-storied tenements, cathedrals.

Paris, Daniel maintained, was at its most beautiful at dusk. Charleston, his hometown, was the same. And just as in Paris, he felt no need to venture out into it, but was happy at what it illuminated. Happy to witness the dying of the day and the manifestation of the night from the comfort of his true home.

Gamble sat upon the stool nearby, an oil lamp lit at her feet. It cast a circle of old gold on the wooden planks of the floor and made her bare legs shine, as if Daniel had painted a line of gilt down her pale shinbones. She insisted on sitting for her portrait wearing one of his linen shirts. Wearing *only* one of his linen shirts.

Her hair was turbaned in a scarf he'd brought from Italy for his mother, which had, by some miracle, avoided being destroyed by moths or mice in the years it had been boxed away. It was silk, dyed in rich blues—from teal and glass green to royal sapphire, and a blue so dark it looked as black as the depths of the ocean. There were ornate patterns stitched in gold at the hems, and the coils in the design glistened whenever Gamble turned her head in the light. He'd not had the chance to give it to his mother. Mayhap he'd have Gamble take it with her; after she left, he didn't think he'd be able to look on the scarf again.

They called Effie to help wrap Gamble's hair; Effie did it with a small smile, then pulled several thick strands out to frame Gamble's face. She said not a word at Gamble's near nakedness, and left.

"If I'm going to do this, I'm not wearing a dress or stays," Gamble insisted. "If I'm going to leave a piece of me in 1804, it's going to be the real me."

"1804 is not ready for a naked you," Daniel replied, and she'd merely blinked.

"Fine. How about half-naked me. Give me one of your shirts, and I'll turban my hair," Gamble said. "You're only painting me from the waist up, right? No one will know."

"I'll know," he said. "And so will everyone else, since you refuse to wear stays."

"Daniel," she said, this time slow and sweet. "Paint me as you would remember me."

Gamble was not adept at sitting still, but for him she sat for hours, well into morning. He filled the lamps twice—he'd surrounded her with them for light—and approached just to adjust the bronze tassels of the turban, where they fell against her shoulder. Once, she asked him to scratch an unreachable spot at the center of her back.

Effie left cups of coffee and chocolate on a tray at the foot of the loft ladder, but Gamble shook her head. "Thanks for the treats," she said. "But I'm likely to spill them all over this white shirt."

Daniel did as Gamble asked. He drew her as he wanted to remember her. He drew her as if hers were a portrait he would wear in a locket, a piece meant only for him, to be held against his body. Something he could carry with him, long after she was gone.

Daniel looked up from his sketch pad. "It's as if I'm making a mourning locket for myself," he said. "You'll have to promise me a strand of hair to put inside. I'll mark the time when you go, and it will be as if you've died."

He knew he shouldn't say it—knew he was certain to ruin the moment, this gilded, suspended time in which they'd found themselves, quite possibly some of the last and loveliest he would share with her. But Daniel had discovered, in these months with Gamble, he could be nothing but honest with her. How else to contend with a woman who laid him bare with a glance?

Gamble looked over sharply. She said, "Do you think this is easy for me? It's not."

Her expression was so markedly different from what Daniel had been sketching, he put down his pencil. He wanted to throw it across the room, but he wasn't a tot in leading strings.

"I do not," he said, frustrated and sad all at once. Perhaps he was bitter, or angered. Perhaps he did think it was easy for her.

Gamble was like a creature from a storybook. She'd wandered into their lives like a lost and wild animal: one of the panthers the fur trappers from the mountains, who brought skins to trade in Charleston, told of in the taverns. They reported that the beasts could drop from a tree onto their prey without sound, kill with quiet efficiency, then disappear into the forest with a mere swish of a tail.

Certainly Gamble was both beautiful and lethal, at least to Daniel. But perhaps he was unfair.

"I do not think it easy for you," Daniel repeated. "But you're returning to someone you love. And you take my love with you."

"You'll find someone else," Gamble said, on a low note of desperation. "I'm sure you will."

Her turban had come a bit loose, and Gamble pushed at it, then yanked a few strands down in frustration. She did not have Effie's skill.

Daniel took up his pencil and began sketching with a fury he had to force himself to quell. "You've seen it, then," he said. "You know what happens to me—to Honor—after you're gone?"

"I don't," Gamble said, lifting her chin. "I should know—I spent enough time researching the two of you when I restored your miniatures. But it's like when you wake from a dream and you try to tell someone what it was about. The memory vanishes the second I try to grab it. It's like history doesn't want me to have it." She paused and took a breath. "Maybe my body knows what my brain can't understand—that it's dangerous, maybe even wrong, to divulge the future. That if I did, it could change what's meant to be."

"It's just as well," Daniel said, calming. He slowed the draw of his hand across the paper. It was not Gamble's doing she was here: she'd not asked to come. He knew he should be grateful for the time they had, for this small miracle, and not be so gluttonous as to demand more than she could rightly give. "No man should know his death date."

"No," Gamble said. "He shouldn't. I'm not trying to placate you, Daniel. It's killing me to leave. Even if I can't remember your real history, I feel in my soul you'll be happy. How could any woman not love the man you are?"

"Yes," he said bitterly. "How could she not?"

They met eyes across the expanse of the loft. The December wind gusted, flapping at the heavy drape drawn over the bay window. Gamble shivered and rubbed her hands up and down her arms. Beneath the thin linen Daniel could see her pink nipples, puckered at the cold. He drew them that way; he drew the shadows her breasts made against her belly beneath the white linen, her neck long where the shirt lay open to the skin, as a man opens it when he's alone and at his leisure. But Gamble was no man, and he'd not painted anyone as he painted her.

Paint me as you want to remember me, she'd said.

So he did.

GAMBLE

Tradd Street
December, 2004

"I left them in the garage," Ham said, as we followed him through the house and out the back of what turned out to be a small kitchen—indeed a Victorian addition, well maintained despite the linoleum floors: a bit of a miracle. I offered Ham my arm at the top of the steps, wincing at his comment. The last place those miniatures needed to be was somewhere uninsulated. I hoped they weren't damaged beyond repair.

We went down the steps together. Once in the courtyard Ham patted my wrist and let go.

Tol and I fell in behind him. As we crossed the courtyard, Tol took my hand. He laced his fingers through mine and squeezed. It was like laying hands on a life raft after hours of treading in dark water.

The garden smelled of tea trees, and I wondered if they were the descendants of the trees Cooper had tended in 1804. But the moment was fleeting, and I didn't notice the details, or whether anything had changed—as it certainly would've—in the two hundred years since. I was too concentrated on the back of Ham's white head. He was so like Daniel.

The huge new garage doors were closed. In 1804, the carriage house doors had been almost always open during the day. Ham stepped to a side door, played with the sticky glass knob for a moment, and after it opened on a scrape of wood against concrete, led us inside.

"I figured they should stay here," Ham said, picking up on his earlier train of thought. "Someone must've hidden them in the loft for a reason."

"And boarded them up so they'd not be found for a very long time," Tol murmured.

Inside, Ham stopped and turned. He nodded, brown eyes bright. "Yep. Wait'll you see the gal. She's a looker."

I swallowed. Could it truly be my portrait? After two centuries, would these men at my side—these good men—even recognize me?

More important, would I recognize myself? And if I did, what would it mean for any of us?

In the main portion of the garage the stable's first stall had been removed; it looked as if the only ones remaining were two large stalls at the back. The floors were lined with old bricks, and even after what had to have been at least two-thirds of a century without them, I caught a whiff of horses.

There was a white pickup truck which had seen much better days, and a trailer with a jon boat atop. Garden tools hung from hooks, and there were metal shelves with buckets and cleaning supplies. Several rusty bikes were propped against the far wall, but there were two banana-seated kids' bikes—bright pink and purple—parked at the front of the pack. The rainbow-colored tassels hanging from the handlebars looked dusty, and I noticed their silver bike bells.

The bikes were covered in still-bright stickers. Since Ham was in his eighties, his grandchildren were likely teenagers, and might think themselves too old now for these fabulous bikes. I felt a surge of affection for this grand old man, who so obviously loved his granddaughters.

We skirted the trailer. Tol ran a hand along the edge of the aluminum gunwale, looking inside. "Ham, do you fish?"

"Used to love to," Ham said. "My joints tend to get creaky sitting too long, and it got tough to launch the boat alone. Haven't been out in some time." He stopped at a ladder nailed into the wall, and looked up. "I'm afraid you two are going to have to do the climbing. The paintings should be in the drawer of the desk up there."

Tol stepped around us and swept a hand toward the ladder. His eyes were bright in the dim light, and I could swear he bounced on his heels. Tol held his power close, but right now energy emanated from him in waves.

What did he know that I didn't?

"After you," Tol said.

∽

The barn loft did not look as it had in 1804. I don't know what I'd expected. It certainly hadn't been used as an artist's studio, as far as I knew, for well over a hundred years. The skinny rope bed was gone, the only trace of it the presence of four shallow indentions in the wood-planked floor, where the legs had stood. I brushed a shoe over one of the small circles, pressing it with my big toe. It was like pushing down on a bruise.

My memory placed phantom items where they'd once been: the bed, the desk with its oil lamp, Daniel's artist's box and assorted paint pots atop. The place I'd sat next to the box of pumice and sharkskin, the sanding tools: I could see it all, how I'd mixed his colors, prepared the ivory. And the easel within the fall of light from the window, the stool upon which I'd posed for Daniel so long into the night.

It was impossible not to think of Daniel here. We'd spent hours in this room, many in that missing bed. What happened here had saved me, in more ways than one. After all this time, the pain and regret I'd felt over my miscarriage—how hurt I'd been over Harry's betrayals, the shame I'd felt when my short marriage had fallen apart—no longer had a stranglehold on me. It was so different than when I'd landed in 1804, hurt and confused, and had found such comfort and even safety in Daniel's arms and in his home.

I was different.

Still, I could easily make a composite of this place. Like a photograph of modern Rome or Athens, superimposed with paintings of the temples, buildings, altars, and ruins in their entirety—the way these cities once had been. All you had to do was scan your eyes across the picture to take in the before and after: to witness what once had existed, what had been lost, and what—if anything—remained.

You may wonder how it was I didn't feel awkward, especially with Tol. How I could stand in a room where I'd loved, and made love with, another man. Or you may wonder if I felt guilt, or remorse, or even shame. My answer to each of these questions: no.

Why? Well, because I am a complicated, smart, grown-ass woman. I have had a *life*.

I looked at Tol. He stood apart but not far away, hands tucked loosely in his pockets. He watched me with that ever-present focus—offering an accord, something like a promise from the depths of those penetrating eyes of his. He took up all the space in the room—he always had—but I'd never seen him push or lord either his superior intellect or his physical size over anyone. By simply being there, without a word, he made me feel both held and free.

He'd always made me feel that way.

At my look, he smiled, slow and sweet so his dimples popped. I smiled back, but resisted going to him. That sweetness in him, in the two of us together, gave me the courage to take a deep breath, to consider my past in this place without fear.

There was an incredible amount of light up here now, thanks to the old hay door having been converted to a large, multi-paned window. There was a desk, but it was not Daniel's. His, I knew, was in gallery 5 of the Galliard Museum. While Daniel's desk had been small, the one here now was bulky and wide—a businessman's desk, I guessed, perhaps late 1940s, a piece crafted before the sharp-cornered and futuristic mid-century style took hold. At some point this desk had been sanded and repainted a matte black, the wide top a thin piece of plywood stained a deep walnut.

I reached out and fingered one of the beveled brass knobs at the small main drawer. There was a dent in the rim of the knob, at the top of the circle and at the bottom...almost as if someone had used pliers or another tool to pull it open. I supposed the drawer could've swelled shut from humidity—it was Charleston, after all. There'd be no reason to break in.

I blew air out through my mouth and snorted. Who was I kidding? There were all kinds of reasons.

Behind me, the floorboards creaked, and I felt Tol. "You going to open it?" he said, the consonants expanding in the high-ceilinged room.

Suddenly I felt the urge to laugh: an uncontrollable case of the giggles, the kind you get in church at the worst possible moment. Like when you're nine years old and expected to pass the offering plate, and the old man beside you smells of menthol, and the scary minister is looking right at you.

This was downright crazy. Insane. Nuts. I slapped a hand over my mouth to keep from laughing. I looked from Tol to the drawer, my hand on the knob.

"I could be naked in there," I said through my fingers.

"Y'all take your time," Ham called from below. "I'm headed back to the house. Come on in when you're done." Moments later, the side door to the garage groaned and scraped as it opened and closed again.

Done with what? Done making sense of the space-time continuum? Done getting a load of a tiny painting of me made two hundred years ago? Done trying to figure out who and what these people were to either of us? What any of it meant to the here and now?

Tol looked heavenward and sighed. "Do it," he said.

I opened the drawer. Inside, folded in a faded piece of gray wool, were two miniature portraits. I spread the wool on the desk and set the tiny ovals atop, careful not to touch the ivory. They were no larger than an egg sliced lengthwise and a fourth as thin.

"I should really use gloves," I murmured.

Tol moved close as I leaned over the miniature portraits. Unable to help myself, I smelled them.

There was a whiff of turpentine. The chalky aroma of ground pigment and the gum arabic Daniel used to bind his pigments. A hint of Ed Malbone's cinnamon and orange cologne.

God. Could it be coffee? And poured chocolate?

Images whipped by like train cars, and me stuck behind the crossing arm: Carriage wheels on cobblestones. Honor's arm through mine. Effie's hand, once, on my shoulder. Daniel's small smile bouncing before me as we danced a cotillion in the Draytons' ballroom. The shock, and regret, in Cooper's deep brown eyes when I'd touched him. Lafayette's courtly bow, his lips on the back of my hand. The call of the lamplighter. The unblemished blue sky above St. Michael's Church.

My gift to you, Daniel whispered in my ear, as I stared down at myself. *You as you are.*

"Well," Tol said, a catch in his voice. "The man certainly loved you."

I steeled myself against a wave of emotion, and I reached out to touch the filigreed edge of the portrait I recognized. It had been painted my last night in the loft—the twenty-third of December, 1804—the night before I walked down Stoll's Alley and returned to 2004.

"We should step back," I said, with a staying hand on his arm. "We shouldn't talk over them." Tol arched an eyebrow. "The moisture in our breath could damage the ivory."

We stepped back, just far enough. I wiped my hand on my thigh. I was nervous.

"They're stunning, Gamble," Tol said.

I nodded, for a moment unable to respond.

Then I managed it. "It was incredibly scandalous for the time, painting a woman like this," I said. "At least in the United States. Some women of the Charleston upper class who sat for miniature portraits would use exotic accoutrements—like an African turban, or an animal stole—to make themselves seem original or unique. But they were rarely painted so intimately."

"You're beautiful," Tol said. When I shook my head, he reached out, ran his warm fingers down my cheek to cup my jaw. I wanted to sink closer, purr like a cat, but resisted. "Gamble," he said. "You are. Look at your eyes. It's obvious you loved him too."

I looked. There I was, painted from mid-thigh to turbaned head. I wore a white linen shirt—Daniel's shirt—undone to my breastbone. The subtle touches of shadow and color gave my body a sensuousness I'd not seen in another portrait from the post-Revolutionary period. My lips were full, open just enough to show a slight glimmer of teeth, as if I were just about to speak. My eyes were luminous and knowing, a hint of a laugh at the corners. He'd even painted my wrinkles: faint smile lines which made the viewer want to smile with me.

My hair hung in loose yellow ropes from the bright blue turban. I looked mysterious and more than a bit wild. Not of this world, yet authentic and fully realized.

There was no adequate way to explain to Tol that my love for Daniel made my love for him no less. Still, I had to try.

"Tolliver," I said, low. "I loved how I felt when I was with him. Daniel was a safe place during a time when I felt like I'd lost my grip on the world. The things I'd thought were solid had become flimsy. I'd been grieving the miscarriage—really, the unraveling of my marriage—more than I realized. I felt untethered. And then I walked down the alley and found this unusual man who gave me a soft place to fall, just for a little while."

Tol watched me, waiting. We did not touch.

"Gamble," Tol said. "You don't owe me an explanation, and you certainly don't need to prove you love me more than you loved Daniel." Here he stood straighter, tucked his hands into the pockets of his jeans and drew a long breath in through his nose. He rolled his shoulders as if he'd been holding tight to something of which he'd been waiting a long time to let go. A muscle flickered at his jaw.

"You're complicated, because life is complicated," Tol said. "There's mystery in you. A hundred stories. I don't begrudge you the experiences, or the relationships you had along the way—just as I know you don't begrudge mine. They don't make us—our story—any less compelling, or any less true."

I smiled. "Get to the point, professor," I said.

Tol bent, encircling me with his body like a bird folding its wings around something it wanted to protect. He curled a warm hand around my neck. I went still, and he pressed his face into my hair, his lips moving against me when he said, "The point is, you're mine. And I'm yours. This is it, for me."

"For me too," I said, rubbing my cheek against his hand. I sure as hell meant it.

We stayed this way for a while, Tol's face in my hair, my eyes closed against the touch. Our bodies a safe half-moon: a place into which we did not have to welcome anyone else—a spot I was loath to abandon.

Outside, a car drove by on Tradd Street, dry leaves at the edges of sidewalks rustling in its wake. The neighbor's dogs barked. I reminded myself it was December on a Sunday afternoon, and history waited for us to fill in the blanks.

"When was the second one painted?" Tol asked, breaking the silence.

I sighed, more at having to move from his embrace than anything else, and studied the other portrait.

"I don't know," I said, picking it up, careful to keep the wool between it and my skin. I held it to the light. Then I set it down again and stepped back. "I don't recognize the dress."

Still, it was unmistakably me. In this one, I'd been painted from the waist up, and wore a more traditional Regency-style gown: high-waisted, short-sleeved, white, with a filmy overlay—a dress more suited to spring. I looked as if I'd stepped from the set of a film based on a Jane Austen novel. As if one of those wonderful British actresses—Kate Winslet, Emma Thompson, or Keira Knightley—might be waiting, costumed, stage right and out of sight.

My hair was pinned in a loose mass atop my head. My cheeks were bright, almost flushed. My eyes seemed knowing and sad, and there were the faintest of shadows beneath them.

"What's that at your waist?" Tol said. I set the miniature portrait down, and we leaned over it at the same time. "Is it a piece of jewelry?"

"It's a miniature inside a miniature—a brooch," I murmured. I really could've used my head loop right then, or even Miss Saralee's eyeglass. "I think there's a face painted on it."

Two hundred years inside an uninsulated wall had done some damage to the second miniature. The lower half of the piece was clouded, likely a result of mold, and that portion of my dress and the outlines of the face in the painted brooch were blurry. I couldn't make out the race or gender of the person inside the miniature Daniel had pinned at my waist. But I knew he would've painted whoever it was as precisely as he'd painted me.

"We need magnification," I said. "I'll have to separate the portrait from the frame and remove the convex glass to get to that mold. I wonder if Ham would let me take this to the lab at the Galliard? I could work on it this week."

Tol straightened. "Let's ask him."

I re-wrapped the miniatures in the wool. But when Tol climbed over the edge of the loft and stood poised at the top of the ladder, I couldn't move my feet.

"Tol," I said. "I didn't sit for the second portrait. I would've remembered it."

Tol met my eyes, wry acceptance in his own. "Yet," he said. "You haven't sat for it *yet*."

GAMBLE

GALLIARD MUSEUM
DECEMBER, 2004

Myron eyed Tolliver and me over his shoulder before swiping his key card at the Galliard's basement door. "It's Sunday. Don't y'all have anything better to do? Christmas shopping or whatnot?"

I crossed my arms against the wind whipping down the alley behind the museum, one hand tight on the box Ham had given us to hold the miniatures. Behind us in the garden, the flower beds between the hedges and English-style urns were covered with sheets; there must've been a chance of frost the night before. I sighed, resisting a petulant groan. As a senior conservator, I'd quite a bit of access to the lab, but before and after hours on weekends remained solidly under Myron's security purview—especially when it came to bringing along a guest.

"I told you," I said, with little-sister-like annoyance. "It's a work emergency."

"And you need *him*," Myron said, doubt apparent.

"Why do you always have to give me a hard time?" Tol said, with a half-laugh. "How long have you known me?"

Myron and Tol had a grudging friendship; I'd introduced them years ago, they played basketball together in a local men's league, and I knew Tol had helped coach Myron's sons. Still, they liked to talk trash.

Tol reached out and wrapped his big hands around my upper arms; he gave them an up-and-down rub for warmth. I grinned up at him—he just couldn't resist his inner white knight.

Myron took definite note: his eyes went straight to Tol's hands on me, then back to our faces.

"Apparently, not long enough," he said, pushing open the heavy door and gesturing us through. "Don't forget to set the alarm when you're done, and don't have too much fun."

Tol and I turned at the same time to retort, but the heavy security door slammed shut and the outside light went with it. Tol felt for the light switches. When fluorescence filled the empty hall, I blinked.

"Ready?" I said, holding up the box. I couldn't wait to get to the miniatures inside.

"Lead on," he said.

In the lab, I gave Tol the largest white coat I could find. It stretched ominously at his shoulders and refused to button across his chest, but would have to do.

I studied the newer miniature under the microscope. I fiddled with the dial, hoping deep magnification would reveal the identity of the person in the brooch I wore in the portrait: the miniature inside a miniature.

"There's just too much mold," I said. "It's clouding the view."

"From being stored outside?" Tol said.

He stood at a respectful distance, curiosity softening the hard lines of his cheekbones and jaw. Even in repose, Tol managed to look as if some ancient Greek sculptor had taken a chisel to his face. Until he smiled, that is. I don't think I'd ever seen a statue with dimples. He clasped his hands behind his back, and despite the ill-fitting coat, at the classic stance was once again a scholar.

"Yep," I said. "Ivory is hygroscopic—its dimensions can alter with moisture—so it needs to be protected from changes in humidity. Especially abrupt changes, like those we get with Charleston's weather. I understand Ham's inclination to keep the pieces where he'd found them, but it would've been better if they'd been stored inside the house."

"Looked like the carriage house had been insulated," Tol said. "But that may have been only recently. I suppose they'd been exposed all those years before the renovation."

"At least a century," I agreed. "But there doesn't seem to be splitting or cockling—any distortion—of the ivory, so that's great." I adjusted the dial one more time. "There's definitely damage, but I think I can handle it. Here, take a look."

Tol leaned over and put his eye to the microscope. He'd been in the Galliard before, had even stopped by the lab, but we'd never examined art together on this level. It felt intimate, and fun. I tried to keep nerdy conservator excitement out of my voice, and failed.

"Notice the thread-like hyphae of the mold," I said. "Right now it's obscuring the face in the brooch. I'm hoping it hasn't disrupted the paint layer too much; if it has, there'll be fading, and the face may be lost."

Tol shifted his feet, but kept his eye to the microscope. "What are those clouds around your body?"

He was such a good student. "Whatever substance was used to bleach the ivory crystallized into those fluffy white areas, which look like mold, but aren't. In this case, I'm thinking it could've been vinegar—that's what Daniel was using in 1804. It's hard to know for sure, since this portrait was painted later than the other one."

"How much later?" he asked.

I shrugged. "Hard to tell. We may never know. But it's not so long that Daniel's technique changed significantly, so my guess is a few years at most."

Tol stood, his expression turning serious. "It has to have been when you went—go—back," he said. "You won't know how much time has passed, there at least, until you arrive."

I didn't want to think about it, leaving him. Walking once again into the unknown. Even if it was for Honor. Not yet.

I cleared my throat. "It's going to take a while," I said. "I can take photomicrographs now, but I'll need to wait until Monday to begin removing the mold."

Tol was quiet, those light-colored eyes of his seeming to hold resignation, or even sadness—some mix of emotions I couldn't make out. Before I could say another word, he stepped close, blocking out the overhead lights. In the dark cocoon of our bodies he pressed his warm lips against the skin at the side of my neck.

"I'll wait," he whispered.

As soon as Tol and I pulled into the drive, Catherine released Kipling out the back door of the main house.

"Find anything in Aiken?" she called, as Kipling bounded down the steps, across the gray bricks of the courtyard, and bum-rushed my knees. I dropped my duffel and wrapped my arms around my dog's neck. God, it's a gift to hug a dog.

"We did!" I said. "Thanks so much for your help."

Catherine waved a hand. "You know we love having her."

"You spoil her rotten, is what you do," I said, smiling. Having Catherine Memminger as a dog sitter was a dream.

"Hi, Tolliver," Catherine said, when he rounded the back of car with my laptop bag and his own leather duffel, each over a shoulder.

"How's it going, Mrs. Memminger?" Tol said.

"Just fine," she said. "Y'all will have to tell me all about your trip later. Oh, Gamble, I've got guests coming in at 353B tomorrow. They say they plan to walk everywhere, but you never know. May want to park on the street this week so they don't block you in."

Catherine used the second kitchen house across the courtyard from mine as a Vrbo. Thankfully, it was rented sparingly, mostly by retirees of means looking for an authentic South of Broad experience.

"I'll keep an eye out," I said. "Thanks again!"

The storm door slammed behind Catherine and I shivered; it was downright cold. It would be hard to wait until Monday, when I could use the details revealed by the photomicrographs to try to identify who-ever it was in the brooch Daniel had painted at my 1800s waist. Still, Tol and I had barely spoken since that brief examination in the lab—since seeing my own eyes there, staring back at me from two hundred years before. I, for one, looked forward to a warm house and a fire.

I shifted the bag on my shoulder and dug in my jacket pocket for the keys. Tol set the other bags at his feet. He waited patiently.

I looked pointedly at his bag. Why had he not left it in the car?

"Going somewhere?" I asked, dry.

"Nope," Tol said. "Staying."

The ancient key slid home and I straightened. "Really?" I said.

I didn't know what else to say. I felt a frisson of anticipation start at my belly, shoot straight up to my shoulders and down into my arms. My fingers tingled, and for just a second I wondered if the ground had dropped. Tol held the storm door as I muscled open the big one. Kipling slipped past us into the house.

There was an icebox feel to the place, the age holding in the cold. I'd turned the heat down to fifty before we left for Aiken, thinking the tem-perature wouldn't drop that far. Though the air had been warm when we left the horse town, the weather had shifted on the drive home, and Charleston felt suddenly like winter.

Charleston at Christmas was my favorite time of the year. Most people visited Charleston in summer and thought of it as a subtropical sort of place. Granted, it was almost always hot here.

Which is why December held a special place in my heart: a lovely, brief window of time, in winter, when the cold swept everything clean. Wind raced down streets and through houses built and arranged specially for this purpose—to catch and funnel it—and the chill often caught folks unaware. What most winter visitors never considered was that the wind blew off a harbor which sat at about 60 degrees in the months of December, January, and February. That wind picked up cold from the Atlantic on the move, then delivered it to a shivering city.

I couldn't wait to get my Christmas decorations out of storage. I had four giant plastic bins of decorations collected over the years—far too many for a woman without children—which I kept upstairs, under the guest bed. Most had been gifted to me by others, or were hand-me-downs from my mom. Some I'd collected on travels, some by browsing through shops on the peninsula.

Tol had given me one, I remembered. A gold-plated ornament from the gift shop at Drayton Hall, made to look like the ceiling medallion in the Great Hall. As graduate students we'd worked together at the house on an excavation project, in the first year of our friendship.

It occurred to me then that there were many gifts in my possession from Tol—things I loved to hold and look at, but which I took for granted. The iron trivet in the kitchen, shaped like a fleur-de-lis, which he'd brought back from France. The mug from Louisa May Alcott's Orchard House, a place we'd explored together when he was on sabbatical in Boston a few years back. Several of the books on my shelves—one of them a signed, first-edition copy of Pat Conroy's *The Prince of Tides*.

Multiple bottles of wine in my armoire came from Tol; there was the Montblanc pen in my desk drawer at work—someone had given it to him, and he'd claimed he didn't want it. There was a grapevine and cotton wreath I'd lusted over on a random walk through the market— one I put on my door every Christmas—which Tol bought for me when I refused to buy it for myself. A fat candle on the ceramic lip of my bathtub, every bit of it—the beveled glass container and soy wax inside—made by a local artisan. I lit it each time I took a bath.

For the past several years, even before Harry and I divorced, Tol went with me to buy my Christmas tree. After hours of walking up and down the rows at several lots, we'd load a tree onto the back of the truck he'd borrow from Kendrick, his closest grad school friend (after me, of course). I never once asked what Tol had had to give Ken in exchange. At my house, Tol would curse and grumble while he manhandled the tree into the stand, because it was inevitable that I'd picked one too tall for the old house and its low ceilings.

But then, when he was done, I'd have a real, live Christmas tree. A Fraser Fir. The glorious smell would spread through the entire house. And I'd feel just that much closer to my childhood home in the North Carolina mountains, a place I missed with an aching desperation during the holidays.

I walked to the far wall and pushed the button on the thermostat until the heat kicked on. While Tol took the bags upstairs, I went to the kitchen and poured us each a glass of water, listening to the creak of his footsteps overhead.

Kipling rubbed her body between my legs and the doors of the bottom shelves in the narrow galley kitchen. I crouched low and hugged her tight. When Tol's heavy footsteps started back down the stairs, her entire head came up, her glossy black ears pricked up. She stared at the kitchen doorway, wagging her tail. It whacked the linoleum floor: *Thump, thump, thump.*

"He's always been the one, hasn't he?" I said.

Tol's footsteps stopped when he reached the bottom floor. "Gamble?" he called.

"Kitchen," I called back.

Then he was there, taking up all the space in the doorway. He wore a suede sport coat in a mushroom color, a pale gray crewneck sweater beneath. The collar of a charcoal dress shirt peeked out from the top. It made me chuckle. We were so different: though I appreciated fashion, and the occasional chance to dress up, it exhausted me even to think about making myself stylish on a daily basis. Style came easily to Tol.

Kipling wound herself through Tol's legs and he bent to rub her ears.

"Hi, handsome," I said. "Thanks for getting the bags." Then I walked right over and wrapped myself around him, burying my face in his jacket. I squeezed as I pressed closer to his big, warm, muscular body, awash in conflicting waves of hope and terror and safety.

"Gamble?" he said, softly. His arms came around me and I felt him kiss the top of my head. "What's going on?"

"It's you," I said into his sweater. "It's been you all along. Since that stupid game of beer pong." I raised my head and swallowed. I felt an inexplicable urge to cry. "Why didn't you say something? We've wasted so much time."

Tol brushed my hair behind my ear and cupped my cheek. "I was scared," he said, in that toe-curling voice of his. He said it without pretense, with complete and utter honesty. Lord, how I loved this man.

"Well, me too," I said, and sniffed. "We could've at least been scared together."

"It doesn't work like that, baby," he said. "You were caught up in Harry. You couldn't see me. But, hey, it's all right, because now you do."

I leaned back from the circle of his arms. "You called me 'baby,'" I said. No more sniffing. My smile was so wide, I felt my cheeks stretch.

"Yeah?" Tol said, drawing it out. His brows went up.

"I *like* it," I said.

"You do?" he said. He walked me backward until we were at the kitchen counter. With an ease that made my girlish heart go all aflutter, he lifted me onto the countertop. I hooked my ankles around his thighs.

"Oh yeah," I said, and licked my lips.

It was the last thing either of us said for a very long time. We kissed in my kitchen like two people who did not care about anything or anyone else in the whole world. We shared the same breath, sank deep into each other, held each other so close you couldn't fit a sheet of paper between us.

"Tol," I said finally, feeling as if I were underwater. "Let's go upstairs."

I kissed a pattern down his neck, peeled back his shirt and ran my fingers along the long line of his collarbone.

"Woman," he groaned. "Do not tempt me."

"I want you," I said. And I meant it. "I don't want to wait."

Then we were kissing again. He was sliding his hands inside my shirt when the ancient front door let out a loud creak. Kip barked and took off from the kitchen, and Tol straightened and turned in a flash, shielding me with his body from whoever or whatever it was.

"Well," said my ex-husband, in his old Charleston drawl. "It was only a matter of time."

"Damn it, Harry," I yelled. "How many times have I told you to knock?"

Tol met my eyes while he adjusted his pants. "It's time to hide that fucking key somewhere else," he said, low and dangerous.

"For fucking real," I said. I adjusted my shirt, wiped my mouth with the back of my hand, and hopped off the counter. This wasn't even awkward. It was flat-out annoying.

I stalked through the living room, planning to spin Harry around and send him straight out the door. But when Harry stood from petting Kip—who writhed in traitorous pleasure around my ex-husband's knees—the look in Harry's eyes gave me pause. He was angry. Dapper, in his corduroy trousers and wool peacoat, but angry.

"What do you want?" I said.

Tol walked in from the kitchen and stood behind me, still as a mountain. "Harry," he said.

"Tolliver," Harry said, giving a curt nod—that thing men do when they're trying to be big and bad. I made a valiant effort not to roll my eyes.

"There is way too much testosterone in this room," I said. I swung around to the armoire, then pulled out three glasses and a bottle of malbec. "Who wants wine?"

This made Harry laugh. I could always make Harry laugh. "It's two o'clock in the afternoon, Gamble," he said.

"When have you ever cared about that?" I said. I didn't wait for an answer. I muscled with the corkscrew until Tol turned and gently took it out of my hands. He unstoppered the bottle and poured the wine without a word.

Harry cleared his throat. "Sorry to barge in on y'all. I'll have to be more discreet from now on." He took the glass when Tol offered. "So. How long have y'all been together?"

"That's none of your—" I started, pissed.

"Since yesterday," Tol said.

Tol took a sip of wine. He did not reach for me, nor try to move closer or to mark me in some unsubtle way as his own, as it's certain Harry would have done if the situation had been reversed. Instead, Tol stood at my shoulder, giving me space. Comfortable with my lead.

Harry sipped his wine, studying us over the rim. He'd had a haircut, I noticed, the sides shaved and the hair at his crown styled up and off his forehead like a hipster model in a J. Crew ad. It made him look younger. Almost uncertain.

But Harry was still mad. (I'd been married to the man, so I could tell). When he shook his head, the movement small and tight, I thought, yep. Confirmation.

"No," Harry said. "It's been a lot longer than that. Tolliver here's been waiting on the sidelines for years. Long before you ever signed our divorce papers. I always wondered when you'd see it."

Tol set his glass on the coffee table. "You know, Sims, I never spent much time on the sidelines."

I watched in fascination as a pulse beat at Harry's temple. But he was in my house, Tol was a lot larger than he was, and, let's face it, Harry had not been the most reliable of husbands. I wondered what he would say next.

Harry set his glass down and rubbed his chin. He said to me, "I always wondered if you'd cheated."

What? Me, cheat? And this from a man who'd come to our home from work functions more than once with the proverbial lipstick on his collar; this, from the man who'd admitted to sleeping with other women within days of my miscarriage. I felt like I'd been sucker-punched.

"You have some kind of gall, Harry," I said, my face blazing.

Harry mussed his hipster hair in frustration. He walked to the fire, likely to cover his reaction, and propped a hand on the mantel. He fiddled absently with the leather strap of the musket. "Yes, well, I suppose I do," he said.

After a moment, Harry turned. He said simply, "Hell, I know you didn't cheat on me, Gamble. You're not built for it. But y'all were together all the time. A blind man could see it. I may be many things, but blind isn't one of them."

"That's why you asked her to marry you so soon, isn't it?" Tol said. He took a seat at the sofa, and when Kipling came and sat beside him, her body pressed against his knee, Tol rubbed the silky sweet spot between her ears.

"I asked Gamble to marry me because I loved her," Harry said.

Fury and confusion roiled in my gut, and I pressed a hand to my stomach. I'd worked hard, in and out of therapy, to recover from that time in my life—from losing a baby I hadn't known I'd wanted, from the scarring and sudden loss of trust in the man I'd chosen, from the resulting dissolution of my marriage. The destruction, and then deconstruction, of the life I'd expected I'd be living, and my own shame over not being able to hold it all together, had taken everything I had in me—and here I was, finally on solid ground. How dare Harry bring this up again. It was like the unearthing of a failed time capsule, one filled with aging, rotting things it turned out no one really wanted to remember.

Most of all, it really pissed me off when people talked about me as if I weren't there—especially when those people were men.

"What do you mean?" I said to Tol. But Tol wouldn't look at me: He watched Harry, waiting.

"Hell," Harry murmured, then slid into one of the leather wingback chairs by the fire and put his head in his hands. He rubbed his face, hard, then looked at Tol. "Yes, I suppose it was. Can you blame me?"

Tol took a sip of his wine and shook his head. If Tolliver was anything, he was honest.

"No," he said. "I might've done the same in your shoes."

I vibrated with anger, arms crossed and hands gripping my elbows, trying to hold myself together. Tol's eyes held love and sympathy when he said, "I always wondered if Harry proposed so quickly because he saw how close we'd become. He thought he was losing you to me."

Everything was clear, and it all hurt. When I'd arrived in Charleston, Harry swept me off my feet. I'd never met anyone like him; I was drawn in by his charm and good looks, his ease with his place in the world, his long family history in Charleston—a lineage that, as a historian, I'd envied. I hated to admit it—hated to see my own shortcomings, my own shallowness—but it'd been exciting to be pursued by a man who could've had his pick of the most beautiful women in the city. Anyone he wanted, really. When Harry picked me, I was stunned. And, I had to admit, looking back at the young woman I'd been, ripe for it.

I took my wine glass from the table and sucked it dry. Then I used it to point at Harry.

"I said yes," I said. If Harry could be honest, I could too. "I didn't have to."

"I know I don't deserve an answer," Harry said. "But there's something I have to know."

I looked at Tol, who lifted his shoulders and whose look silently said, *I have no idea what he's talking about.*

"Okay," I said.

Harry rubbed his knees. "After the miscarriage," he started, then looked at Tol. "I'm sure you know about that?" Tol nodded. Harry continued. "After that, and we had that fight, Gamble, and you left, where did you go? You were gone all weekend, and I just assumed you'd been with Tolliver. When you came back, you told me you wanted a divorce. And I tried—" Here Harry looked at me with a plea in his blue eyes, a sincerity that kept him from being an all-out ass: a quality that would keep him in women for years to come, much longer than he deserved. "Damn, Gamble, you know I tried to convince you to stay. But you were done. Something had shifted."

I sat down, hard, in the chair matching Harry's. At my movement, Kipling abandoned Tol and set her heavy head on my thigh. I knew which fight he meant: more than the infidelities, I'd been devastated by his unfeeling and callous reaction to the miscarriage—it had been the mortal wound in our marriage.

Harry and I had hashed this out long ago. I could not, however, remember what happened after the fight. It eluded me, a literal cloud over my memory.

Where *had* I gone after? I said, with complete sincerity, "Harry, I have no idea."

"I do," Tol said. Harry and I looked at him, startled. "That's when you walked down Stoll's Alley. That's when you went to Daniel."

DANIEL

CHARLESTON
CHRISTMAS EVE, 1804

It was but a few blocks to St. Michael's Church, and despite the cold they all wanted the brace of fresh air. Gamble and Honor walked with elbows linked, the capes of their wool cloaks flapping in the slight wind, Daniel a few steps behind. As they made their way down Tradd Street, Daniel found himself admiring the two women he loved best in the world.

Honor was taller than Gamble, and the hem of her dress kicked up each time she took a step, revealed her thin ankles and the pale blue slippers and silk stockings she wore beneath. It was past time for new frocks. God's teeth, he missed his mother. He was not good at the simple necessities of acting as Honor's guardian. Despite her age, and despite how full-grown she claimed herself to be, Honor was his responsibility.

Gamble's goldenrod flounced hem, on the other hand, dragged through the dry leaves. There was not to be a glimpse of her comely ankles; she was even shorter than his mother had been, and there'd been no time for Effie to take up the skirt. With their hoods up he couldn't see the women's faces. In the dusk light their cold breath floated back to him like smoke.

Carriages bumped by on the street, curtains drawn against the cold so the people inside were hidden. Bells jingled from the harness of a pair of bays attached to a four-in-hand. At the corner of Tradd and King Streets, the lamplighter closed the glass door of the large iron lamp there, his wick still lit. He stepped down from his ladder and lifted the light to snuff it.

"Six of the clock, and all's well!" the lamplighter called, tipping his hat to Honor and Gamble when he saw them. "Evening, sir," he said to Daniel.

"Good evening," Daniel said, stepping up to part the ladies. He took an elbow of each as they crossed over King. "Watch the water," he told them.

Puddles had formed along the edge of the road. It had rained the night before; he'd heard the plunk on the roof of the barn, Gamble asleep at his side. For hours he'd stared up into the dark rafters, wondering, as he found himself doing so often of late, what his nights would become when she left.

At some moment in the deep of night, near morning, an inexplicable calm had come over him. It quelled his anxious thoughts, as if someone had laid a blanket of goose down over his body, and he warmed. Daniel felt—yes, he really had felt it, dream or no—someone lay a gentle hand on the crown of his head and whisper, "All will be well." He wondered, upon waking, if the voice had been his father's.

With her arm still hooked through his, Gamble hopped over a puddle with a laugh. They passed George Laurens's house as they rounded the corner of Tradd and Meeting. Laurens, his wife, and their two younger daughters were emerging onto the street, rubbing gloved hands together and exclaiming against the cold.

"A happy Christmas Eve to you all," Honor called out.

"And to you," one of the daughters, Eleanor, returned. The Laurens ladies were clad each in a fashionable pelisse, swansdown lining the hoods. The mother, Susan, held a white fur muff. Laurens's cotton must have come in well that year.

The enslaved butler who held their door waited until all were out, then closed it behind them, silent and unobtrusive as a shadow.

"Headed to service at St. Michael's, Petigru?" Laurens asked Daniel. The family fell in behind, Laurens's daughters catching up on Honor's side, already in conversation. Gamble dropped back and took Daniel's arm again.

A big man running to fat, Laurens wore his hair in giant lamb chops which curled to meet the corners of his mouth. Daniel tore his gaze from them.

"We are," Daniel said. "Have you had the pleasure of meeting my cousin, Madam Vance of Virginia?"

Gamble smiled prettily, her straight white teeth gleaming in the dark, and Daniel stifled a laugh. "Hello, Mr. Laurens, and Madam Laurens," she said, with genuine happiness. "What a pleasure it is to see you again."

"Yes," said Madam Laurens. "We were seated together at the Bachelor's Ball."

"A lovely conversationalist, your cousin," Laurens said to Daniel, in a hearty aside the entire group could not help but overhear.

"Yes," Daniel said, trying but failing to keep the smile from his voice. "She is that."

"What a shame you'll be leaving us so soon," said the younger of the Laurens daughters, Anne. She said it over her shoulder, with a toss of her ruffed hood. "You'll miss Race Week. It's always the most thrilling society of the year."

Gamble squeezed Daniel's forearm, her grasp warm with meaning. "It is a shame," she said. "I've come to love Charleston. And you've all extended me such a kind welcome. You'll have to promise to force Mr. Petigru into society after I'm gone. I'm afraid he'd stay all day at his easel if allowed."

The girls tittered, and Honor snuck a questioning look over her shoulder, her arms ensconced with the Laurens girls. Gamble winked at her, and Honor made a small smile of relief, her face clearing before turning back.

It was jealousy that made Anne Laurens throw daggers at Gamble, Daniel knew. Which should have been absurd—Gamble was a widow, near to twice the age of the younger woman, without a penny to her name. Yet at each event they'd attended in her time there, Gamble seemed to charm most everyone she met. It didn't matter if they were elderly matrons or young men-about-town in buckskin breeches and snow-white cravats. Daniel observed these exchanges from across parlors and ballrooms, even standing beside Gamble in the park. He felt for these people nothing but empathy.

She was simply…different. There was no artifice, no pretense to Gamble. She spoke, acted, danced—even rode horses—without fear. Her intelligence was not glossed with practiced charm; yet within minutes of conversation it was apparent that she was better-read than most in the room. If she were unattractive, Daniel knew, they'd have dubbed her a bluestocking. They'd have laughed at her.

If seventeen-year-old girls were resorting to cutting Gamble in the street, Daniel mused, perhaps it truly was time for her to go. She was dangerous here, in more ways than one.

Later, when he spoke of this to Gamble in the privacy of the loft, she shook her head in disagreement.

"No," Gamble said. "It's not their fault. The women you know are capable of much more than existing only as ornaments. Plus, people react strongly when faced with someone different—when they feel threatened by that difference.

"These Charleston women," she said, leaning forward in earnest from her seat at his desk, "must endure things I've never had to. Their natural personalities, their dreams, are stifled in ways I've never known. Their lives are small, and whether they're satisfied or not, they don't have a choice. I don't blame them a bit for not liking me."

"Well," said Daniel, "I do. Mary Smythe as much as insinuated we were living in sin, last week at the Charleston Museum. I thought Honor would scratch her eyes out."

"Mary Smythe," Gamble said, "has been forcibly engaged to a man not of her choosing—a man more than twice her age. She is twenty-two years old, has never been given leave to pursue any sort of learning or passion of her own, and has never been out of her mother's sight. I have plenty of sympathy stored up for young women like Mary. She can say anything about me she likes. Besides," Gamble added. "Mary's time will come."

"The Lord help us all," he intoned, making her smile.

"The Lord help men everywhere," Gamble said.

At St. Michael's, the giant brass lamps hissed and sputtered beneath the grand two-story portico, casting light upon ushers who handed out the night's program. People milled about the enormous Tuscan columns, dressed in their holiday finest: beaver hats of every style, English wool and velvet tailcoats, pointed pumps, fine tall boots and spats, and wildly full cravats, even at the necks of the most aged among them. Women flipped back hoods of elaborately stitched and fur-lined cloaks to reveal jeweled diadems which sparked under the lamps. They wore silk dresses and fine, quilted spencer jackets, gowns of rich browns and reds and golds. Along both sides of Meeting Street, horses and carriages sat parked, reins held in the care of liveried drivers. Waiting, of course, to take the people inside to Christmas parties and dinners after the service ended.

"Hi, Cooper," Gamble said, unrestrained affection in her voice.

Cooper stood nearby at the Sims family's carriage. He looked up from making a study of one of the horse's hooves, and his eyes went wide, the whites gleaming like small moons in the dark of the hovering oaks. He wiped the iron pick in his hand against a cloth, and said, so low as to be near a whisper, "Evening, Miss Gamble. Mr. Daniel, Miss Honor."

Gamble slipped from Daniel's arm and went to the young man. "Did Effie give you that book I mentioned? Thomas Paine's *The Age of Reason*? You're going to have to let me know what you think of it." She reached out, and—as if Cooper were a white man, and an intimate—put a gloved hand on his arm. "You'd better do it quick, though, because I'll be leaving soon. For Virginia."

Cooper took a sharp step back so Gamble's arm fell away. Daniel felt a change in the air around them, and several things happened at once. Eleanor Laurens let out a loud gasp, and so did her mother.

Anne Laurens said, under her breath, "She touched him. Did you see she touched him?"

George Laurens coughed, attempted to speak, then coughed again. Giving up, he extended his fat arms and swept his womenfolk into the crowd entering St. Michael's as if he were a human broom and they were dirt in need of disappearing. Behind him, a murmur moved through the crowd, words Daniel could not make out and really did not need to. Through it all Gamble stood like a statue, like a woman frozen in time, horror in her eyes.

Daniel turned to Cooper. "It's fine," Daniel said, steady. "Go to the house and ask Effie to stoke the fire in the parlor. I'll tell Mr. Sims I've sent you."

The young man nodded, but almost as if he could not help himself, looked to Gamble. Regret and fear commingled in almond-brown eyes rimmed with thick black lashes—eyes that looked so much like his older sister's.

"Go now, Cooper," Daniel urged.

Cooper turned on his heel and moved at a clip. At the end of the block, he ran. Daniel waited until Cooper had turned the corner onto Tradd, disappearing into the gathering dark, before he took Gamble's elbow. "Come, let's find a seat. If we wait any longer, we'll be forced to stand."

"Daniel," Gamble said, hoarse.

"I know," he said. "Come now."

If he could have, Daniel would've lifted her bodily and spirited her away. Away from Charleston and these damnable prying eyes. Away from a world of enslavement and subjugation, one he could not change, even for her.

Far away from Stoll's Alley.

"Come, Gamble," Honor said, as if speaking to a child. "You promised to sit beside me and hold my hand during 'Greensleeves.' Remember? I told you how it makes me cry."

Inside St. Michael's the talk had grown hushed, churchgoers settling into their boxes. The candle chandelier gleamed overhead, goldening the native cedar of the pews. The organist played the opening strains of "Hark! The Herald Angels Sing." It was, Daniel, knew, the most beautiful church on the peninsula. He wanted Gamble to see it. He wanted her memories of this place and of him to be good ones.

Daniel took their cloaks and gave them to the porter at the back of the narthex. There was an empty box in the far left of the nave, near the windows. They made their way down the center aisle, and when they passed the box where President Washington had sat on his visit to the city just a decade ago, Gamble drew a hand across the top of the cedar door but did not pause there.

When they had settled into the box, their hips touching, Gamble reached out and took his hand in hers. Honor looked over and saw. She smiled a smile of regret.

Being Quakers, the Petigrus had never been members of St. Michael's. They'd stopped attending Meeting at the Quaker Meeting House on Archdale Square sometime in the years before Daniel left for Europe, long before their parents died. Daniel never truly knew why, but now he wondered if it was not the Quakers' schism over slavery. Why had he never asked? Perhaps, Daniel considered, it was because he had been a young man—a boy, really—full of his art and full of himself, lacking interest in a people and a city he had sworn to leave behind.

Daniel had wanted the world. And Charleston, when he was fifteen years old, had felt small and known.

He did remember there had been a shift in Meeting—a palpable change between the Friends who owned slaves and those who did not, and who believed the practice an abomination. His parents spoke of it with other Friends in their house, in the parlor, long after he was abed. He knew, from overheard conversations, that each of them had spoken up at Meeting. But Daniel couldn't recall what they'd said, only that his father's voice had been low and strident, his mother's full of quiet certainty.

They had been a most excellent pair, his parents. Perhaps it was another reason Daniel had not married again after Simone. Perhaps he was intimidated by the seeming ease of their union. So much so he'd wanted nothing if he couldn't have the same.

Daniel looked at Gamble, who watched the rector step to the altar in his gleaming robes.

A Quaker meeting was a world away from an Anglican service. There was opulence here; it being Charleston, no one did anything in halves, especially at Christmastime.

Daniel had spent many a month in New England and had attended church services there with patrons. Much like the lack of strong drink, the Puritan New Englanders kept their church services long and their clothing drab. Even the meeting of Friends he'd attended there—which he'd already expected to be subdued—made him feel as if he'd visited a world made up entirely of neutral colors. To an artist (one raised in the Quaker tradition), it was a world of earth tones, not sapped of vibrancy but making a conscious choice to be muted. In that Meeting, the color and heat had come from the words spoken by the congregants, male and female alike.

When Daniel had said as much to Ed, his friend said, "Yes, well, Daniel. You are accustomed to Charleston. And Charleston, my friend, being much more attached to Europe and the Caribbean, revels in its audacity. Charleston didn't break from the sins of excess as New England did. Here, rather, excess simply expands in the heat."

When the sanctuary quieted, the rector welcomed a young man to the front. He must've been an altar boy, for he was pale and slight in his white choir robes, his hair black and tied back with a crisp blue ribbon, a circlet of light like a halo gleaming from the candles above.

The rector offered an opening prayer, then took a seat in the chancel. At his movement the priest, his crimson vestments gleaming, gave the boy a nod. The organist struck up "Greensleeves," and the notes filled the sanctuary. Daniel closed his eyes for a moment and let the sensation buoy him, let the warm weight of Gamble's gloved hand in his be his anchor in an unknown sea. His consciousness bobbed on the surface, but he was at peace. He loved the way music did this: how a song could make you feel suspended. A song such as this could have you back in the womb, back in the only place you'd ever been truly safe.

The boy began to sing. The congregation went silent and still. His pure young voice illuminated the room as a candle does the dark. In those moments, as the boy sang, time—which had seemed a conundrum, an aspect of life with which he'd lately been angry—made complete and utter sense to Daniel. He looked at the people around him, young and pink-cheeked, old and white-haired, faces full of lives as individual as a sand dollar. People would still worship here, Gamble had told him, two hundred years from now—some the descendants of the families in this very room. And while the congregation would remain largely white, there would be Negro congregants too. It gave Daniel hope that people would seek refuge here; they would marry here, be baptized here, their deaths mourned here, for ages hence. No matter what, there would be people and there would be life, and it might be different, but the lode seam of sorrow and joy and hope would remain rich and unchanged.

Daniel looked down at their intertwined fingers, Gamble's gloved hand a near to perfect fit in his. He wanted the world to be kind to her. He wanted her to have a place in this city—and finally, at almost forty years old, he felt it was *his* city—where she felt safe and known. If she could promise him this—and as she still seemed unable to shed the sadness over her lost baby and being widowed from a man who betrayed her so, he wasn't sure she could—then he just might be ready to let her go. Able to let her go.

The door to their box creaked open, and Ed squeezed inside. Once settled, his familiar scent of paints, absinthe, cinnamon, and orange oil lifting from his wool split tail jacket, Ed leaned over to Daniel.

"Why is she crying?" Ed whispered.

"Who?" Daniel said.

Ed tipped his fair head at Gamble. She was staring at the altar boy, the track of a tear down one cheek. As Daniel watched, another fell. He said nothing, did nothing. The music soared, the boy's soprano reaching a heartbreaking height. They were all on a precipice. They all stood on the same edge. They all waited for something in this life to make sense, to carry purpose, to awe. Some, Daniel knew, recognized it while they lived. Others felt for it as a man, reckless, stumbles his way through a room in the dark.

Ed leaned in again, his breath warm on Daniel's cheek, and said, "Have you painted her?"

GAMBLE

CHARLESTON
DECEMBER, 2004

"Oh my God," I said. "I think you're right."

Tolliver watched me, very still. Like a biologist observing an animal in the forest, one they don't want to risk spooking. He wanted me to come to it myself, I knew. Tol had always been like this: so certain of a theory, yet willing to test it on the people he trusted. He'd been an astounding professor: he liked to observe, to see if others might be able to find the answer first.

"That's how it works, doesn't it?" I said.

Tol nodded, a quick dip of his chin which belied the calm in his expression. But I knew him, and I knew that the sleek mechanisms in that complicated brain of his were working with furious efficiency.

"I believe so," Tol said. "I believe you were in 1804 for a weekend in our time, but there it was longer. I believe you walked down Stoll's Alley in October, and though you returned here, to 2004, days later, you'd really been gone months."

"Who's Daniel?" Harry said.

I swallowed the lump that had formed in my throat, and looked at Harry with a lost sort of love, an affection I'd always have for him, despite the broken trust and our mistake of a marriage.

"Harry," I said. "I think you should sit down."

There's nothing to telling someone you're a time traveler, if you don't mind that someone looking at you like you've completely lost your marbles. Loosed a screw. Been sent to the funny farm. Got bats in her belfry. You get the picture.

To give Harry due credit, he listened. He did not make a peep until I was done talking. He sat on my ancient, uncomfortable sofa (which is why I always sat on the floor), elbows on his knees, and waited. Then he repeated the salient points, like the attorney he was, asking the most succinct of questions of his client, just to make things clear for the jury.

"You walked down Stoll's Alley," Harry said. "After a girl in a costume. What you thought was a costume?"

"Yep," I said.

"And ended up in 1804. Here, in Charleston?"

"Yep."

"You met a man named Daniel," Harry continued. "An artist. Whose work you'd been restoring at the Galliard?"

"Yep." I nodded. So far, so good.

"And you stayed with him, and fell in love with him. Over a few months," Harry said. He looked at Tol, raised an eyebrow. Harry's expression said, *Sucks for us, brother.*

He cleared his throat. "Then you came back. On Christmas Eve, 1804. But here, only a few days had passed?"

I nodded. "That's right."

"And you came back, same way. Just walked down Stoll's Alley and poof, you were back in 2004?" Harry said.

I turned the knob on the fire so it blazed brighter, hotter. I felt a distinct chill; I couldn't get warm. Kipling curled up next to my legs, pressing her stout body as close to me as she could. I'd not realized she'd returned to the living room.

"That part I don't really remember," I said. I leaned back, welcoming the heat. It reminded me I was alive and in this moment. When my back got a little too hot, I didn't even squirm. I needed to know I was here, grounded. The sting felt earned.

Because it was the truth: I couldn't remember how I'd left Daniel, and Honor, and the Charleston of 1804. I assumed I'd simply walked back down the alley. Thinking now of Daniel, of saying goodbye to him, left a faint ache over the surface of my heart.

Harry slapped his knees, then stood. "Well, let's go remember," he said.

"What, now?" I said.

"Now," Harry said. "Stoll's Alley's just around the corner. Let's see what happens."

Tol stood, and suddenly I was the one left sitting, and I was way down on the floor, the men looming over me. Never would I have imagined Tol and Harry could come to agreement on anything. But there they were, watching. Waiting for me to say "yes."

"No," I said, shaking my head.

"Why not?" Harry said.

I scrambled to my feet, upsetting Kip, who looked up in question. *Why not? Because I might go. I might never be able to get back.*

"You won't go, not tonight," Tol said.

"You don't know that," I said. I heard the note of desperation in my voice. The tiny frisson of fear. "You have no way of knowing."

"I was just thinking we might see the girl," Harry said. "If we see the girl, I'll believe you." The moment he said it, I could tell Harry regretted it. Not enough to take it back, but still.

"Her name is Honor. I don't care if you believe me," I said.

And I didn't. Harry's validation no longer mattered to me. But something about saying it out loud—"Let's go"—pinged the tuning fork inside me. Flipped the switch on a good idea. Maybe I would go and wouldn't disappear. But maybe we would see Honor. And I'd have back-up: reinforcements, if you will.

I knew Tol believed me: he'd more than proved it, with our adventure in Aiken; with his willingness to send me back to 1804. Tol never doubted, because he knew me. And if I went, I went.

It wasn't that I thought I wouldn't make it back from 1804. I'd found Tol: he was my person, and I sure as hell wasn't giving him up—giving *us* up—now.

I didn't know if there was anything I could say to convince Tol I'd cleaned things up in 1804, that I'd officially closed my circle with Daniel and Honor. Maybe returning to the past was the only way he could be certain of me.

There was one thing I knew for certain—I'd never find out why Honor kept saying, "He needs you," and I certainly would never rid myself of this obsession I had with her portrait, if I didn't try.

Damn it. Tol was right. If we were ever going to do it, we had to do it now.

"Fine," I said. "Let's go."

DANIEL

CHARLESTON
CHRISTMAS EVE, 1804

"There are people," Gamble said, "who you never really leave behind, even when you leave them."

She stood on the Tradd Street sidewalk below, looking up. Daniel stood on the top of the limestone stoop. He didn't know why he had yet to step down, why he still held the door, as if he couldn't bring himself to close it. Maybe it was because closing the door of his home to Gamble meant she'd truly be done with them all, her leave-taking real.

Gamble's time there had been brief—only October to Christmas Eve—yet she made as much impact as a meteorite. She'd sent reverberations out into the ground soil of his life, maybe even of this city. A tiny movement no one might feel or even notice at first, its messages subterranean. Waiting centuries to be revealed.

Finally, Daniel stepped down beside Gamble, whose borrowed cloak brushed the leaf-strewn ground. Her hood was pushed back, her hair a candle in the dark.

She took his face in gentle, ungloved hands and pressed her lips to his. Daniel wrapped his hands around her wrists, not to pull them away but to hold her there. When they parted it felt far too quick. She studied his face. Then she smiled, and it was one of regret and resolve. Daniel could see she was ready to go.

"I will always be grateful for the gift of you," Gamble said.

Down the road, beneath the gently swaying myrtle trees, Honor waited. She was to walk Gamble back to Stoll's Alley, and she'd insisted on going alone. Daniel didn't demand otherwise because he knew he'd never be able to watch Gamble walk down that alley without begging her to stay. He was afraid he'd unman himself.

"It's you who are the gift," Daniel said.

The night was bright, full of stars, with an unseen moon illuminating everything. Even a block away, when Honor turned to them, her face revealed was clear. He felt grateful beyond explanation that Honor would do this for him: that she'd send Gamble home.

Gamble turned on her heel and walked to join Honor. The separation was quick, her absence a jolt. The wind rose, and it blew cold down Tradd Street, whirling leaves and clacking palmetto branches high overhead.

The women took arms and were gone.

Daniel sat hard on the stoop. He buried his face in his hands, allowing grief to fill his body. Indulgent, he knew, but so be it.

When the door opened behind him, he didn't move.

"Daniel, did you tell her you loved her?" Effie said. In thirty years, it was one of the few times she'd ever used his given name, without the honorific "mister."

"She knows," Daniel said into his hands.

There was a brief silence—enough time for a donkey cart to come racketing down the street, the driver whipping the horse into some kind of lather—then Effie said, "You might catch her if you run."

It was nearing two of the clock early Christmas morning; they'd indeed left Christmas Eve behind. Church Street was silent. Daniel rounded the corner into Stoll's Alley at a full sprint, his shoulder brushing an ale barrel stacked with others against the house on his left. Empty, it rocked on impact. He slowed, rubbed his shoulder, and drew up at the sight of Honor in the middle of the alley.

"Daniel," his sister said, regret and empathy in the word.

"Is she gone?" he said, breathing hard. He tore at his cravat, wanting nothing at his throat.

Honor stepped aside so he could see down into the darkness of the Bay Street end of the alley. Most of the lamps at the houses lining the alley there had been extinguished, the jessamine growing up and over the walls making the path seem a tunnel. It was difficult to see anything but the night.

Daniel narrowed his eyes, seeking. He didn't know what he wanted— didn't know what he could say that hadn't already been said. He certainly did not know if it was possible to love someone you could never really know, never really understand. Someone incapable of ever being fully yours.

Then there, at the end. Gamble.

"Daniel," she said, and though he knew she whispered, it was as if she stood at his side and spoke into his ear. "Each time I see your miniature portraits, I'll see you."

The wind picked up, sweeping dry brown leaves across the bricks. A single lamp flickered at the entrance to the single house far down on the right, casting wild shadows against the age-blackened alley wall, and it felt as if the air held the knowledge of some dark thing's coming.

The lines of Gamble's body began to fade. To disappear as ink does, on old parchment.

He did not say it. It was something Daniel would regret all the days of his life.

When Gamble was gone, Honor took his hand. Daniel walked with his sister out of Stoll's Alley, into the lives they were always meant to lead.

GAMBLE

STOLL'S ALLEY
DECEMBER, 2004

"Hell, I stepped in gum," Harry griped.

We stopped, an unlikely trio, at the mouth of Stoll's Alley. It was dusk, and perhaps because of the cold, we seemed to be the only people about. A car passed behind on Church Street, its headlights illuminating us for a brief moment, sending our shadows long into the alley. Harry went to a nearby mounting block and scraped his shoe against it.

I couldn't help it. I snorted. "Jesus, Harry," I said.

I looked up at Tolliver, expecting answering humor in his eyes. But Tol stilled. He stared down the alley, his expression fathomless.

I faced the alley and swallowed. Honor was there, mere yards from us, in the center of the brick walkway. Shadows made her young face gaunt, as if exposing the underlines of her skull. She looked about the same age she'd been when I'd left in 1804—she couldn't have been more than twenty-one years old. She wore a long blue dress, edged in delicate flowered stitching, high-waisted in the Regency style. It fell to cover her feet, yet somehow did not seem to touch the ground.

She was pregnant.

"Honor," I said, shock in my voice.

There were footsteps behind me, and Harry whispered, "Holy shit." Honor looked at Tol. "It's you," she said.

The seven o'clock bells began ringing through the city, and it was if their toll made Honor at once desperate and certain. Her gaze swung back to mine, and she placed a hand on the high swell of her belly.

"He needs you," she said. Then disappeared.

When I woke, it was from a dream so fierce it gripped as if it had claws. I strained away from it, and felt large, familiar hands settle about my shoulders.

"Gamble," Tol said, his voice low.

When I managed to open my eyes, the waking world still murky, I found him sitting next to me on my bed. Kip was beside him; she wedged her head between his leg and the bed and whimpered.

"Hey, girl," I said. I stretched out, stroking a hand down the silk of one black ear. "It's okay."

Tol leaned over, blocking the light coming in from my windows. He pressed his lips to my forehead, then touched his head to mine. "Are you okay?" he asked.

"I have no idea," I said.

And at the moment, I didn't. I couldn't seem to pick through time, to decide what was real and what wasn't, and what had really happened the night before. Time felt like an old waterski rope, snapping when a boat engine gunned too soon. Some water-skier waiting to be pulled— Honor, Daniel, me?—was left treading water, a useless plastic handle and a frayed rope in hand.

"Did I really faint?" I said.

"You really did," Tol said.

"My hip hurts," I said. It throbbed, insistent, and I rubbed a hand gingerly over my skin beneath the lace coverlet.

Tol leaned back. I blinked to make out his face. "You fell on your side when you fainted. It's a good thing you didn't hit your head."

He was so serious, I had to smile. I said, "See, normally this is when you'd make some comment about how hardheaded I am." Tol's expression didn't change, and I tapped my head with my fist. "An indestructible noggin."

Tol looked out the window. When he sighed, it lasted a while.

I gulped. "That bad, huh?"

Whereas I wore every emotion on my sleeve and always lost the first hand because I couldn't control my facial expressions, Tolliver was an excellent poker player. He had a ridiculous amount of control over his face and his body and was capable of admirable calm. I'd once seen him silence a classroom of overwrought graduate students—students who'd just been told they'd lost a much-needed grant—with a look, and a deep-voiced "Easy, folks. We'll get this done."

"*Bad* isn't the word I'd use," Tol said. I slipped my hand beneath his on the coverlet, and flipped so our fingers threaded. Tol squeezed. "Why did you faint when you saw her?" he said. "Honor."

"She's pregnant," I said. "And unmarried. You know what that meant then."

"And she hadn't been when you left?" he said.

I shook my head. It seemed a simple explanation, but time travel was a mercurial practice, and age tough to judge on someone wearing two-hundred-year-old fashion.

"I don't know how old she was last night," I said. "But she looked very much like she did in 1804. Except for the belly."

My hip throbbed, and I closed my eyes. Kip gave up any pretense of being well-trained, leaping over Tol's knees and onto the bed. She turned a circle, then flopped heavily across my legs.

"Tol," I said. "I can't shake the feeling I've made a mistake, restoring her miniature and displaying it for the world. Like I was supposed to keep a secret for her, and I didn't. And now this—now she's pregnant? She shows up nowhere in my research after 1804. I'm afraid something awful has happened to her. What if something goes wrong with the baby?"

Tears welled behind my closed eyelids; there was an aching pressure in my chest. It felt like some murky, painful version of fear and regret. Honor needed my help, and there was only one way I knew to help her.

We sat there for a moment in silence, letting my words digest. Tol reached out and smoothed the back of one hand down my wet cheek.

"I carried you, you know," he said.

I opened my eyes. He leaned over again, into Kip, who wasn't about to move. He pressed his lips to mine. They were warm, and firm, and I lifted to get closer.

"Of course you did," I said against his mouth. Tol smiled, and I felt it.

"Harry wasn't strong enough."

"In more ways than one," I said.

Tol kissed me again, once, and sat back. I knew what it meant when he went quiet like this. When he gathered his energy up into that athlete's body, and let it simmer. He'd made a decision, and there would be no backpedaling.

But then he ran his hands over his face, and I held my breath.

"Gamble," Tol said.

"I know," I said. "I have to go back."

PART III

CONSERVATOR

conservator/ noun

1. A person who is responsible for the repair and preservation of works of art…
2. A guardian or protector.

~ *Shorter Oxford English Dictionary, Vol. I*

As soon as you arrive at the past, you're making a choice and there'll be a split.

~ *Ronald Mallett, theoretical physicist*

DANIEL

When Daniel saw Gamble there at the edge of the garden, he knew her to be an illusion. Some shade his addled mind had willed into being: a product of overwrought nerves.

Then Gamble stepped forward, away from the elegant iron garden gate and the shadowy backdrop of the giant tea tree bushes. The sun had mellowed with late afternoon, and it washed her face and body, made her outlines real. She wore a white, sprigged muslin dress, the breeze catching the skirt and pressing it against her legs. Her hair was tied into a topknot; her bonnet, of course, gripped in hand.

It brought back an instant memory: Of the year before, when they'd argued for what had to have been the hundredth time over her absolute inability to keep her head covered. They'd been in the garden, not far from where she stood now. Gamble had laughed at Daniel, promised him she'd at least keep a bonnet in hand. Said she'd be like a person who'd purposely unleashed their dog in a public park: that way, if questioned at her impropriety she'd have the leash in hand. She could claim the hat had gotten away from her, just like the dog.

"Daniel," Gamble said.

Even with the garden between them, he could tell there were shadows beneath her eyes. Before she could say anything else, Daniel took a step forward. "I'm to be married in a week's time," he said, like a half-wit. It seemed the only thing he could say: a certainty she had need of knowing. "Here."

She nodded. "Yes, I know. Congratulations."

Daniel was unable to move. He saw Gamble's jaw work as she swallowed. She came to some sort of decision and walked quickly down the garden path, stopping just before him.

"I can't stay," she said. "That is, I'm not here to stay. I'm here because of Honor."

As if she couldn't help herself, Gamble reached up and tucked the corner of his messy cravat into his shirt, then pressed her hand into his shoulder. When she shoved, it broke the spell. "Daniel, where is she? And what of the baby?"

Finally, he came to life. "Baby?" Daniel said, his voice sharp. "What baby?"

ॐ

"It's true," Honor said. They stood in the parlor, unable to sit.

"How could you keep this from me?" Daniel said, Honor's words like hollow daggers. He leaned against a club chair, his hands gripping the curved top of the backrest. He needed the brace of it; he thought his knees might buckle.

"She kept it from you because Cooper is the father," Effie said. She'd entered the parlor in characteristic silence, flanking Honor. "She needs help, Daniel. Both of them do."

"All three of us do," Honor said, laying a hand on the curved belly he'd not noticed beneath the billowy fashion of her gowns. *Good God, how had he missed it?* The gesture was telling. Daniel knew his sister, and he knew Honor would do whatever she could to protect the life within.

"Effie. You knew." Daniel felt a fizzing at the edges of his body, something between anger and regret. It felt like being on the beach in a high, whipping wind, every bit of exposed skin pummeled by grains of sand.

"Women always know, Daniel," Effie said, and waited until he met her eyes. "We didn't know what to do."

His sister was having a baby. Cooper's baby. Freedman or not, a Negro man's baby. Daniel did not know much—he couldn't, for the life of him, maintain a grip on his wild and whirling thoughts—but he knew how to fear. And if Honor gave birth to a mulatto baby in Charleston, they would every one of them learn with brutal quickness just what it meant to fear for their lives. Especially Cooper.

"You can't stay here," Gamble said, and Daniel heard the desperation in her voice. "It's 1805. There're laws still in place, not to mention support building for the Nullifiers to start their warmongering in the 1820s.

"For God's sake," Gamble said. She paced back and forth on the Turkish rug as she gained momentum, her arms akimbo. "Anti-miscegenation laws won't pass in the United States until the 1960s. South Carolina won't remove its constitutional ban on interracial marriage until the year 1998! That's nearly the twenty-first century! All your lives are at risk."

"Gamble," Daniel barked in warning. Familiar frustration filled him at her inability to ever control her mouth. What was the twenty-first century to be like if people simply did and said what they thought, regardless of consequence?

He looked to Effie, whose dark eyes were wide. He'd no idea how much she knew. While he didn't doubt Effie could be trusted, Gamble's was a tale far too extraordinary to share. It was, he knew from experience, an unbearable weight.

Gamble stilled, and they all looked to the older woman, the evidence of her own mixed parentage written on her lovely face. Effie clenched and unclenched her fists. She gripped the scalloped edge of her muslin apron.

"You think I don't know what you are?" Effie said to Gamble. "I live in this house. Of course I know."

"How?" Honor said. She sank onto the striped sofa.

"Because of my speech, right?" Gamble guessed. She laughed, but it was thin. Trying, Daniel knew, to infuse humor into a room that had grown heavy with all their fear. "I never could learn to talk like a nineteenth-century woman, could I?"

"No." Effie shook her head. "Because you look at me, and see me."

When they gathered later, it was in the barn, in the long run below the loft. It felt safe somehow, concealed—as if in that humble space, nothing could harm them. Daniel looked to Honor. His sister sat beside Cooper on the driver's box of their parked carriage, their legs swinging as they whispered together. As if they were children still, instead of two soon-to-be parents whose decisions held the terrifying power to alter everything.

Daniel considered the young man he'd known since infanthood. Cooper had come to them many years after their parents hired Effie Perrineau, when Effie and Ben's mother died in childbed. Daniel remembered how Effie became mother and more to Cooper.

Trained as footman, Cooper was no longer needed in that position after the deaths of Daniel's parents, when the Petigru household duties had grown small. He went to work for the Sims family then, but as a freedman, continued to live in the Tradd Street kitchen house with his siblings: as much a member of Daniel's household as any one of them.

Cooper and Honor had been born but a year apart. So much younger than the siblings by whom they were being raised, they'd been instant friends: an island of two. Watching them now, together, their lives as inexplicably and implacably intertwined as their light and dark-skinned hands, Daniel knew he'd never persuade them to part. Never persuade them to run.

"You'll have the baby, of course," Daniel said. Beside him, Ben shifted from the wooden post against which he'd been leaning. He set his boots in the dirt like a man preparing to move, but he didn't speak.

Everyone looked at Daniel, four heads turning, four chins coming up. He felt the weight and trust of their regard. He was responsible for these souls—even Gamble's, with her future knowledge. Her awareness of a time to come, of changes in the world and on the earth of which they could only dream. Still, he was responsible for her while she was with him.

"But how?" Effie said. "It's not possible, not in Charleston. Perhaps not any place."

"I will have this child," Honor said, iron in her voice. At once, and perhaps for the first time, his sister seemed a woman to Daniel: cognizant of life's complications. No longer coltish and innocent.

"Is there truly nowhere they can go?" Gamble said.

"Where do you come from, that you think a life for them is possible?" Daniel said, stupefied, on an unthinking burst of words, before he could take it back.

But it was the truth: he couldn't fathom a place where Negroes and whites could form a true friendship outside the walls of a private home, much less a bond such as marriage. And then, to beget mixed-race children, without fear of retribution from society at large—much less the brutal reach of the law.

Daniel didn't wait for Gamble's answer. He cleared his throat and stepped into the dim light of the oil lamp set on the table between them, needing everyone to hear every word. Cleo whinnied in her stall; she put her head over the door, sensing discord in her humans.

"It doesn't matter where they go," Daniel said, answering his own question. "There is no place for them."

"He's right," Ben said, his deep voice full of regret.

"There has to be a place for the child," Cooper said.

It was the first Cooper had spoken since they removed to the barn, Daniel hoping for some semblance of safety. Of secrecy. Now, seated atop the carriage box, Cooper held one of Honor's hands, her pale fingers covered by his dark ones.

Cooper was not a loquacious sort: he'd always been quiet. Good-humored and kind, curious—he and Gamble, when she'd been there before, had formed a bond over books, had pored over newspapers together—but where Honor spoke aloud her every instant thought (much like Gamble), Cooper waited. He considered his audience and weighed his words before speaking.

It was something Daniel knew Cooper had learned from Effie, whose silent regard held an ineffable quality, a strength upon which they'd all come to depend.

Their youth made Daniel's chest tighten. His sister was having a baby. Yesterday, she was as tall as his knees. How could she be of an age to have a baby?

Honor's morning dress fell loose against her long legs, the white folds giving her an ephemeral quality, as if she might disappear on a breath. Honor was so solid, so real to him, the thought of losing her—to an angry, race-baiting mob, or to childbed—made his throat close. He studied her familiar, beloved face: surely it was fuller, a new aware-ness in her hazel eyes. She wore one of their father's ancient greatcoats for warmth. Beside her in his groom's livery, marked by the dusty golds and blues of the Sims house colors, Cooper was broad-shouldered and resolute. He was a man. Certainly, Daniel realized, Cooper hadn't been a boy for years.

Daniel looked again at their intertwined hands, half-hidden in the folds of Honor's skirt, and understood that despite her youth, Honor had been having a life, and he'd not been paying attention. When she looked at Cooper and her expression changed to one of longing, Daniel sighed. He felt at once tender toward and fearful for her.

Daniel realized, in that moment, the sight of them together like this did not shock him. Honor and Cooper were always affectionate in pri-vate; they'd been playmates their entire lives. This new life they'd created was a natural extension of that connection: it must be preserved. *How* was something else entirely.

There was a shift in the room, an exhalation, and Gamble said, "You'll take the child to Paris, Daniel. You and your new wife." She paused, smiled a small smile. "Her name is Lily, is it not? You'll act as foster parents to your niece and you'll paint."

Cooper stood; Honor seemed struck. Before either of them could utter a word, Daniel said to Gamble, "You know this already, don't you?"

No one breathed. It was as if he and Gamble were the only souls in the barn.

"We found a record of your return to Paris after you married Lily," Gamble said. "But that's all I know."

"Niece?" Effie said, cracking the cocoon of silence. "The baby is a girl?"

"It will be," Gamble said. She walked to Honor and reached up, laying a hand on her knee.

"Honor," Gamble said, a host of grief in her voice. It was an enchanter's voice—the voice of a seer. For a moment, Daniel wondered if his legs would hold him. He knew, when Gamble had gone from them forever, he'd paint her like this.

Before Gamble could bring herself to say another word, Honor let out a half-stifled cry, her hand going to her mouth.

"We can't go with her, can we?" Honor said through her fingers. "We have to let her go."

GAMBLE

Two weeks later we found ourselves again in Stoll's Alley, and this time it was just Tol and me. My hair was pulled into a topknot as coiffed as I could make it, bobby pins holding everything together. I'd talked myself out of a rubber hair tie: this was as close as I could get on short notice to early nineteenth-century hairpins. I wore a simple white muslin recreation of an early Regency-style dress, a set of short stays beneath. If you're going to time travel, it helps to work for a museum.

I thought I knew why I stood in Stoll's Alley—why I was journeying to 1805 and leaving Tolliver. This man I loved with a love bound in friendship and companionship, rooted in deep emotional and intellectual curiosity. It was a love tied up in a fierce sort of grace I'd not thought possible.

Too, when I looked at Tol, I saw the things that made me whole, which lined up to my things, as efficiently as the locks on a bank vault snicking into place, a puzzle finding all its pieces. Tol's steadiness and faithfulness, his body and brain kept him rooted to the earth in opposition to all the ways I took flight. When I looked at him, I saw all the things I was not, but could be, reflected.

I knew only this: I had to help Honor, possibly even save her life— hers and her baby's. The memory of Honor in the alley, pregnant and alone, begging me to return, sent resolve sluicing through my bloodstream right alongside my fear. I had no choice.

But I also knew I'd be traveling to the past in order to finally be finished with it: with Daniel and our time together, so Tol could be certain I was done. So I could bind myself to him, to our lives in the present, in the best possible way. So we'd have a future.

Moving on. Traveling back. Walking down alleys—the knowledge that time was nothing but the timber frame of a cabin built upon a mountain bald, and history moved around it, unheeded and brutal as a high wind. How would I ever explain this to our children? I'd have to, you know. Because one day Tol and I would have children. And they'd need to know, well…everything.

It was dusk, as it always seemed to be. Perhaps as it had to be, for the world to shift, the window to open, and time to make its inexplicable fissure in the alley; for the strands of it to slacken enough, maybe, for me to squeeze through.

Before the wind came down the alley, before the sky went from that seductive, wicked pink and orange to its transformational inky blue, I knew what was coming. St. Michael's Cathedral's seven o'clock bells tolled, the gongs rolling through the city and down the long alley as if repaving it in musical reverberation. It made absolute sense that this was a place untethered to time. That it had been a passage for so many, useful for centuries.

I needed for it to be useful tonight. My path had to take me somewhere important.

"It's time, baby," Tol said, taking my face in his hands.

"I love you," I said, whispering. Not because the words were caught, or hard to say, but because this business of walking between worlds was a complicated mystery—because no matter where I went, I knew where I had to end up.

We kissed. It was very much a promise. When we parted, Tol ran his hands down my arms and caught my fingers. He raised my hand to his lips, gave me a smile. It didn't match his eyes, which were somber; they'd lost some of their gold, greening with knowledge in the dark.

"I love you," Tol said, kissed the back of my hand, and stepped away.

There was more to say. Good lord, there was so much more to say. But Honor stood in the center of Stoll's Alley, and I didn't know how long she'd been there. The gas lamps along the brick-and-mortar wall and at the doorways of the houses and gates lining it washed her outlines in flickering light. It was as if she stood inside an arch of light—a glowing entrance. She was still pregnant. Still she needed me.

Honor held out her hand. "It's time," she said. "We must go."

I wanted to leap into Tol's arms, to wrap my legs around his waist and let him suspend me in safety. I wanted to bury my face in that spot between his neck and shoulder, where his muscles grew long and elegant, and where I couldn't get enough of him. It'd always been a space meant just for me. I wanted to kiss him there, to whisper something cool and flippant. To say, *Catch you on the flip side.*

Instead, I ran to Honor and took her outstretched hand. Before we turned away, she looked at Tolliver. And there was something about the way their gazes moved across the alley, over the centuries-old masonry. There was something about the cock of their heads; something shared in the finely drawn breadth of space between their shoulder blades. Despite their seeming differences—in physicality, race, and gender, they were very much alike.

Something was happening. An answer so close, I knew if we'd a moment more, I might catch it. It was in the startling lightness of their hazel eyes. In the knowledge residing there.

"It has always been you," Honor said.

೮

Stoll's Alley, Charleston
Spring, 1805

When I walked out of Stoll's Alley and into the Charleston of 1805, I was alone. Honor was not with me, nor had she been the first time I'd traveled down the alley into the past. I wondered if it would be like before, when Honor herself couldn't remember anything but finding me in the alley. She seemed to operate more as a messenger, rather than as a guide. Sort of like a docent who meets you at the museum, hands you a map of the exhibits, and then leaves you to discover the art for yourself.

I can't explain it. Hopefully, you don't expect me to. Really, we're all better off learning to be comfortable with the unexplained. Trust me on this one.

It had been months since I was last in the 1800s. Since I'd last seen Daniel, Effie, Ben, Cooper, or Honor, save those flashes of Honor in the present. Walking from the alley and out onto Church Street, I inhaled the smell of wood fires, the tang of tobacco, and the sweat of horseflesh, the aching sweetness of the Carolina jessamine lining the cobblestoned street. Here, it was spring.

Being welcomed into the past always felt like a process of disrobing: sort of like the time I was a college sophomore and had returned home from a party on my own because I found I hadn't been safe there. (I'd been a risky young person, there's no way around it.) The next morning I discovered my clothes—top, jeans, undergarments, socks and shoes—strewn drunkenly down the hallway, into the bathroom, and hanging from the doorknob of my bedroom. I'd no memory of it. It was apparent that I'd disrobed on the move, before falling into bed.

Arriving in the past was different, of course. But it was just as mysterious: just as misremembered, as foggy and potentially dangerous. Here, though, the process of coming back was akin to layers of me dropping away—layers of noise and complication—and after, I was left with a pared-down version of myself. I think 1800s Charleston was so hard to let go of—had been so hard to let go of—in the present, because I felt like myself there.

It doesn't make sense, I know. But then again, does life ever really make sense? Even when we're comfortable, when we think we've got it all figured out, we don't. We can, however, be content. This, I believe, is a gift.

I made my way from Water Street and was about to cross over Meeting when a hand gripped my forearm and a loud whinny went up, and I was dragged back onto the sidewalk. A phaeton came to a halt, both horses stomping, flinging their heads in protest. Across the street, a woman—an enslaved woman?—opened the door of a milliner's shop, peering outside to check the source of the hullabaloo. I caught her brief, narrow-eyed look before the door swung shut.

The driver, an aristocratic young man, stood from the red upholstered seat, doffing his top hat. "Madam, are you well?" he said, ready to leap down.

I caught my breath and called back, "Yes, I'm fine!"

The hand released my arm and a familiar soft voice said, "Madam, you must be more careful. You near to missed being trampled."

"You're absolutely right," I blurted. "I was stuck in my head. Thanks for rescuing me."

"Madam Vance?" It was said with such disbelief, the words shook me from the fog of my thoughts. I concentrated on my rescuer's face, just as he said, "I thought you'd long removed to Virginia. Are you returned for the wedding?"

"Ed, how wonderful to see you," I said, with a genuine smile. I'd always liked Edward Malbone. I liked how he loved Daniel. "What wedding?"

A pair of gentlemen passed on horseback, and they tipped their hats to me and called out to Ed, with whom they were apparently familiar. A young Black woman chased a small white boy in a navy-blue skeleton suit down the street toward the harbor; the boy raced alongside a giant hoop, spinning it with a stick as he ran. The sight took me aback: there was a suit like this in 2005, in an exhibit at the Charleston Museum; it, too, had ankle-length trousers, with a short, buttoned jacket. The ruffles at the wide collar of the shirt fluttered as the boy ran. I blinked, feeling as I had so many times during my last foray into the past—as if Fate took time in its hands as a clown does a set of rubber balls, tossing them into the air, juggling at whim.

The woman readjusted a basket hooked at her elbow, fishtails flopping over the rim, and called an admonishment on the move—something I couldn't quite make out. Ed was silent, but I assumed he heard me.

Right away, I knew. "Daniel's getting married, isn't he," I said.

"How is it you don't know?" Ed's sensitive face went from astonished to a bit grim, and I laid a comforting hand on his arm. He'd been there from the beginning, had seen Daniel and me together. He was one of Daniel's dearest friends: the man most likely knew we'd been lovers. There was a chance he knew everything.

"It's complicated," I said.

Ed dipped his chin. Very sweetly, he said, "Indeed."

Ed took his leave of me on Tradd Street, at the side gate of the Petigru gardens.

"This seems to me a moment you and Daniel should enjoy alone," he said.

Ed kissed my hand, offered a sympathetic smile, and left. The long tails of his well-worn and faded green waistcoat bounced against the dun-colored wool of his trousers. He did not replace his top hat, but kept it in hand, a cheery swing at his side. The sun dappled his fair hair from in between the myrtle and oak leaves overhead. *Tuberculosis will take him in two years*, I thought, the knowledge a sharp knuckle to my breastbone. He'd leave a legacy with his art, but it wouldn't be nearly enough. That good man, gone too soon.

See, this was the problem with history, and with time travel—whatever it was I was doing. People remained unchanged, despite the course of the centuries. Love still led us down paths unimaginably beautiful, however littered with land mines. Life still hurt. If love ran like a healthy vein down the heart of it all, loss was its twin—the blue-black shadow line revealing where a nurse might access the lifeblood.

I paused at the gate of the Petigrus' intricate wrought-iron fence and curled a hand around one of the scrolls. I leaned into the iron, closed my eyes, and pressed my forehead against it. I'd not realized how hard it would be to come back.

When I lifted my head and opened my eyes, I saw Daniel step out the back door of the house. Every instinct told me to go to him. It wasn't a romance novel sort of "go": a sweeping, bodice-to-be-ripped moment, a flinging into arms. Instead, it was a quiet "go." A whisper. It was me, and it was Daniel, and if our time together had been anything, it'd been filled with an authentic love—a surprising tenderness—as real as an ages-long friendship. I did not fear meeting Daniel. Did not worry he'd turn me away.

I didn't want to marry Daniel, either. He wasn't mine. But I do believe there are people in this life who belong to us, in more ways than one. In more ways than can be explained within the pages of a book. It's a soul-binding. A relationship free of social custom, of current mores, of even time itself.

To put it simply, Daniel was my friend, and would be forever. History had nothing, and everything, to do with it.

When I opened the gate on a creak of iron and emerged on the oyster-shell path, Daniel paled. It'd been six months. My guess is, he assumed he'd never lay eyes on me again—much less the week before his own wedding.

"Daniel," I said. At least I think I said it. It might've been in my head.

His face changed in that instant; all color returned. I thought it a good sign, and so I stepped forward.

At my movement Daniel said, "I'm to be married in a week's time. Here."

Of course, I knew, and said so. But I didn't say how I knew, and years later I'd wonder on that moment, and wonder if Daniel thought it was because I knew his marriage lines from my work in the future…because I told him I'd studied his history.

But the truth was, each time I stepped foot in the past, I lost bits of the present and retained others, and there was no explaining why. Maybe it was as Tol had said: we weren't going to be able to govern any of it, no matter how much we wanted to. Maybe I'd been granted access to specific memories when it came to history and art—to my work—but not specifics about the people I loved, because those memories could inadvertently alter the course of their lives. Because I could hurt them.

When it came to Daniel, I stretched for what to tell him. The details of his future life felt smudged, foggy—and most of all, as if they were not mine to share.

There had to be some reason time, and time travel, operated as such. Why history seemed so fickle—why it kept the solid things at arm's length. Was this because time, and therefore history, needed mystery to function? Perhaps I'd never do or learn what I was supposed to in the past if I brought the entirety of the present with me. Perhaps this was an answer I'd never get, and I needed to be comfortable with not knowing.

I looked at Daniel and I saw in him all the things I'd loved in 1804. His sweet brown eyes, the sensitive forehead, his thick and unruly hair. The space between his eyebrows which creased when he worked over a problem intellectually, or when he was completing work on a miniature portrait—when he painted the final strokes. Daniel, like so few people in the world, noticed people. He saw them. God knows he'd seen me.

I told him about Honor being pregnant. Really, I said it more as an exclamation rather than as an announcement. I figured he already knew. How could he not know? But right after I blurted the words, it was obvious this was news to Daniel. And I felt an immediate worry: that I'd shared a secret that wasn't mine to tell, but also it was news he absolutely had to know.

I had to touch him. I couldn't help myself. I tucked in his cravat—he'd always let it go messy and loose in our time together, out of artistic forgetfulness. Then the intensity of the situation struck me all at once, and I wanted to shake him out of his fog. Maybe I did shake him, or give him a shove. It's difficult to remember.

When we went inside to find Honor and Cooper, Daniel swept a hand to usher me in. Very much a nineteenth-century *after you*. And this simple act, this courtly, lost gesture, made me miss him, miss this home and this Charleston, more than anything else.

I don't want you to think my coming to this knowledge—that I missed Daniel—was longing. It wasn't. But I've always believed you could miss someone even when they were in the same room with you. You can miss someone, and miss what you shared, without wanting to return to it, or change the life you lived or the people in it.

I think our brains and our hearts are expansive enough, wild and mysterious enough, to do and feel many things at once. I think it's okay not to know how it all works out.

꙳

The baby was Cooper's. How had I missed this? It made so much sense. Not only because Effie, Ben, and Cooper were part of this house and this family in a way I never would be, but because they were attached to Daniel and Honor, as tightly as if they shared a complicated plait of DNA.

Though the Perrineaus had never been enslaved, they were invariably tied to the institution as were all Black Charlestonians. In my years of research, which dealt with the colonial and antebellum periods, I'd never even come close to understanding the institutional horror of slavery. Even after years of conversations with Tol, by all rights an expert on the topic, I'd never reached an intellectual or academic place where I could truly work out how the practice had come to be: how an entire society had decided that the subjugation of other human beings was acceptable.

And not only it was acceptable—it was deemed necessary, willed, designated by a higher power and made into law by other human beings who should've known better. Who, I always thought, no matter how "of the times" they were, absolutely knew better.

Didn't some kernel, some tiny spark of conscience, speak truth, even when the rest of the world drowned it out?

Effie and Cooper, Honor and Daniel, existed in a world wholly foreign to me. And that was saying something, considering that, despite enormous strides in racial equality, race relations in the South Carolina of 2005—hell, the *America* of 2005—were still tangled and stained by the dark side of our history. But it was the state of race relations in 1804, the reality of human bondage, that had driven me, finally, away from Daniel and back to my own time.

That, of course, and realizing—while living in 1804—that I loved Tolliver Jackson. Really loved him. To the ends of the earth and the end of time loved him. That I always had.

Now, as we stood in the barn in 1805, the oil lamp burning and us circling it like a band of gypsies round a bonfire, I felt the puzzle come together. I looked across the flickering lamp and everything made sense. Honor's pale eyes met mine. Eyes that looked so much like Tolliver's. Which held some long knowledge, an innate confidence as rare and spectacular as a night-blooming moonflower. I'd seen that look before.

I backed into an empty feed box and sat down, hard. Cleo snuffled at my hair, and I gave her velvet nose a haphazard pat. Honor and Cooper leaned into each other. Imaginary me traced the bones beneath their skulls. Cleaned the grime of generations away from their faces. I brushed aside the gunk of confusion and age the same as I'd do with my dust brush, allowing the gold to shine through.

I realized what I must've known all along.

"Tolliver is yours," I said, croaking a bit. They looked up.

"What?" Honor asked.

"Who?" Cooper said.

"Do you think—?" Daniel started. But I knew exactly how he'd end that sentence, given the chance.

I swallowed. My throat felt dry and itchy, as if I were catching a cold. "Tolliver. My Tolliver. I think he's a descendant of yours," I said. I waved a hand at Honor's belly, certainty rising in me unrelenting as high tide. "Of your baby's."

Their faces were full of questions. Daniel stepped in. "Tolliver is Gamble's friend, where she's…from. He's a Negro man. A good man. And she loves him," he said.

It couldn't have been easy for him, given our history. I said a brief inner prayer for his brave heart.

"Is he free? This Tolliver?" Cooper asked.

I stopped myself from saying *of course*. Instead, I said, "Yes. There's no slavery there."

Cooper pushed off from the driving box to land lightly on the hard-packed ground. He'd shed his livery waistcoat, and his shoulders were broad beneath his vest and linen shirt, his deep-set eyes dark and certain. I wondered how someone could change so in a year. He was just nineteen years old, but in the time I'd been away, Cooper had become a man. Perhaps he'd always been a man, always endowed with a stillness, a maturity I'd not picked up on, because, well, I was *white and a woman.*

The memory of Tol's admonition made me smile—a sort of smile-through-tears. It buoyed me, and thank goodness for that, because that's when Cooper stepped forward and said, "Then you'll take her. You'll take our baby with you. I want her to live in a place without slavery."

Effie joined him, the siblings a solid wall filled with urging. "That's right," she said. "You take the baby with you when you go, wherever it is you go. Then she can be free."

I did not say to Cooper, Effie, and Honor, *but you were all born free, so the baby will be too.* I'm glad I didn't. It would've been a white woman's comment, but perhaps worse, it would've been a comment from a woman without history.

I knew what the Perrineau siblings really meant. If the baby went with me, she'd be free of much of the fear that came from being biracial: the infinite complications of life as a mulatto woman in early nineteenth-century America. Which, good God in heaven, would only grow more dangerous with each passing year, as the slave trade made a once culturally diverse South Carolina more insular and closed-minded. It was a bloodstain: one that would spread to cover the entire country. It would, of course, culminate fifty-five years in the future, with the Civil War.

But I also knew I couldn't take her with me.

"I'm sorry, I can't," I said. "It doesn't work like that."

I was lost, unable to explain the unexplainable. Whoever it was out there in the ether, whoever knew how the alley really worked—knew how I'd traveled through time, or why—it certainly wasn't me. Still, I felt in my soul it was impossible to bring others along.

I said the only thing I knew to say to two parents: the only thing that would keep them from insisting. "The journey would kill her," I said.

Daniel said, "If the baby is to be who she should be, and your friend Tolliver is to come from her line, then we must keep her safe no matter what. Lily and I will take her to Paris. You and Cooper will come with us. But, Honor"—and with this he took his sister's face in his hands, this man who'd been mother, father, brother, world to her—"you cannot live as her mother. She'll have to be a foundling we've adopted. No one can know. Even in Paris, you and Cooper cannot be man and wife. Can you stand to live like this?"

Honor rose and made herself part of the Perrineau siblings' wall. She took Cooper's hand. They were striking together, dark and light, so well matched. Ready to face whatever came next.

Did Tol and I look like this? If we did, it would be because of them.

"History is a fucking mystery," I said out loud, unthinking. But no one paid any attention to me.

In the dark barn, Honor burned brightest. When she spoke, it was with the righteous fury of a mother.

"I'll never give her up," she said.

DANIEL

Charleston
Spring, 1805

In less than a week Daniel would marry. It was a simple act, a wedding. And Daniel cared deeply for Lily. His love for her was different from his love for Gamble: quiet, uncomplicated, the solid foundation upon which to build the rest of his days. Lily could be his, and he hers, in ways he and Gamble never could. It was a truth that lost a bit of pain with each passing day: Gamble did not belong to him, nor he to her.

Still, he knew none of this was fair to Lily. When they were introduced, it'd been late January, less than a month since Christmas Eve, 1804. Lily was a young widow from Boston—her first husband had suffered from consumption, and so the pair had moved to Charleston in hopes the temperate winters, with more time to be spent outside, would lessen the effects of the disease. But the gentleman died not long after their arrival.

Lily was also a Quaker, rooted in those beliefs—and Daniel found something solid and reassuring in her. As if the presence of his mother had somehow nudged them together. Perhaps, through the ether of time, she'd found a way to ease his heartbreak.

Lily knew much about Gamble, and Daniel's relationship with her, but she did not know everything. In fact, he wrestled for days with just how much to tell her. Lily was quiet and steady, but there was only so much life-altering information a person could manage at once. First, Daniel was going to uproot Lily in a move to Europe, introduce a baby into their lives—his own sister's mulatto baby—and then, in order to explain why they were going to such dramatic lengths to save the child, he'd say it was because Gamble was from 200 years in the future, and she'd told them to?

Good God, it was too much.

Daniel thought Lily would take the move in stride—perhaps even find joy in becoming a mother so soon into their marriage. But there was no telling how she'd respond to the revelation of Gamble's unimaginable origins. Still, he couldn't enter into such a bond with Lily without her knowing the whole truth, fantastical as it might be.

And so this was how he found himself walking along Water Street at mid-tide, the harbor gray-green and choppy under a steely sky, two women he loved by his side. Lily took hold of his arm, and Gamble walked in silence nearest the water, hands tucked into the pockets of the cloak Honor had lent her. Daniel glanced over at Gamble; the green silk lining at her collar, peppered with the tiniest of stitched purple violets, ruffed in the wind.

Gamble returned his gaze with a look that somehow managed to be both bemused and supportive. One that said, *I wouldn't want to walk in your shoes. But you can do this.*

Daniel cleared his throat. He put a hand on Lily's in the crook of his arm, and they all turned to the water.

"Thank you for the walk," he said. "I know the weather is rough, but I thought we could use the air."

A group of gentlemen approached from the south, the tallest gripping a hand to the brim of his top hat when the wind threatened to toss it seaward. They nodded and made their "good afternoons" at Daniel's little trio. He waited until the men had passed, their boots scuffing the shelled path, the tails of their waistcoats flapping against the backs of their thighs in the breeze. It was still early spring, and while in Charleston this often meant warmer days, some still blustered with winter.

"Lily," Daniel said. "I've something to ask of you. I thought it only fair before we were wed, and should you choose to break our engagement and call off the wedding, I'll be devastated. However, I'd most certainly understand. I'd never hold it against you."

Lily stilled, her thick-lashed brown eyes going wide. She was of average height, though taller than Gamble. Her rich brown hair was tucked into a simple ecru bonnet, and she wore the lapels of her cloak high about her neck to ward off the chill from the sea.

After a moment Lily nodded. "Go on," she said.

Daniel told her everything. Of Gamble's arrival the year before, how they'd grown close, how she had left, and what she knew. He told her of Honor and Cooper and the child, of the need for their removal to Paris. Of the danger, his own fears. He kept his gloved hand tight atop hers, concerned she'd pull away. But she didn't.

At times her eyes went wider. Her lips pursed in concentration.

When Daniel finished, Lily raised her chin on a swallow and set her fine jaw at a determined angle.

"Of course we will care for Honora's child as our own, and of course we'll go to Paris," she said. "Daniel Petigru, never did I imagine I'd fall in love again, or even want to share my life with another man. Then I agreed to marry you. Your people are now my people. I shall go where you go."

Anxiety eased its grip in Daniel's chest. He'd no inkling just how relieving it would be to hear Lily's affirmation. Perhaps there was hope for them after all.

He made a move to speak, but Lily's sharp look silenced him. She honed in on Gamble.

"I don't know I'll ever believe you're a woman from the future," Lily said. "It seems impossible. It may be too much for me. But you love Honora and Daniel, and he trusts you. How can I not trust you both?" Lily paused, squaring her shoulders. "You'll be leaving soon, then, Madam Vance? You'll not stay…here."

Gamble smiled, and though it was tinged with sadness, it was as if the sun came out. She reached across Daniel and took Lily's hands.

"You're so good for him," Gamble said. "You're everything he deserves. I'll see you all off, then I'll go back where I belong."

Daniel found he needed to clear his throat. Gruffly he said, "That may be some time. There's much to be done, and I'll have to write to secure work and lodging in Paris, and then passage for us all, which may be difficult, as weather makes spring crossings mercurial. It must be soon, before the baby comes. But the timing may be out of my hands. It could be weeks."

"I also have connections in Paris," Lily said. "We needn't wait for a reply before we sail. All will be well, I'm certain of it. Madam Vance will attend our wedding. And I know Honora will be glad of her help and comfort.

"We're to be a family," Lily continued, meeting Daniel's eyes despite the sudden blow of wind. She held back the wide brim of her bonnet with one small, gloved hand. "This is what families do."

Gamble grinned. "You'd do well in 2005, Madam Robertson," she said. She looked to Daniel. "Time is tricky. I'll wait."

It took but a fortnight to book reliable passage, after Daniel called upon an old friend of his father's, a merchant whose son had taken over when he'd retired. Standing in the son's office, Daniel couldn't help but remember his father behind his old desk, a quill abandoned and a splatter of ink across a flutter of papers when Ramus Petigru grew impatient with numbers or people.

Daniel watched his father's friend cast a disparaging look at his portly, red-cheeked son, who'd made apparent misuse of his father's former office. Likely in his day, the old man had kept it much neater.

But passage was acquired in swift time—they'd lucked upon a merchant ship taking rice to Europe—and so Daniel gave the gentlemen a genuine smile and a clasp of hands, and said he'd ensure that all their luggage arrived at the docks the next evening. In the morning after, they'd set sail.

The next evening, as the seven o'clock bells rang through the city, Ben and Daniel loaded the footman's box with their luggage. Daniel grimaced: along with their clothes came his art supplies, logbooks, and easel—even some of the housekeeping items they might need when they'd secured a Paris apartment. He wondered briefly how the ship's captain would react; already he'd agreed to allow women on a merchant vessel, and now this.

Daniel helped Gamble inside. She caught her skirts up in the door, as per usual, but laughed and whipped them aside. The heavy curtain had been tied back, despite the cold, and she braced both hands on the sill of the carriage window. But her expressive eyes seemed sad, her mouth pinched. She was worried, Daniel thought.

Honor came out to see them off, her arm through Effie's. You wouldn't know to look for it if you didn't know she was with child. But there was a fullness to her face and a slow swing in her step, and to Daniel she seemed much changed, almost as if the babe had made her presence known to no one but Honor.

Twin emotions pulled at Daniel: a tender hope and happiness he couldn't quite name, for Honor and for himself, at the prospect of welcoming a niece. But, too, a resolve buoyed by the fear that they must get Honor and Cooper to safety, now.

Just inside the foyer, before Honor joined Effie on the stoop, the door opened for a heartbeat, maybe two, upon Cooper and his sister. Daniel watched as Honor lifted their clasped hands to her cheek, pressed them there and closed her eyes. Daniel didn't want it to, but the sight took him aback: both in the newness, the fear of them being discovered, and—he considered, with a small, hot shame—because he'd never witnessed a couple of two races before, and there was something about it that felt odd and uncertain. There was still a part of Daniel that doubted, despite Gamble's assertions to the contrary, that a public bond between people of different races would ever be accepted.

At Honor's approach, Gamble brightened, but Daniel could tell it took effort. She tapped her fingers against the door.

"Not to worry, Honor," she said. "We'll be back before you know it."

"I still don't see why you may go and I may not," Honor said, uncharacteristically petulant. She shot a steely glare Daniel's way.

"Because you are in a delicate state," Daniel said, bracing a foot and hauling himself up into the driver's box beside Ben. Ben snorted, and Daniel heard it.

"Delicate, ha!" Honor whispered, but it was fierce. She looked about the street, then leaned in. "You and Ben did not even know I was pregnant."

"That is a subject we'll revisit," Daniel said, in a tone which brooked no argument. "Make her sit down, Effie, please."

"Don't worry, Honor, I'll report back when we return," Gamble said, with a jaunty salute and a straight face. When Honor cracked a smile, Daniel turned to Ben.

"All right, then," he said. "Drive on."

Ben flicked the reins and the horses heaved forward, hooves scraping the cobblestones. The front door of the house shut on a bang, and Cooper jogged down the steps, gave Honor and Effie a brief, cocky smile, then launched himself up onto the rumble.

Daniel cupped a hand round his mouth, and shouted, "We'll be back before ten of the clock!"

GAMBLE

Nothing prepares you, my friend Corey told me once, for seeing a human being die right in front of you, in real time. He told me this overlooking Graveyard Fields on the Blue Ridge Parkway, while we drank local pilsners on the tailgate of his Ford pickup—the one his dad kept pristine for him for over a year while Corey was in Iraq—our legs swinging like kids sitting on the edge of a dock. Getting to hang out was a happy coincidence: we'd both come home one fall weekend—I from grad school and he from his second tour.

I remember how cold it was on the Parkway that afternoon, a full ten degrees colder than down in Asheville, and I'd shivered in my insufficient fleece jacket, my free hand tucked beneath my jean-clad thighs for warmth. But Corey: he wore the same Carhartt overalls and chambray shirt he'd worn in high school, his Tourists baseball cap pulled low over his eyes, and he didn't shiver at all. He just stared straight out over those infinite blue hills, rolling so far into the distance they disappeared into the violet-white horizon. And he talked.

You think you're prepared, Corey said, because you're a soldier. You think you know what it'll be like when it happens, because you've been trained to keep calm under fire, to reconcile yourself to the probability of death. But it doesn't matter. Every time, whether it's a buddy from your unit, a civilian, or an enemy combatant, there is this blip of roaring white blankness, this time out of time, when it feels like all the air has been sucked from the world.

Years later, I'd try with all my might to recall each infinitesimal detail about that night on Adgar's Wharf. I was a historian, for heaven's sake: I studied, observed, and made a whole damn career out of safeguarding historic detail in my memory—out of bringing those details home, sifting the excess, and making them, well, make sense to laymen. But I couldn't remember much of anything from that night on the wharf.

Like a trauma victim, perhaps, I only saw in my muddled mind a bit of the before, and a whole lot of after.

I remember leaving the house on Tradd, waving to Effie and Honor. I recall the sound of the horses' hooves clacking in the dark, feeling the carriage jolt as we made our way down the cobblestones to the head of the pier, where Daniel, Ben, and Cooper unloaded our trunks and bags under the watchful eye of some pock-marked, teenaged sailor ordered to the task. It was chilly on the water, and I stood beneath the arched awning of some rice broker's doorway, next to a stack of barrels. I watched Daniel and Ben from the spot: it looked as if Daniel was placating the sailor; he patted him on the shoulder, then dropped coins in his palm. The sailor turned, held his lantern aloft, and shouted toward the great ship bumping and squeaking against the roped pilings in the dark, her tall masts bobbing high overhead.

Two older sailors jogged down the plank and across the wooden pier; one of them gestured at Cooper, who waited by the carriage. When the three men carried our things onto the ship, I stepped out from beneath the awning. Ben, who was by no means jovial, but always spoke freely within the safety of the Tradd Street house, seemed to fade into the background when he and Daniel were in public. It'd hurt my heart to see in 1804, and it hurt it now, though I was cognizant of the reasons why.

I walked to Ben, but stopped several feet away and tucked my hands in my borrowed jacket; it was the red one of Daniel's mother's, the riding cloak he'd lent me the year before.

"I'm sorry for this," I said, quiet. "I wish they didn't have to leave you and Effie. I wish things were different."

Ben answered without turning his head. To an onlooker, it would seem as if we stood a few yards apart, unspeaking.

"But it's not, is it," he said, his voice low and deep. "And from what you say, nothing'll change for almost two hundred more years. I'm glad it'll happen, but there must be some godawful kind of suffering in between."

I didn't respond. There was nothing I could say.

Ben barely moved, just flicked his wrists as if they needed loosening. As if there'd been shackles there, only recently freed. "It's good they're going," he said. "Daniel's had some trouble since you left."

"What?" I said.

"That Christmas Eve, when you touched Cooper. Folks saw it." At my sharp, indrawn breath, Ben made a tiny movement of his head, a brief shake. "Not your fault. There's been talk about the Petigrus living with free Negroes long before you. It was always going to come to this. Somebody was always going to have to leave."

Ben straightened, and I saw Daniel turn and make his way toward us. The water slapped against the pier: something out in the night-black harbor was making waves.

"I'm glad they're going," Ben added, before Daniel approached.

Daniel stopped, the ship at his back. Light from lanterns hung along the pier and the gas lamps flanking the doorway behind us swung, inconsistent, across his face. He raised an eyebrow, a faint brown dash in the dark.

"That pup's the quartermaster," Daniel said. "Full of himself and mean with it. I had to pay him to let Cooper see to our things. I don't trust them to stay safe through the night, otherwise."

It happened just as Corey had said: a roaring blankness, the feeling of a vacuum. Because that's when Ben made a soft, muffled sound beside me, when Daniel turned, and when it happened.

I've replayed this moment many times in my mind. Two sailors and then Cooper came down the gangplank, Cooper's broad shoulders blocking the view of a third short, scrawny sailor following behind. When they were upon the pier, the scrawny man shoved Cooper hard, his mouth making an ugly shape, the words too far for us to hear.

Cooper's face had already been still and blank, held in that awful, neutral way I'd seen so many Black people in this Charleston hold theirs when encountering white people: empty, void of any emotion whatsoever. He kept his feet after the first shove, but the next sailor was bigger, and Cooper went down. His knees hit the wooden pier with an awful crack, but he braced himself with his hands.

Then Cooper looked up, his expression no longer blank. On his face was a look I'd never seen him make before: he was angry. Now, I know: it was an anger born of hopelessness and exhaustion—the fury of a man who'd been held down far too long. I can imagine Cooper felt as only a soon-to-be father could: as if he'd do anything not to bring his child into a world that would treat them thus.

Cooper rose to his feet in such an athletic rush I gripped Daniel's forearm in fright.

"No," Ben breathed.

DANIEL

CHARLESTON, 1805

In a carriage, at a clip

The carriage hit some bump in the road and lifted for a moment from the ground. Daniel braced a bloodied hand against the ceiling and held tight to Cooper's legs. The boy Daniel had taught to sketch lizards in the garden lay haphazardly across the inside span of the carriage: a heavy, unmoving human bridge from bench to bench. Gamble supported Cooper's shoulders and head in her lap, her arms wrapped round him like an embrace. She murmured to Cooper, words Daniel couldn't understand, tears streaming soundlessly down her cheeks.

The brawl had been so quick, so shocking, thinking on it now made Daniel feel like a man with soldier's fatigue. As if the world around him had gone numb, yet his senses on high alert, every sound a racket. But Cooper had struck the sailor: struck him so hard the force propelled the man off the pier and into the water. And Gamble had flown past Daniel before he could stop her, before he could even think.

Daniel knew Gamble had shouted at the sailors to let Cooper go, to leave him be. He knew she'd slapped the tall one—actually *struck* him—soundly across the face, and the man had grabbed her forearms, squeezing hard so she cried out. Daniel could still see the spittle flying from the sailor's mouth, the moment when the man shook Gamble hard, like a rag doll. He still heard the shot from the third sailor's pistol, watched the blood pool at Cooper's chest as he fell.

As long as he lived, he would never unsee the moment when Ben shoved his mortising chisel between the tall sailor's ribs, and twisted.

The rest was like a fever dream. More sailors spilling from the ship, Daniel keeping them from Ben with every ounce of will in his body. The shouting, Gamble's ashen face as she knelt beside Cooper and pressed both hands against the hole in his chest as if trying to stop a leak from breaking a dike. The blood seeping, scarlet and unceasing, between her fingers.

The captain, Jonas Hale, had arrived in a flurry, taken one look at the situation and ordered his men back onto the ship. He thought Hale had said something about his father—Daniel's father—but he couldn't be certain whether this was a memory real or imagined.

When Daniel said, standing over the body of the dead sailor, "I did this. You'll tell them I did this," Hale nodded.

The carriage lurched again and Daniel gripped Cooper's legs tight against his own, feeling Cooper's lean muscle beneath his trousers, those long legs he'd watched grow from boy to man. Ben must be whipping the horses into a lather, Daniel thought.

Across the carriage, Gamble made a strangled, grief-stricken sound. And Daniel knew.

"He's gone," she said.

GAMBLE

When I walked out of Stoll's Alley, I didn't know how much time had passed. It was still winter, here in 2005. But it was home: my real home, in the present. I'm not sure how to explain it. The air was different. It was lighter.

I know this doesn't make sense. I mean, let's be honest: the air in 1805 would likely be cleaner, free of automobile exhaust and smoke full of chemicals, pumped by modern industry along the Ashley and Cooper Rivers. Still, this 2005 air felt lighter, clearer, as if it'd been sifted.

Maybe history worked like this. Maybe we got better. Learned more. Became all the people we were supposed to be, as the years rolled on, unending swells in the ocean of time. Or maybe we were the sand, and the more pummeled we were by the waves of time, the more pared down and flinty we became. Maybe the real us—the shiny seashell us; the perfect, tiny black sharks'-teeth us—was finally revealed.

Man, wouldn't it be nice if it worked like that.

It was cold, which is how I knew it was still winter. Somehow I'd lost the bonnet. Figured. Lydia Petigru's red cloak, however, I'd given to Effie before leaving, and so my arms and neck were bare. Regency-style dresses are short on warmth.

Effie. Cooper. Oh God.

The gongs from the bells at St. Michael's were fading—I assume having just marked the seven o'clock hour. It was dark, but the lamps flanking the alley lessened the spook of the place. They revealed a way hollowed out by light, as if the ancient brick before me were a passage with an ending, and I, the hero in a storybook, just had to get there.

I turned the corner onto Church Street, and ran.

The only light on at 353 Church was a lamp in the far right, upstairs window: Catherine up reading. I loved that she was a reader; it made me like her even more. I felt a wash of love for her house: the black shutters and glossy door, and the round, patinaed medallion of the Preservation

Society's lauded Carolopolis Award hammered into the stucco. Catherine had worked her entire adult life to save the historic architecture of Charleston; she'd tried to honor the past the best way she knew how—and she did it wearing pearls. She used her time, energy, and money in the restoration, and maybe even the reclamation, of her city's soul.

Catherine and I came from different backgrounds, were of different generations, and probably voted for politicians from entirely different political parties. But here we were, making our complicated lives in this complicated city, trying with all our might to live with purpose.

I'd have to tell her the original shutters on her house had been louvered, I thought. If history had taught me anything, it was that we're all in this together.

My boots slid on the pavers lining the drive, and I wheeled my arms for balance. The pavers were covered in icy moss. Then, there it was: the kitchen house, 353A, my little home. The security light flashed on, and I dove for the hide-a-key under the terra-cotta pot, currently housing the calendula which Catherine kept alive, despite my negligence.

Light filled the stoop and the storm door swung open on a loud protest. And then he was there.

"You're home," Tolliver said. He swallowed—I saw his Adam's apple move up and down in the light at his long throat—and he was down the steps in a flash, lifting me into his arms. "Oh God, Gamble. I wasn't sure. I didn't know if—"

"What? You didn't think I'd come back?" I said, holding Tol as tightly as I possibly could. Surely, he'd not believed I'd leave him. I tried to imagine myself in his shoes: what agony he must have felt!

I gripped his shoulders beneath his thin T-shirt; I tried to wrap my legs round his waist, but it was impossible with the layers of skirts, and so he clutched me to his chest.

Tol brushed the hair back from my cheek and swiped a warm thumb beneath my eye. He started to say something, but kissed me instead. The tenderness of it was my undoing.

"Tolliver," I said, when I was able. It was all I could say.

I thought I'd handled the whole time-travel thing with aplomb. That I was strong and collected, cool as a cucumber: able to leap early nineteenth-century buildings in a single bound. I'd been to the past before; I'd lived a hundred lives. But in Tol's arms, home, the weight of everything I'd seen and everything I'd done—the weight of history—breached my personal floodgates, and I floundered. Emotions I'd held in check, in order to do what I'd needed to do in 1805 and here, multiplied inside me. I felt like a heroine in a do-or-die movie scene, in a hurricane, clinging to roof rafters while water rose roiling in the house beneath her.

Which is all to say, I sobbed. I tucked my head under Tol's chin, and gave up the ghost.

"Okay," he said. "Okay."

Doors opened and closed; there was a rush of warmth, a blanket. We sank into my lumpy old sofa, and Tol pulled me onto his lap.

I opened my eyes to the light and heat of the gas logs, to the gorgeous old mantel mounted with the same two-hundred-year-old musket. I thought of how benign it looked nailed there, as if it'd never done any damage despite being present during at least two wars and some of the city's most dangerous decades. And I remembered Cooper lying bloody and lifeless on cold cobblestones, Daniel holding madmen at bay.

I remembered Effie's face, drained of all joy, when we brought Cooper's body home. Honor on her knees, keening in sorrow. The awful, cold stillness of Cooper's body.

And I bawled. I cried as I never had before in my life.

Tol pressed his lips to my temple. He cupped the back of my skull, his fingers threaded in my hair. After a moment, he spread his arm over my waist like a seatbelt, and his other hand wrapped my hip. I felt it through the morning dress, against my well-padded hip bone.

Still, I couldn't control myself. I cried so hard I gasped to breathe. Tol repeated my name, murmured words of comfort in that delicious voice of his. A voice I'd recognize even if I was elderly and feeble-minded; a voice that would have the power, always, to bring me home.

"Gamble," he said. "Baby, you're home. You're safe."

Home. Safe.

Tolliver was there. Alive and whole. We'd saved him: Honor and Cooper, Effie and Daniel, Ben, Lily, and me. We put history to rights— by God, we'd loved well—and Tol was there, where he was always meant to be.

I know what you're going to say: I know it's a fallacy. For who's to say Tol wouldn't still be here, even if we'd failed? That he wouldn't have been born someone else, somewhere else? I don't make the damn rules. But by God, he would not be my Tolliver. He was meant to be my Tolliver: Honor's and Cooper's Tolliver.

I've no idea how long I cried. No clue how long Tol held me. I was not a pretty crier (really, who is except a Disney princess?), and the story came out along with salty tears and a runny nose. At first, I gasped for air between bouts of sobbing. Each time I'd tell him something—about the baby, or Cooper's brutal death, or watching Daniel marry Lily days later in the garden at Tradd Street—emotion would overwhelm. It was as if I stood, thigh deep in the Atlantic, and though the current was strong I kept my toes curled in the sand. But just when I thought I'd found my footing, a wave came out of nowhere to knock me over again.

And I'd not even told him the most important part of the story: We'd found his family. His people.

Finally, the waves abated. I could breathe again. Beneath me Tol was still; he'd even stopped rubbing my hip. I closed my eyes, just for a moment, and pressed my lips against his well-worn T-shirt. I sucked air through my nose, inhaling the scent of his skin. It was the scent of the future, all done up in laundry detergent, lemons, and leather. He smelled like home.

"I have something to tell you," I said, into the cotton.

The words rumbled in Tol's chest when he chuckled. "You mean there's more? Why don't we give it a minute."

"Okay," I said, and pressed my lips to his throat. I licked him. He'd not shaved in a while, and he tasted like salt.

"Yum," I murmured.

"Gamble," Tol said.

And that was it. I'm not going to apologize for it. I wanted him. I wanted—no, needed—to be enveloped by Tol. To be filled to completeness by someone I knew to be good, to be mine. To feel something solid and real. To ground myself in the here and now.

After all, the only treatment for grief is life.

I shifted in his arms until I sat astride his lap, my knees pressed into the far-too-thin cushions at the back of the sofa.

"Gamble," Tol said. "Let's wait. You're exhausted." But his hands came up, and he fanned his long fingers across my skin where the gown dipped low to expose my upper back.

I cupped his face in my hands. (Only for a moment, because I was in a serious, all-fired hurry.) It was such a good face, the lines of it sharply drawn, time-tested.

Tol wasn't perfect. It occurs to me I may, at times, make it sound like he was. He was opinionated, could even be a snob. He tried too hard to be strong, to keep feelings and emotions in check for the sake of equilibrium. So much of his childhood had been lived in upset: he craved peace more than anything else. And wasn't that a kick in the pants, because he'd chosen me? Life with me would likely never be peaceful.

Tolliver so rarely let people in—*really* in—because, deep down, he was afraid they'd leave.

But who cares. None of us is perfect. Some of us fit so well together, because our imperfections and quirks make up for the other person's. We're all bruised. All burnished. Waiting for the touch of the right human with the right rag to notice our unique history, and to shine us up.

We're all piecemealed. It takes a lot of glue to put us together—sometimes back together. What did Leonard Cohen say? We're all cracked, waiting for the light to get in. Or something like that.

I hitched my skirts to my waist. I smiled so wide, I felt the siren in it. Tol's thick eyebrows went up, and his broad chest expanded on a long breath. This was an opportunity: I took the hem of his T-shirt in hand, and pulled it up and over his head. I tossed it aside, then pressed my body against his, laid my lips against the bronze skin at his sternum.

"No more waiting," I said, into the trunk of him. "Time is of the essence."

DANIEL

Spring, 1805

Aboard the Brig Lady Washington

As the *Lady Washington* neared the mouth of the harbor, the wide silver sea before them, Daniel wondered whether he should look back at the city. There was a chance he'd never again see Charleston. He felt no dark premonition: it was simply the chance every traveler took when sailing across the Atlantic. One never knew what fate waited in the waves.

More so, Daniel knew, better than anyone, how life could change in a heartbeat. How everything you'd thought solid could dissipate before your eyes. How you might round a corner in a place you'd known for a lifetime, and walk into something, or someone, new.

Who knew what Paris held in store for them? She was a city of closely held secrets. He, Lily, Honor, and this baby to be would soon be painted in with as much subtlety as a Boilly figure hidden in a Paris crowd.

The captain had recommended they remove to their staterooms upon entering the sea, as the swells were high and the precipitous rise and drop of the ship was sure to do the same to their stomachs. Daniel thought of Honor, without Cooper. Christ, what a wrenching his sister must feel.

Daniel shook his head as if to fling off grief: he held the loss of Cooper at bay, still—he'd had to, to get them there.

Honor was with Lily in their stateroom below. When Daniel had left them, he'd closed the small wooden door, swollen from moisture and sticky against the jamb, on the sight of Honor seated at the edge of the berth. Her pale face was streaked with tears, arms cradling her belly and her body folded over itself; as if, somehow, she could keep the baby inside safe.

Lily, beside her, placed a hand on Honor's back and gave him a look of pity. There were some things—many things—he couldn't fix, no matter how hard he tried.

Daniel had paused in the saloon outside the door, one hand gripped along a chair back. He could hear Honor's choking sobs and Lily's soothing through the air vents in the stateroom door. Two gentlemen they'd yet to meet sat at the end of the saloon table, going over a log-book. They looked up, a question in the younger man's eyes and a look of sympathy in the elder's. Cotton or rice merchants, Daniel assumed, from the looks of their fine wool vests and trousers. He replaced his hat and gave it a finger tap, and was off and up the stairs to the deck. He couldn't yet stomach introductions.

Daniel had sailed out of Charleston Harbor many times over the years, since that first apprenticeship in Paris when he'd been fifteen years old. It never failed to move him to feel the sway of the boards beneath his boots, the slap of waves against the bow, to come what seemed hair's breadths from the other ships and boats in the harbor. In summer, there could be so many vessels at anchor there, the masts made a small forest of tree trunks against the heat-heavy sky.

Ships were full of action: sailors scaling rigging, men calling orders. Such a different world from his of quiet contemplation, standing alone before his easel. Daniel wasn't meant to be a sailor, but it didn't mean he did not like to sail.

The *Lady Washington* slipped through the treacherous sandbars marking the harbor's mouth, and Daniel watched the low, long islands of Sullivan's and Folly, bright with new green, recede. He watched until the line of marsh grass where land met sea became an indistinct watercolor of golds, greens, and blues, its solidity an illusion. Above him, a sailor called out in warning, and a massive, coiled rope dropped to the deck with a thud. A boom the width of an ale barrel swung round to be caught and tied off by another sailor, and Daniel took a moment.

The air on his face was cool and heavy with salt. Overhead, gulls screeched as they wheeled past the main mast and then circled the stern near the bilge hole, hoping for scraps. The ocean roared against the side of the ship, and Daniel wondered if, when they disembarked in Le Havre, his ears would ring with the sound for days.

He spread his fingers against the thick balustrade and splayed his stance to countermand the ship's rise and fall. Beneath his palms, the wood was slick from the splash. If a truly great wave was upon them, he'd never find purchase.

Daniel turned and wiped his hands down the front of his greatcoat. He moved with caution, a bit like a drunk trying to appear sober, to the starboard side of the ship, to watch the city disappear in the distance. When the last tiny block of color—those pink, yellow, and orange houses along Bay Street, and the rough, brown, indistinguishable wharves—finally faded from view, he faced the sea again.

They'd be at least eight weeks at sea, should the voyage be blessed with smooth sailing and a proper headwind. He hoped, for Honor's sake, it'd be smooth. He remembered when their mother was pregnant, especially the last two pregnancies before Honor. Their mother lost both babes, but for the first few months of her confinement she'd been uncommonly sick—so sick Effie had kept a bucket at hand in every room of the house.

"Daniel!" It was Lily. She and Honor emerged from below deck, Lily clutching at the doorjamb as Honor pulled away from her and made her way across the deck. Obviously discommoded, Lily gave him a fleeting, green look of chagrin before disappearing down the steps.

Sailors nearby nodded, wary, at Honor, though one offered his arm. She took it, attempting to smile. When she was delivered at Daniel's side, the sailor, surely no more than sixteen years old, clutched his hat to his chest and said, "Please watch the rigging, miss. We can't have you falling." He made a surprising European leg and was off across the deck as if it did not lurch at all, as if he'd been born to it.

Daniel took Honor's arm, but she pulled away and placed both hands atop the balustrade. He made a move to speak, but Honor said, "Don't say it, Daniel. Just don't. I cannot remain in that godforsaken cabin where there's nowhere for my thoughts to go. I need the air."

Honor looked out to sea, her jaw set but a pulse beating at her throat. He watched her in silence, his imaginary paintbrush tracing her profile. The older Honor grew, the more she looked like their mother. God's teeth, he could use their mother's presence now. He needed her Quaker steadiness, her iron calm: the belief that with common sense and good choices, all would be well.

There was much he wanted to say to Honor—so much had not been possible in those last, awful hours before morning. When the sun had come up they'd all moved like wooden soldiers, even Gamble. Each completing a small task that would bring them to the next task, so Honor and the baby would be safe. They'd operated like this together, a somber unit.

Daniel wanted Effie to come to Paris—had begged her, in fact—but she insisted on staying. Said she'd take care of the house.

"I won't leave Cooper. Besides, I'm all Ben has left in this world," Effie had said, with a voice so hollow the words curdled in his belly.

They'd been standing on the curb when Effie said it, Ben at the driver's box. Ben had stared into the shadows of Tradd Street, not yet lit by the sunrise. He'd refused to meet anyone's eyes, only waited for them to take their leave. After they'd made their goodbyes, Daniel helped Honor and Lily into the carriage.

Daniel had thought he might not be able to stand it when Honor and Effie parted. It'd almost been his undoing, watching Effie take Honor's face in her hands. Tears spilled down his sister's cheeks, and Effie's light eyes held a sheen, the lines of her face deepening into a mask of grief and anger. Effie had been a mother and more to Honor. She'd held them together after his parents' deaths; she'd refused to let them sink.

"You take care of that baby," Effie had told Honor roughly. "You bring her back to me one day."

Honor threw her arms around Effie, their faces pressed together in the dark. Finally, Ben, without looking down from his perch, said, "We got to go *now*, Daniel."

The street had been empty, but Daniel noticed a drapery pulled aside one of the windows at the Anson house next door. The horses let out soft whinnies of protest at being made to work yet again; Ben clucked and soothed them as best he could. Still, this was dangerous work. They'd put off the constable long enough, and soon he was set to arrive with more questions than they'd have answers. Daniel's request of Captain Hale had given them time at the wharf, but it wouldn't last forever.

On the sidewalk Gamble waited, leaving the family to their farewells. Daniel doffed his hat, adjusting it longer than was necessary in hopes he might think of something—anything—to say to the two women they were leaving behind.

"Effie, you know where the coffers are kept," he said, low and quiet. "Don't hesitate to use them for yourself—for anything you and Ben might need. I left papers; be sure Mr. Porcher gets them. Today, Effie."

Effie put a hand on Daniel's arm, and he covered it with his own and squeezed, not wanting to let her go. Effie had been so much to them for so long, he didn't know how to tell her goodbye. And why it felt like such a goodbye, he wasn't sure. He knew that one day they'd return to Charleston—Gamble had more than insinuated as such. Still, he had to leave Effie with as much support as possible, and if anyone could help, it was their trusted family lawyer, Louis Porcher.

"I know what to do," Effie said.

"You always do," Daniel said. He kissed her dry cheek, then forced himself away from the comfort of her space.

Gamble stepped up, adjusted his cravat, and whispered so low the words stayed between them. She said, "You are loved, Daniel. Time has nothing on a man such as you."

"Be well," he'd said.

Standing at the balustrade with Honor hours later, Daniel thought about that last exchange with a fair amount of chagrin. *Be well?* There was more he could've said to her. Should've said to her. He had the capacity for eloquence—surely such a leave-taking would've been the time to use it.

The ship crested a high swell, and Honor reached for his arm. He took her elbow and steadied them both. The wind whipped rust-colored ribbons from Honor's bonnet across her face, but she didn't swipe them away, vexed, as she would've before. Instead, she pressed at her stomach, her face paling.

"Will you be sick?" Daniel asked, fingers tightening against the quilted fabric of her pelisse. Her arm felt small inside it, and he damnably helpless.

Honor shook her head, brief and fierce. "I think not. But talk to me, Daniel. For the love of Zeus, distract me. What are you thinking about? Your face is pinched—I can tell it's something unpleasant."

Daniel laughed. "Ah, well. I'm thinking on my last words to Gamble. She expressed affection, and I told her to be safe." He hung his head, gave a bitter laugh. "Christ help me."

Honor slid her arm through his until they were pressed side to side. She squeezed. "If there's but one thing I've learned from our adventure with Gamble, it's everything I thought I knew about the world—about time—has been tossed upon its head. I feel as if I'll never look at it right side up again." She cleared her throat. "But love, Daniel. Love remains."

He didn't respond. Together they watched the horizon. It was a cool blue line where sea met sky: seeming touchable, seeming close. The illusion was astounding when you sailed on open water. And it was just that: an illusion, a lie. Because Daniel didn't know, even if they traveled forever, whether they'd ever be able to touch the edge of the world.

Finally, he leaned close to his sister, and said above the wind and water rush: "I believe it was you Gamble came for, Honor. You, and the baby."

GAMBLE

CHARLESTON
2005

"It won't always be like this, will it?" I said.

I studied the ceiling of the kitchen house, noting the long, hair-thin crack in the cream-colored plaster. It looked almost like a tidal drawing: like a line of seawater, winding its way through marsh grass and oyster-filled pluff mud, emptying into sea. Content with being drained and filled daily by the clockwork of brine and life. I wondered how long it had been there. A century? A mere decade?

Beside me, Tol chuckled without moving. "God, I hope so," he said.

"No, really." I turned on my side, the sisal rug burning a bit against the side of my breast.

Yep: breast. Naked breast. I was practically naked, the Regency dress rucked about my waist. There was a two-hundred-year-old set of short stays around somewhere. I cringed, recalling a flinging. I hoped I'd not ruined it in my quest to be as near to Tolliver as was humanly possible.

I reached out and smoothed one of his eyebrows. This time, Tol let me. "There's no way it'll be like this forever," I said. "We'll get old. You'll get tired of me. One day I'll be wrinkled and saggy, and—heaven forbid—you might have a receding hairline and a potbelly, and our kids'll be off to college or Australia or wherever, and you'll decide I'm too much to deal with. You will no longer find my cute outweighs my crazy."

Tol took a deep breath and sat up, stomach muscles bunching, and braced himself on his elbows. He grimaced when the heel of one long foot knocked against the coffee table, which we'd shoved aside when we'd decided to take the party to the floor.

"Gamble," Tol said with admirable calm, considering he was also mostly naked and lying on an uncomfortable sisal rug. "Look around. Things may change, but damn straight it'll always be an adventure."

I rolled onto my back again and sighed. "I guess I'll have to take your word for it."

I smiled. Gosh, I felt good. Languid and delicious and well loved. I stretched my arms above my head, locking my fingers and feeling the warm pull along my muscles. If we kept this up, a regular yoga practice would be in order.

Tol bent over me and pressed his lips to mine. With one hand he took mine prisoner. I blinked when he brushed the hair back from my face, then traced a line across my jaw, down my neck, along my collarbone. One of his eyebrows went up in a half-question, half-leer, and I giggled. Smart and witty were my kryptonite, and Tol had both in spades.

He cupped my breast and rubbed his thumb back and forth across my nipple. I stopped giggling.

"One day, if we're lucky, we'll be old," Tol said. He abandoned my breast, moved his hand lightly across my belly, and skimmed the rim of my belly button and into the dress where it bunched about my waist. His fingers splayed across my pubic bone, warm. All the blood in my body felt as if it rushed to meet it.

"Tol," I whispered, more than a bit undone. All teasing fled.

Around us, my living room was a mess: the chairs pushed almost into the (thankfully turned *off*) fireplace, the coffee table shoved across the floor so far it was near the dining room table. The ancient sofa cushions askew. And us, sprawled across the floor. There was absolutely nowhere else in the world I'd rather have been at that moment. In all the moments, from then on.

"We've got a lot to do before we grow old," Tol said, close to my ear. The sound was deep and delicious, and he kissed my neck as his fingers moved to find me warm and wet.

It was too much. I arched into his hand, arms straining in his grasp. He laughed again, pressed a far-too-quick kiss to my collarbone.

"Will you grow old with me, Gamble?" Tol said.

Before I could respond, he did something with his fingers which sent a fissure of shock through my entire body.

"Yes," I said. Really, it was more of a gasp.

When his mouth replaced his fingers, I begged.

Upon waking the next morning, I knew something was different. Tol was no longer beside me in bed, and he had been during the night. But his absence wasn't the difference. The difference was, I missed him— the sort of missing that meant someone has become a permanence.

That that person has never been, nor ever will be, anywhere else…even when he's not physically present. That he's a given.

Let me try to explain. It's a bit like a heaven-sent friendship (without the sex, of course). Have you had one of those? They mean even more later in life. You meet someone, some friend, and you become so close it doesn't matter that they came into your life years later than anyone else. You find, in the quiet moments, that the shadow of them—the promise—may've always been there, on the edges of your subconscious. That they'd been part of your makeup from conception. Even inception. A star in your universe you'd noticed only on a deep, dark night, though the light from its gases had burned, stretching to find you, for thousands of years.

Being with Tolliver, finding my way to him in both friendship and love after all these years, was like that for me.

I pulled myself up against the headboard. I'd donned one of Tol's T-shirts—his basketball jersey from when he'd been recruited to play on a team with a bunch of students from the Medical University—and it was like wearing a nightgown. It was cold in the centuries'-old bedroom; I breathed out, watching the trail of my breath spin like smoke and disappear.

A snuffle and bump came from the floor beside the bed, and Kipling put her head on the comforter. I reached out and smoothed one of her ears. She wagged.

"All right, I'm up," I said.

Downstairs Tol paced the creaky floor in his flannel pajama bottoms. No shirt. That's right: I was wearing it.

"Yes, ma'am," he said, into his phone. The stair squeaked, Kipling bumped past me, and Tol looked up. He smiled. "I need to speak with Gamble, but I feel confident we can get away today. Yes, ma'am, we will."

"What?" I whisper-shouted. "Who is that?"

Tol held a finger to his lips and rolled his eyes. "Goodbye, Miss Saralee. See you soon."

"Saralee Hutto?" I said, hopping from the last step and sliding a bit in my fluffy socks. I grinned up at him. "Did she call you from a rotary phone?" I cracked myself up.

Tol flipped his phone shut and walked straight for me, all hip-slung, like Wyatt Earp at the O.K. Corral. But with a happier ending. He wrapped me up, and I let myself be wrapped. When we were done he held up his phone.

"We got to get to Aiken," he said. "Miss Saralee and Miss Corrine have a painting they think we should see."

Any time I've ever driven away from Charleston, I've felt an odd combination of euphoria and longing, in a place I suppose most would call the gut. It didn't matter if I crested the cantilevered Cooper River Bridge (soon to be replaced by the new cable-stayed bridge in construction beside it) or waited on the drawbridge at pretty Wappoo Creek on my way toward Savannah—or even if I took multi-laned, concrete-encased Interstate 26 and headed west: I felt it, each and every time. It was both a freeing and a clutch. As if I'd been released into the world, yet at the same time, pulled ever backward.

Now that I'd been in the past—now I knew for sure I'd lived at least one lifetime there—the feeling made more sense. History always seemed to me, as art historian and conservator of old stuff, ever present. I never could shake the impression that time was always doing its loop-de-loops in the air around us when we walked through the present—like a stunt pilot at a Depression-era air show, corkscrewing in a Red Baron biplane and fearless of the unforgiving ground.

And I, a tomboy in dungarees: monkeyed up on some fence with eyes glued to the sky, while everyone else was stuck in the future, looking down at their phones. I just couldn't understand why I alone could see the contrails.

But there was more to it than that. This was Charleston. And Charleston was complicated. The city was well over 300 years old: it'd lived much more than a little. Charleston had seen canoes and U-Boats, hosted pirates and princes, been bloodied and bruised and shamefaced and proud. It told, ever and always, an unflinching American story. No wonder it captivated—no wonder it was so difficult to leave behind.

The city's history was heavy. You can't have been home to the New World's largest slave port and think it's all going to be sunshine and mint juleps, all charm and manners. Every place you set your foot in this city has been touched by human bondage. Black, white, and brown; freed, indentured, and enslaved lives have intertwined here since the beginning. For a visitor, especially, it gives a simple walk through a private, lush, gorgeously fragrant Charleston courtyard a heaviness you might otherwise miss, to know the softening bricks you trod were trod not so long ago by people without freedom.

So maybe it was the past which clung to me as I left the city, or maybe it was slavery. Maybe it's the fact that there was ancestral memory in my bones: that my past self remembered my present. Perhaps we all feel like this, leaving a place we love. Letting go is never easy.

None of the above, however, explained why I felt like this each time I left Charleston on a temporary trip. After all, back then at least, I always came back.

When Tolliver and I drove away from Charleston, we took rural SC Hwy 61 toward Aiken. He drove, and I watched as winter marsh and mudflats turned to sod farms, as young pines broke with yellow pasture. The sky was pale and thin, the sun burning through it like light through a shroud.

I felt the freeing, and the clutch. And wondered if it would always be thus.

෴

We didn't talk much at the beginning of our drive to Aiken. Good heavens, was it nice to sit with someone in comfortable silence. Some-one with whom you felt nary a need to make small talk—to fill those terrifying lulls. I loved weather, but even weather as a topic could be exhausting.

It'd always been like this with Tolliver and me. We could talk, or we couldn't. In fact, we often sat at brunch, he with a newspaper and I with a book, reading in companionable silence, despite any hubbub about us. I think maybe you must have confidence enough in a com-panion to know that every space need not be filled. Being present is enough.

I didn't question why Tol didn't start a conversation, or have anything to say on the two-and-a-half-hour drive through the South Carolina midlands. The truth is, he had plenty to say to me, and I to him. Years of things to say.

Last night I'd come close to telling him everything about his an-cestors. 'Round about two a.m., I rose to use the bathroom. When I returned to the bed, Tol was awake and waiting.

Hands folded in his lap, he'd switched on the bedside lamp I'd left off because I'd not wanted to wake him. The light made an aged, yellow, three-quarter moon on the tatted spread, illuminating Tol's long fingers, his bony knuckles, the richness of his skin.

"Hey," I said, slipping in beside him.

"Hey," he said.

"I tried to be quiet," I said.

"It's impossible to be quiet in a house as old as this," Tol said. If it were possible, his voice deepened in the comfortable silence of the night-filled kitchen house. There was a pregnant quality to it, as if his words expanded to fill the room's corners.

I tucked my hands beneath my head. Something was up. "What is it?" I said.

"You were going to tell me something last night," Tol said. "But then…" He paused.

"Then," I said. "There was sex."

"Yes," he said. "But I've the feeling you need to tell me about what happened back there. It seemed important. This seems as good a time as any."

Oh, Tolliver Jackson. I knew I was about to rock his world. Steady as he might blow, Tol was a man of history. A man who'd wanted to know his entire life about his origins. Growing up a foster kid, in and out of relatives' houses and in strangers', Tol had never felt like he'd truly belonged to anything, or anyone. Instead, he'd adapted, much like a chameleon: able to fit in with any crowd; able to alter himself, on the outside at least, so he blended and made sense, wherever he was.

At first, Tol changed himself to suit others, he'd told me once, years ago, when I'd mentioned it. He said: what young, orphaned boy ever wants to leave a warm house once he's found one? But then as he got older, Tol said, he realized he liked adapting, and he did it well. He liked people—all kinds of people—and had an intense curiosity about them and about his surroundings. He enjoyed putting people at ease, and he felt oddly comfortable almost anywhere.

He was a natural gentleman: just a bit more proper, a bit more courteous, more than a bit more intellectually curious than most. In the end, he realized—no matter where he was or what role he was filling—he was always himself inside.

It made Tol perplexingly self-assured, and I knew it was in part where he got all that innate confidence. But I also knew he'd gotten it from somewhere, and someone, else.

"I do need to tell you something. Lots of somethings," I said. "Are you ready?"

An eyebrow went up. He said, "Of course." As if this were nothing. Of course Tol was ready. The thing was: as it turned out, I wasn't.

A nasty knot formed in my belly and I pushed up to sit against the headboard. I struggled with words that had become oddly gummy and strange in my mouth, like taffy (which I'd never liked, not even as a child). I felt then, that if I told the story, if I revisited Cooper's death one more time, the guilt could eat me alive.

Tol's face gentled in the pale sheath of light coming through the sheer curtains. It was rare that Catherine forgot to turn off her back porch light, but that night she had.

"It's okay, Gamble," he said. "We can wait."

It was *not* okay, of course. Had the situation been reversed, I would've insisted he tell me everything. I'd have made his life hell—certainly sleep impossible—until I got all the information I needed at the exact moment I needed it. However, Tol was not me, which was why we worked.

Remember being a kid at the top of the high dive? Watching other kids jump and flip, squealing the whole way down, emerging from the water with wide, toothy grins. You're ready, excited, and you climb that ladder with all the strength and bravado available in your little body. But once you're there, toes curled over the aluminum edge—in spite of how hard you worked to get there—fear mixes with the blood in your veins, racing all the way to your fingertips. All of a sudden the chlorinated water into which you've been so ready to leap seems dangerous. And despite the other kids cheering you on, despite the promise of a Coke or candy from your dad if you do it, you're paralyzed. You become convinced that if you jump, if you turn the wrong way, you might hit the water at an angle that will hurt.

Maybe, I considered, despite our long journey to this point, Tol was just as scared of upending his history as I was.

Last night, neither of us had been ready. Today, it was time to be brave.

In the car, after I'd said all the words—and there'd been a lot of words—I watched Tol. He tapped the fingers of one hand lightly on the steering wheel, rubbed the others hard at his crown, as if trying to wake himself up. For a moment, in the winter-thin light, I saw both Honor and Cooper in the impenetrable look on his face, in his changeable hazel eyes.

We'd pulled off the highway to talk. At present we sat, car idling, in the forgotten corner of an abandoned country gas station. Sand and dirt had crawled and wind-rushed across the once-paved parking lot, erasing any semblance of painted lines. The storefront was boarded up, a "closed" sign hanging by one rusted nail, swinging in the lazy breeze. The pumps had long been drained, the tanks removed. There were no trees, the store flanked by cotton fields, fluffy as snow and ready to be harvested.

The last time this joint had hopped, I imagined, had likely been in the 1950s or '60s. In my mind I watched an ancient Ford truck pull up, farmhands leap off the tailgate; saw the screen door swing open and slam; heard a jolly greeting from inside. The phantom farmhands walked out with glass-bottle Cokes in hand. They tipped them to the sky, mid-century sunshine flashing off the embossed bases.

Tol took a breath through his nose, and air filled his belly and lungs like a wave unfurling. He blew a long, slow breath out through pursed lips. He did it twice more, and I waited.

"Are you meditating?" I said. He was a constant surprise, this guy.

Tol took three more full breaths before answering. I tamped down on my natural (and toddleresque) inclination to interrupt. My fingers itched to give him a good side tickle, just to see what would happen.

Yes, I realize this was not the place and time and I was a grown woman, and Tolliver had a darned sight more to consider and think about and deal with than me. Still.

"No," he said, at last. "Meditation with you around would be a miracle. I'm doing some diaphragmatic breathing."

I raised an eyebrow.

Tol smiled, and there was a such a combination of affection and indulgence in it, I felt in equal parts enamored and squirmy. He said, "Basically, it's deep breathing. I find it calming, and helpful."

"Hm," I said, nodding. Seemed legit to me. It explained how collected he was, in almost every situation. Maybe I'd try it sometime.

"Maybe you should try it sometime," Tol said.

"It's a lot to take in, isn't it?" I said.

This was the very definition of an understatement. Because I'd just told him he was the descendant of Honor Petigru and Cooper Perrineau. Which meant he was also related to Daniel, Effie, and Ben, and he had a host of Black and white ancestors whose stories he could claim, finally. He had free people of color and Quakers, artists and horsemen, people of great bravery in his blood.

Tolliver's Charleston roots spread wide, like a southern live oak's (*quercus Virginia*, in case you're wondering). Like the Angel Oak on Johns Island—whose branches cast over 17,000 square feet of shade—Tol's roots fanned just beneath the surface of the loamy, water-filled soil. They touched and tangled with the history of the city, knuckling and kneeing up beneath the cobblestones and asphalt. Cracking through to the surface of things.

Here's the thing, though: it wouldn't have mattered if Tol had been none of that. If his people had been plain, average, anybody. History lives within us, and its knowledge can and should be a gut check. But we make of ourselves what we will. No matter what, Tolliver was a *man*. A real man. The best one I knew.

"Effie told me something in the alley, the night I left 1805," I said, and though my voice cracked on the words I soldiered on. "I was despondent, really. Daniel, Lily, and Honor had left for the ship, and I couldn't seem to hold myself together—not like the rest of them could. Maybe it's being from an easier time, especially next to the hardships they'd already had to endure. I don't know. But I fell apart. I felt so guilty. I'd come to help Honor and Cooper, to save their baby. But when Cooper was killed, I felt I'd failed."

I swiped the tears I couldn't keep from falling with the back of a hard, impatient hand, unsure if I could continue.

"What did Effie say?" Tol said gently.

I tried for courage. "She said things don't always work out. That just because I saved paintings, it didn't mean I could save Cooper, or for that matter, any one of them. She said what happened next was bigger than any of us."

Tol reached out and took my hand. "It's mindboggling," he said. He tucked his chin and paused. When he blinked back emotion, the sight clutched at my throat. I set my other hand on top, Go Team-style, and squeezed.

My own tears had already leaked again when Tol said, "These are my people."

"They really are," I managed, words warbly but true.

There was such wonder in his eyes, it took my breath. Tol said, "I never…I just never imagined I belonged to anyone. I thought my story had been lost."

And that was it. I'd carry the guilt over Cooper's death for the rest of my life. I'd always question whether I could've changed what happened on Ancrum's Wharf. I knew, better than most, that when someone is killed it does more than extinguish a single life: it erases the possibility of ancestry, of bloodline, of more than one future. No matter how awful or evil or necessary a killing may be, this is the very fact of what will never come after. A killing is always and only about loss.

In that moment, though, I knew my time in 1805 had been worth it. That it had meaning. And it'd been the right—the only—thing to do. I knew this, because there was Tolliver Jackson.

"You carry within you multitudes," I said.

Really, I whispered it, and thank goodness we were alone in a car on the side of a rural highway in backroads South Carolina, because I could barely get the words out. I swiped a tear from beneath his eye.

Tol claimed my hand, and held it against his heart.

GAMBLE

AIKEN, SOUTH CAROLINA
WINTER, 2005

It was apparent Miss Saralee and Miss Corrine did not often receive visitors, because before they let us see the painting, they had us sit through high tea. There were tiny ham, tuna, and pimento cheese sandwiches; cheese straws and potato salad; dainty Limoges finger bowls painted with cherries (I lifted one, discreetly, to check the maker's mark. I am, if nothing else, a historian) and filled with sliced kiwi, strawberries, and blueberries; multiple pours of black Indian tea with cream; and at last, a silver tray papered with profiteroles, an assortment of chocolate truffles, and, delightfully, Oreos.

"I like double-stuffed," Miss Corrine said, nut-brown eyes flaring with delight, before biting in.

I snickered, Tol squeezed my knee under the drape of the tablecloth, and Miss Saralee smiled, black kiwi seeds caught between her front teeth.

"There's been a change with you two since last time," Miss Saralee announced.

I thought she'd expound, but she sat like the Sphinx at Giza, and didn't so much as blink. Tol and I looked at each other. It was his turn to raise an eyebrow. I knew that look. It said, *Have at it, babe.*

"Oh, leave them be, Saralee," Miss Corrine said. "Can't you tell they're in the first flush? They're like to get all het up if you pry."

See: Miss Corrine said it like this, all sweet and folksy and helpful-seeming, but there was a distinct twinkle in her eyes. I don't think she meant one word of it. I think, just like Tol and me, these ladies had a long and permanent connection. They could say one thing and mean another, and no one else would know what they intended.

Which is all to say, I think Miss Corrine totally meant: *Come on, Saralee, make 'em talk. Get to the juicy stuff.*

"They are grown adults, Corrine," Miss Saralee countered, then swiped a tongue over her teeth. She pressed her lips together and opened them on a pop. "Lord have mercy, Tolliver here is the most fully grown man I've ever seen." She leaned across the table, her shaky elbow bumping a teacup. I reached to steady it. Big mistake: it made her turn on me.

"And you," Miss Saralee said, a lioness recognizing the weakest antelope in the herd. "You're looking rather rosy, rather satisfied. Young lady, you're even more in love than the last time I saw you. I don't blame you one bit. He's a catch."

"Mm-hmm," Miss Corrine agreed on a long, impressively lascivious hum.

"Me!" I said, determined not to remain alone. "What about him? He loved me last time too." Indignant, I rubbed my scapulae against the ornate mahogany backrest of my chair, then crossed my arms. Tol vibrated with silent laughter.

I gave the ladies my best stare-down, then turned to my partner in crime. He should've looked incongruous, at six foot five, in the ornate chair, a full silver tea service set before him. (The ladies had requested he pour.) He'd even dressed down a bit for the trip, as he'd been rather limited with the clothes he had at my house: dark jeans, a round-collared dove-gray sweater, and a pair of matte black leather oxfords, scuffed to perfection. His beard had grown thick in the weeks I'd been away, and I was glad he'd not shaved it yet—it made him look like a medieval knight who could also deliver a lecture at Oxford. This was Tol in informal mode—his darned outfit still looked tailored. And I was almost positive his sweater was one hundred percent cashmere.

Miss Saralee waved a gnarled hand in the air: a physical *pshaw*. "Oh, he was too. Anybody could see it. You just had it written all over your face, dear."

Well. That's true. As I said, I'm no poker player.

Tol folded his napkin and set it to the side of his place setting: an elegant effort at *let's move on*.

"That was delicious," he said, as if we'd not just endured ruthless teasing by two wily nonagenarians. "It was so good, in fact, I can't eat another bite. How about it, ladies: is it time to see the painting?"

Miss Saralee narrowed milky eyes, and they almost disappeared into her wrinkles. For a moment I thought the push had been the wrong move. But then she nodded.

"Yes, I do believe it's time," she said. She looked to Miss Corrine, who gave a regal incline of her head. "I asked Baker to put the painting in the library, under the lamps, so y'all could give it a study."

It took us a while to make it to the library, though it was merely situated on the opposite side of the house. "Cattywampus from here," Miss Corrine said. I took her arm, and Tol Miss Saralee's, and we shuffled across the foyer, into the formal dining room, and through a large cased opening into the library.

It was a classic late-Victorian home library: there was a fireplace framed in Art Nouveau tile and flanked by low, open bookshelves, the highest topped with matching marble busts of Apollo and Diana. The shelves were painted a deep green to complement the dusty mauve walls. A long line of tall windows composed the entire south-facing wall, spilling light inside. Opposite the ornate fireplace was a wall of floor-to-ceiling bookshelves, with a skinny black iron rolling ladder. I cannot lie: I felt lust in my heart upon seeing it. I'd always wanted to live in a house with a library big enough for a rolling ladder.

Nearest the wall of windows, facing in, as if its occupant might address the room with a speech, was an 1870s standing desk. I noticed a very old guest book open atop, which of course had my historian's brain galloping off like a runaway horse.

I took a step toward it, but one of the ladies said, "There, you see? The likeness is uncanny."

I turned. The painting hung on the center partition of the wall of books. Mounted above was a brass picture light, turned on.

Tol and I found ourselves standing before the painting, side by side. We didn't touch.

After a long moment, Tol said, "It's Paris. The *Jardin des Tuileries.*"

"It's you," I said.

DANIEL

Spring, 1812
Jardin des Tuileries, Paris

"I never thought you'd be one for painting *en plein air*," Lily said. It was said with affection and indulgence, and Daniel lifted his head from a study of his canvas. "Neither did I," he said. "But here we are."

Here we are. He took a step back from the easel and considered the words, glancing at Lily, who'd already moved on. She and Euphemia had only just arrived to join him for a midday picnic, and Lily spread the blanket on the grass in the shade of the chestnut trees. He was glad of her company, which was an increasing comfort. And besides—at this he could not help but smile—she kept him fed. He couldn't remember if he'd breakfasted that morning or not. As he awoke with an incessant need to paint, he rather thought not.

Lily stood and brushed down her striped skirts. The pink ribbon at her straw bonnet flitted becomingly in the breeze sweeping south from the Tuileries Palace. She looked past him, wrinkling her nose.

"Coli, no!" Lily said. "Leave her be!"

"She smells the eggs," the girl said, holding a large basket aloft as she approached, skirts bouncing about the ankles of her boots. "*Non*," she ordered, sternly, and the brown-and-white Briard sniffing the underside of the basket ducked its shaggy head.

"Come, Colibri," Daniel said to the dog. He set down his brush with no real regret and clapped once. The dog rushed into his knees and he bent to give her a good scrub. He said, "Why we named her 'hummingbird' I'll never know."

"She was small at first," Lily said. She held out her arms and Euphemia deposited the basket into them. "*Merci, mon cheri.*"

Euphemia's gold-brown eyes went wide, and she tried and failed to hide a snaggle-toothed smile. She had of late lost two front teeth, and it gave her a ragamuffin lisp. "Don't you remember, Papa? Coli flitted from sofa to chair in the drawing room as a pup. She was so quick we could scarce see her paws."

"I remember," Lily said, settling onto the blanket and dispensing with the dishes and food. "She upended the table with the red china urn on it. Your papa attempted to patch it with his glue, but it was lost."

Daniel took the rag from his pocket and wiped his hands, then joined her. He said, "Some urns are not meant for this world."

"Come, Effie, eat," Lily said, but the girl was off, dog bounding in her wake.

"A moment," she called over her shoulder. "I see *Monsieur* Henri and Papillon! Coli needs a run!"

Lily looked to him and Daniel shrugged. "Let her go," he advised, watching as Effie skipped along the white sand and gravel path which had, just two years before, hosted Emperor Bonaparte's wedding procession. "We'll watch from here. She'll return when her stomach growls."

"Effie, too?" Lily said, smiling.

It was their sixth Paris spring. However, each spring felt like the first, for Daniel knew he'd never grow accustomed to the season's beauty, how it washed the city in pastel and petal. Paris seemed more herself in spring than in any other season.

Their first spring, in 1805, was a blur: looking back, it was as if he'd swiped the heel of a hand across a wet canvas, the image smeared beyond recognition. It had been rainy, cold, and gray. They'd all been in mourning, especially Honor. But his sister soldiered on, and when she gave birth to Euphemia in May, just nine weeks after their arrival, the sun came out. At least, he pondered, rather unfairly, it had for Lily and him.

Their Effie was already a beauty at seven years of age, even with her missing front teeth. Her hair was thick, the deep brown of mahogany, and in that sense looked so like her mother's. Her eyes, hazel but with more gold in them than Honor's, were deep-set, framed by thick lashes. She had her father's strong bones, and there was a determined set to her face, no matter her mood. Her skin was much like her namesake's: the color of heavily creamed coffee.

In the first year of Effie's life, they'd wondered who she'd come to resemble most—Honor or Cooper. When Effie first entered the world she was pale as snow, with inky blue eyes. But this, of course, changed, and with that change came an exotic quality to the child which her aura of self-determination—especially in one so young, and in a girl at that—merely highlighted.

It had been luck, her looks. There was no other way to put it. Because it made it so Effie could pass as white. She could rightly call them "Papa Daniel" and *"Mère* Lily," and be the orphaned child of an invented cousin.

"Such lovely skin," came the inevitable comments at the flower market or at food stands in the garden. "Is the child Italian?"

"Her father was Spanish, a minor Castilian lord," they'd answer. "The entire family lost to influenza."

A promise of noble birth overtook the gossips' need for veracity, and Effie was soon left alone, the questions fading. Daniel and Lily, though but a court artist and his wife, were afforded a rather Bohemian amount of permission. (Parisians were no strangers to scandal.) They lived their lives in relative peace.

But each time Daniel looked at Effie he saw Honor and Cooper both. She had Honor's fierce determination and fine sense of humor, coupled with Cooper's innate dignity of spirit, his quiet and keen intelligence. She took to books as quickly as Cooper had as a boy—turning pages as if they might catch fire in her hands.

Honor left them the very week Effie turned nine months old: the week Effie was weaned. Honor loved Effie—Daniel was certain of it—but looking upon the child, remembering the loss of Cooper, proved unbearable. In those first months Honor was despondent, often passing Effie off to the wet nurse, and Daniel wondered, then, if he'd ever again see his sister's smile. When Ben sent word that Effie—grown-up Effie—had taken ill and could no longer manage the house and, in turn, the familial accounts, Honor returned to Charleston, leaving the baby behind.

Seeing Honor to the wharf at Le Havre was a brutal undertaking— one of the hardest things Daniel had ever done. Honor had grown haggard those months in Paris, her face leached of its natural color. Effie had been born premature, and they'd all spent weeks scared for mother and child. At no point had Honor been in bloom with motherhood. Lily told him later that Honor cried each time she nursed Effie; that she handed off the baby immediately after, as if Honor couldn't bear to hold her.

Until that last month, when Honor stopped crying. She stared into nothingness, baby Effie in arms and Honor's face as emotionless as stone.

It was Lily, finally, who said to him, when Honor couldn't, "Let her go, Daniel. Honor will die if she stays."

Daniel would not recall the intensity, the anger and disappointment, of their parting words. Seven years later, he wondered if he knew anything at all about the depths of his sister's despair, the secret inner reaches of her mother's heart. Perhaps it was unfair to judge Honor so harshly. What did he, a man and not a father, know of any of it?

This is how he to tried to think, and to feel.

Long ago, Daniel had ceased feeling pain when he looked at Effie. Now, all he felt was love.

It was rare for Daniel to paint in large scale, as he did that day in the Tuileries. His miniature portraits were as in demand in Paris as they'd been in Charleston. Because of Lily's inheritance they did not rely solely on his commissions, but Daniel loved to work. He found himself daily visiting the Tuileries Palace, or the home of some member of the grand bourgeois, painting couples, wives, children. Once he'd even painted a viscount's cat.

"Be certain to capture her whiskers," the viscount had insisted with a flourish of one ruffled cuff, standing at Daniel's shoulder as he worked a graphite sketch of a portly Turkish Angora. "They have an air of insouciance."

"*Oui*, my lord," Daniel had answered.

Today's work was for fun. For some time he'd wanted to capture Effie in the Tuileries Garden, her favorite of the parks they visited. He hoped at some point that he might send it to Honor, Effie the elder, and Ben back in Charleston. His niece, however, proved as impossible to catch as the small red ball she tossed for Coli.

"Effie, do come," Daniel called, when she and the Briard were back within earshot. He watched as she detached herself from Henri Charpentier and his gaggle of political sycophants. The old barrister blew her a kiss and the girl pretended to catch it. This is how Daniel knew Monsieur Charpentier, despite his reputation of imperiousness, to be a gentleman. He was always tenderhearted with Effie.

Effie preferred the company of adults. Daniel knew he and Lily should remedy this—find the girl companions her own age—but Effie, though generous with her time and attention when it came to other children, was easily bored. She much preferred solitude, and she'd rather be outside in the fresh air than anywhere else.

Effie and Coli arrived at his side. "*Oui*, Papa. What is it?"

"I wish to paint you and Coli," Daniel said. "It'll mean being still, just for a bit. Can you and the dog accomplish this?"

"A miniature portrait?" she asked, her face alight with pleasure.

Daniel reached out and tucked a thick oak-colored curl into her bonnet. He gently cupped her chin and smiled. He couldn't help but smile. "I'm thinking it must be a grand piece, so as to capture your favorite garden in its vernal glory. Perhaps I'll make two, to send one to your mother and your aunt Effie across the sea. But your *mere* and I must have one for ourselves. What do you think?"

Effie's smile widened, and it made a dimple in her left cheek. Cooper had had one in the very same spot.

"I think it a grand idea," she said, like a little grown-up. "But I shall have a time of it holding Coli for long. You must paint quickly."

GAMBLE

AIKEN, SOUTH CAROLINA
2005

"It didn't occur to us until after you'd left," Miss Corrine said. "But the resemblance is uncanny."

"She must be a relation of yours," Miss Saralee said. Still, Tol and I had yet to turn round from the painting. "You can see it in the eyes."

"The bone structure," Miss Corrine countered.

I cleared my throat, leaning forward. "The dimple," I said.

The girl was, quite obviously, related to Tolliver. Or, rather, he to her. He was one of her line. It was written in the indention in her left cheek, which matched his. In the alert and curious cock of her head, the gold cast to her hazel eyes. Her hand where it perched on the dog's shaggy head was slender and long-fingered. You could already tell she'd be taller than most: she was gangly, but would one day be graceful.

I wasn't sure Tol would see it. We rarely see ourselves as we are. It's difficult to find anything familiar in an ancestor's painted face, though many try. I've seen this happen time and again at the Galliard, especially during fundraising galas. Members of old Charleston families clad in custom tuxedos and glittering designer gowns, standing before portraits of Draytons or Middletons or Pinckneys, wondering aloud at the seeming unflattering line of an ancestor's long nose (*it was the style, an effort at ancient elegance*, I tell them: an attempt at appeasement) or the irregular arch of an eyebrow. It's not often they truly see themselves there.

Daniel's portraits were different, though. I'd noticed this years before, when I'd first studied his miniatures. Like the work of Ed Malbone, Daniel's held a sort of luminescence: a glow, or flush, in the cheeks; a pearl to the skin, which others of the period lacked. His people lifted off the ivory, fully dimensional. They were life-like, animated—so real and rich in detail I always imagined I might see the sitter on the street two hundred years later, choosing a piece of fruit from a produce bin in the grocery store, or even buying a taco from a food truck. Great artists are always like this: their influence takes on an expansiveness, widens its circle like the orbit of a far-flung planet.

Historians know the masters can step out from the ether of time and into the present, and create as if nothing has changed. Great artists do so much more than chronicle a place in time: no matter the form imaginative interpretation takes on the canvas, they paint us as we wish to be, as we could be, as we are. The truly gifted create images that—no matter how magical, rare, or even odd—ignite a sense of recognition in the viewer. Because of this, the faces they illuminate serve as mirrors. It's entirely up to us to decide whether we believe what we see.

"I've walked in that garden dozens of times," Tol said. He leaned just a bit toward me but didn't break his gaze from the painting. "You remember the ornament I brought you from Paris? It came from a market not far from here."

The tiny silver figurine of Notre Dame. I hung it on my tree each Christmas, by a loop of red velvet. "Did it really," I said.

Miss Corrinne piped up: "She looks a bit like my aunt Sadie."

"She sure does!" Miss Saralee agreed, turning toward her. "Remember, Sadie married that Marvin Eggleston who wanted to sell the lawyer's file. Said it was 'too heavy and dark' for the house."

"Oh yes," Miss Corrine said. "They liked the modern style." Both women grimaced as if someone had made an untoward odor.

Tol and I met each other's eyes. "This is surreal," I whispered.

Miss Corrine shuffled over to a green damask sofa and plopped herself down. She brushed off her trouser legs. "Wasn't Aunt Sadie named after some Frenchwoman?" she said. "The last name started with a P."

"Perrineau?" I said, my voice pitched high.

Have you ever experienced *déjà vu*? Yes. Of course, I know everyone has. I don't mean the slight impression that you've been in a similar situation or repeated a conversation with a friend. I mean serious *déjà vu*: the kind which sends an animalistic prickle down your spine, to the base where Darwin insisted that once upon a time we all had tails. The kind of remembering that stops you in your tracks—which makes it feel as if time lays its hand, palm down, on the nape of your neck, and curls its cool fingers in toward your throat.

I felt *déjà vu* in that library, and I know Tol felt it too. The low afternoon sun broke the window line on the south wall, blazing in through the 1880s panes. It sent dust motes into the air—invisible until now, but present in any old room, especially libraries—glinting, as if someone flung grains of mica. If those grains materialized into a swirl above our heads, some wizardry of classical physics, I wouldn't be surprised.

"That's it!" Miss Corrine smiled broadly. "Sadie Perrineau. She married a Hampton."

"Uh-huh. Regretted it, too, I bet." Miss Saralee made her way to the couch. "I need to sit down," she announced.

See, this is the part where you'd have thought I'd say something like *my sentiments exactly*. Because the realization that time has been playing a game of high-stakes poker with your life, and the lives of your loved ones, should take the legs out from under just about anybody.

But I didn't say it, because I didn't feel that way. I felt...relieved. Fully realized, there in that made-for-sci-fi moment. As close to content as I'd ever been.

I felt as though our story was, despite its plot twists, heading toward the conclusion it was always meant to have.

I went over the names in my mind: Sadie Perrineau. Daughter of Benjamin, from his first marriage. Married a Hampton.

Corrine Hampton Wilson. The lawyer's file. The miniature of Honor found inside. It was all connected. We were all connected.

Then, a thought sparked. It was just like the time a bird flew into a pristine, clear window in the house where I grew up. It was spring, and I stood at the kitchen sink, washing dishes while admiring my mother's native azaleas blooming a peachy orange just beneath the sill. And out of nowhere, *wham*. Right before my eyes.

"Tol," I said, hollow. "Have you been back before?"

Tol stepped back from the painting, rubbed his chin, and just as I was about to repeat myself, looked down at me.

"No," he said. "No, I'd feel it." Then he reached out an arm and folded me into his side. I wrapped my arms around his waist and clung, comfort and relief and the simple, strong sense of safety washing through me at the connection. Tol's wingspan was wide. Thank God for that.

And it *was* a relief, I thought, looking again at the girl's face in the painting—at the familiar intelligence in her familiar hazel eyes. Because one time traveler in the family was enough.

Tol shifted our bodies without releasing me. "May we take the painting down and turn it over?" he said to the ladies.

They'd sunk into the couch like sand dollars in wet sand, and the room was warm in the sun. Miss Corrine had dozed off.

"Go right ahead," said Miss Saralee.

"Okay," Tol said, under his breath, like a prayer.

I let go, and he took the thick gilt frame gently in hand and lifted the painting from its nail. He paused for a moment, not turning it over yet. I watched his face. I'd rarely seen it this uncertain. The lines of his bones had gone soft, and there was a pensiveness, a wonderment there, which made him look like nothing so much as a boy.

"By the window," I suggested.

When we stood beneath the window in the streaming sun, Tol turned the painting over. Like many aged works, it'd been reframed and perhaps even re-matted over the years, and stock plywood board covered the back.

Tol took one of his yoga breaths. Holding my gaze, he said, "Miss Saralee, does Baker have a toolbox we could borrow?"

It is delicate work, prying the lid off years of people's stories. This is what one does, of course, each time one peels back the layers on a piece of art. It could be as simple (and as discommoding) as cleaning away the grit and age from an urn found buried in a nineteenth-century privy, or peeling (ever so gently) the tacking back from a painting to see what other colors (and therefore, other paintings) may lie beneath, or even wiping dust from the fragile, mud-stained pages of a soldier's journal. There's delicacy in all of it, and a conservator trains for this. Because, honestly: you never know what you're going to get.

There were two other layers of fiberboard beneath the painting, discovered with the help of Baker's trusty toolbox. We relocated the guest book, then draped a tablecloth over the standing desk by the window and laid the painting face down upon it, and everyone—including Baker—watched closely as I used his tiniest straight-edge screwdriver and a small iron pry to pull the pieces of fiberboard away. If I'd been in my lab at the Galliard, I'd have had access to my scalpels and brushes. But you've got to work with the gifts you've been given, as my mom always said.

Tucked between two layers of fiberboard was a piece of paper folded into an envelope. It was twice the size of a modern envelope, vellum, made mostly of rag and straw, and I brushed off my hands before I peeled it from the board with painstaking care. Beneath, something had been written on the wood in scrolling nineteenth-century penmanship, with what was sure to be India ink. The removal of the envelope kept the words inside a pale frame of virgin board, freeing them from the darkening cast of age. The writing looked as clean and crisp as when it'd been written. It was Daniel's hand.

I read aloud: "Euphemia Honora Petigru, aged 7 years & her dog, Colibri. In the *Jardin Tuileries*, her favorite. May 1812. By her papa the artist, Daniel Matthew Petigru. For her family in Paris and in Charleston, now & ever after."

I looked up at Tol. "It's the baby," I breathed. "Baby Euphemia."

There was an odd expression on his face—it's difficult to describe. But joy and wonder were there. And everything else fell away.

Tol turned the painting over. He touched Euphemia's face, lightly, with the tip of one long finger.

I let him: the conservator in me didn't even flinch. For one, I get to lay hands on all the art I want, and I am well aware it's a privilege. It's just like what they tell you about the benefit of kids learning to write in cursive: there is an undeniable hand-mind connection when you write this way. Something clicks with the curving, unbroken line of ink and language. Something keeps. This is because you touch it: you do it yourself. It's the same with art—any art, but especially the old stuff.

When you lay hands on the layers of paint or the aged wood or the slick of carved stone, you feel the artist reach out from the past—from a past which becomes less of a past, more of a just-a-minute-ago. You hear it when the artist whispers in your ear: *I made this. See, we're not all so different.*

Second, I let Tol touch the painting because it was his. Euphemia was his.

The library of the Hutto house felt *right*, even in its high-ceilinged grandeur and the unblinking marble gazes of Diana and Apollo. *We* were right—all five of us, the two old ladies, the horse-loving Irishman, Tol, and me. Light sifted inside the room as the sun banked behind some cloud—some conglomeration of water molecules recycled a thousand years over. The sunlight drew its blanketing shadow across the careworn Turkish rugs, over Baker standing solid and silent near the fireplace, over the damask sofa where Miss Corrine still snoozed, over the matching chairs, over the priceless furniture and the crackled leather spines of the well-loved books. The shadow was not foreboding, but instead a welcome shade, gray with our shared humanity. With our inexplicable human affinity for mystery and doubt, love and nonsense. We were the shade.

I got the feeling I always did when history moved through a moment like this, when it left me shaky from some sort of divine adrenaline: from the knowledge that something *big* was happening. I wanted to spread my arms wide, proclaim my love of the world and everyone in it. In short, I wanted to dork out completely, to Pollyanna the heck out of everything.

But this moment was not mine.

Tol traced the dimple in the girl's cheek. It matched the one currently revealed in his own, which had popped out with his smile. He did not take his eyes from the painting.

"I'm hers," he said.

DANIEL

Tradd Street
1832

The morning light in the barn was dim, his joints stiff and his step uncertain, but Daniel was determined to climb. It had been twenty-seven
years since he'd last been in this place—twenty-seven years since he'd
returned to Charleston. There had been a time, when their Effie was in
middle childhood, when he thought he'd surely come home, after all,
but the years had passed with inexplicable swiftness.

There were new horses in the stalls, Cleo having died long ago. They
were beauties—thoroughbreds bred for show and efficiency. Ben had
seen to that. Years ago, Ben and his family had taken up residence in the
kitchen house, and in addition to acting as de facto head groom for two
neighboring families, his son, Erasmus, was a renowned saddle-maker
with an office on the peninsula and a tannery outside town.

Daniel had gifted his portion of the Tradd Street house to Honor
years before, and Honor refused anyone but Ben. She did not want to
sell, but she didn't live there, so Daniel didn't know how she used the
main house. He thought perhaps it was for meetings with like-minded
women, other proponents of southern anti-slavery, like the Grimke
sisters and the rest. Theirs was a hushed and relatively secret society—
certain to be small in number—but it existed, and Daniel wouldn't have
been at all surprised if Honor, and the house, had something to do with
it.

If not that, then what else Honor did with the house, he couldn't
guess. She'd married for the second time, to Parker St. Denis. A man
surprisingly well suited to Honor, younger than she by eight years, theirs
his own second marriage. St. Denis seemed equipped for Honor's tendency toward individualism, allowing her unusual freedom and space.
Daniel was glad of it. He did not believe Honor would've survived
otherwise.

Daniel appraised the ladder to the loft. It still seemed sturdy. He
could climb it: he was sixty-seven years old, not for the grave yet. He

touched the pocket of his frock coat, feeling the small package inside. *There*, he thought. He didn't want it falling out. He gripped a rung overhead, then set a foot on the rung nearest the dusty and hay-strewn barn floor. His boots were scuffed, he noticed, in need of a shining. He tested his weight on the bottom rung. It gave, but held.

If there wasn't a more suitable adage for the trajectory of Daniel Petrigu's life thus far—*it gave, but held*—he didn't know what was. He took a breath, took heart, and climbed.

After heaving his aging bones over the edge of the loft, Daniel needed a moment. He sank atop the stool there, next to the skeleton frame of an empty wooden easel. How many times had he sat at this stool? How many times had Honor, or Effie the elder (when he wore her down with asking), or had neighbors and friends? How many times had Gamble Vance, his woman from the future, sat there and told him of miracles, of future events both impossible to believe and impossible not.

Famous, and infamous, men and women had sat for him at Tradd Street and in their own gilded rooms: the Marquis de Lafayette, John Calhoun, Eliza Pinckney, aging signers of the Declaration like Thomas Heyward the younger and Edward Rutledge; dignitaries, politicians, their wives, and more. But none had stayed so long in his consciousness as Gamble.

Daniel looked about his former studio. His things had been kept in good shape, sure to be Effie's and then Ben's doing. The small bed sagged rather precariously in the middle, a few tufts of fur there indicating the respite of a neighborhood cat or some other barn-dwelling creature. The rug beneath was hardly moth-eaten, and his chair and desktop were covered in but a thin layer of dust, meaning someone cleaned it with regularity. The colors and tools he'd not taken to Paris were arranged in a receding half-moon at the back of the desk, to the right of the half-empty oil lamp. Daniel couldn't stifle the brief smile at the sight, nor the grimace that came after.

Effie kept oil—had she thought he might return? And also the paint pots (surely crusted over and dried), and his most well-used of brushes, which Daniel wished had been gifted to students at the College of Charleston, or even local children. They'd gone to waste sitting so long. He wondered if Honor had insisted the brushes remain.

He liked to think so. He liked to think, despite their parting and the years between, his sister missed him, loved him still. Perhaps, if he could work up to it, he'd ask her.

Daniel stood, his knee joints creaking, and went to the desk. He bent and blew off the dust. Then he took a deep breath and felt for the latch beneath the middle drawer. It gave as easily as it had nearly thirty years before, and he reached inside, feeling for the miniature portrait he'd hidden there. When his fingers touched wool, he stilled.

Life was funny, Daniel mused, when the miniature lay before him atop the thick piece of gray wool in which he'd wrapped it so long ago. Not funny *ha-ha*, as Gamble once quipped, but funny *odd*. Daniel had regrets about his life, yet he regretted nothing that might change its trajectory: he liked where he stood. He wished Lily were still alive—he missed her constancy and goodness intensely; he felt the pain of her loss each and every day, though it'd been five years since—but he wouldn't change most anything else that would in turn change where he'd ended up.

Still, if you asked Daniel to write the story of his life all those years ago, before Gamble appeared in the alley, it would look a stranger to what it was now. It would certainly never have included a time-traveling, unapologetically frank woman from the future, a career as a miniature portraitist, and a late marriage. It would've included time spent in Paris, but not an entire life there, and not acting as a father figure not to his own children but to a niece, beloved as she was.

You think you know how things will turn out, but time is the great mystery, and it sees no need to explain itself. Daniel knew this to be a truth as reliable as sunrise and sunset, the regular changing of the tides.

He looked down at the tiny portrait atop the desk. It was too dark there, and so he took it to the stool, turning and sitting in a great beam of sunlight coming in through the large loft window. He'd rather depended on that sunlight, so long ago and for a good many years, to illuminate what he most needed to see. Miniature in hand, he hitched the legs of his trousers. Out of habit he loosened his cravat. Daniel lamented that the blasted neck cloths had yet to fall out of fashion.

Take it off, Gamble would've said, had she been there. He knew he should imagine Lily saying something so intimate, not Gamble, but there it was. It was the room: the loft studio, and what they'd done there. It was Gamble's lack of inhibition, her rare ownership of her own body, and the freedom with which she wielded it, which had been a large part of why she entranced him. God's truth, he'd let himself be entranced. If she'd not also been kind, and funny, and sharp, Daniel would've thought it sorcery.

He'd painted the miniature portrait in December of 1804, at Christmastime, the night before she left. Though an unconventional pose—in it Gamble wore his white linen shirt, open at the neck, and his mother's blue scarf turbaned about her head—no one knew she'd been naked beneath the clothes, no one quite willing to admit they could see a sliver of flesh-colored leg at the base of the portrait. No one, that is, but Daniel.

He pulled the package from his pocket. It took a bit of juggling, because he still held the miniature, but he shook the paper wrapping to reveal another small oval of painted ivory. He held the two pieces side by side in the light. It was a second portrait of Gamble, one he'd painted a year after the first, when she returned briefly to their time. She wore a simple white dress, high-waisted, with short sleeves. Her hair was pinned up but loosened from the events of the day, and the shock of the news she brought. There were shadows beneath her blue eyes—a hint of age and knowledge at their corners.

At her waist, in a rare moment of sentimentality, he'd painted a brooch—with a miniature portrait of himself inside. Now, decades later, he did not feel embarrassed to see it, but instead glad he'd marked his role in her life, if only in this tiny way.

Daniel laid the portraits down, one on each thigh. He scarcely breathed. It was obvious now, how much Gamble had changed in the months she'd been away between that first visit and the last. How, inside the startling intellect and shining personal beauty, she'd come to herself like a soul returning to a somewhat abandoned body. He'd not noticed it before, the difference, though he had been her portraitist. Perhaps he'd not known to look for it, then. Perhaps he'd paid less attention than he thought.

"Daniel?" The voice was hesitant, but Daniel would forever be able to pick it from a host of others. He took a deep breath and stood, laying the miniatures on the desk before walking to the edge of the loft.

Below stood Honor, in a deep-blue dress. She wore a rose-colored bonnet, her thick brown hair fixed below the wide brim in complicated curls. Her face showed traces of her forty-nine years, and her eyes, which she blinked and narrowed in order to see, had fine lines emanating from their corners. She wore a cloak with billowed sleeves, and she held the hand of a young boy in trousers, who was dressed like a smaller version of a man. They looked up at him, waiting.

"Hello," Daniel said, more to the boy than to Honor.

He wasn't quite sure what to say. The last they'd seen each other had been in Paris: in 1823, Honor left St. Denis and her children behind, and with Effie the First (as Effie Perrineau had insisted on being called) had sailed to France, to celebrate young Effie's eighteenth birthday. It'd been nearly a decade since.

Honor smiled. "Would you never consider you're too old to be bandying about in barn lofts?" she said. She dipped her head to the boy. "This is my youngest son, Montagu. Monty, say hello to your uncle Daniel."

"Hello," the boy called up, his voice clear and high. He had a cowlick of rust-brown hair, which he pushed from his face, his freckled nose scrunching in annoyance when it flopped back.

With that, the delicate spell was broken. Daniel laughed. "Hello, Monty. 'Gads, Honor, did they really make you name him Montagu? You couldn't have put a stop to it?"

"My first name is Daniel," the boy said. "But everyone calls me Monty."

Daniel felt a wash of emotion, heat like a flush, and he steadied himself against the railing. Honor had given her youngest son his name.

"Pay no attention," Honor said to the boy, shaking his hand in her grasp. "Your uncle Daniel has grown batty with age."

The sun, full up, illuminated the upper floor of the barn. The horses stirred, one knocking at its feed bucket. Honor shaded her eyes while Monty scuffed a shoe in the dirt.

"Will you be coming down or will you wallow in memory until nightfall?" she said. "I'm inviting you to supper. And letting you know we'll be using the house for a meeting or two while you're here. How long will you be here, by the way, brother?"

So many questions, Daniel thought. First, how she could flit his memory about like a white flag, when hers was so clearly full of dark spots. Second, what was her life like, now she'd remarried? And third, who was "we"?

"I'll tell you all of it," Daniel said. "Including news of your daughter…after I complete one last task here." He knew the mention of Effie was a low blow, but he couldn't keep himself from it. It might buy him time.

Honor looked sharply at her son, who seemed intent on the thoroughbred in the nearest stall; the horse curved its big head over the stall door, watching the boy with liquid brown eyes. Despite the tension humming between his mother and uncle, Monty seemed oblivious.

Honor narrowed on Daniel. Monty tugged at his mother's hand and whispered something, and she nodded, releasing him. Daniel felt a brief shame—he'd allowed old frustrations to get the better of him.

But Monty grinned up and said, "Goodbye, Uncle Daniel. Mama." The boy took off from the barn, disappearing in a flash of light at the dark-edged entrance.

"Only until six! Listen for the lamplighter!" Honor called.

There was no way on heaven and earth she was a stiff and unyielding parent, Daniel considered. Though, mayhap he knew nothing at all. Once he could've recited each of his sister's dreams, every one of her idiosyncrasies. But it had been a long time since he'd figured on anything certain about Honor.

Honor brushed gloved hands down the front of her dress and met his eyes. "I missed you," she said. "I'm glad you've come home."

"And I you," he said, clearing his throat because he'd started soft. "Always."

"It *is* your home, Daniel, no matter whose name is on the deed. Ben feels the same," Honor said. "I do hope you'll remain as long as you like."

Daniel found he could not speak—the rush of emotion, memory, and words he couldn't say crowding the cavity of his mouth—and so merely nodded.

"I'll see you inside," Honor said, before turning and disappearing as her son had, into the bright Charleston daylight.

Daniel turned back to the desk, and the miniatures. He studied in the earlier piece the fine line across Gamble's forehead, the one he'd smoothed with a fingertip while she slept. He drew inward, let memories beat about him like seagulls at a scrap. But then he remembered their parting, what Gamble had done for them all by insisting they save Euphemia, and Daniel breathed. He banished the gulls, instead thought of sea and sand, and found a bit of peace.

Daniel folded the miniature portraits carefully in the wool, layering the fabric so they'd not touch. He put them back in the secret drawer, listening for the unmistakable click when it latched.

It would be the last time Daniel looked upon them. Someone would move the portraits later, some Petigru or Perrineau descendant in the centuries hence. But for now, at least, they'd remain hidden in his desk, a small whisper of a woman who came and went, and who changed everything.

GAMBLE

"Euphemia Honora Petigru," I said, peering as deeply as one could into the eyes of a painted person. I leaned back, considering. "Gosh, Tol, you look so much alike. It really is uncanny."

"See," Miss Saralee said, nudging Miss Corrine, who snorted upon waking. "Told you 'uncanny' was right on the money." Tol went to the window. He blinked in the sun, rolled his shoulders. Taking a moment, maybe. Considering the history.

I looked at the girl. Daniel had painted such a winsome, sparkling look in her hazel eyes. She seemed full of life. Memory flickered, and I glanced back at the ladies and then said, under my breath, "Daniel did write 'papa,' didn't he?"

Tol said, "It's likely Daniel knew that with his name, Euphemia could inherit property, or better secure a marriage. It was simpler if she passed as white. Definitely safer."

Miss Corrine perked up. (So much for subterfuge.) She tucked her chin as she shifted on the sofa. "Mm-hm," she agreed. "Lots of folks passed. Up through the '60s even."

"Makes sense," I said. "Sucks, but it makes sense. Pardon my language," I added, with a sheepish look at the old ladies. Miss Saralee rolled her eyes, and Miss Corrine gave a pragmatic shrug of her bony shoulders.

"It does suck," she said.

Tol returned to the painting. I couldn't help it: I reached out and squeezed his waist. He wrapped an arm about my shoulders and squeezed back. Good lord, was it a relief to have a true partner.

Good lord, I thought. *Please don't let me screw it up.*

"Now we have a name," Tol said. "Now we can find her."

Miss Saralee cleared her throat, exasperation apparent. She said, "Aren't y'all going to read what's in that letter?"

DANIEL

PIERRE–ST. DENIS HOUSE
CHARLESTON, 1832

Standing in the second-floor front room of Honor's house on Queen Street, watching his nephews jostle for position and tug at their stiff new clothes, Daniel could see that Honor had made a good life. She raised her eyebrows at the boys' tussling but couldn't keep the smile from her face.

She said dryly, "Enough, you monsters."

Honor's husband, Parker St. Denis, reached out and scuffed the acorn-brown head of the oldest boy, Percival, aged fourteen. "Cease, Percy, you lout," St. Denis grumbled, but with affection. "If you will, they will."

"'Gads, Pa, this cravat is choking me. I look a right fop," Percy moaned, giving his neck cloth a tug. Still, he quieted, and so did the two younger boys. He bumped his middle brother, Henry, behind the knee, which almost made the boy's legs buckle. Henry, though aged eight, had yet to have his growing spurt, and looked close enough in age to six-year-old Monty to be his twin. He twisted to give Percy a half-hearted swat.

Daniel knew the feeling. Cravats were a gentleman's menace; they ought to be banned from existence. Percy, being older, was clad much like his father, but his younger brothers were lucky to be dressed as they were in their robin's-egg-blue short jackets and comfortable, high-waisted trousers.

Percy's half-sister, Catherine, at eighteen years the oldest of the siblings, sat serene in a cane chair Daniel had pulled up at far left, to give the situation a bit more depth. She seemed incognizant of the family hullabaloo. She propped one elbow on a delicate card table, a book in hand—an open book, one she actually seemed to be reading. She dropped her other hand and caressed the sleek head and ears of the family's black brindle Plott hound. The dog leaned into Catherine's full skirts. Daniel stifled a chuckle: he'd love to paint the rapturous look on the beast's face, but Honor would maim him.

"Elegant, but *us*," his sister had insisted, when commissioning him for the family portrait.

Catherine was a product of Honor's first marriage to Gabriel Huger, the only child who had come from that union before Huger was killed by a British bullet when he stood too tall beside an otherwise capable earthworks at the Battle of New Orleans. Daniel observed that the girl seemed at home with her stepfather and half-brothers, and if one didn't know it, one would never guess she was a product of a different marriage. Well and why not, he mused. Catherine had been a toddler when Honor married St. Denis. He was the only father she knew.

As if sensing Daniel's study of her, Catherine raised her head and gave him a serious, considering look from blue eyes she must have inherited from her father. As if she were weighing just who he was and what he was about. It reminded Daniel so much of Honor that he dipped his chin and made a slight leg, sketch pad and graphite rising in hand like a courtier's doffed cap. The corner of Catherine's mouth went up.

St. Denis shifted, and Honor smoothed the rounded collar of Henry's white shirt. The boy jerked back from her mothering. Time to forge ahead, Daniel thought.

"You, Monty," Daniel said, and the boy perked up.

"Yes, Uncle Daniel?"

"Go and sit cross-legged before Cat," Daniel said.

The boy did, and the big hound wagged her tail—really, her entire back end—at the prospect of being so close to two beloveds. She licked Monty's cheek with a long tongue, and Monty giggled. Then the dog rested her head over the boy's shoulder and looked up at Daniel with large, adoring eyes; her pose was perfection.

Daniel laughed. "Wonderful! Good dog," he said.

Daniel had placed Honor in a chaise, with St. Denis standing behind and to the right. Daniel stepped up and adjusted Honor's wide skirts with a flap of the pleated fabric, so they fell with an insouciant flourish against her crossed and tucked ankles, exposing the pointed, embroidered toes of her blue leather slippers. The low neckline accentuated Honor's long white throat; the fashionable gigot sleeves of her gown, the same blue as the boys' jackets, made it seem as if she could quite possibly float.

Daniel preferred the women's fashion of their younger years, the simple—and, in his mind—more sensuous fall of a high-waisted gown, the lack of nonsense about the shoulders. Even so, Honor was tall, and she could carry the outsized drama of the look. Her hair had been looped and braided elaborately, and her face was flushed with happiness—her countenance, as she observed her family, one of good humor and matriarchal benevolence. How beautiful she was still.

Daniel put graphite to paper, sketching as he stepped back.

St. Denis shifted on his heels. He wore a deep blue morning coat with a fashionably dark cravat, crisp dove-white breeches, and a pair of tasseled Hessians, the black boots shined and still stiff with newness. Daniel wondered if Honor had attempted to talk the man into wearing a pair of more fashionable full-length trousers.

Honor turned chin over shoulder, amusement in her voice when she said to her husband (much in the same tone she'd used with her boys), "Cease twitching, my love. I know you abhor the boots. Be thankful you aren't in trousers and pumps. Daniel will be quick and it'll all be done in a shake. And think how our posterity will thank us."

St. Denis took his black top hat from the table and shook it out, grimacing. "These Hessians will have our posterity thinking I was a dandy. They've not yet been ridden in." He made to doff the hat, but Daniel stopped him.

"No, leave it in hand," Daniel said. "Just held loose at your side, there. Henry," he continued, his concern shifting to the middle brother, who wore a leather sling of arrows and a bow over his shoulder. "Adjust the strap of that bow. There, to the right a bit. Percy, place your left hand on his shoulder. Ack, don't pinch him, lad."

Henry bent his head against Percy's hand in reaction, rubbing ear to shoulder. "That tickles," he complained.

Daniel moved his graphite in rapid strokes over the paper as he backed up. This room of the house was perfect: high-ceilinged, with a pearly, satin-finished paint on all the molding, shelves stacked with books, the walls papered on each side in an elegant pattern with tiny Chinese fishing birds and exotic flowers. Atop the lavish papering hung two portraits framed in gold: his and Honor's parents, each an individual portrait, made when they'd been in their thirties.

His rice-broker father looked as if he'd brook no foolhardy: Ramus Petigru stood at his desk in the counting room, one hand hidden in the folds of his hunter-green waistcoat. There were stacks of papers and logbooks on the desk, an inkpot and feathered quill—the marks of a successful merchant. He wore a gray wig tailed with a blue ribbon; he was unsmiling but not unhappy. The artist had caught the strength of character in his father's face, had drawn a sharp intelligence in the slight narrowing of his striking hazel eyes.

His mother, in her portrait, was seated atop a fine chestnut mare. She wore a red riding habit and a cocked hat with a white plume. Her cheeks were flushed; two thick strands of her blond hair fell across the gold-stitched lapels of her waistcoat, as if she'd galloped up moments before from an invigorating ride. There was a quirk to her lips, a bit of irrepressible humor about the corners of her green eyes.

He must've really known them, the artist. How Daniel missed them both.

Daniel stopped his backward momentum when he fit the family neatly into the imaginary frame he'd drawn in the air with his mind's eye. That frame appeared about Honor and her family as a rectangle, as distinct as if the lines had been laid with the aid of a wooden ruler, and he couldn't help but again consider his sister and the life she'd made for herself—this family.

Honor touched a hand to a locket pinned at the low neck of her dress. Daniel took a breath of surprise: inside was a miniature portrait of Effie in her toddling years. He knew, because he'd sent it from Paris two decades before. Apparently, Honor wanted all her children included in the portrait.

Daniel missed Effie with a pang. The last post he'd got from the wild Carolina frontier had arrived months before, to his lonely house in Paris. It was full of life among homesteaders, farmers, and the Cherokee—not at all savage, Effie insisted—of her life as a frontier tutor, tales of foaming white rivers, and mountains as blue and infinite as waves upon the sea. It seemed to Daniel a world apart.

Daniel caught Honor's clear hazel gaze, and she released the locket. She looked back at St. Denis, who took her hand. The couple left their ungloved hands clasped against Honor's shoulder and looked forward, their faces similarly set.

Quickly, before he could change his mind, Daniel sketched a figure standing at Honor's right, just behind St. Denis and a step away from the other children. He added an eagle's feather in his absent niece's thick oak-brown hair.

GAMBLE

AIKEN, SOUTH CAROLINA
2005

The letter was not addressed. When we opened it and laid it flat, its only announcement was a crackle of protest at such an intrusion after one hundred seventy-three years. Tolliver took a pair of wire-rimmed eyeglasses from his shirt pocket, slid them to the tip of his nose, and leaned over the letter.

He read aloud: "Whoever you are, this is for you. We were bade by my papa, Daniel Petigru the portraitist, to keep it safe and in family. I do so to my best, but cannot promise where it will end up. I cannot promise where any of us will end up. However, I am still here." Tol paused, then continued. "She signed it 'Euphemia Honora Petigru, daughter of Honora Petigru and Cooper Perrineau.'"

Tol pressed down on the letter, palm flat, as if he needed a moment—as if he were feeling for the meaning in the words like a shaman laying hands on a sick person whose body must be coaxed to reveal its secrets. As if, by touch, something healing could be created there.

"Tol—" I began, not at all sure what I meant to say.

"There's another page," Tol said.

He used a gentle thumb to peel the letter apart at the edge. It was stuck to a second, large sheet of paper beneath. I put a hand on Tol's forearm; he'd pushed back his sleeves, his skin warm.

"Don't," I said. "We need steam."

The kitchen of Miss Saralee's house was rather turn-of-the-century in nature, though it was obvious that updates had been attempted over the decades since. The linoleum floor peeled at the corners, decorated in a descending 1960s pattern of brown, orange, and lemon-yellow chevron and diamond shapes—the Depression-era cabinets a rather unfortunate shade of lima-bean green.

A black iron teakettle sat on the gas range. I weighed it for water and turned the appropriate knob: this resulted in repeated clicking, but no hiss of gas.

"There's a lighter in the drawer nearest the fridge, dear," Miss Saralee croaked from the library.

There was. I turned to Tol, who'd followed me. "You do it," I said, handing over the red plastic lighter. "I'm afraid I'll blow us all up."

He bent to the task, executed it, and returned the lighter to the drawer with aplomb. "You're so brave," I said, grinning. "The last time that gas was checked could've been when Warren Harding was president."

Tol took my face in his hands, and I went still. Against my lips, he murmured, "See, I am good for something." Then he kissed me.

A few minutes later, breathless, I pushed back against his chest. "I'll say," I said, tucking my hair behind my ears. The kettle whistled, and I took it off the hot eye. Tol winked at me.

"I'll get the letter," he said.

Steaming a letter goes exactly how you'd imagine. Though an almost two-hundred-year-old document takes delicate handling, when done so properly the paper itself is not as fragile as you might think. Made from an amalgam of rag cotton and linen, sometimes even wood pulp, paper—if cared for and left in appropriate conditions—is fairly sturdy, if it hasn't gotten wet in the interim. It's the ink that tends to fade over time.

The two pieces came apart intact but not easily, and only because I peeled with painstaking slowness. It's funny, really, how patient I always was with my work, though not with much else. We steamed the paper just enough for it to soften the stuck-together edges, but not so much as to dampen it. Tol set the painting of Euphemia in the Tuileries Garden on the floor against the wall beneath the library windows, and we placed the found papers side by side on the standing desk. At the sight of the hidden document, my historian's heart skipped a beat.

"It's an original sketch," I said. "Daniel used graphite to draw from life."

My fingers moved a hair's breadth above the drawing. It was a pre-liminary sketch of the painting Daniel had made of Honor's family with Parker St. Denis: the painting we'd discovered in Miss Saralee's barn the month before. But here, there was the addition of someone not present in the finished product.

I traced the figure of a young woman. She wore a plain, wide-necked dress in the style of the 1830s, and since it was a graphite sketch, we'd never know what color the dress had been, at least in Daniel's mind. Though her hair was pinned up in the elaborate curls of the period, he'd drawn a long feather tucked there. It made her look exotic, insouciant. Somehow, I knew—I just knew—that because the girl was not present in the painting, she must've been absent from the sitting.

She stood a step behind forty-something-year-old Honor and her husband. By the way Daniel had drawn the girl—apparent, immediate, but not as sharp as the others—you could tell she was different. Present, but not really there, almost like a ghost.

"It's Euphemia," I said.

"Effie," Tol said.

The second I heard him say it, I knew he was right. My mind fogged then cleared, the drawing before me wavering and returning to focus, as if someone had adjusted the lens of my internal camera.

Of course. Tol knew the girl's nickname not because he'd time traveled himself, but because he'd listened—really listened—to my story, to his story, to the whole convoluted and beautiful mess of it.

I'd not realized—I'd been far too distracted by my jumbled journey through time, my own painful history, and by Daniel—that Effie Perrineau, the free woman I knew in 1804 and 1805, had a more formal given name: Euphemia. I remembered the regard the Petigru siblings held for Effie, a woman who'd accepted me into her home with no small amount of grace. It was more than regard: it was love.

And as Cooper had been Effie's much-younger brother, Cooper's child by Honor—Tol's Euphemia—would have been Effie's niece. Daniel's niece.

"Of course," I said. "Of course, they'd call her Effie."

Tol stepped back from the standing desk and rocked on his heels. He drew off his glasses and rubbed his eyes.

"That's what Honor meant, in the alley," he said. "When she said, 'It's always been you.'"

I nodded, my brain awhirl with connections trying their damnedest to click. I made a concerted effort to calm myself. "Yes," I said. "Honor meant you. All of it—her traveling down the alley, coming to the future to find me. It was all to save Effie, her baby. To in turn save you."

Good God, I considered, as I never had before: was it possible the sheer will of a mother was so powerful a force it could propel a person through time?

"Tol," I said. "Euphemia's note here means she knew. Someone told her, at some point, that Honor and Cooper were her birth parents."

Tol took a very deep breath. He took my shoulders in his large, capable hands. Off to the side I heard soft snuffling and the occasional sleepy snort coming from the library sofa. Both ladies were dozing, Baker having excused himself while we'd been in the kitchen. Sunlight made a blinding frame around Tol's big body, and I blinked against the glare.

"Gamble," he said. "I need to tell you something."

"Okay," I said, swallowing the sudden and proverbial lump in my throat.

Tol said, "Once upon a time, when I was in Paris, I met a girl in a garden."

EFFIE

Effie Perrineau Wolf stood at the open doorway of their cabin, a two-story frame home so new-built it still smelled of sawdust and fresh-cut timber. Sam Hawkins was coming up the hill earlier in the day and earlier in the month than usual, his mail sack bouncing against his thigh. Behind him the rising sun had yet to break the lush green forest, but the light in the air lit dew on the grass, making everything shine.

"Sam," Effie said, and he raised a hand in greeting.

"Thought I'd bring this on," he said, digging in his pack as he walked. "Came from Charleston. Looked important."

When Hawkins reached the edge of the steps he handed over a large brown envelope. Effie recognized the writing on the flap as Honor's. Her mother's sprawling script was looping and graceful, the ink dark with the pressure of a purposeful hand.

At once, she knew. It was about Papa Daniel.

At the look on her face, Hawkins cleared his throat. "You all right?" he said. "Want me to fetch Abe?"

"I'm here." Effie's husband, Abraham, had come up silently, in his typical fashion, so neither she nor Hawkins had noticed. Effie felt Abe's warmth as he stepped close and put his hands on her shoulders. She reached up and curled her fingers over his.

"Sam," Abe said, acknowledging the man with a nod. "Thank you kindly."

The post rider touched a finger to the brim of his hat. "I'll leave you to it. We'll see y'all soon," he said, before turning.

Often when he stopped at the Wolf homestead, Hawkins would stay for a meal or a drink. But the couple didn't offer, which was odd. Sam felt nothing but hope the news in that letter of theirs leaned toward good.

Hawkins liked the Wolf couple. Effie had taught his own children all their letters. His nieces and nephews too. They were good neighbors, worked hard, always had an open door and a seat at the table for any-body down on their luck—which was often on the frontier. They never looked their noses down at anybody. Hawkins didn't care one bit that she had a Frenchie accent and skin a shade or two off white, and him a half-breed Indian.

The couple watched until the post rider disappeared down the trail into the forest. Effie looked down at the letter in her hands.

"I know what this is," she said, swallowing sharp-edged grief. "It's from my mother. It must be Papa Daniel."

"Yes," Abe said. He raised their clasped hands to his lips and lightly kissed the back of hers. The skin there was rough from work, and ever so precious to him. "You felt it'd be soon."

They stood unspeaking until the sun broke the trees, until sunlight washed up and over the grass like an unfurling golden wave, until it paled all the boards on their new, wide-planked porch. Effie rested her hand, the one holding the unopened letter, on the high swell of her belly. Inside, the baby pushed out: a tiny foot protesting the cage of her ribs.

Abe squeezed her hand. "He loved you," he said.

Effie took a deep breath—as deep a breath as she could, consider-ing—and said, "I know."

GAMBLE

AIKEN, SOUTH CAROLINA
2005

Once upon a time, Tolliver said, he met a girl in a Paris garden. Once upon a time, just like in a storybook.

After this announcement, Tol took my hand and urged me out of the library, away from the snoring old ladies and out the front door. On the wide Victorian veranda, he let go, paced a bit, and returned. Then he told me a story.

Less than a year after we first met at the dean's house in West Ashley, he'd led a group of undergraduates on a spring-break trip to Paris. One day, after a morning of lectures on the Black Arts Movement and the influx of African-American musicians, artists, and political refugees in the Paris of the 1930s and '40s, Tol released his charges to the lure of the city in spring. And he, not immune to its charms, headed out himself.

Tol sat on the ground against a chestnut tree, sipping on the largest cup of espresso he could find. He'd been laughing to himself, recalling the smirk the Parisian barista had given him when he requested their largest to-go mug, when the wind kicked up.

It was as if, he said, the season changed in an instant. The air grew cold. Leaves went racketing down the white gravel paths and green lawns, and branches whipped overhead. Suddenly, the gardens were cleared of people, and Tol felt very much alone. When the girl appeared, he was not so much as struck by her strange, old-fashioned dress as he was by the pleading in her hazel eyes, the desperation in her voice.

"I didn't believe, not right away," Tol said. He shrugged, chagrined. "I thought she was just a disturbed kid."

It took one more visit, he said—or visitation—for Tol to believe.

"I was with my students," Tol said, with a remnant of awe. "We'd come from the Musée de l'Orangerie, and the wind did the same thing it had the first time she appeared—but no one seemed to notice but me. Then there she was, standing in the middle of the lawn, just waiting."

Tol rubbed his thumbs together, as if he could bring himself back to the present. "I told everyone to take five: go grab lunch and we'd meet back up. And I walked over the lawn to meet her.

"Every time I walked through a garden in Paris," Tol continued, "kids chased after me, chanting 'NBA!' Like they were convinced I was some famous athlete. But everyone'd vanished. It was just the girl and me."

I walked to the nearest white wicker sofa and sat down hard. Pollen dust mushroomed. "It was Effie," I said.

"No." Tol shook his head. "It was Honor. She looked about twelve or thirteen years old."

"Honor," I said. It came out as a whisper, so I tried again. "She came to you too. And this was, what…1998?"

"Yes," Tol said, his pale eyes pinning mine.

When it hit me, I leapt to my feet. "But that's years—*five years*—before I saw her in the alley!" Hollow, my heart fluttered and dropped in my chest. "Why did you not tell me? What did she say?" I demanded, wringing my hands as dramatically as a high school theater geek in the role of Ophelia.

Tol knew, all these years? How could he? What else did he know?

"She told me about you," Tol said.

What Honor told Tolliver was that I, Gamble Vance—the woman he'd met, and had fallen in love with, just the year before—would one day make an unbelievable trip back in time. That I'd meet Honor in Stoll's Alley, and at her urging would travel to 1804: to Honor at age nineteen, to her family, to Daniel.

Honor also told Tolliver that one day I'd marry another man. That my marriage would be brief and troubled. That my time in the past would help me heal—from Harry's betrayal and from the miscarriage. That it'd be years before I realized I loved Tol too. And Tol must stand by through all of it, and wait for me.

She said it was imperative that Tol believe me. That in the end, it would all be for him—for us. And she couldn't say why.

Honor said Tol could do all of the above, no matter how difficult, because of how much he loved me, believed in me, and because of the stout fortitude of the people he came from.

I rubbed my hands over my face. "Holy shit," I said, rather inelegantly.

When Tol said nothing, I looked up. The sun had nearly set behind the poufy green tops of the long line of loblolly pines. In the field facing the main house three thoroughbreds grazed lazily, their elegant necks curved and long tails swishing. The last of the sunlight glanced across the white fence posts, making everything gleam. It was an achingly pastoral scene, sweet as an artist's dream.

"You must really love me," I said. I didn't know what else to say.

Tol walked to the wicker sofa, dropped the long way down to his knees and put a gentle hand against my face. He stroked the skin at my neck, just behind my ear, and I practically purred. Then he smiled his real smile, the one that showed his dimple.

"I really must," he said.

GAMBLE

2006

I used to believe we were only once for this life. That history ran in a long, impenetrable timeline, with nicks on the page marking the decades: indicating famous births, marriages, and deaths; the upheaval of weather, war, and pestilence; a nod to grand events, major cultural shifts. That our personal historical timelines began with our ancestors, as far back as could be researched, and would end long after we were made dust.

This is not to say I'm immune to the mystery of history: to the surprises that are inevitably revealed when we dig into the past, or when we wipe clean the aged grime from our familial artifacts, or dig through the multi-colored strata of a place we love. What kind of conservator would I be if I did not ready myself, professionally at least, for the way history likes to play games of chance like a big-city street-corner magician, sliding cups over a hidden pea with a practiced sleight of hand.

Now, I know: it's possible to live more than one life. Now I know there are fissures in the story of things. That, as the loquacious and maddeningly circumspect Hamlet tells his buddy, Horatio, and therefore all of us, "…there are more things in heaven and earth."

Now I know we carry all our lives with us, swirling and snapping like sheets on a line in the wind.

Sometimes our lives are like lightning bugs, appearing just in the summer season, blinking gold along dark roadsides while we rush by in our midnight cars, headed forward along the highway, always forward. Sometimes we must look into the deepest parts of the forest—into the overgrown and secretive side roads—to catch the shine.

Now, older, wiser, and travel tested, I know this also to be true: Time is a flicker. A brief magic. There always, but with light banked until we're in need of a little waking up.

ॐ

In December of 2006, a little more than a year after Tolliver and I chased his history and mine down Stoll's Alley and into the past, we found ourselves on opposite sides of the Rotunda Gallery on the second floor of the Galliard Museum of Art. Beneath the green- and gold-stained glass of the Tiffany dome—the colors a bit banked from a century of dust—a grand party of people milled about in their finest evening wear, champagne flutes and wine glasses in hand. They were our loved ones, and it was our wedding reception. We'd been married not an hour earlier in a small ceremony at St. Michael's Church, right at dusk.

It was a Wednesday in December, my favorite month in Charleston. I wore a candlelight white gown with simple, medieval lines: long sleeves and a square neckline, neck free of adornment. An Art Deco pair of sapphire chandelier earrings hung from my ears—a wedding gift from Tol—and I wore a circlet about the crown of my head, a delicate weaving of cotton vine, fern, and purple thistle. Tol, of course, looked like he'd stepped away from a photo shoot for a bridal magazine: he wore a black custom Dolce and Gabbana suit and tie, his size 14 feet encased in shoes that probably cost more than my car. He looked like Idris Elba set to play James Bond, but better.

As a couple, at least in appearance, we were incongruous. But we fit. We always had…it just took us a while to figure it out.

I watched Tol move through the crowd—how handy that he was always easy to spot—and smiled when his foster sister, Deborah, straightened his tie. She'd been deep in conversation with our friend Ken and his wife, Hailey, and Alice Duggar and her partner of thirty years, Meg—half as short as Alice and a third as wide. See: opposites attract. It's a real thing.

If you're wondering, Harry was not invited. I met him, though, the week the invitations went out, at The Golden Whale. I bought him a beer as we sat across from each other in a black leather booth. And I told him the entire story from start to end, not knowing—and, to be honest, not caring—whether he'd believe me or not. But one thing I knew for sure: I owed him the whole truth.

To his great credit, Harry listened, his handsome face still, as I laid everything on the line: what happened to me in 1804 and in 1805, Tol's ancestry, our discoveries. Harry took a swig of his oatmeal porter and set the bottle on the scarred wood tabletop.

"See, we were never really meant to be," Harry said.

I opened my mouth to protest (I'm not sure why, just it didn't seem fair or right to make such an excuse—to assume either of our actions over the years were without consequence) when Harry continued. "Or, perhaps we were meant to be, but only for a little while," he said. "So you could find Tolliver."

Well. It surprised the hell out of me.

When I apologized for not inviting him to the wedding, Harry laughed. It was a half laugh, debonair even, but I heard a pang of remorse in it. (Or maybe I imagined it. Still.)

"Don't apologize, Gamble," Harry said. "I'm not made of steel. I don't need to watch."

Even now I think it may have been the most authentic thing Harry ever said to me. I wished him joy.

At our reception guests stood around candlelit tables draped in appetizers and desserts from our favorite Charleston restaurants, the sheen of their gowns, tuxes, and suits gleaming in the magic light. I saw Ham Dubose holding court with Miss Saralee and Miss Corrine at a set of cushioned chairs we'd arranged for our older guests; my mother with Catherine Memminger by the steamed oysters; my older brothers, Mac and Doug, doing their best to demolish a silver tray of barbeque wings with Xavier and Michael Gadsden, Myron's teenaged sons. In the corner, our band played Al Green's "Here I Am," the brass line with volume low but thumping, to fit the space.

Looking at all the faces, I felt happiness—a right and good joy— light me up from the inside. As if I weren't already glowing like a candle.

Beside me, my soon-to-be-former boss cleared his throat. "So, after all this, you're really going to leave us?"

I took a long, slow drink of my champagne, savoring the fizz and pop of bubbles as it slid down my throat. I smiled over the crystal rim.

"I really am," I said to Mark Whitman. When I'd handed in my resignation letter—giving the Galliard, I thought, a rather generous two months' notice—Mark offered me a raise and a sabbatical. Which had been similarly generous, and harder to turn down than he'd ever know.

When I didn't elaborate, Mark smiled. Patient, charming, with a razor-sharp intellect, Mark knew all his chips had been played. "The Smithsonian will be lucky to have you," he said. He looked across the room as Tol made his way through the crowd toward us. "Both of you."

"Thank you, Mark," I said. "For everything."

Mark clinked his glass to mine. He said, "The Petigru-Perrineau Exhibit. Truly, Gamble. It's a credit to you and to Charleston. Thank you."

Tol arrived, bent to press a kiss to the top of my head before taking Mark's outstretched hand. "Thanks for being here, Mark," he said. They shook, like men.

"I suppose I forgive you," Mark told Tol with a wink, then disappeared into the crowd.

Before anyone else could waylay us, I looked up at my new husband. "Can we go somewhere?" I said. "Just for a minute?"

Tol nodded. "Of course. Think we'll make it?"

I tipped my ear toward a seemingly innocuous door at the nearby wall, half-hidden by one of several drinks stations and a tuxedoed bartender sporting a David Beckham mohawk.

"Don't worry," I said. "I know a secret passageway, and I've still got my keys."

This was how we ended up in our wedding clothes, all alone in gallery 6. The temporary wall had been removed between it and gallery 5, so the *Miniature Portraits* exhibit flowed into this one. I looked up at the embossed copper script on the long gallery wall: "Mulatto: A Reclaiming of Color and Family in Post-Revolutionary Charleston."

Here, Tol and I had worked together—with help, research, and personal art on loan from the Cox Research Center, the Quaker Society of Charleston, the Huguenot Society, and several Charleston families, Black, white, and anywhere in between—to offer a view of this family. Of the Petigrus and the Perrineaus, and the complicated, American, uniquely Charleston lives they'd led.

We included Daniel's miniature portraits, sketches, paintings, and Paris work; his desk, journals, tools, and jars of color. We grouped together miniature portraits and sketches of Effie, Ben, and Cooper; set the deed of the Tradd Street house under lighted glass—the deed Honor had signed in 1808 with the help of the wily attorney Louis Porcher, indicating Ben's claim of habitation. We commissioned an art student from the College of Charleston to paint a family tree for each family along the walls, but instead of lines linking one generation to the next she drew cargo ships at sea, barrels of Bahamian rum, myrtle and oak, cotton bolls and indigo, verses from African spirituals and

French poems. There were dogs and horses, elegant stirrups, saddles, and other tack-and-groom accoutrements, along with easels, paint pots, and brushes. Between these painted things were names—so many names—linking everything. One long, unbroken, unfinished story.

At the center of the room, on a set of interlocking, multi-leveled display tables, we featured works of past and present Charleston artists of mixed-race heritage. There were paintings, sculptures, and samples of book binding; woodwork, handcrafted tools, sheets of music, pottery, fabric art, and more. There were sweetgrass baskets of all shapes and sizes, bright-patterned quilts, and in a corner of the room, standing sections of intricate wrought-iron gates. Beside each piece was a photograph of a contemporary artist holding a portrait, or the name on paper, of one of his or her ancestors. Because the point of art, of course, is more than to connect us. The point of art is to make us feel less alone.

The exhibit was not perfect. Tol and I had agonized over the details, the presentation, the academic blowback we might receive from our very personal attempt to reclaim, as individuals and as an interracial couple, the word "mulatto" for the city and the people we loved—past and present.

People we loved, but whom we'd soon leave.

I tugged Tol across the exhibit space to a single display stand made with metal legs and a reclaimed mahogany top, crafted by a Gullah metalworker from nearby McClellanville. On the stand sat Daniel's journal, open to his penciled self-portrait. The placard read, "Daniel Matthew Petigru, 1765 – 1843, Portraitist."

While there was a full biography on Daniel in museum advertising and in the exhibit brochure, I'd struggled over the content of this placard. Daniel was much in his life: a son, brother, lover, husband, uncle, and friend. He was a chronicler of the people of this city, of decades of history. He was so much more to me.

"I felt—" I said, then stalled. Tried again. "I felt like he should be here."

Tol raised his glass to Daniel's portrait. "To Daniel," he said, low and quiet. "Thank you."

"Thank you," I whispered. Knowing full well how love permeates centuries.

☙

Not long after we moved to Washington, D.C., I dreamed of Honor. In the dream we stood together in Stoll's Alley on an October night. It was one of those perfect Lowcountry nights: with a warm breeze like a caress, a hint of woodsmoke and history on the air. This time, the lamps did not flicker. This time, the moment was still and quiet.

Honor was nineteen, the age she'd been when I first arrived in 1804. She wore the gown she'd worn to the Draytons' ball, the night Daniel and I danced a cotillion. She was beautiful and sad.

"This can't be how my story ends," Honor said.

"It doesn't end," I told her. "It goes on. Time is flimsy. There are no promises in it. Our lives are leaves on the wind—the ages never pass. We make the same mistakes, over and over. You are just as real, just as alive now as you are in 1804. Would you like to see? I can show you."

But before I could show her whatever it was that dream-me intended, I woke in our bed in the short-term apartment we'd rented in the Adams Morgan section of D.C. I rubbed my face and forced my blurred vision to sharpen, to focus on the popcorn ceiling and the whirring fan overhead. I heard the shower: Tol was already up. That morning we planned to take the Metro to Alexandria, to check out a house in the Old Town—one a colleague in the Smithsonian Institution Offices was selling for his elderly uncle. It had yet to go on the market, so we were getting first dibs.

Ah, but the dream. Frustrating, isn't it—not to know what happens? Despite everything, I feel the same.

The house was perfect, at least for us. Our colleague's uncle had bought it from the family who'd owned it for generations; he'd raised his own family there and lived there until he lost his wife the year before. His children and grandchildren lived in other states and had no interest in holding on to the house. We made an offer that afternoon, after several phone calls to our bank and a handshake with the uncle, who insisted on sharing cigars on his stoop. We walked away light on our feet, Tol's long arm slung round my shoulders. We both knew it was a beginning— fresh cut and all ours. It was, as my favorite Anne, the redhead of Green Gables, would say, "… a new day with no mistakes in it yet." Or, in our case, a new home.

We spent the day in Old Town Alexandria, celebrated at a cafe with coffee and beignets, and wandered the three-hundred-year-old streets.

It felt familiar: the town, in subtle ways, was a bit like Charleston. The cities were similarly aged, steeped in American history—places time had taken for a dance through a hodgepodge of centuries. There were colonial-era single houses, renovations of Civil War-era buildings, modern and ancient flags flying, gas lamps, cobblestones, bricked streets, and more. And the distinct feeling—that is, if you allowed for it; if you remained open—quite a lot of *something* had happened here. That something always would.

We were easy with each other, though there'd be years of laughter, arguments, and tears ahead—the stuff of a shared life. Late that night, we walked a side street to the parking garage where we'd left Tol's car. The bartender at the pub where we'd enjoyed a leisurely nightcap recommended the route, after hearing we were historians.

Soon we found ourselves at the head of Ramsey Alley: an old, skinny walk located behind a long line of restaurants. The historical marker at the alley's entrance said it was also known as Lafayette Alley, for the French general. The marker reported that the cobblestones may have been laid by Hessian mercenaries who remained in the area after the Revolution.

Tol and I leaned into the marker, the better to read it in the dark. It was well on into night, and the streetlights flicked on, a pair of tabby cats trotting down the alley past trash cans, trees, and several parked cars. A few houses across the alley from the restaurants had gas lamps flanking their back doors, and the flames inside the copper shades flashed orange.

Tol and I took a step back from the historical marker at the same time. In unison, almost like a pair of toy soldiers, we turned on our heels.

"No way," I said.

"Nope," he said.

We took hands and found another way home.

EPILOGUE

GAMBLE

CHARLESTON

So here I sit, on this bench in White Point Garden, looking out onto a blue and busy harbor as storied as any in this country. I add my own story to it, just like you do. Just like any of the thousands of tourists visiting Charleston each year do: the beleaguered parents allowing their kids to clamber over the cannons, or the middle-aged couples under the oak trees, shaking their heads at the statues. Just like the newlyweds wheeling by on rented bikes, getting the history good and wrong.

Here's the thing, though. Charleston is an uncommon city. But it's an anybody kind of town. It always has been.

Still, I left. We left. The truth is, we might never come back, at least not to live—we're just here now for a visit. Tolliver and Ham took Cooper out fishing on the river, so I'm enjoying the rare time alone to trace my old walk around the peninsula. Taking a moment to breathe in my own history, to ponder on the choices I've made.

Here's something true: you really know a place only when you're brave enough to leave it.

When you do, time becomes soothsayer, mirror, microscope. When you walk away, you grab a piece of a place; you peel it back. Sometimes it drags after you, like Linus's dirty blanket. Sometimes you tattoo it onto your skin. And, as with any tattoo—no matter how adept the artist—the ink fades, the words or drawing stretching, changing with time and with you.

I wonder what people think when they see Tol, Ham, and Cooper out fishing together. When they observe the occupants of that puttering metal jon boat: a tall, handsome Black man; an elderly, distinguished white man; and a four-year-old girl with curls the color of sorghum honey, her skin brown as a cedar tree. What do they think they see, those folks in the speedboats, pleasure yachts, sailboats, and day cruisers, setting out from their private docks or hired slips in Shem Creek or the downtown marina to the wider water of Charleston Harbor, or for the Gulf Stream, to deep-sea fish for mere hours, at hundreds of dollars a pop?

Do they think the three make odd companions? Or do they notice the ease of their bodies, the odd, similar cock of their heads when listening to the river or the egrets or each other? Do they look past age and skin color, and see—*really see*—the shared strands of DNA, cast like shimmering fishing line across ever-moving, ever-changing waters?

Those boaters would be remiss if they didn't consider that the men and the girl are related. They'd be remiss—ignorant, or just plain unlucky in their lesser powers of observation—if they couldn't see that the three in the jon boat share the same story.

But this is Charleston. A town that has flipped the pages of the ages, seen just about all that the beautiful and awful world has had to offer for over 300 years and counting. A town that, despite its missteps—and there are plenty—knows deep in its painfully arrogant, stubborn, independent and multicultural soul, that we're all related, one way or another.

When I rise from the comfort of this bench I'll head to my last stop. I can't, after all, visit Charleston without popping by the Galliard, to see friends. And I've friends there, you know, both alive and well, and also looking back at me from a couple hundred years of paint. (You'd have friends like this too, if you looked hard enough.)

I still feel the same way about the miniature portraits. When I sit on that bench in gallery 5, I can't help but wonder at the faces—even with everything I've seen and all I know. For me, they are people in crystalline: there's an undeniable clarity to their expressions, to the flush of their cheeks, to the individual purpose in their eyes. To some, these miniatures may seem a mere remnant of the past, so past as to make the people in them unreal. But all I think is, how can they be long dead?

To me, they're not old or musty or forgotten. Instead, the faces make sense. They're real. Their stories wait in the ether. An ether through which I have both wittingly and unwittingly traveled—with my research and with my bones.

Because I've traveled, I know time is nothing but a construct. You, however, might wonder: how can we trust time when it feels so ephemeral, so flimsy?

The truth is, time cannot be trusted—not at all. I know this better than anyone. Why should you believe me? Well, because I walked down an alley. Because I have a story to tell, and it's never been mine alone. And if there's anything I've learned, it's this:

We're made of the same stories.

AUTHOR'S NOTE

Dear Reader,

First, and foremost, thank you for choosing my book. I realize there are other books you could be reading, and I hope I've taken you on a satisfying adventure in the time you've dedicated to mine. My greatest wish is that you've been transported, because this is what I long for as a reader myself.

The idea for *The Miniaturist's Assistant* came to me because I miss the days when Charleston had a true quiet season—when you could hear history in addition to see it. There's something magic about standing in the quiet of an old place: its stories seep into your bones.

One hot Charleston night, my husband and I picked our way along the bricks lining Stoll's Alley. The gas lamps at the pre-Revolutionary houses flickered and hissed, bending the light. There, at the far end of the alley, I saw a girl: fully formed, in early 1800s dress. She was desperate. And she said, "Come back."

Like Tolliver, I yearn to know my own history. I'm an eleventh-generation Southerner whose family settled in South Carolina at the turn of the seventeenth century. If I know anything, it's this: the past is fickle and porous—and there are fissures in the surface of things.

I've been around Charleston, South Carolina, my entire life. As a graduate student in the early 2000s, I lived on Folly Beach: one of the sea islands marking the entrance to Charleston Harbor. I've biked down the middle of Meeting Street in the dead of winter without encountering a car—you can't do this anymore; too many tourists—paddled saltwater creeks, waterskied the Wando River, skinny-dipped on Sullivan's Island, wandered empty cemeteries and centuries-old alleys at night, and enjoyed far too many servings of Charleston Light Dragoon Punch. Charleston is a town built for a storyteller, but you must pull yourself from its wonders in order to actually do the writing.

If you're familiar with Charleston, you'll recognize many places in the novel—some long gone and some unchanged, some with names and details altered. My story's Galliard Museum is inspired by the Gibbes Museum of Art (and the sculpture described in the opening scenes by Patrick Dougherty's gorgeous *Betwixt and Between*), and the Cox Research Center (where Tol is director) by the Avery Research Center for African American History and Culture. Gamble's kitchen house is modeled after a kitchen house on Church Street that my husband rented for friends and me in celebration of my fortieth birthday. Much of this novel came about because one day, I wandered into the *Miniature Portraits* exhibit at the Gibbes, and stumbled out, in a writerly fog, hours later. The centuries of stories in those tiny, intricate faces— all those complicated lives—made me breathless.

My stories are always steeped in place. They ask what it means to be fully, audaciously human, no matter the time period. With this novel, I wanted, more than anything, to show what I believe in my soul to be true: that time is nothing but a construct, that we live history in liminal layers, and that there's a mystery to memory which may remain thoroughly unsolvable, beyond our ken. Charleston is a place where the complications, beauty, and brutality of the American experience are on full display, but you have to be open to all of it.

This being said, historical fiction can be a tricky horse to ride. I love writing it—and I don't mind when the horse I'm riding veers off into the woods, or gets spooked and makes a leap over a fence. Long as I keep my seat, I feel I'm doing my job. But since this is historical fiction, and not a history book, I've taken a novelist's liberties with the historical timeline.

When Gamble first alights in Daniel's barn studio, she refers to the fairy tale "Rapunzel." The German brothers Grimm first published their version in 1812, eight years after Gamble climbed into Daniel's loft. Gamble would've of course been familiar with the tale, but (if this was the historical record instead of fiction) Daniel would not—at least not yet.

General Lafayette—Marie-Joseph Paul Ives Roch Gilbert du Motier, Marquis de Lafayette, to be sure—is a fascinating figure, and was, by many accounts, a resourceful, dashing, brave, and intensely patriotic man. After the American Revolution (which he helped us win) Lafayette returned to France and worked tirelessly for her liberty and that of her citizens, getting himself into a good bit of trouble along the way. He returned to the United States in the year 1824-25, near the end of his life, visiting old friends and rekindling patriotic energy in the still-new republic. Lafayette was beloved by Americans and feted wherever he went, especially in Charleston.

I've had a crush on Lafayette since I was a child pouring over Revolutionary history, and I wanted him in my story. I allowed him an earlier, fictional return to the United States, so Daniel could paint his portrait and Gamble could meet him. Lafayette did say, "It is the pride of my heart to have been one of the earliest adopted sons of America," and that, "Charleston is one of the best built, handsomest, and most agreeable cities that I have ever seen." I think, if he could've, Lafayette would have visited us more than once.

Other real-life early nineteenth-century figures appear, some only by mention, and some as cameos: Edward Greene Malbone, a lauded miniature portraitist (who did, sadly, die of tuberculosis), the Quaker feminist Ann Tuke Alexander, and painter-poet Washington Allston. Though I employed them fictionally, I tossed historic South Carolina surnames into the air, juggled, and let them land on my characters. (I also co-opted a few excellent friends' names.) And though I'm an alum of the College of Charleston's graduate program, my fictional use of the department enjoying a party is exactly that.

Lastly, Daniel's work and reputation was inspired by the nineteenth-century Charleston artist Charles Fraser—a famous miniature portraitist who painted many of the city's people. You can find Fraser's self-portrait, his account book, paint pots, and astounding work in the Gibbes Museum of Art.

The older I get, the more I'm convinced we share the same story. I hope you've enjoyed Gamble's.

In friendship,
Katherine

RECOMMENDED FURTHER READING

Aiken, C. (1990). *Techniques and Methods of the American Portrait Miniaturist.* American Portrait Miniatures in the Manney Collection. D. Johnson. New York, The Metropolitan Museum of Art.

Aiken, C. (1997). Ivory and the Art of Miniature Painting. Looking for Eulabee Dix. J. A. Ridley. Washington, D.C., National Museum of Women.

Aiken, C. (2000). Literature that Addresses the Characteristics and Conservation of Portrait Miniatures. Reviews in Conservation. S. Woodhouse. London, International Institute of Conservation. 1: 3-9.

Robertson, Emily, ed. (1895). *Letters and Papers of Andrew Robertson*, Eyre and Spottiswoode.

Avery Research Center for African American History and Culture: https://avery.charleston.edu/

B.R. Howard Conservation: https://brhoward.com

Gibbes Museum of Art, Miniature Collection: https://www.gibbesmuseum.org/miniatures/

Philadelphia Museum of Art: https://philamuseum.org/collection/curated/art-when-were-apart- american-miniatures

ACKNOWLEDGMENTS

*If the only prayer you say in your life is 'thank you,'
that would suffice.*

~ Meister Eckhart

Writing a novel, especially a historical one, is an endeavor neither quick nor entirely solitary. A novelist is a magpie—at least I am—and we hold seemingly useless information, random conversations, innocuous interactions, the slant of light on the side of a centuries-old building, in the treasure chest of our imaginations, the importance of which is difficult to explain to others. All of it is breathed into our books.

First, my thanks to you, dear reader. Thank you for spending time with my stories, for adventuring with me, for wanting more. You've shown up for me in countless ways over the years, whether through your emails and letters, attending my events, inviting me to your book clubs, subscribing to my newsletter, connecting with me on social media, reading my newspaper column and other writing, sharing my books with your family and friends, and so much more. I never forget that you're the reason I get to be a writer.

I am deeply thankful to my literary agent, Joelle Delbourgo, who from our very first conversation spoke of Gamble and this book as if she'd known both all her life. Joelle, thank you for your wisdom, talents, insights, experience, and humor—for loving and championing this story, and for wanting to be on this ride with me.

To my wonderful editor Jaynie Royal, Pam Van Dyk, Elizabeth Lowenstein, and the entire Regal House Publishing team, thank you for cultivating a literary oasis in the publishing world, for nurturing this book, and for bringing it to life.

To my publicist Lauren Harr, of Gold Leaf Literary, thank you for your energy, sense of humor, and kindred spirit.

My everlasting thanks to miniature portraits expert and art conservator Carol Aiken, who I interviewed for this book, who shared with me details of her life and work, and who pointed me in the direction of other scholars. Gamble would not be who she is without Carol's generosity. (Any mistakes in the novel on the topic of portrait miniature and art conservation, it should go without saying, are mine.)

In the decade between my first novel and this one I earned a MFA in Writing from the Vermont College of Fine Arts, and while I didn't write this book there, my teacher-mentors and fellow students strengthened my craft in innumerable ways. A special thanks to my fellow alums, especially my dear friends Amy Wallen and Amanda Silva; faculty advisors Trinie Dalton, Clint McCown, and my beloved mentor, Connie May Fowler, who helped me access my story's inner light. Connie, this book would not be the same without your creative alchemy and boundless generosity.

For Callie, Erin, Liddell, Danielle, Charisma, and Ashley, who walked the streets of Charleston with me and patiently listened as I nerded out on every historic detail: I am in your debt.

Merci beaucoup to Sandy Leder for the French translations.

Having an artist's brain is tricky, and I'm thankful to Debbie Klingender and Kate Hannon for helping me point my ship toward true north.

And to Gentle Pain Relief in Hendersonville, North Carolina, especially Nonnye Lucky and Rita Kotsias: your magic on my former-dare-devil's banged up body has literally saved my life.

For my Charleston family, Bill and Linda Yaeger, for golf cart rides around The Citadel, answering random texts about peninsula streets, and a soft place to lay my head.

My first readers are always my mother, Karen Crawford, and my sister, Callie Caldwell. Others who read early versions of the novel include my dear Aunt Kathleen, my sister-friends Christy Altman and Alyson Mountcastle; Janna Laughridge, and Laura Sullivan. You all made this book better.

Heather Bell Adams, Kimberly Brock, and Gina Heron—beta readers, gifted authors, beloved friends—the day each of you came into my life is gilded. I am blessed by your friendships, your storytelling magic, and the largeness of your hearts. Kim, you are a story sorceress whose phone calls kept me going.

To my in-person and virtual community of writer-friends and fellow book lovers, old and new: What a joy it is to connect, to share this literary life with you.

I'm grateful for the words of South Carolina-born actress Viola Davis, who in a moving speech at the 2017 Oscars, said that the point of art "is to make us feel less alone."

Thank you to the docents and tour guides at the Gibbes Museum, the Charleston Museum, the Heyward-Washington House, the Nathaniel Russell House, the Charleston Library Society, and others, for sharing your expertise and enthusiasm with me. To the servers and bartenders at too many Charleston establishments to name, for the sustentation, conversation, and libation, I say "cheers" and "hear, hear."

To the historical preservationists and conservationists of Charleston: you do work that is profoundly meaningful and good—work which tells a uniquely American story, reminding us how irrevocably connected we are. Thank you from the bottom of my heart for fighting the good fight so what is rare, precious, important, and hard about Charleston is preserved for future generations.

To the booksellers who hand sell my books and others, I wouldn't have this career without you. Especially to Leslie Logemann and the crew at Highland Books in Brevard, North Carolina, whose gift of a bookstore makes our mountain town an even better place to live.

For the family members, friends, and neighbors who have supported me over the years of writing this novel in myriad ways, whether through lending me writing space in your homes, checking in on me, understanding when I cancel plans or need to hibernate for weeks on end, picking my kids up from school or practice, writing me notes of encouragement, celebrating my achievements along the journey, and buoying me with your belief: I'm eternally grateful.

I am a wealthy woman because of my family and friends, and I'll never be able to name you all. But this time, I must thank the following: my beloved Aunt D.B. and Uncle Cool for lifetime lakeside support (and so much more); and Charisma Arbogast, Ashley Dickson, Rachel Durant, Erin McManus, Sarah Grace Montgomery, and Lisa Presnell—fierce, remarkable women whose friendship has kept me afloat in rough waters, especially these last two years. I'm so damn lucky we get to do life together.

I simply wouldn't be a writer without my parents. Karen and Newell Crawford, my everlasting thanks for your continued love, support, and confidence in me, no matter what. For loving my family so well. For letting me use up all the firewood at the lakehouse. I love you to infinity.

Sister—thank you for being my champion and compatriot, for sharing DNA and an inappropriate sense of humor with me, and for loving our people so well. It's some kind of miracle that you are my person for life.

For Merlin, our resident house angel.

For my husband, Stuart Dodson: None of this is possible without you. You make it all work, and you do it with silliness, humor, endless optimism, studly shoulders, and a great big heart. I love you like crazy.

Wylie and Willa, you make everything magic, including my stories. You're the loves of my life.